A FRAYED SATIN NOVEL
UNVEIL
GREER RIVERS

Cover Design: Simply Defined Art
Editing and Proofreading: Christine George, Lynda Hambright of Hambright PR
Formatting: Kayleigh King

ASIN: B0F8159LGM
eBook ISBN: 979-8-9988945-1-0
Paperback ISBN: 979-8-9988945-0-3
Hardback ISBN: 979-8-9887592-9-4

CONTENTS

ACT THREE
SWAN LAKE

UNVEIL

He's her curse, she's his salvation, and he'll stop at nothing to make her his.

Rebellious ballerina Luna Bordeaux can't wait for her birthday. One last performance, one necessary breakup, then? Freedom.

Except her white knight boyfriend proposes on stage.

And her black-masked stalker just crashed the engagement party...

Orion Fury protected his future wife in secret, impatiently waiting to enforce a near-forgotten marriage pact. After his enemy crosses the line, a night that began with a party ends in kidnapping and murder.

Now Luna is a stolen bride trapped in the wilderness with the man who hunted her. But Orion isn't the only predator in these woods, and their enemies will do anything to stop the Fury-Bordeaux alliance.

She's determined to hate her villain, but is he dangerous enough to keep her alive?

PLAYLIST

"Change On The Rise" by Avi Kaplan
"MONEY & FAME" by NEEDTOBREATHE
"Figure You Out" by VOILÀ
"Beauty" by Layto
"Start A Riot" by BEGINNERS, Night Panda
"Ballerina" by VOILÀ
"it is what it is" by Abe Parker
"Dangerous" by Sleep Token
"Let It Go" by Chandler Leighton, Lø Spirit
"Magpie" by The Unthanks
"Take It out on Me" by Bohnes
"Après Minuit" by Felix Räuber, Schlindwein
"babydoll" by Ella Boy
"Gravedigger" by Livingston
"Even In Arcadia" by Sleep Token
"Wait For You" by Myles Smith

Get the full playlist here!

TRIGGER WARNINGS & CONTENT ALERTS

Frayed Satin is a series of interconnected standalones inspired by classic ballets, reimagined with dark and twisty happily ever afters. While best enjoyed in order, each book stands on its own.

This series is a second-generation legacy of the *Tattered Curtain* series, but one can be enjoyed without reading the other.

Unveil is a dark, spicy reimagining of *Swan Lake*, and the legacy sequel to *Phantom*, a modern-day *Phantom of the Opera* retelling. All books have a guaranteed HEA.

TRIGGER WARNINGS

Unveil is a dark romance and should only be read by mature readers (18+). The following content alerts and warnings contains spoilers.

Trigger warnings include, but may not be limited to: mental health discussions and depictions (bipolar disorder), arranged marriage (forced), kidnapping, stalking, threats of violence, graphic violence and murder (on-page), gun violence, knife wounds/injury, toxic family dynamics, gore, alcohol use, car chase, bloodplay/bleeding, power imbalance (between captor and captive), death of a loved one (on-page), burn/fire trauma, harsh language, off-page death of a parent

SEXUAL CONTENT

Primal play, rough sex, praise kink, marking/biting, light bondage/restraint, breeding kink/language, size kink, dubious consent, aftercare, bloodplay/bleeding during intimacy

TROPE ALERTS

Southern Gothic Romance, Arranged marriage, "touch her and die", secret identity, mistaken identity, stolen bride/kidnapping, stalking, villain gets the girl, obsessive/possessive MMC, ballerina heroine, second-generation/legacy, one-sided enemies-to-lovers, only one bed, wilderness forced proximity, morally gray MMC, he falls first and harder, one night stand that won't quit

Protect your heart, friends. Reader discretion is advised.

ONCE UPON A TIME...

AUTHOR WITH BIPOLAR DISORDER EDITION

The following is some insight about little ol' me and mental health. If spoilers bother you, maybe come back after reading the story. But if you don't mind, then keep going!

The first book I wrote with serious mental health discussions was *Phantom*, a *Phantom of the Opera* reimagining where the heroine, Scarlett, has Bipolar Disorder Type I, like I do. I shared a similar foreword to this one in that book about my experience, including psychosis and all the fun stuff that comes with it. If you're curious, I invite you to check it out.

Writing *Phantom* healed something in me, a part that was afraid I'd be villainized or dismissed. But that didn't happen. Instead, I was met with an outpouring of support for Scarlett's portrayal and for my own story. I will forever be grateful to my readers' compassion, and I ask for the same with the character in *Unveil*.

Once again, I pulled from my own experience to write this book. Every symptom is one I've personally lived through. If you or someone you love has bipolar disorder that looks different, that's completely valid. There's no one-size-fits-all version of this disorder, and mental health is not a monolith.

For me, writing has been an extremely therapeutic outlet. I honestly don't know where I'd be without it, my husband, my therapist, my medication, and the kindness of family, friends, and strangers.

All this to say, if you've been searching for answers to the secrets your brain insists on hiding... *keep going*. It's hard. It sucks. But your health and happiness are worth it. *You* are worth it.

Never, ever forget: You are loved. You are wanted. You matter.

To the mood readers who've ever said, "I wish I could read a Southern Gothic, primal, omegaverse vibes only, kidnapping stalker dark romance all wrapped up in a contemporary dark romantic reimagining… but, like, make it Appalachian."

Because same.

"...THE BONDS OF *Love* BIND HIS FURIOUS SPIRIT."

-JOHANN KARL AUGUST MUSÄUS
THE STOLEN *VEIL*

$\mathscr{P}$ROLOGUE
LUNA

Ten years ago

"**Y**ou did what?!"

At the sound of my momma's shout, Lucy and Brylie fall out of their pirouettes. I stutter mid-fouetté, forcing my adopted cousin, Benoit, to catch me for the billionth time.

I growl my frustration, but he chuckles.

"It's okay, *cher*. We'll try again later. Rest for a minute."

He's a saint for putting up with me while I figure out this new turn. I'm almost twelve, and my teacher says I'm not ready, but I *swear* I nearly have it. Kind of.

As much as I want to try again, my momma's still yelling. My twin, Nox, and I exchange confused glances as he straightens in his seat in the corner. All five of us stare at the closed stage curtain, where my dad's voice echoes from the auditorium beyond.

"*Ma muse*, I was drunk, young, jaded, and so fucking foolish. I never dreamed I'd have you, let alone a family. None of us did."

"Don't you '*ma muse*' me, Sol. I can't believe you'd gamble your daughter's life away! I can't believe any of you did! Especially you, Kian. I thought you were a romantic!"

Lucy stills at the mention of her father.

"Obviously, it's no fecking excuse, but in our minds, we were betting house money that night," Uncle Kian answers.

"*Cazzo*, I thought my vendetta would kill me sooner rather than later," my Uncle Sev, Brylie's dad, adds.

"Exactly," Uncle Kian agrees. "What does it matter to lose something you thought you'd never have?"

"Well that's funny," Lucy's mom snaps. "Considering you claim you were in love with me before we even met. Where was *that* energy, hm?"

"At the bottom of a liquor bottle," Lucy's dad grumbles. "*Tine*, there's a reason I quit drinking."

I motion for us to sneak closer to the curtain. There's no way we'll finish practicing *Swan Lake* with this as our background noise, and we're all too curious to keep going anyway. At least, I know *I* am.

"What if we get c-caught?" Lucy's so nervous her stutter's back, even after a year without it, and she's twisted her strawberry-blonde ponytail tightly around her finger, turning the tip purple.

Nox snorts. "Never have before. We've gotten too good at it."

Lucy's eyes widen. "You d-do this a lot?"

"Of course not, Loose," I whisper.

She's younger than the rest of us, and her kitten, Dinah, is braver than she is. When my friends are here at Bordeaux Boarding School from their real homes—Lucy from Las Vegas and Brylie from Italy—we try to convince Loose to join in on our fun, but our skittish little rabbit would sooner read about adventures than have them. She used to be wild like us, but ever since she was kidna—

I close my eyes.

We don't talk about that.

When I open them again, I lean around her so she can't see me stick my tongue out at Nox for worrying her. He smirks and shrugs. Butthead.

Momma's yelling again, but there's a sadness in her voice too. It tugs my chest forward, leading me to push aside the curtain—

"What're you doing?" Brylie hisses, yanking me back by my practice tutu before I can reveal our hiding spot.

I know she saved me from blowing our cover, but I still glare at her. She gives me a sassy look back, and I sigh before peering out, opening the heavy curtain enough for her to look beside me, with Nox and Benoit sneaking in above us.

My parents are in box five, where they take business meetings and hear updates from Daddy's shadows, the people who secretly work for him. They're the ones who help with his "dirty work," as Momma calls it. He says they're a "necessary evil." Whatever *that* means.

There's a bunch of people up with them now, crowding the not-so-big space. Uncle Ben—who I haven't seen since his family moved to New York—the McKennons, Lucy's parents, and the Lucianos, Brylie's. Both their families flew in for our end-of-summer recital, but why are they up there now?

I squint until I make out a man and woman standing apart from them in a dark corner at the back of the box. I can't see their faces in the shadows, but my dad isn't wearing his mask, which only means one thing. They're either friends... or enemies.

"Luna, d-do you know who those other p-people are?" Lucy asks in her barely-there southern accent as she squeezes underneath me to eavesdrop with the rest of us. Stutter, disobeying rules, *and* an accent? She must be *really* anxious.

"No clue," I answer.

"What're they talking about?" Brylie asks in her own light southern and Italian accent, her green eyes as confused as ours.

I shrug again. "How the heck should I know?"

"It's your mom who's doing most of the shouting." Her eyes dart from me to Nox.

"You know what? No. This is bullshit!" Aunt Tallie, Brylie's mom, hisses like a snake. "This was at McKennon Casino, wasn't it? Why the hell didn't you just cheat?"

I arch an eyebrow at Bry, who rolls her eyes. She's my best friend, but she's so dang prickly. That's how Antonia Rosalee got

her first nickname, 'Briar Lee,' when we were kids. She's thorny as
a briar patch, and between Lucy's speech impediment and our
mess of accents, now we've got "Brylie."

Lucy's mom sighs. "Kian would never cheat in his own
casino... no matter how *crazy* the bet."

"If I may..." a man starts.

"No, you may not," Aunt Tallie growls.

"*Dolcezza*..." Brylie's dad murmurs, almost too low to hear.

"Please, Talia, everyone..." a woman begs softly, and my ears
perk up. "Once we explain, you'll understand."

"Fine, Queenie," Tallie snaps. "Go ahead. Explain how these
fools gambled our daughters' lives away."

A sudden, loud bubblegum pop draws my eyes to three boys
sitting in the auditorium seats, stage left.

One is sitting up straight, his tanned cheeks aglow with the
light of his bright tablet. The boy in the middle looks younger,
maybe Lucy's age, around ten. He's got a wild mess of black hair
flopping into his eyes as he lounges across several seats, a sketch-
book propped on one splayed leg. And the third boy...

A scowl clouds his face as he rests his arms over the back of the
seat in front of him, flicking a pocketknife open and closed.

A *knife*.

How creepy is that?

The other boys seem to be paying serious attention to
anything besides the argument in box five. And the third one
stares right at my hiding place. At *me*.

My fingers clutch the curtain to close it, but the rest of me
can't move. I'm stuck staring back at him as the man who must be
his father begins to speak.

"'Gambling lives away' is a nasty way to put it. Arranged
marriage is much more civilized."

Momma scoffs. "Civilized? You're one to talk, King Fury.
Everyone back in Appalachia knows about the Wilde and Fury
families. How is a Capulet-and-Montague-style feud remotely
civilized?"

King? And Tallie called the woman "Queenie." Are those their real names?

Cool. Weird… but cool.

"Great question, *ma muse*," my dad says to my mom. "And why the fuck would we sacrifice our daughters to save a family of criminals?"

The man's easy voice turns cold. "Pot calling the kettle black, don't you think? We're all criminals. Powerful ones. That's why I chose your families when I made the bet. I knew this day would come. The Furys are infighting. The Wildes are gaining ground. The King Fury branch needs alliances and all the muscle we can get to keep everyone in line, and most importantly, *safe*. We *need* the Troisgarde."

Troy-guard. He actually pronounced it right. Momma says even though it's a made-up word, it's the Louisiana French way of saying it, like how Calliope Street is "Kal-ee-oh-pee" around here. Our three families use the name because we like each other… or something. I don't know. There's more to it, but Nox is the one who wants to follow in the "Phantom of the French Quarter's" footsteps. They tried to teach me all that boring stuff, but I'd rather dance.

"Is this real?" Benoit scoffs. "It sounds like *Raymonda*."

The ballet we did last summer had fun costumes and choreography, but the story of a rich guy kidnapping a girl who's already engaged felt make-believe. Until now.

"They can't really be talking about marrying you off," Nox mumbles behind me. "Over my dead body." He crosses his arms like Daddy does when he says the same thing.

Up in box five, our dad hums thoughtfully. "Don't you have your own secret club to back you up?"

Mr. Fury huffs. "The fact you know about it is why I didn't go to them."

"Don't be so hard on yourself, Fury," Uncle Kian says smugly. "We make it our business to know other peoples' business."

"And that's my point. All of us have our own territories.

Bordeauxs have the Deep South. McKennons hold the West, Lucianos, the Northeast. The Furys and Wildes control Appalachia and the Southeastern Coast, with the Furys barely hanging on. *For now.* We're being chopped down branch by branch, and the Wildes keep coming. Everyone wants the throne, and I won't be the one to bend the knee. They're already pushing into Mississippi and Pennsylvania, Bordeaux and Luciano territory. You don't want that. Trust me."

"My cousin controls the Northeast," Uncle Sev corrects. "I'm no longer a player on the board."

"What the fuck, Severino?" Uncle Kian growls.

"Look, I'm on your side up until the point my Brylie has to marry a monster."

"A monster?" Mr. Fury snarls.

"He has a point," Uncle Kian agrees. "You can't tell me the one with those crazy eyes is entirely sane. No way I'm letting him marry my girl."

"They're not monsters." Queenie's soft voice is harder now. "Orion, Dashiel, Hatton... they're *boys.*"

King's tone roughens too. "And each of them have been through more in their lives individually than your pampered princesses have combined. You can't imagine what we've lost to this feud. My own sister—" he chokes.

The sketchpad boy scowls up at the box. The tablet held by the boy beside him goes dark. The one who hasn't stopped looking at me flicks the knife open one last time, then crosses his arms, breaking eye contact as he leans back.

His gaze moves to the doors like he's waiting for an intruder to burst through. Which is kinda funny since Bordeaux Conservatory is neutral ground. Everybody respects that rule. It's the safest place in the world.

I drag my eyes back to box five.

Queenie murmurs words I can't catch, then speaks louder, gentle but firm.

"King lost his sister recently in a Wilde retaliation against another Fury branch. That's why we're here. This feud won't just defeat the King branch. Our enemies want to wipe us off the map. Everyone knows our ambitions up there. They know we intend to make our blue mountains safer. Still lawless, in our Fury way, but built on family, community, and land. Not shaped by greed or bought by power-hungry men clawing for control. We need your help."

There's a moment of silence that reminds me of a funeral.

"I'm sorry for your loss," my dad finally replies before his voice turns shockingly cold. "But we're not handing over our daughters as sacrifices to keep your feud in check. You losing a family member, no matter how tragic, is only more reason to protect ours."

"He's right," Uncle Kian adds. "My wife and I abolished arranged marriage in our own society over a decade ago, before we formed the Troisgarde. We won't start them again. We won't take away our daughter's say in her own life."

Lucy finds my hand and I squeeze. I grab Brylie's too. Even though she hates this kind of thing, I'm not surprised when she grips mine fiercely. She's soft sometimes. Especially when she's scared.

Benoit's right. All of this sounds like the ballets we dance in. But in real life, there's no way our parents will make us marry someone we don't like. Right?

"You will honor the Troisgarde-Fury pact," King insists, each word heavier than the last. "Or are you not men of your word?"

"Of course we are," Kian says. "But a drunken bet is a different animal. Hell, we'd give you anything else you fecking well please—"

"It'll be my boys or no one!" The shout ricochets from box five. "Marriage is the only power in our world that means something anymore. The legacies made from them are sacred. The Troisgarde-Fury Pact means survival for us all. We won't just protect the bride. We'll inherit the right and privilege to defend her family, and they'll protect ours in turn. I won't risk you forming that kind of loyalty with men who intend to hurt me and mine."

Lucy's hand tightens, and she huddles against me. Even Brylie moves closer. Sweet Benoit and Nox stand as tall as they can, like they're ready to fight.

The staring boy's eyes are back on me.

"You're treating them like pawns," Aunt Lacey argues.

"That's where you're wrong, Mrs. McKennon. They'll rule the Fury kingdom. The King kin will make them queens in their own right." His voice softens. "Like I did when I claimed Ruth. My Queenie."

"Don't worry, *cher*," Benoit murmurs, squeezing my shoulder, making me realize I'd been fidgeting. "Nox and I will protect you with our lives, I promise."

I nearly snort. "Don't be so *dramatic*, Benny."

He scowls. "Well, if this guy tries anything, Sabine would be the first to tear him in two."

Benoit is as loyal as they come, especially to the woman who found him after the last big hurricane destroyed his home. My dad's security manager has never stopped helping him look for his parents. But in the meantime, one of my grandmas, Madam G, adopted him.

And he's right. Sabine and her police officer wife run this town when my parents are touring for Momma's shows. They'll protect us. Everyone will.

"Pawns. Queens. Pretty words disguising ugly threats," my dad rumbles. "No wonder you have no alliances. You've got a lot of nerve."

"What I have is desperation. You think I want to sell off my sons? Of course not. But by being here, calling on *our* pact, I'm admitting that I can't protect my own family anymore."

His voice grows more pained. "I want my boys to have what my wife and I have almost more than anything. But what I want most for them, for everyone, is to stay *alive*. My boys will do whatever it takes to protect our family, *your* families, and the innocents in this feud."

No one answers, the auditorium quiet as a graveyard.

King's barely controlled anger edges back in. "What's your motto? Blood of three, power of many? *Your* families need these alliances too. You think the Wildes aren't a threat, but they will be. Dealing with me is the lesser evil, I assure you. Your daughters will either be protected by all of us or left up for the slaughter by a ruthless Wilde."

The tension in the auditorium thickens, making it hard to breathe. Then my father's deep voice chills me to the bone.

"You've threatened our children for the last time. If a Fury sets foot in any of our territory again, it'll be the last thing you do. Are we clear?"

"You can say that a-fecking-gain," Uncle Kian says, followed by Uncle Sev's "*Sì*" and what I'm sure is an Italian curse word.

There's a heavy sigh and the creak of a seat. A man with black hair and a beard steps into the light, his expression unforgiving. The boys look exactly like him.

Below him, another squeak echoes in the auditorium. A woman appears from one of the side doors and glides down the stage-left aisle with the grace of a dancer. All three boys glance over their shoulders the instant she appears, before the door even closes. Her blonde hair curls at her shoulders, and her long black dress flutters around her feet. Her eyes brighten as she finds the boys.

Queenie Fury.

She ruffles the sketchpad boy's hair, and one by one, each lifts his chin, waiting for the light peck on his forehead without even looking, like the gesture is so familiar they hardly notice anymore. When she's finished, the boy who stared at me smiles up at her.

His *smile*. It's so *sweet*. Something I never would've expected on such a surly boy.

As they gather their things and get up—gosh, they're so freaking tall—they surround their mom in practiced formation.

The boy with the knife takes the lead, the one with the tablet follows at the end, and the youngest with the sketchpad gravitates to her side. Their heads are on a swivel as they move through the auditorium.

They're not just walking with her. They're protecting her.

Her warm eyes flick to mine, trapping me with her gaze. For a split second, I'm afraid she'll out us. Instead, she smiles so wide I can't help grinning back until hers falls into something... sad. Like she feels sorry for me. Or worried? I don't know, but the look is gone before I can decide, and King's voice grabs my attention again.

"You have until their twenty-second birthdays."

"What are you talking about?" my dad growls.

"My boys won't make a move before then, that's my promise. Not unless the girls are in danger. Otherwise, as soon as the clock strikes midnight on your daughters' twenty-second birthdays, you'll honor the Troisgarde-Fury Pact, and my boys will have their wives. I warn you. Once the first birthday arrives, the Wildes will use brutal tactics to interfere. If that happens, I won't stop my sons from doing what they must."

"Twenty-two?" Uncle Sev asks. "That seems arbitrary."

My dad grunts his agreement. "Most rules do until they're followed."

"Or fought over," Mr. Fury adds. There's a beat before he continues. "You're lucky I didn't say eighteen, since time is of the essence. The Troisgarde-Fury Pact has already made waves—"

"You *told* people?" Uncle Kian growls. "Bets between honorable men are kept private."

"No, *I* didn't tell anyone, but there were more than just us in your gambling Red Room that night. In any case, I'll spread rumors that the birthday clause is for twenty-five. If I know the Wildes, they'll take the bait and bide their time just to fuck with us. Our families will have already united before the Wildes realize they've been played. I'm counting on you to keep your daughters safe until then. The moment my boys can protect them, they will.

They understand the stakes and will guard your daughters with their lives."

The boy at the front of the line—the first to defend his mom —stops at the doors and locks eyes with me again. It feels like *his* warning as his father speaks.

"Your princesses shall wear the Fury crown. Because without us, we'll *all* die by the Wilde sword."

Queenie wraps her arm around the boy, turning him toward the door. His eyes leave mine, and his mom gives me a small wave before she and the Fury boys slip out of the auditorium.

Above them, another door opens and closes. King Fury must have left too, because I hear Uncle Ben's voice for the first time.

"It's war if you break this oath, Sol."

There's a pause.

"Then it's war."

ACT ONE

THE DANCE OF THE BORDEAUX

1

CORPS DE BALLET

LUNA

Present Day

Twenty-eight.
Twenty-nine.
Thirty.

My heartbeat races, my thighs shake, sweat prickles my brow. I'm sure my smile is blinding every time I turn and the spotlights zero in on me as I fling my leg around in a perfect spin. I'm dancing the best I ever have, rising up on my pointe shoes. Flying.

Thirty-one.

This is it.

Thirty-two.

And I land the final fouetté during the last performance of my life, tears in my eyes.

The auditorium erupts in chaotic applause as the rest of the senior class floods the stage, cheering and hugging me. Our celebration is barely audible over the orchestra blasting "When the Saints Go Marching In," and it stays lost in the music when someone from sound switches on an early '00s graduation song. As soon as it starts playing, the orchestra leaves their instruments in the pit to hop onto the stage and join the huge pile-up.

I somehow hold back my tears, but it's hard. We wrapped our college career with the show that was the most fun we've ever had performing. And now? It's over.

Technically, we graduated months ago, and the point of Bon Temps Senior Night is to usher in the freshman class. The seniors who stuck around after graduation work on the production all summer before we scatter across the world to chase our dreams. We're welcoming the new students, but it's also a goodbye. To college, New Orleans, and each other. And, damn, was it a good time.

Our rehearsals usually consisted of running over parts we already knew by heart, then partying on Bourbon before heading to Frenchman Street. Partying instead of practicing meant tonight wasn't our best work, but this audience of new students, friends, and family would've cheered if we'd played patty-cake for the last hour and a half. Most were probably one drink away from being trashed *before* the five-dollar cash bar opened.

Us performers had our fair share of alcohol, but I only had one shot, and that was just because Brylie and Lucy twisted my arm. No way was I doing thirty-two freaking fouettés, one of ballet's hardest turns, while drunk. Sure, I've done that a time or twelve for funsies in soft shoes, but en pointe? Hell no. That's a broken leg waiting to happen. Broken toes have been enough for me, thank you very much.

Flowers pelt the stage, and a bouquet of red and white roses bounces off Lucy's head, knocking her ribbon headband askew as she squeezes into the crowd. Brylie and Benoit find their way to the center and tug Lucy inside as she scowls. Or scowls as much as she can. Lucy's the nicest of us and wouldn't hurt a fly.

"Watch it!" Brylie and I defend her in unison, although my tone is *much* gentler than Bry's husky shout. None of it matters, really, because popcorn, pecans, and Mardi Gras beads are flying from all directions too.

As I try to find the culprit, I spy box five instead. I'm not surprised to see Momma dabbing her eyes with one of Dad's handkerchiefs.

What does surprise me is that she only has her best friend, Uncle Jaime, and his husband, Robert, beside her.

Where's Dad?

I frown, until a heavy arm slaps over my shoulders and a hard hand musses up my hair, knocking my black feathered veil off my head.

"Nox! You *butthead*! You're lucky Benny and I even let you back here."

Nox, Brylie, and Lucy shouldn't be backstage since they're not Bordeaux Conservatory seniors. But Bon Temps Senior Night is always a madhouse, and no one cares so long as you're having a good time. As I fix my hair, though, I'm regretting it now.

My twin chuckles. "Now, now, that's no way to respect your elders."

"Seven minutes does not deserve elder status."

"Technically a whole day," he points out with a grin.

"By a *calendar* day," I counter. Being born at 11:53 P.M., today's Nox's birthday. But as soon as the clock strikes twelve, it's mine. We'll have a countdown to switch the party over, and I can't wait to lord it over him like he does me. "Now get your ugly ass off me!"

I escape his clutches and glare at his grin. Aside from not having any scars, he's the spitting image of our father, six-foot-four, black hair, fair skin. Although, we have no idea where his golden hazel eyes came from.

"If I'm ugly, you're ugly," he cackles.

"Are you calling Momma ugly?" I joke.

"Nope." He smirks. "Can't see the resemblance whatsoever. Your feral side gets in the way."

All I can think to do is stick out my tongue, and he snorts. Even after all our low-key bullying, I'm still terrible at comebacks. Plus, he's kind of not wrong.

Other than our eyes, Momma and I could be the ones who are twins. Mine are more like a clear lake compared to her moonlight ones, but we're both short and fair-skinned. I've done my best to look different where I can—gotten tattoos, straightened my unruly curls and dyed them cherry cola red. After the thousandth time of being asked to sing an aria instead of perform an arabesque, a girl can get a complex.

Living in the spotlight, spending my life here in New Orleans at Bordeaux Conservatory—totally not awkward that it's my family's school, by the way—and never leaving anywhere without my overprotective parents, I've always been in Scarlett Bordeaux's stunning shadow. I'm ready to break free, and I have just the plan.

We visited Appalachia, where Momma's extended family used to live, a lot growing up. I loved the green and blue mountains. Hiking through the woods was so different from running through the Garden District's pungent flowers. That freedom calls to me more than the stage ever has, much to my helicopter father's dismay.

Which makes it strange that he's not here, watching the last performance of my life.

"Back up, everyone! Curtain, curtain!" someone calls, and we all move in unison to let the curtain drop and give our final bows.

A song blares through the speakers as each senior group goes out for a bow. First the reluctant sound and backstage crew. Then the costume designers in their favorite pieces, the orchestra, who raise their instruments as they're called. Next, the directors, actors, singers, and dancers begin to take their individual turns.

This production was nothing short of chaotic. The playbill credited *Phantom of the Opera*, *Moulin Rouge!*, *Sweeney Todd*, *Alice in Wonderland*, *Cinderella*, *Giselle*, *Raymonda*, *Manon*, and *Sleeping Beauty*, all remixed into a gothic contemporary piece created by the senior playwrights.

I couldn't pick one favorite dance, so I choreographed a mashup of *Giselle*'s Mad Scene and my Black Swan duet with Benoit. I've even combined costumes with my *Swan Lake* feather bodice, a black feather crown, a veil, and a flowy, tulle romantic tutu that lands below my knees. I skipped the pounds of tattoo concealer I normally wear, so the gorgeous colored skull pieces on my upper right shoulder blade and left thigh are proudly on display. Any other tattoo and Dad would've freaked, but skulls are our family symbol. Pointe shoes finish the look, which I'll miss in a masochistic kind of way. I don't know if pain's my kink, per se, but maybe if I ever lose my virginity, I'll find out.

Speaking of getting laid, my boyfriend, Ozias, couldn't make it tonight due to a last-minute family thing, and to be honest, I'm kind of glad. We've dated for six months, but I'm still not sure if he actually even likes me.

We've barely been physical, and believe me, I've tried. But it's either Dad's overbearing "someone must be guarding you at all times" philosophy or Zy's "I respect you and Mr. Bordeaux too much" ridiculousness that gets in the way of anything past closed-lip pecks.

It's gotten to the point that I can no longer stand Ozias's white knight, goody-two-shoes nonsense. His straitlaced personality should've been my first red flag, not the fact that he barely touches me.

And the worst part? I know the difference. I know what it's like to be needed in that passionate, all-consuming way, thanks to a masked stranger during my last birthday masquerade. One hot, steamy makeout in a dark corner behind a haunted pirate bar and I was ruined, I tell you. Ruined.

Then he was gone.

So actually, fuck that guy for leaving me hanging.

I wince at the annoyance building hot in my chest. Even my irritation at a stranger is stronger than anything I feel with Zy.

"You guys killed it!" Brylie shouts as she gives me and Benoit a pale-yellow shot.

"*She* killed it." Benoit lands a sloppy kiss on my cheek, reeking of beer. I didn't notice while we were dancing, his natural talent kicking in at the time, but someone clearly didn't care about breaking a leg tonight.

"Ewww. Gross!" I give him a fake glare as I wipe the spit off my cheek with my sweaty shoulder, not much better, but then I smile and raise my glass to him. "*Laissez les bons temps rouler*! To you taking the Manhattan Classical Ballet by storm as principal!"

A blush creeps underneath his light freckles. "Please. Corps de ballet, first. You know that. I'm not a prodigy." Before I can argue, he raises his drink. "And to you! May your dad loosen the leash enough for both of us to roam."

We clink the plastic cups and down something that tastes suspiciously like straight gin. I shake my head at the burn but keep a straight face, even though I'm dying inside, so I can win the game. Benoit gasps, his expression contorting.

Yup. He always loses.

"Luna's Liquor Poker Face streak is still alive!" Brylie laughs.

He groans. "I can't help it. I'm like Loose and her tea. If there's no sugar, I can barely keep it down."

"Hey! Stop making fun of my Long Island Iced Teas." Lucy crosses her arms, then adds smugly, "And y'all somehow forget that I'm the only one who can drink absinthe without throwing up."

"Gin, absinthe... and she's only twenty," Brylie groans. "We've corrupted the good girl."

"Cheers to that," Benoit snorts, clinking another plastic cup —*where the hell did that come from?*—with Lucy's. "But touché, little McKennon. Touché."

He sips while Lucy downs hers. When she displays the empty cup proudly, he tips an imaginary hat to her and laughs.

God, I'm glad he's having fun. Tonight was hard for him, even though he'd never show it.

Madam G passed last year. With her gone and his parents never found, he was heartbroken over finishing senior year alone. We were there for him, celebrating every moment, of course. But when you long for a home that no longer exists, nothing compares.

Brylie and Lucy disappear to find more drinks, but I grab Benoit by the suit coat from his *Manon* costume.

"Hey. You know my dad will let you go. Being one of the Phantom's shadows isn't for life anymore, and you're like a son to him. He's thrilled for you about MCB. We all are."

His smile doesn't reach his glossy blue eyes. "I... I worry about leaving New Orleans. It'll be like they're actually gone."

My chest squeezes, and the gin dries on my tongue. I have no idea what to say. I've never been good at this stuff. I open my mouth to try, but a wistful smile crests his face as he takes in the stage we grew up on.

"You guys are my only family now. I know it's time. It's just hard." He smirks. "And what if I don't even like it up there? Maybe I'm meant to be here forever. It's home, you know?"

I nod. A lump clogs my throat, because I do know. I just feel the opposite. I'm dying to get out, an itch deep in my soul that only open roads and blue skies can scratch.

"Let's take it one adventure at a time, okay?" I finally say.

He grins. "You're right. I leave next week for rehearsals, but I'm still your shadow until then. So no funny business with Ozias Thrasher until I'm gone. Your dad would be so pissed."

I roll my eyes, barely keeping myself from muttering, *Fat chance.*

Benoit is a shadow, one of Dad's men. Uncle Jaime was Momma's shadow before she officially met my dad, so bodyguard besties are kind of his thing. With all the training my friends and I have had over the years, it's questionable who's guarding who on our wildest nights.

"I know you can't wait to get rid of us," I joke.

"Actually, kinda." He laughs. "No chick talks to me because they think I have a thing for you."

We both gag. Dating Benoit would be the literal equivalent of dating my brother.

"Good thing you've got Nox to wingman you."

"Don't get me started. When it's not your fault, it's his. Girls can't even see me past his tall ass." His brows wiggle. "Good thing I don't mind sexy seconds."

He tilts his forehead toward Nox, now surrounded by dancers and actresses who apparently don't care how big of a player he is. My brother doesn't go to BC, attending New

Orleans State instead, but his reputation precedes him anywhere he goes.

When he catches us looking, he makes a show of turning his baseball cap backwards. I roll my eyes so hard I swear I see my brain.

"Oh shit," Benoit laughs. "He brought out the big guns."

Lucy tsks as she appears. "That boy's read way too many of my spicy books."

"Hey, the manuals work," Benoit counters, pointing a thumb back at Nox, happy as a clam amidst all his starry-eyed fans.

Brylie's nose crinkles. "Do you think he's gonna do that thing again? The one where he dances with everyone until he finds the perfect girl or two, then leaves the rest hanging?"

"It's his schtick." Benoit shrugs, then grins. "Which means at least one will need a strong shoulder to cry on when he's done choosing. Wish me luck! Gotta go protect the Prince of the French Quarter from the swarm."

"You're gonna miss your turn to bow!" Lucy reminds him.

"Listen, if I find a girl between now and the time I'm supposed to go out on stage, I couldn't care less about bowing."

She frowns. "But it's your last one."

"You'll understand when you're older," he jokes and snatches her cup, downing it with a smack of his lips.

"Benny!" she yelps.

"Sorry, Loose. It was either Brylie's straight liquor or your middle school Screwdriver. See ya!" He starts but stops to point hard at me. "I mean it about Zy." He backs up, pointing two fingers between his eyes and mine. "Don't get me in trouble."

"I won't!" I raise my hands in mock surrender.

"Kinda hard to do that if she's breaking up with the guy," Brylie mutters.

"Bry!" I whisper-shout, but Benoit's thankfully already out of earshot.

"What?" She shrugs while Lucy huddles closer to us both as

we wait for my turn to bow. "Maybe Benny will be able to convince you to do it."

"*Are* you gonna do it, tonight?" Lucy asks.

"She should," Brylie says. "The Troisgarde girls need guys who are obsessed. Anything less and he'll never be able to stand toe-to-toe with our dads."

I groan, "Agree, except my dad actually *likes* Zy."

Even Lucy grimaces at that. "Eww."

"That's the worst," Brylie agrees. "Any guy my dad is even nice to instantly gives me the ick. I swear they only like the boys we don't." She shudders for effect. "But my Spidey senses are telling me you've gotta do it quick, Lu. Something's up. I can feel it."

Benoit's name is called, and we look around, only to find him laughing with Nox and three girls in tutus from *Cinderella* and *Sleeping Beauty*.

"Typical," Brylie snorts. "You're up soon. What'll it be? Single or sad?"

I arch a brow. "'Single or sad,' Bry? Really?"

She lifts a shoulder. "I said what I said."

Lucy gives me a knowing smile, so I answer her instead of the prickly one with the humor drier than a desert. "My cutoff is midnight. I refuse to be with someone at twenty-two who makes me feel"—I tug at my suddenly too-tight bodice—"unwanted."

Lucy pouts. "We want you."

"Thanks, Loose," I snort. "But I'm already in one platonic relationship with—"

"And last, but not least, our Bordeaux black swan," the emcee announces.

"Oh, gross." I grimace at the phrasing and my stomach twists. "He wasn't supposed to say that. Now I look like a narcissistic bitch."

"Oh my God, no one thinks that," Lucy laughs.

"Who cares?" Brylie slaps me on the ass, making me squeal before she pushes me toward the curtain. "It's your last bow, babe. Make it count."

"Don't break a leg," Nox calls from the back.

"Butthead!" I shout over my shoulder as I stop at the red fabric wall.

"*Giselle* and *Swan Lake*, danced by Luna Bordeaux!"

I sweep through the curtain, rise en pointe, and perform one last fouetté. The fact that I nail it, even after a couple of shots, goes to show I've danced my whole life. The crowd goes wild, nearly deafening, as I land and bow.

Tears blur the sea of friends and family who've supported us. And I quickly open the curtain to wave everyone out to soak in this moment too. It's not mine. It's all of ours.

We bow together, our pride, nostalgia, and anxiety over the future palpable. The emotions swell in my chest like a balloon.

I shouldn't even be here for many reasons. For one, I was supposed to be a junior like Brylie and Nox. But I couldn't wait to start my life, so I took my core curriculum over summer breaks.

Part of me also expected to get kicked out before I ever got my degree. I didn't think I'd make it to high school graduation, let alone college. After all the shit my friends and I have pulled, we should've been expelled several times over. It was mostly harmless stuff. Tourist pickpocketing, underage drinking, trespassing...

Of course, there was that time when I escaped handcuffs before Nox took the cop car on a joyride. *That* was certainly a bad idea.

The worst was when we were caught breaking and entering a Bourbon Street "toy" shop at fifteen. We'd been swordfighting with the questionably large appendages, eating edible underwear, and laughing loud enough for Sabine's wife—the absolutely zero fun police chief—to hear us. Momma forced us to apologize to the shopkeeper in person, and my cheeks still flush with embarrassment thinking about his horrified face.

The fact of the matter is, I've been cleared of too many crimes to count, but everything I did was in the name of chasing a thrill. I crave adventure, like the ones in the ballets I've danced my whole life. I just hope I can find that freedom outside of New Orleans. You know, without getting arrested.

"And that's it for Bon Temps Senior Night, folks. You've been a great... wait, what is... *Oh*."

The clapping and laughter die down as the emcee reads a card a stagehand delivered.

"Alright, well this is, uh, exciting!" His uncertain chuckle says otherwise. "We're making Bon Temps Night history with this one. Ozias Thrasher, come on up."

My chest seizes, murmurs ripple through the audience, and the crowd around me backs away, leaving me alone at center stage. I glance around, catching Lucy's and Brylie's confused faces in the wings.

Then boots thump up the stage-left stairs, and Zy's dark mop of hair, wide smile, and golden tanned skin light up in the spotlight as it follows him to me. The auditorium falls silent. I try to school my "what the fuck are you doing" face.

He really is handsome. Tall—even taller than Dad and Nox—and his broad shoulders fill out a dark jacket, reminiscent of Siegfreid in *Swan Lake* but with dark jeans.

"Hey, Luna." He smiles, his deep voice soft, white roses in hand. Momma's favorite. Not mine, but still pretty.

"Uh, hey Zy, what're you doing here?"

Okay, I couldn't resist, because what the fuck?

He laughs nervously. "Hey emcee. Can I have the mic?"

What the hell?

My cheeks heat. I'm used to the spotlight, but not one that literally overshadows everyone else.

As the mic is passed, the faces that were full of tears and excitement a moment ago are now colored with confusion. Some people even look pissed. Stealing the limelight from theatre kids and dancers is *so* not the move.

"Sorry," I mouth, grimacing.

My gaze flicks to box five where Mom gives me a bewildered

shrug. Whether that's because she has no clue what's going on or because Dad's still MIA, I can't tell.

Frustration and embarrassment heat my cheeks. I resist the urge to cross my arms, gripping my tulle tutu instead.

Flee. Flee. Flee.

I don't know what's happening, but my legs literally itch to run—hell, leap—anywhere else.

Zy has the mic now. He's talking. I can't process the words, my brain fritzing out like dying speakers. Something about us dating, running into each other by chance several times at my favorite bars before he asked me out. Cool cool cool.

What. Is. Going. On—

Oh my God, he's... is he kneeling?

Nonononono.

"What are you doing?" I whisper. "Stand. Up."

But he doesn't hear me, or doesn't care, as he reaches into his pocket.

"Luna Bordeaux..."

My eyes flit around, searching for my dad, because why in God's name is he letting this happen? Something pulls my gaze to the right this time, and I find him in box six, the glossy ridges of his scars catching the light.

But my attention doesn't stop there as a guy beside him leans into the light, black hair falling over his forehead. His dark stare demands my eyes stay on him, his deep scowl sweeping a cold chill along my flushed skin.

When Zy takes my hand, for some reason, it's the guy in box six I mentally beg for help.

My gaze remains his captive, even as Zy asks, "Will you marry me?"

2

NEVER WHITE ROSES

ORION

"Damn, her tattoos are sick. I don't know if I could draw them that well," my brother, Hatch, murmurs behind me, his rough voice low. But I can hear him loud and fucking clear. "Especially the one on her thigh. I mean, look at that. When her skirt rises, you can see how far up it‑‑"

"Watch it," I growl.

He snorts. "This guy's too easy, Dash. He needs some of your 'Dr. Dashiel' monkhood discipline."

"Not like you have *any* discipline to speak of, Hatton," Dash mutters as he taps his tablet.

I'd think it was med school shit if I hadn't caught him checking a certain someone's daily post earlier. None of us have social media, but that hasn't stopped us from watching on burner accounts the past few years. With time almost up, keeping tabs is more necessary than ever.

I tune them out, leaning forward with my forearms resting on the golden railing lining box six.

My thumb traces my mouth as I mentally count.

Twenty-nine.

"You were right," Hatch tries again. "She's pretty good."

Thirty.

"Swinging her leg out like that can't be easy."

Thirty-one.

"Bet she's bendy. Tattoos, red hair, probably a freak in—"

Thirty-two.

Her raised foot lands, and I turn to slam my fist into Hatch's thigh, forcing a mix of a groan and a cackle. It doesn't matter that I've thought all those things already. What matters is she's going to be my fucking wife.

"Damn, man," he rubs his leg, his face contorted in a pained smile. "The closer you get, the easier you are."

"You'll feel it soon enough," I warn.

"Give it two years," Dash grunts, swiping his screen. With Brylie's birthday only a couple of months behind Luna's, Dash's part of the pact is coming up soon. The wait's gotta be getting to him too.

"Trust me, I'm beginning to fucking feel it," Hatch grumbles, still rubbing his quad. "Being charmingly funny helps the madness. Y'all should try it sometime."

Luna's radiant smile lights up as everyone from backstage swarms her. My reckless little rebel has gotten quite the fanbase. But there's a sadness at the edge of her eyes, and I've been trying to figure out why this entire show.

She has no plans that I know of after graduation, and I know *everything* about Luna Bordeaux. Maybe she's sad this part of her life is over? In the same beat, though, she's happy too, ecstatic even. Throughout the night, there've been glimpses of grins I've seen countless times right before she does something impulsive that I have to clean up. Her mischievous side makes her the life of the party, but the girl should at least think before she acts once in a while. Then again, she wouldn't be my Luna if she did.

The curtain falls on the celebrating seniors, making my heart stutter with anxiety that she's out of my sight so close to midnight.

"Where's that after-party again?" Hatch asks, pulling my thoughts away.

"Masque. The speakeasy underneath the opera house," I answer.

"Underground? I thought New Orleans is below sea level," Dash pipes in.

"Everything but the French Quarter. The Bordeauxs built underground tunnels during Prohibition. It's how the speakeasy is still just a rumor..."

I drift off as something in the air changes. My brothers shift, setting off alarm bells in my head.

"Mind if I join you, boys?"

The blood in my veins freezes solid. I push off the railing slowly, leaning back in my seat, arms crossed.

"It's your place, Bordeaux." I toss over my shoulder, loud enough to be heard over the music. My brothers remain silent.

I'm the eldest, which makes me in charge in our father's absence. And if anyone's going toe-to-toe with my future father-in-law, it's me.

"You're goddamn right it's my place," Sol Bordeaux growls as he slides into the seat to my left. "And it's neutral ground, in case King didn't mention that before you entered my territory unannounced and without permission."

"You forced my hand." I shake my head. "I tried reaching out last year. You know what tonight is, and you've still refused to see me."

"Correct. Because I'd have to be in my grave before I let a Fury near my daughter."

The amount he doesn't know about his daughter is hilarious. The Phantom's princess is pirouetting circles around her father, and he has no idea.

I scoff. "You didn't even ask her if she wanted to meet me, did you?"

He shrugs. "Didn't need to. I know my daughter. She'd never want to involve herself in your feud. She's my little rebel, but in matters such as this, she's—"

"Innocent." I finish quietly, nodding. "I know. I don't want to corrupt her. Despite what you think. I want to save her."

"She doesn't need saving," he snaps. "She's perfectly safe here. The last person she needs to be around is an Appalachian outlaw. Your *dairy farm* and real estate holdings don't fool the Troisgarde."

"We prefer to think of ourselves as the Robin Hood of Appalachia." A sly grin lifts my lips. "Robin Hood needs his Maid Marian."

He snorts. "Robin Hood dies in the old versions, you know."

Prick.

"Bordeaux, I'm not doing this with you," I growl. "You know the pact. If you try to 'remove' me, you'll lose an ally in King Fury's bloodline. And trust me. Right here, at this very moment... You want allies."

He stills for a second, chin tilted in my direction, like he's waiting for me to elaborate. When I don't, he settles back, playing it off like he was never interested in the first place. I'll tell him when my wife is safe by my side. Not a second before. If I tip my hand, he could hide her away from me, send her to the Lucianos in Italy like I heard he wanted. There's no chance in hell I'm letting that happen.

"You're arrogant and self-important, Orion. You're forgetting I know everything that goes on in my city. With how many shadows followed you after your arrival this morning, you might as well have had a Second Line welcome party."

This morning?

I don't let my surprise show, but Sol smirks anyway. "Like I said. I know everything that goes on in New Orleans. Never forget that."

Not everything.

"Your point?"

"My point is that I know when you arrived, and I already know when you'll leave."

"Oh?" I raise a brow, resisting the urge to smirk back.

"I want the three of you gone by dawn. The Troisgarde never agreed to King's pact. As far as McKennon, Luciano, and I are concerned, it is null and void. Three drunk men have no business betting shit like that."

"On that, we agree. But... you did. And the Wildes are picking us off one by one, and the other Fury kin are too conceited to work together. We need the blood of three on our side."

"The blood of three, boy. Not four."

"It won't be four once the pact is fulfilled. It'll be one unified alliance, connected by King Fury's bloodline."

"The Troisgarde are *not* Furys."

"Not yet. It's *your* vow we're calling on you to uphold. We're just trying to make honest men outta y'all, Bordeaux." My lip quirks, unable to stop myself this time.

Unamused, he scowls, but the killer scars on half of his face barely move. Those wounds are nothing we haven't seen before, but my own tight, rough palms itch in empathy. I wonder if Hatch feels it too.

I look away, wishing the curtain would rise already and unveil my little bird again. I need her to help me ignore the ghostly scream in my mind.

Even six years later, it's deafening.

As if he hears it, Sol's voice lowers reverently. "I'm sorry about Queenie."

I bristle and feel my brothers doing the same.

"She was a good woman, and the reason I didn't have you kicked out immediately," Sol adds, no heat behind the statement, just facts. "It's hard when they're gone. The loss..." He shakes his head.

The lump in my throat feels more like a serrated blade as I clear it. The suffocating guilt remains, though, its weight caving my chest in since that night.

"I heard you've suffered the same losses," I offer. His mother died a few years ago, and, more recently, Madam G, a woman

Luna considers a second grandmother, passed too. "My condolences."

There's a beat of silence in box six as pandemonium reigns below, the contrast as stark as two enemies confronting the other's humanity.

This is why I believe in the pact. The Troisgarde may despise us, but we'll do whatever it takes to ally with men who have the capacity to both kill for their family and mourn with the enemy who's lost his. Those are people the King Fury branch can trust.

At this point, Troisgarde or not, after watching Luna Bordeaux as long as I have, I'll do anything to make her mine, even if she hates me for it.

It's not exactly a new concept in the King Fury playbook, after all.

My phone vibrates in my hand.

Speak of the devil.

I peek at the screen.

KING

Midnight.

My eyes roll. Of course he'd send this reminder. Only catch is, *I'm* not the one who swore to be hands-off until the stroke of midnight on her twenty-second birthday. I tried, I really did. Hell, I'm still trying. King would skin my hide if he ever found out I've already broken that part of the pact. Not that it'll matter after tonight.

"How's King?" Sol asks dryly as I slide my phone inside my pocket unanswered.

He couldn't have read past the privacy screen, but he filled in the blanks. Or the Phantom's fucking psychic. Wouldn't be surprised, honestly.

"Did you tell him that my daughter will never marry into a family that ranges from professors to criminal lowlifes?"

Can't argue with that one.

"Sounds like she'll feel right at home," I drawl, earning another scowl. "And that we're the perfect fit to protect her."

"So you say, but if my daughter needs protecting, it's only because King started this war."

"No. You did, with a vow you're now trying to break."

"Vow or not, you've lost. If you knew anything about my daughter, you would've known she's in love with someone else. The Thrashers are good folks. Ozias's father and I have been friends for years. Shame you wasted your time—"

Luna's name is called, and we both fall silent as she glides past the curtain, spinning into an almost perfect fouetté.

"Flawless," Sol whispers. "That's my girl."

I chuckle. "*Our* girl's about two shots deep."

He frowns at my observation, but I just watch with pride as she beckons everyone out from behind the curtain, encouraging them to experience the most deafening roar of applause yet.

Sol's voice grates through the noise. "She'd never drink before a performance."

A response is on the tip of my tongue when the emcee fumbles and the music quiets. A man climbs the stairs to the stage, approaching a shocked Luna, who tries her best to act natural.

But I can see the forced ease in her shoulders, the tilt in her eyebrows. I can *feel* her anxiety rolling off her in waves as the spotlight homes in on—

"What the fuck?" Sol and I growl, both of us leaning forward to get a better look at Ozias crossing the stage.

He's dressed in a *Swan Lake* costume of all things, complete with a crossbow slung across his back that looks kind of like mine back in my car. And he's carrying white roses.

Luna twists the gauzy tulle of her tutu and lightly bounces on her pointe shoes, a nervous tic she's had since the first time I saw her a decade ago.

"Does that look like love, Bordeaux?" I snap, darting my eyes from him to her.

My vision tunnels, zeroing in on the stage where Ozias and Luna stand. The arms of my chair creak under my grip as he drones on about his bullshit feelings. Then...

He. Drops. To. One. God. Damn. Knee.

"What the fuck is he doing?" My voice hardly sounds like my own.

Ozias was supposed to be nothing to worry about. If the rumors are true, he has his own reasons for holding back.

Or so I thought.

But here I am seething as a ring glints in the spotlight. Luna's face blanches to a sickly pale hue, made starker by the black feather crown and veil on her head.

He takes her hand, and I can't hear a thing over the thunder in my ears.

Don't do it, little bird. Don't you—

She glances to the crowd, searching for something, until she looks up.

All feeling drains from my body.

Is she looking at me? There's no way she can see my murderous expression, but I will her to hear me anyway.

If you say yes, he's a dead man. All bets are off.

She doesn't take her eyes off mine as she crushes me with five words.

"Yes, Zy, I'll marry you."

The auditorium erupts in applause, swallowing up the *crack* of wood underneath my hands as the antique chair's arms break off. Ozias hugs her, giving her a chaste peck on the cheek.

I force myself to look away and focus all my fury on the man I was counting on to protect her whenever I couldn't.

"Did you know about this?"

He doesn't answer and I huff, shaking my head.

"Un-fucking-believable. You know what? You wanted to play ball, Bordeaux? Let's play."

His brow narrows as I continue, spitting all my venom.

"You think I don't know your daughter? She wobbled in a

turn she's been perfecting since she was twelve, which means she took a celebratory shot between her performance and her bow. White roses are her *mother's* favorite flower, not hers. And she hates that Ozias made a night meant for everyone about her." I jab my finger toward the stage. Sol's jaw ticks. "I also know this is a mind game, and her 'fiancé's' days are numbered. No one steals my wife."

No one but me.

Sol stands slowly, the rage that was on his face a second ago now placid after my outburst, like a murky lake hiding clay that can suck you under if you dive too deep.

"I meant what I said, Orion Fury. My daughter's made her choice, and it wasn't you. Which means your 'pact' means nothing. The New French Opera House and Bordeaux Conservatory are neutral ground. Start a fight here and it'll be your last. I'm only letting you stay now out of respect for your mother, but I want you out of my city by morning."

"Believe me, I'll be gone by midnight," I seethe.

He appraises me, fists clenched and vibrating at his sides, then he's gone, vanishing into the shadows of some secret passageway only he knows. I've found this place is full of them.

I turn back to the chaos below. Ozias shakes hands with congratulators while Luna looks adrift, stunned, brow bunched in confusion.

Then she looks at me.

She's probably wondering where her father went, but I lock eyes with her, leaning forward so she can see the promise there.

Hatch whistles. "Look at that Fury jealousy in full force."

"Shut the fuck up, Hatton," Dash snaps, dropping Hatch's real name like a pissed-off parent.

Hatch waits a beat, then he murmurs low, serious for the first time since they arrived, "This changes things. They figured out King's rumor was bullshit. Waiting until tonight was to mess with your head."

My teeth grind. "I know."

That's the thing about Hatton Fury. He loves fucking with people ninety-nine percent of the time. But that means one hundred percent of the time, he knows exactly how they tick.

Dash leans forward. "It's neutral ground. What do we do?"

I keep my gaze on my future bride.

"First, I'm going to take this outside. Then I'm stealing my fucking wife."

3

CORPS DE BORDEAUX

LUNA

"Pretentious-looking thing, huh?" Brylie inspects the ring, a gold band with an I-have-no-idea-what-carat boulder sits on my finger. "Ugh," I groan, snatching my hand back and turning the ring so the diamond faces my palm.

Brylie has her thinking face on while Lucy worries the feathers on her tutu from the *Swan Lake* corps de ballet she and Brylie wore to match my bodice.

For the after-party, I freshened up and changed into something more comfortable and less sweaty, while still matching the masquerade theme. Now I'm in satin ballet flats, the white swan feathered bodice without the leotard, and my *Giselle* romantic tutu. A white-veiled feather crown pins back half of my hair with the rest tamed in loose barrel curls that fall over my shoulders.

I would've felt pretty, but ever since Momma showed up, I might as well be a Troll doll. At least if I decide to dramatically cry from rage or pity, my feather mask will hide my tears.

Brylie shrugs. "Take it off. It's not like he'll notice. He's barely talked to you all night."

I wince. "It sucks that you're right."

Lucy analyzes me in that curious way she has of reading people like a book, right down to the last page. Which is a relief at the moment because I don't want to have to spell out the confusing mix of emotions inside me.

"You're spiraling, huh?" she finally asks. "That's why you're in the darkest corner of Masque?"

"Yup, I'm spiraling." I wrap my arms around my stomach, where fear, anxiety, and regret churn like a hangover from hell.

"And I don't blame you!" Brylie whisper-shouts around her drink cup. "That was like proposing at someone else's wedding."

"Not helping, Bry," Lucy scolds.

"I know, okay?" I answer anyway. "I feel awful about that too."

"*You* shouldn't feel bad," Lucy insists. "It's *his* fault."

She glares at the back of Zy's head while he probably brags about how he came up with the idea to sabotage Bon Temps Night.

I mean... propose.

"I bet he did it to corner you into saying yes," Brylie spits. "He's even telling people this is your *engagement* party. He made tacky flyers and everything."

She points to the black and gold invitations on a nearby table, save-the-dates I never agreed to.

I snort. "I appreciate the enthusiasm, Bry, but not everyone is a villain."

A strobe light flickers over her scowl. "They are in my book. At least until they prove they're the hero."

Lucy shakes her head. "In *my* books, Zy is as white knight as they come." Her nose wrinkles. "I'm partial to the villain myself."

"Really, Loose?" Benoit melts out of the shadows, resting his arms over our shoulders. "I would've expected you to fangirl over the blond romantasy prince."

"They're always the real bad guys!" Lucy scoffs. "I thought you said y'all read my books. That's romantasy 101!"

"Eh, maybe I just skim to the spicy parts. Nox is the one who actually likes them." Benoit's smirk grows as he slips her drink from her hand and downs it in one fluid motion.

"Benny!"

"I take my shadow responsibilities *very* seriously, and you know the rules. No underage drinking in Uncle Jaime's bar." He points to the man who's been in our lives since before we were born.

Jaime took over Masque when Madam G passed, and suddenly, our fun uncle became a stickler for the rules. Now he crosses his arms, wearing a raised "don't try me" brow. Lucy pouts back, hands on her hips. She's much sassier with a liquor coat on, but Jaime takes her threatening posture for what it is—adorable —and grins back.

She huffs and drops her bravado. "Okay. Y'all are rude, but whatever. I'm gonna go dance." Grabbing Benoit and Brylie, she drags them to the dance floor. They'd probably go willingly, but she's too annoyed to give any of us an option. "C'mon, Luna!"

"In a minute, I should talk to my boyfriend."

"Fiancé, you mean?" Brylie grimaces, then salutes. "Godspeed."

I automatically salute back. Godspeed, indeed.

Despite my resolve to confront Zy and my messy emotions, I slip deeper into the darkness to gather my courage.

Everyone from the auditorium has packed into Masque. Jaime outdid himself, decorating the speakeasy like an idyllic forest lake with classical ballet songs playing between mainstream dance tracks. The floor shimmers beneath my friends' feet as Benoit twirls them around. Blue strobe lights flash over Bry's and Lucy's white feathered costumes, their arms elongating like wings splashing water. They're lost in a pas de trois until two guys in light blue and gold masks spin the girls away into a waltz, leaving Benoit to eagerly head back to the bar.

All around, vines and flowers hang from the ceiling, hiding me from well-wishers and anyone I pissed off by taking their shine tonight. Only my friends know I'm in turmoil.

Is it bad to break up with a guy on your birthday? If not, it's definitely a faux pas at your "engagement party." But tonight was my personal ultimatum, and, considering that peck on my cheek after proposing out of the blue, I'm more certain than ever that there's no spark. Nothing like my last birthday.

Warm hands grip my thighs like he needs me, opening and spreading me around his hips as he holds me up, our masks keeping us anonymous, letting me just be me. His soul-destroying kiss brings me to the brink as he grinds into me, then—

He vanished like a ghost.

"The nerve," I growl, then snap my hands to my sides when I catch my fingertips tracing my lips. The guy had to be a tourist, because I never saw the clit tease again, and if I ever do, I swear I'll knee him straight in the balls. Right after he finally gets the job done, obviously.

I sigh.

Yup. More passion during fifteen minutes with a stranger than in six months with the ever-respectful Zy. Before tonight, I would've even sworn he liked someone else.

"Now what am I supposed to do?" I mutter.

"Didn't see this one coming, huh, Madam Boudoir?" Nox jokes as he strides up to me. "Oh, that's right, you were a *fake* medium before you were arrested for swindling people. But hey, at least you got a thigh tattoo out of it, right?"

There's an edge in his words, sounding just as conflicted as me.

"Like you have room to talk," I try to taunt back. "You were arrested right along with the rest of us."

"Except Lucy. We gotta learn to listen when she says to run. Our records would be a lot shorter."

We laugh halfheartedly, his temper heating his golden eyes. I wait for him to break the ice. He's almost as good as I am at avoiding emotions, but he never lasts as long.

"So, you really had no idea he was going to propose?"

"Of course, I didn't," I snap. "Did you?"

His brow lifts. "You think Dad or I would've okay'd that? I know Dad likes the Thrashers, but I don't buy his white knight act for a second. And Dad only likes him—"

"Because I don't like him," I groan. "I know."

"Well, consider that goodwill gone." Dad approaches with Momma on his arm.

He wears all black but for an owl mask and a skeleton ribcage costume beneath his cape. Momma's bronze and navy gown sparkles under the twinkling lights and matches the feathers pinned into her updo. She's stunning, and once again, she's the moon and I'm a mere shadow in her orbit.

It's not just her looks, though. She's self-assured in ways I'll never be, and graceful, like the spotlight's always on her. If I'm not en pointe, I've got all the confidence and finesse of a baby bird falling out of a nest. There's no way I'll fly if I keep getting lost in the moon.

I blink that depressing thought away and try to grin at them. But they greet me with stiff postures and hardened expressions, and I highly doubt their *Swan Lake* costumes are to blame.

Like Nox, they're clearly gearing up for a heart-to-heart. That's the last thing I want when I'm happily wallowing alone. After years of practiced avoidance, playing it off is my go-to defense mechanism to keep myself from combusting.

As soon as they leave, I'm doing it. That's my deadline. We chat, laugh, avoid, then I break up with my 'fiancé.'

Momma lets go of Dad to take my hand. "Do you know what made him propose? And so publicly? I knew you liked him, but... not enough, right?"

"No, not enough. He's so... *blah*," I sigh, then smirk wickedly. "Why can't guys be like they were back in your day when kidnapping was all the rage?"

The unscarred side of Dad's face scowls to a comical degree. "This isn't a joke, Luna."

Momma plants her hands on her hips. "And that was absolutely a 'do as I say, not as I do' situation, young lady. You're incorrigible."

"I prefer sassy, but toe-may-toe, toe-mah-toe, and all that."

Try as I might to keep the banter as just that, my stomach

twists. The joke is one of those that's laced with truth. As much as I want out of my parents' shadows, I've seen how they look at each other, filled with love, compassion, and something deeper. Their souls are forever entwined in a pas de deux, a dance so seamless one can't move without the other. Compared to that, Zy and I might as well be strangers.

Momma takes my hand again and pats it like she can read my mind. "We'll figure this out, okay?"

"She's right," Dad agrees. "As soon as the festivities are over—"

"As soon as the festivities are *over*?" I yelp, panic thrumming through me, all pretenses gone as I cross my arms. "Screw the 'festivities.' How about right now? What's going on? And why were you in box six while I was stuck center stage having my life ruined under a spotlight?"

"I had a meeting concerning Troisgarde matters." His lips thin. "The details of which you've refused to participate in."

I open my mouth to argue, but nothing comes out. Dad continues in my silence.

"I've respected that decision, *ma luné*. However, that means tonight's not the night to delve into those details. What I'll say is this engagement couldn't have come at a better time. Celebrate tonight. Come dawn, I'll explain everything."

He's right, and it's my fault. I've always played the rebellious ringleader, but that impulsive, devil-may-care attitude has gotten me helicopter parents who treat me like I'm fragile the moment things go sideways. To them, I'm the baby of the family, and not just by seven minutes.

So I do what I'm best at, apparently. I throw a tantrum like a child.

"Screw that. I promised myself I wouldn't celebrate my birthday with someone who doesn't care about me. I'm telling him tonight."

"No. You're not," Dad says firmly. "You could've avoided this if you'd have let me ship you off to Italy like the Lucianos offered."

"I wasn't going to miss my showcase! This was my last dance with my friends."

He raises his hand, calming me, but just barely. "Since you *didn't* leave, you'll have to play the part tonight. I don't want to ruin your night, *ma luné*, but you have to trust me."

"But—"

"No buts. I'll explain tomorrow. Tonight, try to have fun, okay?"

I scowl, confused, hurt, and angry. But I finally bite out through gritted teeth. "Fine."

He nods, then kisses my mom's temple, lips brushing her soft, black curls. "Come, *ma muse*. Let's get you a Cinderella drink."

Momma squeezes my hand. "Stay close tonight. Don't worry. We'll sort this out."

They turn before I can answer, so I glare into my empty cup instead.

He hasn't even gotten me a drink.

"Hey, you know I got your back, right?" Nox asks, reminding me he's still here.

I nod and initiate a side hug that bumps our cups together.

"Enough about me. Go. Have fun. Your birthday's almost over, and there's no reason both Bordeaux twins should sulk."

"True. And it's not a good look on you." He smirks and lifts his cup. I hide my smile, pretending to sip as he realizes he's coming up empty.

"You brat," he snaps with sibling outrage. "Give me back my drink!"

Spinning out of his grasp, I down his gross vodka, enduring the taste before shrugging. "Whoops! All gone. You snooze, you lose, twinny."

"Jesus, remind me to never feel sorry for you again."

"Fine by me. Go dance with your adoring fans, manwhore."

"Fine by me, little sis." He smirks, then slides into his patented "In-Nox-icating" smolder and scans the crowd. Benoit nicknamed that look as a joke, but Nox ran with it. Unfortunately.

A gaggle of Conservatory girls spot him instantly. He skipped a mask so they'd know exactly who he is.

I follow a few steps behind him, but now that my family is gone, I'm back on edge. The stares have returned, stronger than before. I swear it's from one particular direction, though.

Behind me?

I pivot slightly on the ball of one foot to squint at the dark corner I emerged from. Heat flares up my neck, my heart thumps in exhilaration, but... there's nothing there.

My breath leaves on a huff. "Weird."

"What's weird?"

I yelp, spinning around to find Zy and his two cousins flanking him.

4

WHITE KNIGHT PAS DE DEUX

LUNA

My hand flies to my chest as my heartbeat slows, but not by much.

"You scared me!"

His cousins' mouths curl into unsettling, triumphant smirks, making me shudder.

Zy frowns. "Sorry, I didn't mean to."

"Jumpy, aren't ya?" Bart laughs.

"It's fine." I ignore Bart, waving off Zy's concern. My gaze darts between the three of them. "Why aren't you wearing masks to a masquerade?"

"We don't play dress-up," Rufus rumbles, his arms crossed.

I resist rolling my eyes. *Okay, cool guy.*

Zy cuts him an annoyed glance, then gestures to his breast pocket, where two masks stick out, one black and one white.

"Didn't know which one you'd want me to wear." He nods toward my outfit and grins. "White it is."

"Fitting," Bart snickers.

"Why is it fitting?" I frown.

"Don't mind him." Zy sets his drink down and ties the white mask on. "He's an asshole. His whole family is. My mom barely claims them."

Bart purses his lips but then seems to think it over before shrugging like he agrees. Moving on, he points at my ring.

"Now that you're getting hitched, what's next?"

I bristle, but with my dad's warning ringing in my head, I fumble over what to say.

"She'll join the New Orleans Ballet Corps," Zy answers in my silence, flabbing-the-freaking-gasters out of me. He squeezes me into a side hug, beaming with pride.

But I scoff, Dad's warning be damned.

"No. I'm doing no such thing."

His face falls. Guilt needles me, but seriously, how does my *fiancé* know so little about me?

"Really?" he asks. "But you're so talented."

There it is. The expectations. God, I can't wait to get out from under their weight.

When you're in the public eye, there's this weird phenomenon where people stop seeing you as a person and start seeing you as a thing they've taken a stake in. Choosing not to pursue something you're "so talented" in becomes "unable to hack it" or "a waste of potential" just because you're not living the life they've already bizarrely mapped out for you. They don't care about your dreams if they don't align with theirs.

Those are strangers, though. It hurts most coming from someone who's supposed to know you, and the disappointment in Zy's frown makes me feel like I'm actually screwing up.

I curl in on myself, holding my stomach. "I don't know. I guess I've always wanted to travel. Be on the open road? Explore the mountains where my Momma's family is from?"

Why are these questions? Just answer the man.

A song plays for half a measure. Then he bursts out laughing, putting more gusto behind it than necessary and making me jolt.

"Oh my God, you got me good. Your dad would kill me if I let you do that."

"*Let* me?" Anger twists my lips, but he doesn't seem to notice as he and his cousins double over laughing like my hopes and dreams are a comedy show.

"I'm serious," I insist. "I wanna get out, explore, maybe hike the Appalachian Trail."

"Hike?" Bart sneers. "Sweetheart, you wouldn't last a day in those mountains."

I prop my hands on my hips. "Watch me."

The challenge thrums a defiant chord in me. If I could, I'd stomp off right now to start learning about backpacking. Just to prove the asshole wrong.

Zy pulls me in. "Come on. Why would you ever leave NOLA? Your friends, your family, your home?"

"I..."

I swallow.

Play the part.

I shake my head and pitch my voice higher. "You're right. I'm being silly. New Orleans is home."

"There ya go. You've come to your senses."

The hell I have, but I'm not here to convince three knuckleheads what I want. The only person I need to talk to is Zy, that's never been more clear.

Jesus, tomorrow can't come soon enough.

A tray of shots comes by, and Bart pulls out a wad of cash that makes my eyes nearly bug out as he signals for the waiter to stop.

"For the birthday girl." He grabs four, flashing his canines in a grin over his shoulder that makes him nearly drop them. "Help me, will ya, Rufus?"

I go up on tiptoe to figure out what the shots on the tray are, but the waiter disappears in the crowd, and I plop back down on my heels. Honestly, I'll take any liquid courage at this point.

Bart passes the shots out, leaving me last. "You look stressed. Maybe this'll help."

Zy's eyes narrow at his cousin. "I can get my fiancé a drink."

"Sorry, Thrasher. Figured I'd give my future cousin-in-law what she needed since *you* couldn't do the job." He snickers. "Damn, man, you act like you didn't have your daddy around to teach you manners or something."

Ozias's cheeks flush crimson. I want to defend him, point out that my dad wouldn't even speak to Mr. Thrasher if he didn't like the man, let alone allow me to date his son.

But something's... off.

I glance between them, trying to figure out where this tension is coming from. Rufus and Bart are practically twins with blond hair that's slicked back and teeth so big I feel like little red riding hood, their eyes watching my every movement like a predator.

Zy is undeniably handsome, dark eyes and hair, always clean-shaven, showing off his sharp jawline, although I like him best scruffy. And how could I forget Mr. White Knight's easy smile that never, ever, *ever* goes away.

Except for right now.

Zy's jaw clenches, the muscles ticking as I wait out this weird standoff. I reach up to cup his cheek, but he flinches away.

I sigh.

Typical.

The motion broke the moment for everyone though, and Zy looks his cousin up and down before he takes my shot from my hand.

"I'm getting you a drink. Be right back."

What the hell?

My eyes dart between my empty hand and his back before I eventually mutter, "Jesus, what was that all about?"

Bart chuckles behind me. "Thought he'd do that." He taps my shoulder. "No worries, princess. I always think ahead. Here."

His shot enters my field of vision, and I take it before he can spill it down my chest.

"Snagged an extra one before the waiter left. You looked like you needed more than one."

Damn right I do.

He and Rufus raise their shots, and I do the same as Bart says, "Let the good times roll, Princess Bordeaux."

I don't dignify the "princess" remark with a response, toasting instead. "*Laissez les bon temps rouler*, indeed."

We down our shots in one go, but I come up sputtering. The

overly sweet concoction makes me forget all about my Liquor Poker Face game, and I scrape my tongue with my teeth.

"What was that? Straight sugar?"

Rufus snorts. "Just like a city girl not to take her liquor."

"Aw, be nice, Roofs. The girl can't be good at everything. Nice dancing earlier, by the way." Bart backs up the compliment with a reproachful brow. "Though I was surprised to see the tats. Skulls? On a pretty thing like you?"

"Your point?" I cross my arms and settle on one foot, popping my hip.

"Kinda slutty, don't you think? Especially that one." Bart gives my legs a once-over that makes my skin crawl even though my tutu completely covers me down to my shins. "Just an observation."

"Keep your observations to yourself then, how about that?" I ball my fists at my sides. "The skull is the Bordeaux family mark."

Bart tsks. "You're not gonna be a Bordeaux forever. You don't wanna be mistaken for a Fury fucker, do you?"

The hair on the back of my neck raises.

"What did you just call me?" I haven't heard that last name in years. And *no one* speaks to me like that.

Bart shrugs. "Calling it like I see it. Skulls are the Fury's mark too. You ever met one?"

He doesn't wait for my answer. "They're these assholes that try to throw their weight around, kind of like your daddy, come to think of it." He leans in, cupping his hand around his mouth like he's telling a secret. "Trust me. Being a Fury fucker is the last thing you wanna be."

I step closer, lifting my chin. "You don't know me very well, but call me that again, and I'll go do it to spite you, asshole."

His toothy grin turns to a scowl, and his chest puffs up as he towers over me. If I hadn't had a ruthless crime boss for a father and years of mixed martial arts training, I might be more than just a little bit scared. As it is, though, I'm mostly furious.

"What'd I miss?" Zy reappears, handing me a drink that takes every ounce of restraint not to throw in Bart's face.

"Just getting to know my cousin-in-law," Bart settles back, winking at me like nothing happened.

I'm not a snitch. I'll get back at him someday, and since Rufus hasn't said a thing, he can go fuck himself too.

"Zy? I think your cousins were about to leave. Weren't you, Bart?"

A glimmer in Bart's eyes spikes my adrenaline, but I stand my ground.

Zy's gaze bounces between us and he clears his throat. "Can I talk to my fiancée alone?"

He takes my hand without waiting, the soft fabric of his gloves warm and cold at the same time.

"Sure thing, cuz." Bart grins, checking his phone, then claps Rufus's shoulder. "We're gonna grab a smoke. Join us when you're done. We've got some things to iron out."

They shoulder into the crowd, leaving me with a frown and Zy scowling at their backs. I've never seen him like this, but his temper is kind of... hot?

Jesus, I'm so starved for passion, I'll take hate at this point.

"What was all that about?" I ask.

"What? Oh, uh, nothing. Come on. I wanted to talk to you."

My chest jolts. If ever there's a time to break this news, this is it.

Sorry, Dad.

"Yeah, I wanted to talk to you too," I admit. His brow quirks up. "Do you, um, wanna dance and talk?"

Movement helps me sort my thoughts, especially when they're all over the place like now.

Apparently, that's not Zy's style.

He scratches the back of his head and points toward a corner with his thumb. "Let's just go to the back. Somewhere quieter."

He takes my hand again, and I sigh, wishing he'd... I don't know, grab my arm? Throw me over his shoulder? Anything to show he can't wait to ravish me right here and now. But, of course, he'd have to *want* to do that in the first place.

Instead, he sits us at a table near the back. The twinkling, starry lights flicker over his furrowed brow.

I swallow. "Ozias, I—"

"No, me first, please," he interrupts.

My "Okay" deflates out of me on a sigh.

This better not be like the movies where I one hundred percent wish I'd gone first.

"I know you want to leave New Orleans, but my cousins are starting their own business down here and asked me to join. My family... they need the money. And there are people I care about that rely on me to work with my cousins. So, I figured after our honeymoon you'll have the travel bug outta you, and we can set up roots here? My grandmomma would love that..."

Yup. I *one thousand percent* wish I'd gone first.

I zone out. I can't help it when I'm now the star in the movie I dreaded watching.

But the worst clichés are the storylines where the girl just suffers in silence.

So... I don't.

"*Icantdothis!*" I blurt.

"What?" he asks.

I swallow. "I can't do this."

His shoulders sag.

Oh God, did I hurt his feelings?

"I mean, I just... Zy, before tonight, I didn't even know you liked me this much. Let alone loved me."

His face clouds. I follow the thick gulp down his throat. When he speaks, his voice is rough.

"You said yes, Luna."

Okay, weird response.

I shift in my seat. "I did. But I couldn't exactly say no in front of a whole auditorium, could I? And what's with this proposal at all?"

Silence stretches between us until he slouches in his seat.

"Shit." He tries to swipe a hand over his face, stopping at the white mask and snatching it off to tuck back into his jacket pocket with the black one. "I've fucked this up, haven't I?"

I grimace, but don't disagree.

He trills his lips in defeat and pulls out a pack of cigarettes from his inside jacket pocket. "Look, I need... I need some air."

My nose wrinkles at the thought of him smelling like an ashtray when he gets back, but I keep my mouth shut. I must really have hurt his feelings. He only smokes when he's stressed.

A glance at his phone makes him curse. "Fuck. Thirty minutes until your birthday." He squeezes my crossed knee and stands. "I'll be back before then. I just need to think. We'll talk when I come back."

I nod, because what else can I do? As platonically, boringly chivalrous as Zy's been the past six months, it's still been six months. I can give him twenty-nine minutes.

"Don't worry." He chuckles as he rounds my chair. "I'll take my jacket off, so I won't smell as much."

He pats my shoulder in a way that screams brotherly. Then he's gone.

My trapped breaths rush out of me so quickly I get light-headed, like I'm no longer treading water but sinking to the bottom of a lake.

He wants to talk? What else is there to talk about? Unless Zy comes back a completely different person, I'm done.

I have to be, or I'll never get out of this town.

5

DANSE MACABRE EN SIX

ORION

"**W**hat the fuck did you say to my wife?"

My shout bounces off brick as I burst through Masque's hidden passage door and bow up on the three guys hanging out in the alley.

Rage has been riding me since I saw Luna curl in on herself when they were talking to her. The only reason I didn't charge out from the shadows was because my girl gathered her anger like a shield and stood up for herself. That, and starting a fight inside neutral ground would be a surefire way to get my ass killed before I could save her. Even then, I almost couldn't handle sitting idly by, but King's text kept me in check.

KING

Don't fuck this up. The family needs you.

Now, with a crossbow on my back, these Wildes grinning at me, and fake-ass save-the-date flyers littering the dead-end back alley, all bets are off.

"*Your* wife?" Ozias chuckles dryly as he stubs his cigarette on the brick wall. He pushes off it while his cousins uncross their arms, fight glinting in their eyes. "You mean *my* fiancée?"

"Oh, fuck off, Thrasher. Or should I say *Wilde*? Considering who your real dad is and all."

They scowl, and triumph pulses through me. Our intel was right.

But the win only proves what I've feared. Sol's slipping.

Ozias's mother had every reason to hide the truth, cheating on her husband, for one. I doubt even he knew. But the Wildes did and helped her cover it up, while Sol trusted his friends and believed he'd done his due diligence.

Which means the Wildes have gained enough influence to trick one of the most dangerous men in the country. It also means Sol's territory has grown too fast for him to keep up.

He never would've missed this if he'd let us watch his back. Instead, I had to sit on the info, banking that the rumors about Ozias were true and Luna would be relatively safe until I could make my move. Exposing the truth too soon would've blown everything wide open before we were ready.

"Wondering how I know?" I ask. "Family trees are kinda our thing in this feud. No matter how deep you bury those roots, we'll dig them up. Your mom giving you your *stepdad's* last name doesn't make you any less a Wilde."

"You don't know what you're talking about," he sneers.

"Oh? That shit proposal was only because your Wilde blood thought you could screw over the Troisgarde-Fury pact. Well, I'm here claiming what's mine. Something I understand you haven't done yet?"

I raise my brow, doubt drumming in my chest—until his twisted expression confirms my suspicions, setting me at ease.

Obviously, Luna would still be mine no matter who she chose to give herself to. But the thought of this lying son of a bitch taking her virginity under false pretenses makes me murderous. My brothers can't afford me escalating the feud to that level. Not yet.

"Christ, Ozias. That was the easy part," Rufus mutters.

Ozias's glare cuts from me to Rufus and back. My hands lift in mock surrender.

"Hey, no judgment. If I were in love with someone I couldn't have, I'd be stuck pining too."

"Keep her out of this," he growls.

"Happily." My smile drops. "Call it off with Luna, Ozias."

His fists tighten. "We'll never allow Fury filth to secure a Troisgarde alliance."

"Face it," Bartholomew, the wisecracking motherfucker who pissed off my bride, chuckles. "We beat you this time. And if Ozias can't get it done, in more ways than one, Rufus and I ain't got no problem falling on that sword."

Mother. Fuckers.

I'm vibrating with rage, but I nod and let this pent-up hatred flow through my limbs.

"Alright. Just remember, it didn't have to get bloody." I sigh dramatically. "*But* if you insist…"

I set my crossbow against the building, tucking it behind a trash can, and slide my knife from the sheath strapped to my ribs.

Bart cracks his knuckles. "Three against one doesn't seem fair, but if *you* insist—"

Two sets of heavy footfalls sound behind me. I can *feel* Hatch's maniacal grin and Dash's cold gaze as they come to back me up. Their blue and gold masks clatter to the ground.

"If you think I came alone," I shake my head, "you Wildes are dumber than I thought."

"Nah, we figured you'd be too much of a coward to face us yourself. The King Fury kin ain't got no spine. Y'all should just run off to the coast like the rest of you," Bart muses, tapping his scruffy chin. "Speaking of, how's your cousins? Heard the boy's gonna be going to that school of y'all's. And the girl…" He grins. "Well, I heard she's growing up nice and pretty."

"Shut up, you sick fuck," I snap.

He shrugs. "Think she'll take after her older sister? You know the one, Zy."

"Barty," he warns, hands clenched. "I swear to God—"

"Just like Wilde trash to have infighting. Not surprising, though. You've already got inbree—" Hatch cackles. "Well, you know."

"Speak for yourselves," Rufus spits. "Don't act like that guy who got offed for raping and murdering one of ours had all his teeth. It's a wonder y'all ain't killed yourselves off yet."

It's a wonder we haven't *all* killed ourselves off.

Enemies are closing in from all sides, especially with tensions flaring again. A spark from up North reignited it all, leaving a Wilde mother murdered, her Fury attacker dead, and her son sentenced to life. I don't blame the kid, but now every family is pointing fingers, and the fallout keeps yanking us into the fray too.

Bart's smile widens. "You know what, Rufus? I don't think they know how much we got in common. Sounds like they have no idea what's going on up in their family tree."

In my periphery, I check my brothers' expressions to see if they know what he's talking about, but they're as unreadable as I am.

Rufus snickers. "Too bad your momma fucked up sacrificing herself for you three. Or at least, that's how Daddy tells it. He says he sleeps like a baby dreaming about her screams and the crackling of that fire."

"The fuck did you say?" Hatch bursts forward, only caught by Dash with an arm across his chest.

"You heard him." Bart juts his chin at me. "He said your crossbow did fuck all that day. You even let two Wildes get away."

"And took one out," I snarl.

"Enough," Dash snaps. "With our histories, we'll run our mouths to death." He and Hatch flank me, mirroring the Wilde cousins beside Ozias. "This is between Orion and Ozias. If we're doing this, we go by Devil's Mountain rules. One-on-one fights only."

The words grate out of him like he regrets having to say them. He wants blood too. None of us are safe until the Wildes are put in their place, and he and Hatch have as much riding on this as I do.

Rufus pops his neck and all three draw blades that gleam in the alley's dim streetlamp.

Bart smirks. "Only problem there is we didn't go to that fancy-ass school."

"Yeah?" Hatch chuckles, nodding at me. "Neither did we."

A crack echoes against the brick as Hatch sucker punches Rufus, snapping his head back.

The storm breaks.

Dash and I collide with Bart and Ozias, fists and knives swinging. My blade slices a shallow line down Ozias's chest. He nicks my arm, but I barely feel it past the rush.

It's a brutal dance, Hatch and Dash in tandem against the Wilde cousins, me with Ozias. We're evenly matched, but Bart still somehow manages to run his mouth.

"Once we're done here, we're taking her with us. She won't even put up a fight."

"The fuck's that supposed to mean?" I growl over my shoulder.

"Let's just say I know how to loosen her up."

Ozias and I both hesitate before he turns on his cousin. "And what the hell does *that* mean?"

"Oh, don't act like you didn't know what was in that last drink—" He's cut off by Dash, lost in the fight as he kicks the guy's ribs, cracking bone.

"Stay away from the Troisgarde daughters," Dash grunts, fending off a right hook and slashing Bart's thigh.

Hatch seizes the opening and drives an elbow into Bart's chin. Dash spins to cover our brother, facing Rufus. My brothers and I are a well-oiled machine, and it's never clearer than when we fight.

Rage and urgency war inside of me. I need to get to Luna, stop her from drinking whatever's in that cup—

A fiery slash burns up my side, and a fist slams my jaw, clacking my teeth into my cheek.

Stars flash. Iron floods my mouth as I meet Ozias's eyes. His grim expression and bloody teeth mirror mine.

"You'll only get her killed, Orion," he seethes. "That's what happens to the women in your family. Your aunt, your cousin...

You couldn't even protect your own mother. Why do you think you can protect your wife?"

A roar tears out of me as I drive a kick into his chest, sending him crashing to the ground.

Then I'm on him, punching hard enough to whip his head sideways with every blow, making him groan, "You son of a—"

An engagement flyer flutters through the chaos, and I snatch it midair. Before I can stop myself, I rip Zy's own knife from his hand, slap the invitation against his cheek and drive the blade through both.

His face seizes, stunned by the pain, but his body still thrashes, reaching for the weapon, until I pin him under my knees.

I lean over him as he fights me. "It's sad it had to come to this, Zy. You should've left my girl alone."

Rage enters his eyes, and I smirk, twisting the knife.

"So, consider this my and my wife's 'regrets.'"

Warm blood seeps through the paper like ink, soaking my fist around the hilt. His limbs go slack under me. His eyes roll back. Then he's out cold.

I leave his knife in and wipe my hand on his dress shirt before climbing to my feet. My arm wraps around my torso as I suck in sips of air, but I still pivot to help my brothers.

Rufus is shit-talking now, both Wildes' backs turned on their cousin.

"We either get the Troisgarde daughters or remove them as Furys. I'm partial to that feisty one. What's her name? Brylie?" He laughs. "God, have you seen that ass? All I want to do is fuck it raw until she cries—"

Dash snaps. I don't see what happens with Bart in the way, but I hear it. The sickening slice. The thud onto brick. The death rattle as air leaves the lungs for the last time.

Everyone freezes.

"Goddammit," Dash breathes. Bart shifts, revealing my brother as he jumps off Rufus, knife dripping blood.

Rufus's eyes are wide and empty.

Lifeless.

"Well, shit," Hatch mutters.

"What the fuck did you do?!" Bart screams, swinging wildly at Dash, but Hatch and I grab his arms.

Dash staggers back, tearing at his hair. "*Fuck!*"

"You killed my brother..." Bart scans for his backup, finding Ozias unconscious on the ground. "And my *cousin*? You're dead. You hear me? Life..." His voice falters. "Life for life."

"This already was life for life," I counter harshly.

"No! No. *You* did this!" He wrenches free, crazed desperation in his eyes, his knife swinging frantically between us. "The Troisgarde daughters have been in danger from the moment we heard about the pact." His eyes blaze. "Dead or alive, we don't care. But we'll *never* let you have this alliance."

"And you still think this wasn't already about life for life?" I snap, taking one stride to yank a bolt I designed from my crossbow's custom quiver and point it at him. "You Wildes think this is a goddamn game, but you're killing our people, threatening our *wives*. This feud isn't a game." I grab my bow from against the wall and use the stirrup to load it, but when I finish, I keep the weapon hanging at my side. "Why the fuck do you think we'd let that slide?"

"And you killed *two* Wildes," he counters. "You just started a fucking war."

"This *was already* a war!"

"Zy will live," Dash interrupts in his detached, clinical tone. He's kneeling beside Ozias, hands bloody from taking the guy's pulse at his crimson-streaked neck. "The wound isn't life threatening. He's passed out. Get him to a surgeon, and he'll recover. Just with a gnarly scar."

Even in this loud city, silence sits heavily between us, leaving only the sound of Ozias's steady, ragged breaths.

A crow caws farther down the alley, breaking the moment, and sound rushes back in, including Bart's shout.

"All y'all are still dead—"

Before he can react, I fire a bolt into his leg. He yelps, grabbing his thigh.

"You..." the rest of whatever he was going to say gets lost in a garbled cry as he lurches forward, hitting cobblestone with a thump, face first.

"Please tell me that was a tranq dart," Dash groans, his bloody hands driving into his own hair.

"It was," I answer. "He'll wake in the morning. But Ozias is a hiccup. We need to get him to the hospital. We can't have him dying on us too."

Dash stands, eyes dragging to Rufus. The weight of what we've done settles in.

One of us was bound to fuck up, but I'd planned for it to be me. I'm already throwing down the gauntlet by taking Luna, but with one dead, the Wildes will want vengeance. This feud's never over, and while the Wildes sprinkled gas on an ember, the King Fury kin just blew shit wide open.

I have to get Luna out *now*.

Hatch looks to Dash, then straightens. "I'll drop them off at an ER and take care of the body. Dash, work on the diversion. We'll deal with the rest later. What matters is the alley's clear like you needed, Orion. Go get your girl. We've got this."

"Wait," Dash says, fishing out a plastic baggie from Rufus's coat pocket. He holds it up to a distant streetlamp, and the light gleams against a makeshift blister pack.

My heart stutters. "Bart said he knew how to 'loosen her up.'"

"He mentioned something about her last drink..." Hatch curses, "Fuck, I swear I kept an eye on things the entire time, even when I was with Lucy, but I didn't catch that."

"Same with me and Brylie." Dash shakes his head. "Zy only bought them both one, and he downed his before he came out here."

"Fuck, fuck, *fuck*," I shout the last, pacing. "Can you tell what they are?"

Dash narrows his eyes at the pack. "I'll try. Looks like only half of one is missing."

Hatch whistles. "That's a first strike as far as I'm concerned. Putting a woman in danger like that? Rufus is a sanctioned kill."

"I don't give a fuck about that. I've gotta go."

I wipe my face, checking for blood. When I finally come away with none, I grab Ozias's jacket from the chair he'd hung it on, taking the black mask and gloves from the pocket, then yank them all on. He and I have dark hair, similar builds, and I'll pop my collar to hide my neck tats. Thank fuck my mouth isn't bleeding anymore.

Between the dark, strobe lights, mask, and flowing alcohol, I can pass as my enemy. I just have to move fast if I want to make sure the cuts burning all over me don't seep through the jacket, so I turn to go.

"Orion," Hatch calls, catching me before I enter the hidden passage to Masque. "Give us till midnight for the distraction."

I check my phone. "Twenty minutes?! I need her out now. Especially if she drank that last drink."

"You want Sol's men on you?" He asks, his pierced brow lifting toward the thorny rose inked along half his black hairline. "If she didn't drink whatever they gave her, we have to stick to the plan. So, midnight."

"If she's safe..." I exhale, then nod once. "Midnight."

6

BLACK MASKED PAS DE DEUX

LUNA

I would normally *never* be the girl hiding in the corner of the bar, scrolling social media while everyone else has fun. I'm usually the life of the party, the one dragging people to the dance floor and buying shots for the whole place.

But every congratulation for this sham of an engagement stifles me more than the last. I'm suffocating, *this close* to calling it. The night. My relationship. Hell, being in New Orleans at all.

Lucy and I have talked about it, the expectations that come with being part of the Troisgarde, the elite in this city. Brylie's prickly attitude makes her immune, but Lucy and I get bombarded everywhere we go, online and in real life. Our actions are heavily scrutinized, and not just onstage.

That's why leaving is so tempting. Just... disappearing. Lucy and I fantasize about it all the time. Being anonymous, normal. That's what I want right now. Rebellion and sabotage itch under my skin, telling me to flee and never come back. It'd devastate my parents, but I need to do something or I'll combust.

I press my fingers to my temple, trying to massage away an impending headache.

My emotions are everywhere. I'm running on fumes, adrenaline, and alcohol—a terrible combo, but that's what I get for pregaming two nights straight. A surprise proposal by the guy I was one conversation away from breaking up with doesn't help either.

"May I have this dance?" a deep voice says, barely audible over the thumping music.

A black-gloved hand enters my vision, palm up. My gaze rises to find Zy in the Siegfried costume jacket, its high collar raised to his jawline, a crossbow peeking over his shoulder, and his dark hair tousled over his black mask. The costume team really went all out on the prop weapon. It looks real, not that I'd know the difference. And Jesus, I knew Zy was big, but sitting down like this, he looks as massive as a Saints football player.

His sharp focus needles into me like he's searching for signs of... something.

"You feel okay?" he asks, an edge to his voice. His posture is stiff but his hand is still out casually, waiting for me to hold it.

I blink. "Yeah... of course, I just..." Even with all that running through my mind, only one thing comes out. "You changed your mask."

His lips twitch, and I swear his shoulders relax. "The white wasn't me."

"Fair enough." I laugh.

A small smile curves his lips, then he blinks quickly, shaking his head.

"Hold on." He pulls a bouquet out from behind his back—*where the hell did he get that from*? "For you."

I blink, taking in the wildflowers and blush roses amidst sprigs of green, with downy feather accents. A lush meadow fills my hands as I slowly take it and inhale deeply.

The scent reminds me of family road trips through mountain parkways, my hand surfing the wind outside the car window. After the awful meeting that changed everything, we never went back.

My eyes sting, my voice suddenly watery, and I have to clear my throat. "But you already got me flowers."

The ones my mom loves.

"You like these ones," he says simply, like it's no big deal.

"Did you go to Saint's Petals?" It's our family's favorite store, and the only place in the city that always stocks my favorites for me.

"Is there anywhere else? I got them before your show. My... cousins brought them from my car before the party, and I hid them in the corner until I could have my first real moment alone with my fiancée. Miss Mabel's son says, 'Hi,' by the way."

His words are slower than usual, but maybe that's the shots catching up to me. Or the fact that this guy I questioned everything about a few minutes ago just asked me to dance and gave me my favorite flowers from my favorite store.

He closes my dropped jaw with a gentle lift of his gloved finger.

"You sure you feel okay?" he asks again, but with less worry behind it this time. "You look a little confused."

"I am." I tilt my head at him. "I think I'm not used to this side of you."

"Ah. Makes sense." His grin suddenly sends my stomach all a-fluttery, and he motions to me with two fingers. "Come on, Luna Bordeaux. Dance with me."

For the second time this conversation, my lips part in surprise, entranced by the man who most assuredly got hit on the head during his smoke break. But hell, if he's asking me to dance, I'm not gonna pass up the opportunity.

I use the tablecloth and mountains of tulle in my tutu to covertly slide my phone back into the carrier garter on my thigh that Brylie's mom, a costume designer, made for me. Zy tracks the movement, and I swear there's heat there I've never seen before.

Or maybe that's wishful thinking.

Before I take his hand, I reach for the drink I've barely touched, but it's snatched from me.

"Zy, what the hell?"

"How much of this have you had?" he growls, almost to himself, but the emotion behind it makes me shiver.

"Maybe a sip? Why?" I grimace. He *did* buy it for me.

"*Maybe* a sip?"

"Ugh, okay, you got me. None of it alright? I'm sorry, but it smelled like rotten cotton candy and overly sweet drinks aren't my style."

His lips purse, but the tension in his forehead eases, his voice gentling. "And this is the only one I've gotten you?"

"Weird question," I say, barely resisting being a sassy bitch. "But yeah, Ozias. That's the only drink you bought me."

He blows out a deep breath and nods.

"Good."

Then he chucks the damn thing into a nearby trashcan.

"Hey!"

"Don't worry." His smile returns, fully carefree and wide this time. "If we have time, I'll get you another one after our dance."

"You really want to dance with me?" I ask, a little starstruck by the way the twinkling lights highlight the excitement flickering in his eyes.

"Yeah, Luna, I really wanna dance with you." His gloved hand finds mine, not letting me stall anymore and laying the bouquet on the table. "We can grab them before we leave tonight."

I frown at the wording, but then the music shifts into a sultry, slow beat as he leads me onto the dance floor. In the crowd, I see Brylie and Benoit dancing together, and Nox twirling around two girls I've never seen before, both of whom he'll probably take home. Lucy's nowhere in sight, but we're in the safest bar in New Orleans, and my dad is literally stalking us all from the corner...

Wait, where is he?

Zy wraps his arm around me, spinning me to the beat, and catching me off guard. I giggle as he pulls me into his chest and leads me away from Dad's usual corner booth. One gloved hand slides into mine, and the other rests on my lower back. Even through the fabric, my skin tingles underneath his warm palm, radiating a flush of desire through me.

Now he decides to pull out the stops? I exhale through my

nose and can't help my scowl, allowing myself to daydream about throttling him for turning my mind and body into an emotional wreck for the past few hours now. It's not like he'll see the expression through my mask.

He glances down and his lips quirk before he rumbles, "Don't look at me like that, Luna."

Oh God, Jesus, Mary, and Joseph, has my name ever sounded that sweet off his tongue? Like he's tasting it slowly, savoring it. Pressed against him, I can feel every syllable vibrate from his chest and into mine. I want to curl into him until what he said hits me.

Oh.

Could he tell I was scowling at him?

Oops.

I swallow and ask hoarsely. "Like what?"

His head dips, brushing featherlight lips along my cheek.

"Like you can't decide if you want to make love to me or hate-fuck me right here on this dance floor."

My eyes widen, and I freeze, but his hands just tighten around me as he twirls me again. I glide with him, my body flowing in his embrace like we've danced for years, all while my brain short-circuits.

"I... I don't want to hate-fuck you."

"Not yet anyway. We're young. It'll happen eventually." A sinful smile graces his full lips. "But the alternative sounds damn good to me."

Any response I could have disappears in my watering mouth because...

Oh.

My.

God.

He's shocking me. I am well and truly shocked, and it feels like I'm seeing my fiancé for the very first time.

We're hardly ever this close, and now I can't take my eyes off him. Is there more stubble on his jawline? Five o'clock shadow is just a saying, right? It looks hot as hell on him, outlining those lips that I'd love to taste.

No. I'm *ending* things tonight. Just because he's acting the exact way I've always wanted him to, and then some, getting knocked on the head during his cigarette break doesn't mean any—

Wait.

I sniff.

Huh.

I'd expect the pungent scent of cigarette smoke, but instead, I get crisp river air winding through pine forests, cut with sweet bourbon. I breathe him in without meaning to, and his arm tightens, pressing me against his chest and making my lower belly clinch.

"You don't smell like smoke," is all I manage.

Smooth, Luna.

"I decided against it," he murmurs into my hair, then his thumb brushes my shoulder. "I like these. Your tattoos. The skulls are... fuck, they're perfect."

I pull back. "You like them?"

"Yeah. I'm surprised your dad let you get them."

I snort. "He didn't have a choice once I bribed someone outside New Orleans to do it." I shrug. "I wanted to wear our family's mark."

His dark eyes flash. "And so you do."

Those words are thick like caramel. He tugs me impossibly close as he guides me through the chorus, placing my hand on his shoulder before skimming down my torso. His hand drops low, grazing where the skull's wreath of flowers bloom up my upper thigh.

"I especially love the one here."

I shiver from the heat in his voice and touch. But I bite my lip until anger and uncertainty drives the question from me.

"It doesn't make me look like a Fury fucker?"

His steps falter. His gaze hardens. "*What*?"

I shouldn't have said anything, but my tongue's looser than usual—*thanks, alcohol*—and here I go spilling things I shouldn't.

"It's what Bart called me."

His lips thin. "And what did you say back?"

My eyes widen. *Whoops.*

"Nothing."

"Luna..." he warns, eyes narrowed.

I wince. "You're not gonna like it."

"Try me."

"Okay... but remember I'm a brat sometimes."

He snorts. "Noted."

I worry my lip. "I said if he called me that again, I'd go fuck a Fury to spite him."

I brace for impact, ready for hurt, or disappointment, or anger to hit me.

But instead, he bursts out laughing.

The sound is deep and rough as it tumbles from his chest. But most of all, it's carefree. Like his lungs aren't used to releasing something so unburdened. It's heartwarming, and I... I've never seen it before.

He finally catches his breath, sighing as he leads us back into the dance, and I'm so enthralled, I barely stop myself from tripping.

"And what did he say to *that*?"

"Nothing," I answer, a little dazed by how happy he looks. "I think he was afraid I'd go do it, and I was afraid I'd let it slip about the pact."

"The Troisgarde-Fury Pact?" His focus sharpens on me, and my stomach drops.

Double whoops.

"You know about that?"

He clears his throat. "Everyone where we're from knows about it."

I groan. "Jesus. I didn't realize it was public knowledge. It's not like there's anything to even talk about. My dad shut it down years ago. It would've been a nightmare if I had to go through with it."

Zy's jaw ticks. "You sound like the pact is a curse."

"Isn't it? We're not in medieval Europe, and I certainly didn't choose to get married to a stranger."

At that, I swallow. I guess this is as good a time as any.

"Uh, not-so-tangential segue here, but did you... think about what I said?"

I wish I could see his expression, but even without his mask, the strobes have started to cast a weird blur over his features.

"Uh, yeah," he hesitates. "I did."

I blow out a breath. "Like I said, I don't want to stay here. I know you want to settle down in New Orleans, but I need out. I need to roam. I've been dying to go back to the mountains, and I need to leave the nest at some point."

A soft smile quirks up his lips. "So do it."

"You said you wanted to stay here." I smirk, confused.

"What can I say? You've convinced me to change my mind."

I want to laugh, but it's just too little too late.

"Don't you feel like there's something missing between us? Some... spark?"

His thigh slides between mine as he dips me, going higher than any of my partners onstage ever have. My lower belly swoops, and my core clenches. I've performed moves like this thousands of times, but never like *this*.

"No," he finally answers, eyes hard, and... darker than normal. "I think we're fucking made for each other."

My breaths catches in his thrall. "Made for each other?"

He nods. "You wanna roam? I'll go with you. So..."

Then he whisks me back up, and lifts me, making me feel light and fluttery. Weightless in his hands. My tutu swirls as he pulls me back in and whispers in my ear.

"What's it feel like to fly, little bird?"

My heart soars. Maybe this is what it's supposed to feel like. Maybe this *is* the spark.

Dizzying pleasure dances over my skin, stealing the breath from my lungs and making me lightheaded, but I focus on him. He dances with me so effortlessly, skilled, *practiced* even. It's exhilarating, and I can't help chuckling in disbelief.

"Who *are* you, and where did you learn to dance like this?"

"I'm your fiancé," he says seriously, the word that felt like a cage fifteen minutes ago now giving me that same floaty sensation that I had in the air. But then he swallows before answering the rest. "And my momma taught me to dance."

The weight in his voice presses on something tender in me. "You don't talk about her much. Only your grandma. Grandma B, I think you called her?"

"Grandma B... yup, that's what I call her. Good ol' Grandma *B*." He scowls. "She prefers to go by Bossie, and trust me, she lives up to the rep. That lady's mean as a snake."

I chuckle awkwardly. "I thought you liked her?"

"Nope. She's a bit of a ruthless bitch if I'm honest. Don't worry. She'd say the same. Proud of it, actually. My Grandma Francine is the sweet one. Fancy lives on the land with us. Still works Momma's dairy farm."

"Dairy farm? Grandma *Fancy*?" I shake my head. "See? This is what I'm talking about. It's like I barely know you. Before tonight, right this very moment, I've felt more chemistry being reckless with strangers at Pirates than the entire time we've dated! We haven't even really kissed!"

Yikes. That was harsh. But it *is* true. Aside from tonight, I've never felt that same needy, breathless desire that I did on my twenty-first birthday. These past few songs, I've tasted it again, and it solidified for me how badly I need it. What if he goes back to being the boring white knight tomorrow?

"Strangers at Pirates?" he finally muses, a sly smile forming. "That's awfully specific."

He stops our dance long enough to check his phone, and murmurs.

"Thirteen minutes to your birthday."

That grin creeps further up, and my chest flutters as he pulls me into his embrace again.

"Wanna do something reckless, little bird?" His lips caress my neck, right under my ear, before hovering over my mouth. "Let me show you just how fucking bad I want you, Luna Bordeaux."

7

BACKSTAGE ENTANGLEMENTS

LUNA

I barely get out the word "Yes" before Zy whisks me to a dressing room for Masque's visiting bands. I have no idea how we got past my dad—the whole bar was a blur—but the second we're inside, Zy locks the door, tipping back a chair one-handed to lodge under the doorknob. He dims the lights before sweeping off the makeup counter with one arm, then plops me on the surface with my bouquet next to me. I hadn't even realized he grabbed it.

Excitement sparks across my skin. Emotions I haven't felt in a year make me lightheaded. I was supposed to break up with him, but my white knight boyfriend is *finally* making a move, venturing into this dark, sensual side I've begged for. I'm ready to see where this goes, my body feeling looser and more free than I ever have as intoxicating anticipation rolls through me.

In my periphery, he removes his crossbow off his back and sets it against a chair, then tugs off his gloves before resting his hands on the counter on either side of my hips. The bright lights behind me cast a shadow around my head, and that, combined with his black mask, make it hard to see the details of his intense expression. What I can see, though, has my mind swimming with heady need and my sex pulsing as he leans closer, taking up all my vision.

I suck in a breath as he reaches under my tutu without touching me and pushes it up my upper thighs to step between my bare legs. My panties are a measly piece of fabric against his rough jeans, barely shielding me from his hard length trapped behind his zipper. If the bulge against me is any indication, he's *huge*. How had I never noticed that?

Oh yeah, he's never been turned on by me before. At least not that I could tell. But there's no denying it now.

My mouth waters, body aching for touches and sensations I've craved since my birthday last year with a stranger.

I bite my lip, and his gaze drops to my mouth. Have his eyes always been this dark, or is it just the lighting?

When his low voice rumbles from his broad chest, I stop caring.

"You have no idea how long I've wanted to do this."

My voice is hoarse. "Do what?"

He cups my neck, palms both rough and smooth, and lifts my chin.

"Make you mine."

His lips crash with mine in a possessive claim, not kissing, *taking*, as his tongue demands to be inside. I open on a moan, greedy to taste him. My hands grip one of his wrists, and my legs pull him into the cradle of my hips. His grip stays on my neck, keeping me exactly where he wants me while his other hand grabs my ass under the tulle, grinding me against his cock.

"I've missed your taste so goddamn bad."

My brows bunch, but I resist pointing out you can't miss something you've never had. Only one person has kissed me like this, and it was definitely not him.

As if he's greedy to prove me wrong, he bites my lip hard enough to make me whimper, then soothes the sting with his tongue. I clutch the lapel of his costume and pull him closer, my hips moving with his as he thrusts how I hope he will when I finally get those jeans off.

The jacket goes first though, with him shrugging it off and revealing a black T, stretched tightly over his shoulders and biceps.

Didn't he have a dress shirt on before?

He nips my jaw, sending an electric shiver down my spine while he murmurs, "*Fuck*, Luna."

Oh right, *who cares*?!

I knead muscles that I've never explored, tracing rolling hills and valleys as they flex beneath my fingers.

God, he's big. Bigger than I realized. Then again, I've never been *this* close to him. Or maybe the alcohol is making me forget.

If I don't remember this, I am going to lose *it.*

His hand returns to grip the front of my neck as his tongue dives into my mouth again. I love the pain when his scruff scratches my chin. I love this intimacy, this desperation. All of it. He's giving me everything I've needed.

I wrap my legs around him, pulling him flush to the apex of my thighs, afraid it'll end like last time.

Don't leave.

"I'm dying to be inside you... but I don't have time. Not to prep you and take you the way I want you."

"*What*?!" My eyes widen. "No, no, no. We have time. We have all the time in the world."

His thumb brushes my jaw as he chuckles darkly. "Oh, you're right about that. Just not tonight."

I almost whine. God, how embarrassing. But then his lips quirk up, and his hand on my neck molds down my curves.

"Aw... don't cry. There's something else I've been dying to do too."

He jerks me forward, until my ass hangs off the counter's edge. I yelp, catching myself on his shoulders as makeup products clatter to the floor.

I blink at his neck, my vision doubling at the black design there. Huh.

"When did you get neck tatt—"

A loud *rip* interrupts the thought. My gaze jerks from what I swear looks like a blurry inked skull to the strip of tulle he's tying around my wrist.

"Hands behind your back."

"Behind my back?" I echo with a bewildered laugh as I obey. "Uh, why?"

"You're a flighty little thing, birdie," he says, giving me a pointed look. "Now be a good girl and let me tie up my fiancée so I can feast on her cunt."

My eyes widen, and I straighten, eager to help him do exactly what he promised. This side of him is positively delicious, and he knows I love it. It's in his smirk as he huddles over me, pressing to my chest, while he ties the tulle around my wrists. Desire pulses in my lower belly. Bondage *and* my virginity in one night? I'm a lucky, lucky girl.

He tests the tight knot once then slides something off my finger as he backs up. The ring glints in the mirror lights. My focus zeroes in on the unfamiliar, glossy grooves lining his palm, but the anger in his clenched jaw draws my attention before he pockets it.

"What're you doing?"

"That one didn't fit you." He leans me back against the mirror, a devilish smile lifting his mask. "But don't worry, baby. I'll give you the ring you really want."

His hands slide over my breasts and squeeze, making me moan, and I forget everything else as his fingers curl under my sweetheart neckline.

"Mmm, I love your tits."

He pulls my bodice down until my nipples pop free, forcing my small breasts to rise obscenely to my chin. I gasp as he dips in, licks, blows, and sucks on one, making it pebble while he tweaks the other with his fingers, then switches. The connection zings to my clit.

"*Zy!*"

He jolts, pinching my nipple and biting into my other breast *hard*, making me inhale sharply.

"That's not my name," he growls.

"What?" I ask, confused.

He nips again, making me yelp. Then his lips skate up my

chest and neck with open-mouthed kisses, tongue, and teeth, ending with his hands cupping my breasts and his lips over my pulse at my neck.

"I am your *fiancé*, Luna Bordeaux."

I hum, "My fiancé."

For the first time tonight, I *love* the sound of that.

"Only mine," he says low, erupting goosebumps down my neck and chest.

"Only yours," I pant, lust clouding my mind.

"Perfect," he murmurs, then nods to the standing mirror across from us. My tutu is pushed up to my hips now, and I have the perfect view of my legs splayed out for him as his hand drifts down to cup my sex. "Now watch me taste this sweet cunt for the first time."

My heart stops and my mind is a foggy cloud of lust as I obey him. He hooks a finger under fabric that's slick with my arousal and pulls it aside, tightening the elastic around my upper thigh. His long finger teases my clit before gliding through my arousal to barely enter me.

"Please," I moan.

"Tell me you want me to taste you. Tell me you want your *fiancé* to taste you."

"Please…" My eyes are locked on the version of me begging in the mirror, needy and willing to do anything for him, despite this sham of an engagement. "*Fiancé*. I need you to taste me."

His voice lowers an octave. "Anything for you, my bride."

He kneels for me and curses. My gaze snaps away from the man in the mirror to the one looking at my sex like he's starved for me all this time.

He grips my thigh over my tattoo with one hand, and the other spreads me to swipe his tongue through my arousal.

I cry out as he swirls the bundle of nerves at the top. His eyes lift to mine, and I suddenly ache to see the rest of him behind the black mask, but my wrists are still tied behind my back.

He pushes tulle higher around my hips, giving me a better

view as his tongue laves into my core, up and down through my arousal and around my clit.

"Mirror," he murmurs, and I drag my gaze back to our reflection.

My body heaves, a rosy flush blooms from my breasts up to my cheeks as I bite my lip and ride his tongue. I look wanton and desperate, rebellious in the best ways.

He moans into my core as he feasts on me, and his growing hardness tents his jeans. That reaction? It's for *me*. He grips both thighs to spread me now, putting his whole body into making me feel good. And it feels *amazing*, but now all I want is him in my mouth.

I lick my lips and swallow so I can gather my courage to tell him so, but my throat's gone dry.

Strange. I'm mentally salivating for this man, but my body hasn't gotten the memo.

His tongue dips into my core, swirling around the entrance, and I moan as sensation rips through me. I try to keep my eyes open to watch him devour me, but I'm barely hanging on by a thread as it is. I slip against the mirror, and catch myself by digging my heels into his upper back.

He chuckles against my core, making me shiver. "Patience, my little bird."

I don't know where this nickname came from, but I'm digging the way his accent drips over it like syrup. He grips my leg like he owns me, hand slipping under the lace garter that holds my phone to palm my tattoo. His own skull tattoo cover his hand and letters cover his knuckles—

I frown.

Zy doesn't have hand tattoos...

He nips my clit. "Give me those pretty eyes."

I moan, "Oh God."

"Not God. Fiancé."

"*Fiancé*," I echo instantly.

His chuckle rewards me with a teasing vibration against my

clit, making my muscles tighten and my toes curl. That feeling I've craved since I almost captured it a year ago builds again. I can almost pretend this is a continuation of that feverish night, like time never passed, and I'm already right on the verge of coming as I grind against his mouth, chasing it.

But I'm exhausted. I'm usually keyed up after a performance, but I'm afraid the last few nights have caught up with me. My strength has almost completely drained from me.

Outside, the crowd cheers the countdown to midnight, the switch from Nox's birthday to mine. I'm missing it, but I don't care. I'm ringing in my twenty-second year with a damn bang.

He circles my clit, and a soft moan escapes me on a heavy breath.

My vision's fading at the edges, and my orgasm fades with it despite how hard I'm fighting to keep it.

Wait. Is that normal?

I blink, trying to focus, but my head's too heavy, my eyelids like sandpaper. I slump against the mirror. My legs lay limply over his shoulders, no longer pulling him in. His mask shifts over his narrowing eyes.

"Luna?" His voice is even slower and deeper than before.

My body shudders weakly. Almost like an afterthought.

"I'm... I feel..."

"Fuck, Luna." He shoots up, snapping my panties back in place, pulling my bodice over my breasts.

"Wait! No! Come... Come back! Please," I whine. "I want you."

He takes my feather mask off and sets it aside before cupping my cheeks.

"Your hands... they're rough and soft at the same time," I mutter.

Ignoring me, his eyes scan my face. "What the fuck did they do to you?"

Worry narrows his dark brows and concern swirls in his eyes —one hazel-brown with forest green specks swirling around the center, the other its stunning opposite. Were they always that many colors? I feel like I've seen ones like that before... once.

I gasp.

"It's *you*."

He ignores my revelation that he's the same guy who disappeared on my birthday and squeezes my cheeks, holding my head up.

"Focus, baby. You said you didn't drink that drink I gave you. What else have you had?"

What's the big deal?

My voice croaks as I form the words past the Sahara Desert in my mouth. "Shots backstage..."

"No, Luna. *Here*, in Masque."

"Oh... " I try to think. "There was Bart's shot."

His eyes narrow as he mouths the last two words, then curses, "*Fuck!*"

Still holding me upright, he jerks his phone out and puts it on speaker.

"Dash. Question."

Why is he talking about punctuation?

"Yeah?"

"How much did Rufus have left again?"

There's a pause that lasts an eternity. Or maybe a second. I don't know. I'm hot and want my fiancé back.

Using my limp legs, I try to tug him closer, but I think I'm falling because his arm bands around my waist.

"Best I can guess is they used half a pill. Maybe crushed Molly or some kind of party drug into her drink? Not a lot, but enough."

"Symptoms?" The stranger from last year watches me closely.

The other voice curses. They kinda sound alike. Even their drawl is the same.

"*Ten!*"

The countdown outside makes me smile. "It's almost my birthday!"

"Can't know for sure, but these things usually cause drowsiness, arousal, dry mouth, euphoria, mood swings."

I giggle. "Sounds like me."

A tinny growl crackles over the phone. "With as little as they used, it'll run through her system fast. But they probably dosed her with enough to make her compliant."

"Son of a bitch."

Death enters the stranger's eyes. Not at me. Past me, or about me maybe? He brings me into his chest, arm locked around my waist as he asks, "Is Hatton ready?"

"Three!" The crowd continues.

"Hatton? Wait. I think I know a Hatton."

"Two!"

"Shh, baby, I'm listening."

I pout. "Don't *shhhhh* me. I'm twenty-two now."

"One!"

"Yeah. Good to go, hoss."

"Hoss?" I huff. "You guys have such weird names."

"Be there in five. Y'all take your cars back. Throw them off track."

He hangs up and then looks at me, grimacing. His thumb rubs my numbing cheek. "Just remember that I wanted to do this the right way. I *would've* done this the right way. But I've been given no choice."

"Happy birthday, Luna!"

Something slams against the door. I jump. Oh God, someone's trying to break it down.

He exhales. "It's showtime, birdie."

"Get your fucking hands off my daughter, Fury!"

"Wait... " My eyes snap open. "You're—"

"Your husband," Orion Fury says proudly. His apologetic frown lifts into a smile as he rips off his black mask. "And it's time you come home with me, pretty bride."

8
FLY AWAY DEAD MAN
ORION

She opens her mouth, but I quickly cover her scream.

"Shh, shh, you'll be safe soon. Just don't fight me."

Naturally, she doesn't listen, her clear lake eyes blazing as she sinks her teeth into my scarred palm.

"Fuck!" I snatch it back.

"Orion *Fury*?!" she shouts, adrenaline overpowering the drug in her system. "You *asshole*!"

The door behind me rattles with every staccato bang.

"I think you mean hubby," I chuckle, trying to play off the fact I need to grab her sweet little ass and get out of here before her father breaks that door down.

In true Luna Bordeaux fashion, "compliant" isn't in her blood. She's the Phantom of the French Quarter's daughter, a fighter through and through. Her limber body lands a few painful strikes against my ribs, slowing me down.

She's been mine since the night our fathers made that bet before we were born, but this fury in her right now—my fucking namesake—is the hottest confirmation I could ask for.

One particularly sharp knee lands above my dick, making me double over around her right as the door breaks open. Sol fills the frame, his finger stabbing the air at me. His owl mask hangs crooked, and even the scarred half of his face twists with rage.

"You're a dead man, Fury!"

In a burst, Sol lunges toward us. Goddamn, even thirty years my senior, he's still fast.

I snatch up my crossbow, spin, and fire in a smooth motion. The bow *clacks* as the cable's tension releases the dart that sinks deep into his thigh. He'd already crossed half the room, but the dart stops him in his tracks.

"Sorry, daddy-in-law. Not today," I tsk, slinging the crossbow over my head and onto my back. "I've got a wedding to plan."

He stumbles backward into the door frame, wide-eyed as he tries to steady himself. Luna's tired, pained cry falls from her lips.

"What the fuck?" Nox growls, his voice somehow lower than his dad's. "Did he shoot you?!"

"Sol!" his wife, Scarlett, yells, nearly making me double take between her and her daughter.

But Luna's at my side, her kicks weakening.

"Hold onto me best you can." I scoop her up bridal style, cursing myself for tying the restraints behind her back. It kept her from pulling off my mask or hitting me, but now she's helpless.

"What?" she asks faintly, her blown pupils now hidden behind long lashes. But she curls into me anyway.

I shift her higher in my arms, getting a better hold of her, accidentally shaking loose a white feather from her bodice. Her breath kisses my neck, making me shiver even though her feverish cheek burns my skin.

The way she's huddled into me, her intoxicating Carolina jasmine and honey scent flooding my senses, dusts up everything I've had to bury so that I could stay in the shadows and keep her safe. And now, after years of desperately needing her, giving in only once... I'm finally holding my fiancée.

But this reaction isn't because she wants me back. It's because she's been drugged.

Fear that I haven't felt in a long time exploded in me the second I saw the spark leave her eyes, my Luna drifting away. I'm furious that those Wilde bastards drugged her, and even more furious I didn't catch it sooner. But she'd said she'd felt fine, had acted normal outside the dressing room, and I'd asked about the drink—just the wrong one.

The fact that the Wildes wanted her aroused... *compliant*? My stomach churns. If I could go back, they'd all be in the ground. I've already started a war over Luna's safety. I'll raze the battlefield to keep her that way.

"I'm gonna kill 'em," I vow, grabbing the bouquet and placing it on her lap.

"My dad?" she whimpers.

"Shh, shh, no, baby, everyone's okay. Just sleep, alright? I've got you."

I look back at Sol struggling to stand, unintentionally blocking the door and keeping anyone from coming in. Nox catches him, and Scarlett cries out.

"Please! Someone get my Luna!"

"I will... kill you, Fury!" Sol shouts past the fast-acting tranquilizer dart.

I open up the secret door behind the mirror and pause.

"I've been here, Sol. The whole time."

His face contorts, and the words land like I hoped they would, freezing everyone.

"My *brothers* arrived today, but I've been here for years, protecting her." I shake my head. "And you never knew."

I'd hoped Sol had a better handle on her safety. But I was her real shadow. And the moment I looked away to set things in motion, she was fucking drugged.

My face hardens, showing the full extent of my fury.

"Your daughter's safer with me. The Wildes know about the pact. They're *here*, and they won't stop until the Troisgarde daughters are theirs. Or dead. So I'm stealing my wife. No one will protect her better than me."

I shut the mirror door behind me, silencing his enraged roar.

Inside the dark tunnel, I squint as I walk us through the narrow corridor until we exit into the alley behind Masque. I kick an empty dumpster with my foot, rolling it in front of the door, nearly losing my balance.

Soon, Luna will be a sack of potatoes in my arms. I need to reach the car before that happens *and* before Sol's men come after us.

But in my rush, I nearly trip over the body on the ground.

Wait, what?

"I thought you'd take care of this by now, Hatch," I mutter.

Then it hits me.

Fuck.

Where are my brothers? Are they okay?

Can't think about that right now.

I curl Luna closer, hoping to shield her eyes from the scene, but it's too late.

She yelps, "Did you *kill* him?"

I hold her tighter. "Don't scream. You've done so good for me."

"No, no, no, he's dead. Why is he d-dead?"

"Believe me, if I could go back, I'd kill them all. *Slowly.*"

If she responds, I don't hear it. The world around us explodes with fireworks, flashing above and thundering against brick, plaster, and concrete. They rocket up from the heart of Bourbon Street—just as we planned—crackling and booming overhead, spooking police horses and drawing beat cops past me toward the chaos.

I turn into the wall, so it looks like Luna and I are in a lover's embrace rather than a kidnapper carrying his victim. When the coast is clear, I leave the shadows, sidestepping a pile of manure left by one of the horses.

I smirk, then I take the pettiest second to fish Ozias's engagement ring from my pocket and drop it onto the pile.

"Told you it was a shit proposal."

Then I cut through a few alleys, a side street, and a courtyard garden before finally reaching my destination.

The Nyx Headhunter SUV chirps as I approach, doors

unlocking and engine rumbling to life thanks to the proximity start Hatch helped me set up.

Balancing Luna against my chest, I open the back door and lay her on the pillow I packed for our long drive home. I'd take off her restraints or tie her wrists in front of her if I could. But I have a feeling she's gonna want to kick my ass the second those pretty eyes open, and I can't risk her blind rage careening us off a mountain.

She whines softly as I reach for the seatbelt.

"Shh, it's okay. Just sleep."

"My... dad?"

"He's safe. I promise. Your dad got your dose, and he's a big dude. He'll be up and furious in no time."

"*My* dose?"

"Uh... okay, yeah, fair question. I'll explain later."

With Sol down, I might have a couple of hours before he can come after us. My goal is for my bride to be safe in my bed on Fury land before her father can catch up.

After buckling Luna in, I tuck the blanket tight around her.

"By the time you wake up, we'll be home."

"But... I am... home," she murmurs sleepily.

I shake my head, brushing her hair back before stealing a forehead kiss in a second I can't afford.

"I'm your home now, baby."

I shut the door, lay my crossbow in the front passenger seat, and slide behind the wheel. Adrenaline and satisfaction race in my chest as I look in the rearview mirror and see my future, right where she belongs, tucked into an adorable, sleepy ball.

My reckless, hellion of a wife will hate me in the morning, but she's finally fucking mine. That's all I need for now, at least until I can convince her to love me back.

ACT TWO

SWAN DIVE

9
THE CLITBLOCKER IS THE ENEMY
LUNA

My hand surfs the waves of mountain air as we drive. We round each bend and switchback up and up to the peak, where we'll picnic after this long ride. Momma and Daddy tucked me and Nox into the back of the car late last night, so when we woke up, we'd be in a different world, one that feels old in my bones and untamed in my blood. Now mist kisses my palm, crisp and light despite the same heavy humidity that feels like a thick coat back home. Pine and maple trees pass in rows or tangled thickets until the road curves and a valley of mountains dips and rises in layered blue hills. A deep, low croon fills my ears...

...in time with the rhythmic *thumps* against leather. I smile at the handsome voice singing along with the folk music on the radio and snuggle into a warm blanket and pillow that smells like maple, bourbon, and pine.

But my eyelids scratch like sandpaper as I try to peek them open. It takes several blinks before I can see the tattooed fingers drumming against the steering wheel. The driver leans back, one arm resting on the center console, slowly bobbing his head to the murmured lyrics. His five o'clock shadow might as well be midnight, and the guy's strong jaw is free of scars like my dad's.

His hands tell a different story, though. Red and glossy scars peek between the webbing of each finger. A cool skull glares out from the top of his hand, and I squint at the black letters rolling beneath the knuckles on his long fingers.

F

U

R

Y—

"Fury!" I bolt upright, and a blaring headache pierces me behind my eyes. My arms hang uselessly at my back, but fiery pins and needles explode as life pours into them again. "*Jesus*, what the hell?"

"I guess that answers my question as to whether you're feeling okay."

"I actually feel enraged, thanks for asking," I hiss.

"Well, good morning to you too. Or afternoon." Orion Fury's stunningly mismatched, two-toned gaze locks on mine in the rearview. "We're almost there. Just a couple hours left."

There?

I glance out the window of the high-end off-roading SUV, expecting to see city streets, brick buildings, Juliet balconies, and shotgun houses. But nope.

Walls of thick trees block the view on both sides. We're climbing a mountain, the winding road ahead as empty as behind us, its faded yellow lines barely visible. Colors are richer, green, brown, a touch of yellow and orange on turning leaves, all more vibrant under the overcast sky.

My heart squeezes. This is just like the autumn family vacations we used to take. We haven't been back in ten years, not since...

... not since King Fury came to New Orleans and threatened my family into an arranged marriage pact.

Fuck the Furys.

"You *kidnapped* me?"

This is what I get for making fun of how my parents met. I don't care how cute they are, I will not be suckered into loving a black-masked stalker. No matter how hot he is.

"Well... you're an adult, so, there's that." He shrugs. "Maybe call it a honeymoon, instead?"

"No, jackass! I'm not calling it anything, because I'm not going anywhere with you," I rasp around my dry mouth then kick the back of his seat. "Let. Me. Go!"

"Shoot, really? But I got you a pillow and everything."

"What do you want me to say? Gee, thanks for the blankie with a side of *kid-nap-ping*?"

"Ah, now that's not nice, little bird."

"Little bird?" I mock. "How cute, *Fury*."

It actually is kinda cute. I loved hearing it until he enacted his deranged, evil plan to steal me. Especially in that deep Southern drawl, a lyrical, mountain hollow accent that dips and flows like something sinful.

Of course I'll never tell *him* that. Not when my bodice digs into my underarms and its white feathers stab my boobs. I've worn this same piece for hours of rehearsals, but lying in it? I'll take torture instead, thank you very much.

I shift against the seatbelt to scratch where the feathers itch me, but my arms won't move, numb from being immobile behind my back for so long. And why?

Oh right. Because this madman *kidnapped me*!

"Why am I still tied up?" I snap, tugging at the makeshift cuffs that dig into my wrists. There's barely any room to loosen them. "Thanks for ripping my favorite tutu, by the way."

"You didn't mind before," he chuckles.

I lift a brow. "That was before I realized you were the same guy who couldn't even get me off the *first* time. If I'd known, I would've never gone to that dressing room with you. You... you *clitblocker*."

He snorts before a full-throated laugh breaks through.

"Don't laugh at me! You left me hanging! I had to use a vibrator and spicy romance books for *weeks* to get rid of you."

And I never really did.

I bite back that truth, but it still thickens the air between us as hotly as if I'd said it out loud. A second ago, his gaze in the rearview mirror was warm with laughter. Now his eyes smolder, and the intensity there forces me to squeeze my legs together.

"Shit, Luna." He shifts in his seat. "Is that what all this attitude's about? I'll pull over and make up for lost time right now."

I blink, only now realizing what I blurted out.

Wow, embarrassing.

"No, God no. I can't stand you. Everything that happened back there was only because you were pretending to be my fiancé!"

"Ain't no pretending about it," he growls. "I *am* your fiancé. And you knew who I was the moment we kissed. I could tell. Which is the *only* reason I went as far as I did."

I want to argue, but... he's right. On some level, I knew he wasn't Ozias. The bouquet alone was a major tipoff. Ozias treated me like an obligation. The fact I stayed with him so long proves how desperately I was looking for something. Probably the same something only this man's ever given me.

And now look where that's gotten me.

"We wouldn't have gone far at all if you hadn't tricked me!" I insist. "If it isn't obvious, I don't want you anymore."

"Really?" he asks slowly, leaning his elbow on the center console, running his finger over his lips in thought before his brow raises in the mirror. "So if I buried my face between your thighs again, right now, you wouldn't be ready for me?"

I shiver, all the heat in my body pooling in my core.

He chuckles low in the back of his throat. "Thought so. You're pretty bold for a girl I can still taste on my tongue."

Oh good God, don't think about that. You're angry, not turned on. Angry. Angry. Angry.

"You. Are. Infuriating!" I writhe against the seatbelt, stretching the tulle cuffs as far as I can while wishing I could smack the ever-loving shit out of him.

I know exactly what to do once I've got a little movement. Nyx model SUVs have much more space than the back of a cop car.

"Take these off me and maybe instead of drawing your death out long and slow, I can convince my dad to—"

I suck in a breath.

Momma crying. My brother cursing. My dad getting shot with an arrow...

Guilt fills my chest, and I can barely breathe.

"Orion?" my voice breaks. "Did you kill my dad?"

His eyes soften at the edges. "No, baby. As much as Sol may hate it, Bordeauxs are family to the King Fury line. Plus," he blows out a breath, "we need him. The bolt was a low-dose tranquilizer dart. It put him out for a few hours tops. Enough time for my brothers and me to get away."

"So he's safe?"

"Of course. The Bordeauxs aren't our enemy."

Relief courses through me, sagging me against the seat, until the rest of the night's memories catch up.

"And Ozias?"

His face clouds. "In the hospital last time I knew."

"The hospital?"

He nods. "I stabbed him. Dash said he'll recover, but I made sure he'd never smile again."

"Oh my God. You really are monsters," I whisper, my voice hoarse again.

"That reminds me. I got something for ya."

"I don't want anything you give me."

"Oh yeah, you do."

He props his knee under the wheel to steer and plucks a bottle from the passenger seat. The bouquet he gave me mocks me beside his crossbow and a detached metal tube with a needle on the end. A tranquilizer dart.

My pulse skips, but I flick my gaze to the window pretending like I'm trying to get comfortable instead of working up a plan. As I shift, my phone and garter dig into my upper thigh. If I could just reach it, I could call my dad...

Orion flicks open the plastic bottle cap with his thumb, pops in a straw, then angles it so I can drink from my seat.

"Would a monster give you water? I bet your tongue feels like fuzzy peach skin."

In answer, my dry tongue darts out to lick my even drier lips. But I stand my ground.

"I'll drink if you untie me."

"So you can attack me and run us off the road?" he scoffs. "I don't think so."

"Then I don't want it," I croak.

His good mood drops with his voice. "Drink your water, Luna."

Now, *why* did that command vibrate through me down to my core? My inner muscles need to stop it with their freaking grand jetés and pirouettes.

I narrow my eyes. "What, are you trying to drug me again?"

His fingers crinkle the plastic, expression darkening with anger as he sets the bottle in a cup holder.

"I didn't drug you. I *did* plan to tranq you—"

"Semantics much?"

"—with the very low dose that I wound up using on your father." He eyes me. "I was only going to use it on you to get you out of there safely. But Luna, you were already fading before that, and the motherfuckers who actually drugged you had worse intentions. You can thank your sham of a fiancé for that."

"*Zy*? Please. Ozias is a gentleman. A white knight. He wouldn't hurt a fly."

"You think?" He grabs his phone from another cupholder, scrolls, then shows it to me.

The photo's blurry, but I can make out a blond guy with a deadly slice across his throat laying on the bloody ground.

"Oh my God, you killed Rufus? Is Zy really in the hospital, or did you kill him too?" I cry, remembering the hazy scene from the alley.

"No. If I'd wanted to, I would've. But believe me, if I could go back in time, he'd be worse off than his cousin. Because this—" he zooms in on a blister pack of pills on the body, "—is a new party drug, Pining. My brother confirmed it from the tree stamp on the pill. It's basically Rohypnol mixed with Molly. You remember how I took your drink before we danced?"

Dread pools in my stomach. "Yeah?"

"We found the drugs on Rufus after Bart hinted at making you more 'compliant.'" That last word rumbles out on a murderous growl as he carelessly tosses the phone into the passenger seat. "I thought *that* was the laced drink. Then you said it was the shot." He massages his forehead. "What were you thinking, babe? Taking a drink from Bartholomew Wilde?"

"Wilde?" My eyes widen. "No, no... they're Thrashers. Family friends."

He shakes his head, face grim. "Your dad's intel was wrong. Ozias's *stepdad* is a Thrasher. Ozias and his cousins? Wildes. But besides all that, you just met Rufus and Bart last night. It was reckless."

"I'm not *reckless*. Nothing bad like this has ever happened to me."

"Yeah, because *I* was protecting you."

"What are you talking about? My dad protects me. His shadows. My brother, Benoit—"

"And me," Orion cuts in, jabbing his chest. "I've been in New Orleans for years. Watching you. Making sure no asshole did exactly what happened when I wasn't there for just five goddamn minutes."

I glare. "Blaming the victim much?"

"Hell no. If anyone, I blame myself. But fuck, babe, you've gotta be more vigilant. Your father's a king on this board, but that makes him and everyone he loves a target. He's tried to protect you, but he's stretched too thin after taking over most of the South. Ozias and his cousins slipped past his defenses. The Wildes had the Troisgarde daughters in their sights since they found out about the pact."

I sift through all that information, deciding which facts to argue over and which ones open doors to more answers. He's singing like a songbird now, but Dad taught me to ask the right questions before the answers dry up.

"My father said I had nothing to worry about with that pact. He refused to comply because it was bullshit and you Furys know it. If I'm in danger, it's because *you* dragged us into a war by telling your enemies there's an alliance that's never gonna happen."

"The fuck we did," he snarls. "Your father's the one trying to renege on a vow *he* made. My family's followed the pact to the letter, including keeping quiet. We know more than anyone what's at stake, and we'd never put our brides at risk. We even put out rumors that we weren't coming for y'all until you were twenty-five, and yet the Wildes struck hours before your twenty-second birthday. Which means there's a rat in the Troisgarde. Your father needs us."

I scoff. "My dad's more afraid of me running away and getting into trouble than anyone hurting me."

"Your father's not afraid of you running away. He's afraid of you being hunted."

My pulse stutters. "What do you mean?"

"Think about it. You're not allowed anywhere but Masque anymore. You've been locked down at Bordeaux Conservatory for weeks."

I shift. "I was rehearsing. Benoit and Nox are the ones who always want to go to Masque. That's nothing new."

"Exactly, it's nothing new, because they know the city isn't safe for you anymore. People like your father can sense restlessness like that, like a storm's coming. You didn't notice because he shielded you from everything, but he closed ranks. Hell, he didn't even let you be alone with your disappointing boyfriend for longer than two minutes."

I scowl. "He's overprotective."

"And why would he be *so* overprotective in a world he owns?"

I glare at the back of his head. "Maybe he sensed *you* were coming."

"Except he didn't. I've coasted under your dad's radar all this time. Way before your twenty-first birthday. I'm good at staying hidden, but not that good. And with the way the Phantom of the French Quarter used to haunt his streets, I expected him to find me like"—he snaps—"that. But he didn't."

He lets that reality rest before continuing. "I was the only one who saw the Wildes close in. That's a problem. But our family can help yours. Together, we could make the Wildes think twice before they burn shit to the ground."

I huff. "No one's burning anything to the ground."

"They already have!" he snarls, making me bite my tongue.

That reaction was too strong, the deep growl torn from his chest too raw and pained. My chest squeezes. He's not speaking metaphorically.

He releases a harsh exhale. "Look, the reality is, no one up here is a cohesive front. Whether you're in Dark Corner, Old Bridge, or Foxfire Hollow, we all use old-school guerrilla warfare tactics more than anything. And don't get me started on what they're up to on Devil's Mountain and Ravenstree. Point being though, certain Wilde and Fury factions want to stake their claim farther and wider than they ever have, including the Southeast, the North, and even the West. We'll wipe each other out if the King line doesn't take the throne."

"And you're so much better?"

His brow raises. "Yeah. We are. We're lawless, but we at least *abide* by pacts and codes. But without the Troisgarde-Fury alliance, we can't expand. None of our families will survive." His gaze returns to the curving roads. "Bottom line? You aren't safe in New Orleans anymore. It was time I brought you home."

Home.

Outside the window, the walls of trees break to a gorgeous view that surrounds us on all sides, and I suck in a breath.

The mountains' mist lifts under a single ray of sunlight,

unveiling hills, valleys, and hollows, with lakes and meadows scattered between. Orion rolls the windows down and I breathe deep, closing my eyes. Pine, rich earth, crisp air. Freedom fills my lungs, my veins. I've never lived here, but I've missed it like it was home.

Still, Orion is the *last* person I want knowing that Appalachia, *his* home, is what I've always craved.

I lift my chin. "If they were so dangerous, why didn't you come before now?"

"I wanted to. If something's mine, I guard it with my life." His knuckles whiten on the steering wheel, pulling the inked letters taut. "But the amendment to the pact said we let the daughters live without interference until y'all's twenty-second birthdays. I waited as long as I could, but then Ozias went rogue, proposing like that. He probably thought your engagement would keep me away from you. He was wrong."

I nibble at my lip, unsure if I should bring it up, but go for it anyway. "What about my twenty-first birthday? Didn't that break your rules?"

His slow, creeping smile has my cheeks flushing at the memory. Him whisking me from the dance floor, maple and bourbon kisses in the shadows, grinding against my core until we were seconds from throwing all caution to the wind...

Then my friends appeared, and he vanished.

When Orion answers, his voice is delicious caramel, like he was thinking about it too.

"Kissing you that night was the best rule I've ever broken. Until last night, when I devoured you until midnight." His eyes flick up to mine, crinkling at the edges. "Seems you make me reckless too, little bird."

I worry my lip. "And Bart? What happened to him? Is he...?"

"Not yet. But go ahead and decide how you want it done, because that motherfucker ain't long for this world." His gaze holds mine. "The Wilde-Fury feud has a code. Blood for blood, life for life. I'll risk both to protect what's mine, and he hurt what's mine." His jaw ticks. "I don't know where that coward ran off to, but my brothers are on it. Once they're done running inter-ference, Dash will find him."

"And how would he do that?"

His brow raises. "I can't spill *all* our secrets, yet. That's wife territory, and I'm gonna need you to at least like me first."

"Hm. Guess I'll never find out, then."

"We'll see about that, baby."

I resist a shiver. His delicious accent grows thicker when he calls me "baby." Slow and intentional, curling his tongue around the word like he wants me to feel every letter, and good God, it's working.

"Now come on. Be a good girl and drink your water." He picks up the bottle again and tilts it back.

I have half a mind to reject it again, but my throat aches, so I lean forward and drink like I've been lost in a desert.

As soon as I see my reflection in the review mirror, though, I almost recoil. My hair is still half-up, held in place by my feather crown, but hairspray clumps strands that fight to tighten back into their natural curl. Mascara smudged, foundation smeared, and my lips are swollen from last night's makeout session. A freaking mess is what I am.

And yet Orion's focus is solely on me, his eyes darkening.

Why is he looking at me like that?

I follow his gaze as it glides from my lips around the straw and down my body like a caress... stopping where my nipples peek out, trying to escape my bodice's sweetheart neckline. Jesus, the little sluts are begging to be sucked by his sinful mouth again, and I will not have it.

Calm your tits, ladies. He's the damn villain.

I suck the last of the water, and slowly sit back against my numb arms.

His eyes flash like he can read my mind.

"Luna... don't you d—"

I lurch forward and spit the water in a powerful stream right at his face.

He doesn't even try to stop it, just accepting his fate. I lick the leftover drops from my lips and grin, anticipating an argument.

But he shakes his head good-naturedly and chuckles.

Chuckles.

His huge tatted bicep flexes as he untucks his black T-shirt to use the hem to wipe his face. The fabric rises, revealing the hilt of a sheathed knife, an F burned into the leather. My eyes drift from it to the rest of him, and my lips part.

"Damn, baby, I didn't expect you to squirt all over my face before I even get to fuck you."

"You're disgusting," I murmur, but I'm only half paying attention, because his tanned, corded back muscles ripple as he swipes the water from his face, rolling underneath fresh, angry cuts that crisscross his flesh over intricate tattoos.

I wince. They must be painful. Did he get them from fighting the Wildes?

I shudder, unsure what to do with that thought now that I know what happened last night.

My eyes snag on one tattoo in particular—a macabre ballerina skeleton with a gorgeous, painted skull face, dressed like the black swan, performing a fouetté turn en pointe up his ribs. She's absolutely stunning, with her cherry cola hair flowing around her in waves...

Holy crap.

That's me, right? This sexy stalker lunatic—who claims that one day I'll magically agree to marry him—tattooed me dancing my favorite ballet on his droolworthy body before I ever even spoke to him.

He's insane... *right*?

And am I also insane because I think that's hot?

Okay, yes and yes. Great. Awesome.

But in my defense, I've been influenced by Lucy's books about fictional men who bestow mind-numbing orgasms and can't *actually* stalk and kidnap me. This guy's done all of the latter, and nary an orgasm in sight.

Bastard.

Said bastard's shirt is back down and his lips now quirk sinfully. I scowl, but his eyes flick past me in the rearview mirror, brows furrowing.

My interest piques. "What?"

"Nothing." He straightens, eyes darting between the road and mirror. "Just a bump in the road. A little company is all."

I almost snort. These roads are nothing but bumps and potholes.

But I crane my neck to see a blacked-out Nyx Z2, a sports car model that's not even released yet. Which means...

"That's my dad and brother!"

10
FAST AND FURY

LUNA

S ure enough, my dad's head peeks out from the passenger seat window, and even though the tint is darker than what's legal, I know Nox is behind the wheel. Their car is so close I can see the scars on Dad's face as he waves at two more cars behind him. All three take up both lanes, gaining on us fast.

Orion sucks his teeth. "Well, I'll be. Wonder how they figured out where we were."

"I don't know, but you are *so* screwed."

"We all might be," he mutters to himself, whizzing by the only road I've seen in miles at a dizzying speed. "Of course they'd catch up right outside Old Bridge. Mighty fucking inconvenient."

I almost frown at the cryptic complaint, but I'm too giddy that I'm about to be rescued.

Orion increases speed around a bend, but Nox matches him, getting closer even as Orion hugs the mountain on another curve.

"Where the hell did he learn to drive like that?"

My gleeful grin mocks Orion in the rearview mirror as I discreetly work the tulle at my wrists and run my mouth to rattle him.

"Oh, you know, my dad's just friends with Felix 'Phoenix' Santori, the *owner* of Nyx Automotive. My brother learned to drive on Phoenix's racetrack. He's been hanging out with F1 and NASCAR drivers since he was sixteen."

"A racetrack, huh? Is that a fact?" Orion relaxes in his seat, one hand on the wheel, the other on the center console. He traces his lips, gaze flicking to the rearview mirror again. "So he's pretty good at offensive driving. Defensive too?"

"All of it," I say proudly. "And the cars following him? Probably Benoit and my Uncle Jaime. They all took the same classes. So just call it quits and pray for mercy before my brother T-bones you into a guard rail."

Orion snorts. "He won't do that. We both know I've got precious cargo."

"So what? I don't give a crap as long as he stops *you!*"

"Now, now. We can't be reckless." He tsks. "You're always trying to go and get yourself hurt. What am I gonna do with you, hm?"

"Pull over and beg for forgiveness on your knees, for starters."

His smile grows. "Next time I'm on my knees for you, sassy bride, *you'll* be the one begging."

My jaw drops and it takes a second to realize what's happening when he reaches back toward me, steering with his knees.

"What're you doing! Eyes on the road!"

"Please," he snorts. "I could do these switchbacks blindfolded."

I squirm away from his hand, but he just snags the crossbody strap and stretches it to join the waist seatbelt he must've buckled before we left. Then he tugs both, checking their tightness.

Panic tussles with something fluttery in my chest. "I'm in danger!" competing with a totally unhealthy, "Aw, how sweet, he's protecting me!"

It's official. I'm fucked up.

Once again, I blame dark romance books, and maybe the fact this so-called "meet-cute" runs in the family.

I harness my sass. "A seatbelt isn't going to keep me from escaping."

"True, but child locks will. The seatbelt is to keep my little bird from flying around when I do this."

Both hands back on the wheel, he swerves the SUV from side to side, jerking it across the entire road like a total maniac. If I weren't buckled, I'd be slung around the back seat.

"What are you doing?!"

"Keeping what's mine, *mine*."

"I'm not yours!" I slam my feet against the passenger seat but keep them clear of his side. Despite my bluster, my hatred hasn't *actually* given me a death wish.

My brother's engine roars behind us as he speeds up.

"See? He's going to catch up and pit maneuver you right off the mountain!"

We round a bend, heading straight toward a fog-covered mountain looming ahead.

"Don't think so." He chuckles. "Your brother might've learned to drive sports cars when he was a teenager, but *my* brothers and I have raced backroads since we got our first side-by-sides at four years old. Brace yourself. You've given me an idea."

He barrels toward the tunnel on the wrong side of the road, edging the guardrail overlooking a sheer cliff dropping thousands of feet.

"Are you *crazy*?" I screech.

He speeds up, then slams the brakes. Tires screech, and my brother barely has time to stop from ramming the bumper. Orion brake checks again, whipping wind through the half-open windows and tangling my hair as glass crunches behind us, lurching us forward.

"What is wrong with you?!"

My brother's bumper is mangled, but he revs again as Orion floors it.

"What are you doing?" I scream. "You're *insane*!"

"Believe me, you haven't met insane. His name is Hatton Fury." A strange glint flickers in his eyes as he smiles at me in the rearview.

"Do you think this is *fun*?" I shout, but my gaze locks on the pitch-black void framed in a semicircle of stone ahead.

"We're coming up on a tunnel, baby. Better hold your breath, but don't pass out on me. It's a long one."

"Hold my breath?"

"Yeah, so you can make a wish." He nods, as if he's not hurtling me and half of everyone I love into our doom.

"Ready…"

He slows.

"Set…"

Kills the headlights.

"*Go!*"

He catapults into the void as I scream bloody murder.

The other cars' headlights are out, probably from the collision earlier, and the only way I know they're in the tunnel too is the engines' roaring ricocheting off stone.

Orion jerks forward then brakes, forward, brake, forward—forcing me to cling to anything I can with my arms still behind my back. Tulle whirls around my legs, and wind lashes my hair into my wailing mouth.

I want to be free. I want to be free. I want to be free…

So I can kill him.

There's a bang behind us, and a shower of sparks. If I wasn't shrieking air from my lungs already, I'd be holding it now.

Light is a pinprick ahead of us as Orion slows. A car rumbles past, scraping us, and popping something off the SUV. He curses, and his arm lashes out behind him to cover my face with one hand, while his other smacks the window button, rolling it up and protecting me from debris before it hits.

When he removes his hand, the light in front of us has brightened, so I can see the other car as Orion whips the SUV to the right, slamming into the back with a god-awful screech. It spins out and he easily skirts around it, tearing ahead as the other twirls in place. This close, I glimpse my dad bracing himself against the door while Nox wrestles with the steering wheel. Behind us, Benoit and Jaime veer into the tunnel walls to avoid hitting Dad and Nox, but in their effort, they ram into each other.

I peer past Nox as he rights his car, holding my breath as Uncle Jaime and Benoit climb out, guns raised. But Orion was right. They won't shoot, and their faces twist with something like rage and defeat when they realize it too.

We burst into the sunlight just as Nox regains ground. My seatbelt bites deeper into my chest with every tight switchback, until my breath runs out and I gasp clean air.

A teary choke rips from my lungs. "I did *not* give you that idea!"

"You're right. It was the 'right off the mountain' part that inspired me."

"What does *that* mean?"

He rounds the next curve, every tread of the Headhunter's four-wheel drive hugging the guardrail on the drop-off side of the road, the forest plunging below. My calves press into the seat's edge, bracing for the next turn around the mountain.

But instead of bearing left, he keeps going—aiming straight for the woods.

He's going to turn.

He has to.

Right?

Right?

"Orion!"

The guardrail ends and we blast past two narrow trees onto a long-forgotten dirt road overgrown with thin brush. Branches snap against the frame, tires spraying gravel, until the SUV's brush guard splinters through an old gate. Orion fights the wheel as we careen over the bumpy path before finally, mercifully, straightening out and decelerating.

"You almost killed us!"

The grin Orion flashes me in the rearview is all dangerous confidence and adrenaline. "Nah, we were fine. I know what I'm doing, baby."

But the smile vanishes. He glares past me. "But *they* don't. Goddamn, Nox. Stop already, man."

The sports car skids down the dirt road, no match for the rocks and roots pitting the ground. Horror chokes me as my brother loses control, clipping a massive oak before the bumper anticlimactically crunches into a boulder. The car zigzags, finally ending up wedged between two trees, smoke pouring from the hood and tire wells.

After a beat, my dad and Nox climb out. My dad roars, but this far away, I can't hear with the windows up. Nox slams a fist on the smoking hood. A shuddering breath leaves my chest as relief drains my adrenaline.

"They're okay, Luna."

I suck in a breath, remembering my captor, then my head swivels to find Orion looking at me, concerned eyes watching me, his lips a hard, unforgiving line. He shifts back to take the SUV out of park and my eyes flick to the barren, rocky road in front of us. I hadn't realized he'd stopped.

In a daze, I turn around as the SUV kicks up gravel and drives away. Tears sting my eyes as the tunnel of trees close in behind us, swallowing my family until they disappear.

"You know," he begins casually, "I never thought about it, but running away on 'crush and run' gravel is perfectly poetic."

The woods blur, a watercolor of greens and browns, reds and yellows.

After a moment he tries again.

"So... what'd you wish for?"

I whip around. My shock and anger glare into the rearview mirror, where Orion's mismatched eyes are overly bright with mirth.

But there's a tremor in his hand as he rakes it through his hair, and his voice is pitched a little too high.

"Wait, don't tell me. It's bad luck. It won't come true if you tell." His smirk is tight. "We don't want that, do we?"

I answer through gritted teeth. "You won't want it to come true. But I sure as hell do."

His eyes narrow, then a slow smile curls his mouth. "You're

hot when you're mad. I like that in a fiancée. You'll fit right in with the Furys."

"Had many fiancées, have you?" I snarl.

"No, Luna." His gaze locks on mine, all humor gone. "I'll only ever have you."

I let him see every drop of my hate.

"Be careful what you wish for, Orion Fury."

11

SKULL TATTOO

ORION

uck, that was close.

My fingers shake as I inspect every bolt, wire, nook, and cranny of the SUV's undercarriage, heartbeat thundering like the clouds rolling down the mountain. Adrenaline and exhaustion rattle through me as I work, not easing up even when I find the black box glued to the frame and start to pry it free. Without Luna watching, waiting to pounce on any sign of weakness, the anxiety that's been pent-up since my brothers and I hatched this plan releases.

She's given me the cold shoulder since the chase, eyes glued on the view. Fine by me. She can take in her new home without having to see how on edge I was while getting us out of enemy territory and into Lost Cove.

The past twenty-four hours have been a shit show.

This wasn't the way I wanted to claim my bride. In all the time that I watched Luna Bordeaux, only once did I manage to get close enough without detection. Her needy moans from that night were the soundtrack to my fantasies for three hundred and sixty-five days. When I finally had her in my arms again, I wanted more of *that*—less murder, kidnapping, and car chase.

But Sol and the Wildes gave me no other choice but to steal back what's mine.

And to top it off, before the deep woods swallowed my signal, my brothers texted that while they were checking on the other

Troisgarde daughters, Bart slipped out of the hospital, somehow shaking my tranq dart within an hour. Which means Bartholomew Wilde is in the wind. Not good.

Dash and Hatch had to split up to search for him, which meant no running interference for the trackers Sol planted on their cars. We'd checked all our vehicles before the performance and removed the one from mine, leaving it in a local dumpster to keep their cars the decoys and mine in the clear.

We should've known something was off. The devices were in easy-to-find places and shitty models. It never crossed our minds that Sol would plant two, but he's not the head of one of the most dangerous crime families in the country for nothing, and the smart motherfucker outplayed us. With my brothers stuck in New Orleans and a tracker still hidden on my SUV, Sol followed the only vehicle moving. Mine.

I grunt, leveraging my knife under the box. The thing's stubborn as a tick. Granted, *this* one is a BlackJack, a BlackStone Securities model, so I wouldn't expect anything less. But thankfully, after another twist, it pops free.

"Got you, fucker." I drop it into my hand and exhale, resting my head on the dirt.

Knowing I had this tracker on me for the last three hours in Wilde territory was enough to fuck me up.

Of course, Sol caught up with us right before the exit back to Dark Corner. With Nox racing me like a madman, I couldn't risk taking a sharp turnoff and getting cornered, so into the lion's den we went.

And not just any lion's den. Ruth "Bossie" Wilde's land. She's the matriarch that runs these parts, grandmother to none other than Bartholomew, Rufus, and Ozias, and she's as ruthless as they come. The last place I want Luna is anywhere near the Wildes, and I had to drive for hours in a land full of their proverbial landmines, each corner and bend a possible trap.

After an eternity, I finally got us into the red painted woods of Lost Cove, neutral territory in our world. We're still hours from our Dark Corner holler, but safe from the Wildes, so I took the first dirt road turnout that could hide us to ditch the BlackJack.

The overgrown path led to a rocky cliffside where a river runs twenty feet below. Rain upstream has filled it to the brim, flooding banks and cresting over boulders. Humidity clings my shirt to my sweaty chest under my leather jacket. A gust whips under the SUV, bringing the earthy scent of petrichor and some relief from the early autumn heat.

Normally, I'd skip the jacket, but the heavy air, plummeting temps, and whistling wind means a storm's brewing. A bad one, judging by the thunderclouds veiling the highest mountains on the horizon. The radio forecaster said it'll rain buckets for the next week. "The storm of the century," they said.

Folks 'round here don't place much stock in catastrophizing like that. Meteorologists rarely get it right, focusing on the plains and valleys rather than the peaks. We're a different biome—in every sense—but whether they're right about the severity, a storm *is* coming, and I need to get my girl home.

These mountains are prone to mudslides, rockslides, and washouts in the best conditions. Once we're out of Lost Cove, we still have hours more off-roading to go, and it's already dusk. I won't feel safe until we're in King Fury land, and I just want my bride home, where she belongs.

Once she's there, I'll do everything I can to convince her to be mine. I know I can do it. Like my father was able to with—

Don't think about that.

I shove the tracker into my pocket and scan the chassis, this time for damage. The Nyx Headhunter's fender and tailgate are fucked from the love taps I gave the Bordeauxs, but it's nothing I can't fix with Hatch's help. Everything under here looks fine.

The SUV shifts above me.

I still.

When nothing moves, my eyes narrow at the frame.

Did I imagine—

It happens again, and a smile slow curves my lips.

I knew Luna Bordeaux would be an adventure, and she hasn't disappointed.

Basing my direction on the shifting above, I grab my crossbow from beside me and silently shimmy out the opposite side—no small feat for a six-five fella even with the lift kit I installed. Once I'm out, I loop my crossbow around my back and stay low, listening.

Somehow, my dainty little city girl manages to rustle leaves, snap twigs, and curse under her breath louder than the rumbling sky. I'll have to teach her how to walk in the forest, but for now, I bite the inside of my cheek to keep from chuckling. She's as graceful as a swan on stage, but out here, she's got all the subtlety of a coal train.

I lean against the SUV, waiting for her to notice.

But with absolutely *zero* survival instincts, she looks off into the woods instead of checking behind herself. I wait, plotting the best way to catch my little bird.

Her tulle-cuffed hands are somehow in front of her now, a pity since her perfect, round tits are no longer propped up like a meal on a platter. I admire the rest of her—slim curves, fragile neck begging for my skull-tattooed hand around it, gauzy tutu struggling to conceal a perfectly delectable ass I can't wait to sink my teeth into. Half her hair is still pinned back with a feather crown, the rest spilling in vivid cherry cola waves against the green forest backdrop.

Fuck, she's gorgeous.

The incoming storm's cool air gives her a cold chill. Won't be long now before it's pouring. We need to get moving.

I push off the SUV, standing at my full height, ready for when she finally turns or runs. I'm surprised she hasn't fled already, but I kind of hope she does. I've sat in the car for hours, so I'm up for a good chase.

But she does neither, still just scanning the trees.

Damn, she'd get herself killed out here without me.

"Go on." My voice rumbles out like the storm. "Run."

She freezes, then slowly turns on one slippered foot. Her eyes, clear blue as a spring river, widen.

I cross my arms, smirking. "I dare you. I haven't chased prey in a good long while."

She scowls, and I let out my chuckle as I force open the dented trunk with a jerk that makes it creak in protest.

"For what it's worth, you wouldn't make it far. That Garden District pavement running ain't got nothing on rocks, hills, and roots. You'd sooner sprain an ankle than get free of me." I nod to her bound arms. "Especially with your wings clipped. Even if you did, there's no one for miles. City girl like you'd get ate up by wampus cats and bog mud before morning."

Her eyes narrow. "You just made those words up."

"I assure you, I did not. There's all sorts of shit out here I don't know about, let alone what *you* don't know about."

"Maybe I'll take my chances," she sneers. "Anything's better than being held captive by the guy who tried to kill my family."

"This again?" I roll my eyes before riffling through my gear. "If I wanted them dead, they'd be dead. But you said yourself Nox knows how to drive."

"Yeah, but he's never had to go up against a maniac with a death wish."

"Like I said, that's Hatch, not me. But I bet he loved the challenge." I tap a mocking finger against my chin. "He could've, I don't know, let my wife and me have a lovely drive through the parkway."

"A lovely drive? You were reckless!"

"You'd know a thing or two about that, wouldn't you?" I snort, resting my hands on the trunk's edge as I peer into the cabin.

Front door's open. Tulle handcuffs in front of her. I thought getting out of the seatbelt alone would've been damn near impossible.

"How the hell did you get out, Houdini?"

My eyes sweep over her, clinically this time as I try to figure out the answer. But her hooded gaze is trailing up from my boots and rests where my raised shirt and jacket reveals my lower abs. I never want her to stop looking at me like that.

Thunder rumbles low and long in the distance.

We have to go.

I clear my throat.

She shakes her head like she's rattling out thoughts I'd do anything to make come true.

My brows raise and my lips twitch. "You good?"

She straightens and adopts a smug look that just makes me want to kiss her.

"I'm a ballerina, so I'm flexible and I have a high pain tolerance. I loosened these restraints enough to tuck my knees through and loop my arms forward." She lifts a shoulder nonchalantly. "It was a lot easier with tulle in a crossover than handcuffs in a cop car."

"Impressive." I whistle, then waggle my eyebrows. "Flexible *and* a high pain tolerance? Don't tempt me with a good time."

"Asshole," she grumbles, fisting her hands together. "You're disgusting, you know that?"

"Only for you." I wink, and a blush blooms over her ivory cheeks.

Everyone says she looks like her mom, but to me, the differences are stark. Her eyes are lighter, her smile wider, more carefree in their similar porcelain features, and she's slimmer with a more athletic build, gliding everywhere she goes—except the woods, apparently.

And her sass? That's *all* Luna, and I love it. Meek and mild ain't for me. That's more Hatch's speed. The way she cares for her friends and snarls at her enemies makes her perfect for me.

Finding what I need from the SUV, I balance the items in one arm while I force down what once was an automatic trunk door and then kick it shut. Hatch would kill me if he saw me do that, but I'll fix it later.

Not taking any chances, I prowl around the woman who has no idea she's in my trap.

Wary eyes analyze the plastic bag and one child's arm float swimmy, but then her gaze lands on the crossbow on my back.

"Why do you casually have a crossbow?"

"Ain't nothing casual about it. I hunt."

"So, you're one of those guys who sits up in a hut all day and drinks beer?"

I scowl. "I'm a hunter, not an aimer. Those guys set up bait, then point and shoot. I like the chase."

"The chase? You brought that thing to New Orleans," she snorts. "What were you gonna hunt there?"

I can't help the smile that breaks free. "My wife."

Her eyes widen, and I chuckle. "In all seriousness, I'm the oldest in my family, which means once King steps down, I'll be the head of the King Fury line. Until then, I guess you'd call me an enforcer, or a second-in-command. We all protect each other, but Hatch and me are more... hands on. Me especially. Dash is the one who'll actually be something someday."

She frowns. "So you're saying you hunt people. With a crossbow? That's ridiculous."

"Caught you, didn't I?" I flash a grin.

She rolls her eyes. "Why can't you use guns and knives like everyone else?"

I almost laugh at the phrasing, *like everyone else*. Only people in our world think "everyone else" is as strapped and ready to fight as we are.

But her question brings a lump to my throat that I have to clear. "I do have those things. But I guess you could say the crossbow's got sentimental value."

Her eyes narrow on my face this time. I don't know what she sees there, but they soften at the edges, a balm to that ache in my chest, before she sighs.

"You're weird."

I snort. "I don't think I've ever been called that before. That's usually reserved for Hatch."

"Yeah, well Hatch didn't kidnap me, nearly kill my family twice, *or* insist I marry him, a complete stranger. So, you know, just going by sheer facts on this one."

I laugh. *Laugh.* Last night was the first time I'd even smiled, let alone laughed, since I can remember, and I haven't shaken this goofy grin since my little tyrant woke up.

It feels... good. Lighter behind my ribcage where I've been heavy for years. Momma would've loved her for that alone.

My heart jolts painfully. *Fuck.* It's usually easier to not think about it, but I don't know, Luna makes me feel all types of things. Shit I'd hoped I'd buried.

I swallow past the hurt in my chest and drop the tracker into the plastic bag from the last barbecue we had on Fury land. Which was... ages ago. My cousins are old enough that they don't even need the arm swimmies anymore.

After sighing at that depressing thought, I inhale and begin filling up the airless plastic float.

"What're you doing?"

"Blowing up this here swimmy." I hold it up before I blow another lungful into it.

She huffs and leans back against the SUV with a *thunk*, looking around the forest behind me. Then she fixes her gaze on me again.

"Why do you call your own dad 'King'?"

I speak through puffs. "It's how we identify the branches of our families. Just easier to call him that when we use it all the time anyway."

"You call your mom Queenie too?"

Call. Present tense.

Guess she doesn't know.

I look toward the trees. "Nope. Just Momma."

There's a beat, then she asks again. "So you're the King branch?"

"Inquisitive little bird, aren't you?"

She grins proudly. "Am I getting on your nerves?"

"Nope." I pop the 'p', taking pleasure in her fresh scowl, then answer. "We go by patriarchs and matriarchs as heads of families here. There's lots of Fury kin. Good, bad, ugly—"

"You're the ugly ones, then, huh?"

Giving more breaths into the plastic floatie, I give her a once-over before saying, "Didn't think I was too ugly last night, did you?"

She smirks. "Only because you were wearing a mask. Now that I see you in all your 'glory,' I know exactly what kind of Fury you are."

I fill up the rest of the floatie then stuff it inside the bag before dropping it to the ground.

"Is that so?" Standing to my full height, I stalk toward her. "Because there's another kind of Fury. The dangerous ones. The ones who will do *anything* to protect what's theirs."

She swallows, and some deep part of me craves the flash of fear in her eyes as she backs into the SUV.

"So let me ask, after last night... which one do you *really* think I am?"

And another part of me craves the rest of her reaction as the fear disappears quickly and defiance takes its place.

"The only thing I *really* think is that you need to take me back right now, because I don't want anything to do with you and I..." she drifts off as I close in around her. "...w-won't... marry..."

Leaning around her, I rest my hands on the roof rack as I cage her in, taking over every angle of her vision. Her breath hitches, her skin flushing down to her rounded tits.

"You gonna finish that sentence?"

The first droplets of rain hit the top of my head, but my position protects her from the chilling moisture that drips down the back of my neck. I tower over her, nearly a foot taller, and with my leather jacket open, I easily shelter her small frame.

"I-I won't... marry—"

I cut her off by slipping my knee between her thighs and planting my foot on the running board, lifting her up and forcing her to straddle my leg. She clutches my shirt for purchase, one sharp nail digging into my abs. I shift to press my cock against her hip, and her pretty river eyes flutter closed as I let her feel the full extent of the want I have for her. The *need* I have to taste her again.

"*Orion*," she breathes, and *fuck*, do I want to claim her right here and now. But I've already waited this long, I can handle another day.

I can't help taking a little for myself, though. I haven't stopped wanting her since I almost came at the taste of her last night. Having her only a few feet away the past several hours but being unable to touch her was a special kind of torture. The truth is, from the moment I arrived in New Orleans the day after her eighteenth birthday, when I finally saw her in person, I've *only* wanted this rebellious girl.

My hand drifts down her body, the other gripping the rack like it's the only thing stopping me from hoisting her onto my cock. There's a purpose for what I'm doing right now beyond taking what I want, and the only way to keep her safe is to hold back and remember that.

Ruby red flushes up her chest, but she doesn't stop me, not even when my fingers trail down her tulle skirt. Our gazes lock in this battle of wills. I'm testing how far she'll let me go. She's daring herself to keep pretending not to care.

When my fingers brush her thigh, she breaks, grabbing my shirt and scratching my abs with one of her sharp nails. I groan at the sting and hike her leg around my waist, pinning her against the SUV to fully cage in my little bird. She bites her plump lip, and her thigh tightens around my hip.

I stroke over her garter, stopping at the crease of her hip, right over the stunning ink staring up at me.

"You're gonna keep fighting me, and I crave it. But what you don't realize is you're already mine. You wear my mark." I squeeze the tattoo hard, earning a gasp.

Her eyes go from half-lidded to angry in an instant. "Skulls are the *Bordeaux* mark."

I nod. "Furys too."

Letting go of the rack, I tug down my shirt's neckline, revealing the birthmark above my heart, a skull marred with a scar through its crown.

Her mouth parts as she studies it.

"The Fury birthmark," I explain. "An odd phenomenon that's lasted generations. Anyone born into it has one, and anyone sworn in—married or otherwise—gets a skull tattooed. You're ahead of the curve, pretty bride. And isn't it so *very* interesting that yours..." I brush my thumb where the blush roses and wild-flowers highlight the crack through the skull's crown. "Is *exactly* like mine? Down to the eyes. Almost like someone planned it."

I circle my thumb over each eye, one a swirl of dark green ringed around brown, the other its mirror image.

"No..." she breathes, gaze darting from my birthmark to my eyes, then down to her tattoo and back.

"Just putting it together? Bet you thought my eyes were familiar from *somewhere,* didn't you?"

"But... how—" She tries to push me away with her closed fists. "What the *fuck*?"

I chuckle. "You were reckless that night. Raising hell on Bourbon, swearing you'd go to anyone brave enough to tattoo you. So I called a girl Hatch knew up the bayou and told her what to give you. Once you called the rideshare, I helped you get there."

"But you couldn't have known where I was going! The driver got lost and took me to a different artist..."

"Or maybe he knew exactly where he was going."

She groans. "That was you too?"

I nod. "You *really* should double-check your rideshare info. Any ol' depraved bastard could drive right up and steal you."

"There's no *way* that was you," she scoffs. "That was forever ago!"

I lean in, sneaking my fingers under her garter as I whisper against lips I'm already addicted to.

"You're right, that was *forever* ago. Imagine how hard it's been to keep my hands off you all. That. Time. I only slipped twice, but god*damn* were both times worth it."

I roll my hips into her, like I will when we fuck, and she whimpers.

"You're so responsive," I growl. "I'm barely touching you."

"I... it's just been a long time," she insists.

I chuckle. "I agree. Never *is* a long time."

She gasps. "How do..."

"Come on. I'm an obsessed motherfucker. You think I'd let anyone else take you?"

I press harder, enjoying the way she squirms. "Last night, I wanted nothing more than my future wife's virgin blood on my cock. But a quickie in a dressing room isn't how I'll claim you. I'm going to take my time to give you the attention you deserve, and I want you to know it's your husband fucking you, not some coward."

"What if Ozias and I had sex?" she throws out.

Jealousy burns my chest, but I tamp it down and answer evenly, "I know Ozias. He and I are the same. Loyal to a fault and ruthless about keeping our loved ones safe. His heart's with someone else, so I never worried about him."

Understanding flashes across her face, like some distant pieces have fallen into place.

"Besides, even if you had, there's no way he could do what I can for you. No one else knows what you *need*."

I follow the swallow down the vulnerable column of her throat, my mind fantasizing about all the places I'll lick, suck, choke, *bite* as I claim her.

"Y-You don't know what I need."

"Sure about that?" I stroke up against her, hitting that bundle of nerves I can still practically taste on my tongue. It's got to be so swollen and sensitive. If I didn't have another agenda, I'd kneel in front of her and wrap her legs over my shoulders again.

She clutches my shirt as her head falls back, but my hand slips in to stop her from hitting the window. Her body grinds on me, and I have to grit my teeth to continue.

"I know you're a virgin." Her eyes widen, and she tries to fix them on me, but I squeeze her thigh, my fingers sneaking under her garter. "And I know I'm the closest thing you've ever gotten to an orgasm from someone else."

"How...?" she asks, lust making her voice husky.

"Because no one else can give you what you need. You want to be claimed, ravaged, you want a dirty, reckless fuck for your first time. And you want to feel like you're the only girl that matters."

"You... don't know what you're talking about."

"Don't I?" I cradle the back of her head and grind into her harder, making her moan, the sound rising above the thunder. "Only I know how to draw noises like that from you. No one else has any idea how to tame you."

Her cheeks flush a gorgeous shade of pink down to the pristine white bodice's neckline, where her tits strain against it with each breath. The darker pink of her pebbled areolas teases the top, and I almost pull the damn thing down for another taste.

Focus.

I swallow, dragging my eyes up to hers. Fire, need, and... is that hope? It all mixes like rushing waters in her clear blue depths.

"I-I don't want to be tamed."

I tsk and let my hunger for her color my tone as I wrap my hand around the garter. "Oh, baby. Yes you do. It's why you test boundaries. You're dying for someone to push back, and no one has measured up yet. You want to be taken, to give your decisions to someone you trust."

"That will *never* be you." She tries to sneer, but it melts into a shaky breath, sending a hot curl of satisfaction winding up my spine.

"See, the thing is, you already trust me. It's why you didn't run earlier. It's why you didn't get behind the driver's seat and take off." Having what I need, I slowly let her down and back away. Her full lips purse into a pout of disappointment that I'm sure she has no idea is written all over her face. "And it's why I was able to get close enough to do this."

I hold up her phone, the one I grabbed from her garter, and give it a little shake. All the flush of the lusty haze I stoked in her drains from her face.

"What the hell? Give me back my phone!"

I chuckle as I pick up the plastic bag and plop the phone inside.

"What do you think you're doing?"

"Putting this tracker into this here baggie," I answer, fishing out the BlackJack from my pocket and adding it to the bag. "You know, so we don't get our alone time interrupted again." I wink.

She turns green. "A tracker? Like... like from my dad? How'd you find it?"

I shrug. "It was where I would've put it."

I blow air into the bag itself and snap it shut before turning around.

"Wait! Wai-wai-wai-wai-*wait*." She tries to run after me, but my strides are longer, and I'm already at the ledge looking down at the river below us. "Please, don't do what I think you're gonna—"

I chuck the bag into the river before she can stop me.

She skids to a halt on the slick dirt. My heart leaps to my throat, and I catch her with an arm around her waist, holding her to me with her back to my front. Her breaths heave, and my pulse still hammers over how that could've ended.

My forehead hangs for a moment, pressing against her nape, and my hands squeeze her tighter. She doesn't seem to notice, and when my head raises again, I find her eyes locked on the bag as it tosses in the waves, bobbing along until it disappears over a distant waterfall.

"What did you *do*?"

The hopelessness in her plea *almost* makes me feel bad. But then I remember why it was necessary.

"I did what I had to. That waterfall at the end could take that bag and the tracker in it all the way to the New River. With that current? Your family will think we're two states away by morning."

I easily pick up her limp, defeated body, and carry her back to the car. Shit, I hate the way she's giving up. But I had to do it.

At the crossover, I set her on her feet. Her gaze stays on the ledge, so I lift her chin to face me.

"Now they can't find you. You're mine, Luna Bordeaux, and I fight for what's mine. The Wildes, the Phantom of the French Quarter, anyone who tries to get in between me and my bride. *Including* you."

"You're a monster," she seethes.

Thunder rolls, and lightning flashes through the dusk, making me realize how dark it's gotten.

A fat raindrop smacks me in the forehead. "Call me what you want, but be a good girl and get back in the car."

I reach for the door, but she stomps in front of it. Rain pelts us, cascading down her forehead and clinging to thick, black lashes that frame the return of that obstinate fire surging through her veins faster than the river beyond the ledge.

"I know that look." I arch my brow. "You're about to do something reckless."

"You don't know 'my looks,'" she spits.

"The fuck I don't. I've seen that one plenty of times. Two instances off the top my head? A year ago... and last night." I step closer. "Right before I felt your pussy clench around my fingers for the first time."

Her rosy cheeks make me think the shiver racking through her has nothing to do with the rain dripping down her chest and into her bodice. I lick my lips.

She swallows, trying to keep her composure, then says, "You

know what? I'm ready to tell you what I wished for back at the tunnel. It has to do with why I didn't run. Wanna hear?"

I snort. Thunder rolls ahead. I've gotta get us out of here before low visibility and mudslides make the roads too treacherous, but this is too fun, and now I'm curious.

"Sure, I'll bite, birdie."

Her lips curve into a sinfully wicked smile that I'll now strive to see every day of the rest of my life.

"Your *birdie* wished she could fly away from you."

My brows shoot up as she presses against me, one sharp nail jabbing into my left pec.

"So that's what I'm gonna do. First, I'm escaping. Then I'm coming back with an audience to watch me stab you with my pointe shoe shank."

My grin goes lopsided. "That's quite some plan. Except..." I snap my fingers and frown. "Shucks. Now that you've told me, your wish won't come true. Too bad."

She smiles sweetly. Something silver glints in her closed fists as she draws them back. "Watch me."

Thunder and lightning rend the sky as she slams a needle into my chest.

12
SWAN DIVE

LUNA

"Ow."

One, unemotional word. That's it.

I've planned this big cinematic moment from the second I saw the dart in the passenger seat—a sneak attack to tranquilize Orion so I could steal his SUV and drive back to New Orleans—and *this* is the only reaction I get?

I expected him to start stumbling like my dad did last night. But as I pivot on the ball of my foot to run, Orion grabs my wrists and tugs me in, as strong as ever. The hard angles of his face are carved with annoyance, hurt, and... pleasure?

What the hell?

"Did you... did you *like* being *stabbed*?"

My inner muscles clench as he grins. "I told you I like it when you fight back."

Rain pelts us, and he leans over me almost like he's trying to block the cold drops from landing on my head rather than intimidate me—which he's clearly trying to do. Holding both my tulle-cuffed hands with one of his large ones, his jaw clenches as he pulls the tranq out and holds it up. Lightning streaks across the sky beyond a mountain up ahead.

"Funny thing about these tranquilizer darts," he muses. "I made them myself. The crossbow's force depresses the dart's plunger, delivering the sedative to the prey." His brow raises at me as his thumb rests over the bottom of the tranq. "Like it did with your father."

I gulp.

"Unfortunately for *your* little stunt, you didn't do that part." He depresses the plunger and the sedative I'd hoped would jam straight into his heart shoots into the sky, mingling with the rain. "So, all *you* did, you reckless little thing, was stab me with the equivalent of a needle," he growls. "Here's a little rule of the woods. If you're taking out a predator, finish the fucking job."

He tosses the spent tranq inside the SUV.

"So, I'll give you two options. The first is to get into the damn car without a fight."

I swallow. "And the second?"

His lips tick up. "I'll give you a chance to make your wish come true. Try to escape me. I'll even give you a five-minute head start."

My eyes flit around, scanning the surroundings before meeting his gaze again. "What if I scream?"

"During a thunderstorm in the middle of the woods, miles from anyone? Good luck." He chuckles darkly. "Your call, though."

Then he pulls my wrists in with one hand and digs behind his back with the other, pulling out his knife.

"No!" I try to jolt away, but he knicks the tulle, well away from my hand, setting me free.

I rub my wrists, and he scowls at the red marks. He takes them in hand, massaging them before I can stop him, forcing me to bite back a moan.

"Let me say this, little bird. *When* I catch you? I'll show you *exactly* how you crave to be fucked."

When he lets go, his eyes flick to the SUV and back to me. "So, what'll it be? Get in or flee?"

I shake my head, taking a step away from him.

"I was hoping you'd say that." He chuckles so deeply that the heady depth of it stops me in my tracks. Then he rocks toward me on his toes, his lips a whisper away from mine as he taunts me, "Fly away little bird. I crave the hunt."

I fly.

Raindrops are sharp pellets on my skin, coming down so hard I can barely see ahead of me, and I barely have enough time to dodge trees after I see them. As treacherous as it is, I can't help but look behind me, to see if he makes good on his word.

But he leans against the SUV, filling his crossbow quiver.

Why on earth does he look kind of hot doing that? Is something wrong with me that I like seeing him nonchalantly waiting to run after me and ravage me as he checks a weapon, inserting another dart into—

Oh my God, run!

Orion stuffs one hand into his pocket and gives me a little two finger salute off his forehead before calling playfully, "Watch where you're going, fiancée. Stay safe! Don't want you to get hurt!"

"Well, I'm certainly not safe with you!" I shout back, turning around anyway.

He laughs nervously. "Just... give me a challenge, not a concussion, yeah?"

Run. Run. Run.

My heart races as I navigate the woods in ballet flats, slipping and tripping on mud and dirt, and trees, and roots, and—

A *thwick* through the trees has me stopping like a big dummy, and a dart lands in a trunk a foot away from me.

My eyes widen at the sight of the arrow embedded in the tree, the plunger depressed inside.

I hear him rack and reload the crossbow as he whistles.

"You have three more minutes, and this next dart goes into that sexy ass cheek."

"Keep dreaming!" I shout, but my adrenaline kicks up as I start running again and snap at myself. "No excuses, Bordeaux."

It's the mantra every ballet instructor has drilled into me my whole life, and it helps me focus on my flight.

I have no idea where I'm going, but all I know is it's downhill and it's away from him, so I push on, boomeranging from one tree to another, holding onto trunks to keep from falling.

"Just keep thinking about how I'm gonna find you, then fuck you," he calls behind me. "Fill you with my cock and give us both what we need, because we've waited long enough. It's time I claim my bride, little bird, and fuck you how we need it."

An embarrassing, needy whimper rushes out of me. Is it wrong that I feel more alive than ever at the mere thought of him catching me? My adrenaline pumps all to one place, and I don't think about how my nipples peak behind my bodice, how desire pools in my lower belly, or what it'll feel like once he finds me.

"Be careful!" Orion growls way behind me, but I ignore it, trying to see through the plummeting, torrential rainfall. Visibility's so difficult that I can't even see the ground a few feet in front of—

The ground drops away beneath my feet.

"*Luna!*" Orion's guttural shout follows me as I fall, voice full of the same terror that lurches from my belly up to my throat and out into a scream.

"Orion!"

I scramble in the air, but there's nothing to grab onto.

Orion's horrified face appears over the ledge. He stretches out his arm, but there's no use. A feather drifts off my bodice up to him in a cruel joke as I slam into the rushing waters below.

Frigid cold engulfs me. Shock makes me gasp, and water floods my throat, choking me. I thrash, but the rapids roll me under, smashing me against boulders. Branches catch my hair, tear my tutu, and whip me around. My lungs burn as I fight not to cough, but a rock twists my ankle and my muscles seize from agony, losing all the fight in me. Water roars in my ears, blinds me, and crushes the breath from my sternum.

Something grabs my arm, yanking me up, and it's only then that I realize I've been screaming his name.

"*O-ri-on,*" I beg for relief.

"I've got you, baby. It's okay, I've got you." He clutches me to his chest. I cough and sputter as we bob in the current. "There you go, cough it out."

My body racks with the effort as it obeys. I look up through burning eyes, my lashes heavy with water.

Orion's face is hard with worry, before his focus shifts to the river violently rolling us. "Shit. Hold on."

He grabs the back of my head, curling over me as I grip to his jacket. We sail through the water until we crash into something, making his body tense at the impact, then the current wrenches us from the boulder he protected me from.

I want to ask if he's okay, help somehow, but I'm still fighting for breath and clinging to him like a life raft. Hell, he *is* my life raft.

"Fuck," he mutters. "Alright, whatever you do, don't let go, okay?"

I nod but can't help looking over his shoulder. My eyes widen.

Just ahead, the water stops. There's nothing on the horizon but dark, blue-gray clouds, sheets of rain, and surging brown and white waves.

"There's a waterf—"

"I know," he grits out, huddling over me. "Close your eyes, hold your breath, and make a wish. Pretend it's like the tunnel, okay?"

The water crests. I suck in my last breath as he one-arm hugs me to the point of pain and wraps the other around me to cover my nose and mouth with his hand.

Keep us alive.

Then we fall.

13
GRATITUDE
ORION

*P*rotect her. *Protect her. Protect her.*

The mantra fills my mind, my veins, every fiber of my being as we career over the edge of the waterfall. My stomach lurches into my throat at the weightlessness.

I.

Am.

Her.

Shield.

I squeeze Luna flush to me so hard it must be painful, but I won't—I *can't*—let her go. My heart beats out of my chest harder the longer we're mid-flight, until we plunge into churning water so unyielding it feels like breaking through concrete.

Water fills my ears, and Luna screams into my hand as we tumble around, but I don't let her escape, keeping my palm against her mouth and nose so she doesn't suck water into her lungs. We roll in the icy-cold depths, pinballing rocks along the way. I twist us to avoid impact, but I can't see through the mud, silt, and debris displaced by the storm. Pointy, hard, objects of all shapes and sizes collide into me, but it's when Luna flinches from getting hit that I wince.

All the while I kick, trying to right us. When Luna tries to do the same, she cries out into my palm.

Fuck, she's in pain.

I did this to her. I hurt her. If it wasn't for me, she'd be safe—

No. Can't think about that now.

The water is equally violent the further up we go, but we finally break the surface with a heave, and I let go of her mouth. We both suck in huge breaths, our lungs desperate for air.

We sail in the rapids, and I grab every branch I can, cursing when they rip from their trees, until my shoulder smashes into a boulder. Air bursts from my lungs, but I claw for a crevice and keep Luna in the vise of my other arm.

Something tugs on the crossbow that's still miraculously strapped to my back. The water pulls at Luna's tulle skirt, trying to take her away from me. I squeeze harder around her waist and slingshot us from one boulder to the next, pushing off at an angle to use the water's momentum to hurl us through a pitch-black fissure.

We're shot out the other side on another waterfall, quickly plunging into a pool below. My feet touch the bottom this time, and I propel off, shooting us through the calmer water with my arm out to keep us from hitting anything else.

We splash through the surface, sucking in oxygen, but hearing her *alive* is the sweetest sound. Catching my breath, I swim one-armed to the rocky riverbed and drag us into shallow water.

Luna slides out of my arms onto all fours, coughing and sputtering. Pain radiates over every inch of my body, but I'm behind her, gently pushing her forward to help her up as she crawls over pebbles and sharp stones.

Finally, the soft, silty bank dips under my hands. I grab a thick exposed root and wrap my arm around her waist to pull us both onto land, collapsing beside her on my back, not caring that my crossbow jams into my spine as I quickly check for paint on the trees. I don't know where we are, my crossbow might be wrecked, and depending on the paint color, we're either safe or we're fucked.

I squint through the rain dripping from the canopy. A lightning bolt flashes, revealing a beat-up shack beyond and a splotch of paint on the closest oak.

Red.

Relief sags from my bones until lightning flashes and thunder claps a mere second later, the electricity in the air raising the hair on my arms. We need shelter *now*.

I shake out the water from my ears, and the first thing I register in the cacophony of the cascading waterfall, the rumbling storm, the roaring rain, is Luna hyperventilating.

"Luna?"

She tugs her bodice, trying to get it off, and I curse, sitting up and grabbing the fabric at her back to rip the shit in half. But the water's shrunk it so tightly I can't even get my fingers down the back. Her arm stretches behind her, trying to reach the clasps, and my heart pounds painfully as I wave her hand away.

"Fuck, I'm getting it. Just hold on for me."

I tremble as I undo one impossible clasp after another until the whole thing falls off her chest and onto the ground. She sucks in a ragged breath that shreds me in two, and I roll her onto her back so her lungs can fill, keeping her arms splayed out with my hands on each wrist so she doesn't curl around herself.

"You're okay, Luna. You're okay. Breathe, alright?"

At a loss of how to help, I wait for her breaths to finally slow, then exhale the terror gripping my chest and let her go.

"Jesus, you scared me." One of those strange, stressed, manic laughs bursts out of me, and I sit back, raking my hands through my hair. "Thank fuck you're safe."

Even in the dark, I can see her eyes shine with rage.

"I'm *safe*?" she growls, her voice a ragged rasp. "No thanks to *you*."

"No thanks to me? You would've died if I hadn't jumped in. Those were damn near Class VI rapids. Some *Olympians* don't even attempt those."

"And I wouldn't have had to if you hadn't forced me to run and fall in!"

"Ah hell no. I gave you the choice." I throw my arm up. "You're the little bird who decided to go swan diving off a cliff to your death."

She sneers, sitting up on her forearms. "And I'd do it again to get away from you."

"Be my guest." I gesture tiredly with my arm. "River's right there."

Her only response is crossing her arms and scowling.

I scoff. "You're a piece of work, you know that?" I lean over her, resting one hand beside her head to block the rain from dripping into her eyes. "I saved your life, yet you think *you're* the one that gets to have the attitude?"

Anger thins her lips... until she suddenly melts underneath me. Her brows furrow in something I'd swear was guilt, and I'm immediately on high alert.

But then she touches me.

Her hands slide over my shoulders and cup my neck, fingers brushing through my hair. Entranced, I climb over her more to slip my knee between her legs, caught in this tenderness so freely given that I'm not sure I trust it. But... what if it's real?

My mind goes hazy. I've *starved* for her softness.

"You're right," she whispers.

"I... am?"

She nods slowly, then squeezes her legs around my knee. "I haven't been grateful, and after that? I don't want to think about what could've happened. God, just thank you."

Holy shit. I was afraid I'd never hear those words, at least not until I'd convinced her to love me.

I swallow as she bites her lip. For the first time, I truly register that she's naked from the waist up, and like the dog I am, my eyes drop to her breasts. I want to lick them, flick my tongue over the small buds, peaked from the cold rain and icy spring water.

A shy look crosses her face. I wipe her hair off her forehead to better see that sweet expression, tugging free a feather that clings to her hair for dear life, the crown itself long gone. When she slowly pulls me down, I close the gap, my heart pounding faster with every inch. My hand shifts from caging her in to holding her waist.

Our lips brush tentatively until she teases my mouth open. I'm lost in her touch as her nails scratch my scalp, and my hands glide up her slick torso to cradle her head.

"You're mine, Luna. No one else has had you, and no one ever will."

"*Orion,*" she whispers, shivering. From cold, rain, or from us, I'm not sure, but I press my body heat into her anyway. I sink my tongue into her open mouth again, mimicking what I want to do when we finally have the time. This will have to tide us over until I can get us safe.

But my cock is rock-hard right now, and it's taking everything in me not to give in. I've waited this long for her, hopefully a few more days won't kill me.

"Say it for me, baby," I beg. "Say you're mine."

"Orion, I'm... I'm your..." She swallows, gathering her courage, then whispers, "I'm your worst *fucking* nightmare."

My jaw drops, and she brutally bites my lip and slams her knee into my dick. Blinding agony shoots from my crushed balls to my dumbass brain, nausea rolling through me.

"Fuuuuckkkkkk," I groan.

"I am *not* yours," she sneers with a cruel, satisfied smile, then shoves me off.

I collapse onto my back and crossbow, curling into a fetal position and clutching my junk, fighting the urge to throw up.

"Don't chase me this time, asshole. I'm escaping you whether you like it or not."

She breaks into a jog, but two steps in she cries out and stumbles over a root.

I can't even check on her, because, *Christ*, did her bony-ass knee hurt. When I finally turn my head, she's already climbing rocks and exposed roots onto drier land, favoring one leg.

She's hurt.

I suspected as much, but seeing it sends a pang of guilt through my chest. *Why* I have guilt while doubled over from her kneeing me in the balls, I have no earthly idea. I'm fighting delirium.

She finally hobbles onto raised land, half-naked, feather bodice in one hand, and catching herself on tree trunks with the other. There's no way she'll get far, and now I'm even more pissed because she's made it impossible for me to go after her and stop my reckless little bird from getting lost—and who knows what else—in the forest.

Breathing through the throbbing ache, I crawl to my knees and unhook my crossbow from my back. How it survived those boulders slamming into me, I don't know, but the attached quiver's still full with a mix of real bolts and darts. The one already locked and loaded seems unaffected too. Hopefully I don't have to use it, but if I do, it should work like a charm.

With her in my sights, I call out, my voice rough.

"Stop."

"No!"

"Alright, but you're forcing me to do it for you. You already proved once that you'd get yourself killed in these woods, you don't gotta prove it again."

"Go... fuck... yourself!" she yells, limping around a tree.

I sigh. "How about the other way around? As soon as you wake up, that is."

"As soon as I... wait, what?"

I brace the crossbow on a root and pull the trigger.

The bolt is so fast I can't see it, but Luna jolts with a yelp as the dart finds its target. She plucks it out and turns unsteadily on her feet to glare at me, holding it up.

"You shot me... in the... *ass*?" she yells.

She stumbles, catching herself on a tree trunk. Angry eyes bore a hole into me as she slides down, all the fight leaving her slower than it should with a full dose. But that's just a testament to how strong she is.

As her eyes flutter closed, I can't resist one more parting shot.

"Looks like I was right. Your wish won't come true after all, birdie. There's no flying away from me."

14

HE'S A GENTLEMAN

LUNA

My eyes snap open, finding a wood-beamed ceiling. The clap of thunder that woke me still rattles the warped window beside me.

Where am I?

A fire crackles and pops, splashing yellow and gold figures that dance across the stacked log walls. The most delicious smell tickles my nose, and I breathe deeply. My fingers twitch on a rough sheet, my head rests on a lumpy pillow, and my leg is inexplicably raised on a pile of blankets. The one on top of me is much softer, the lining of a leather jacket that smells like maple, bourbon, and pine. I almost curl into it, but the memories roll in faster than the river that got me here.

Kidnapping, murder, car chase, almost drowning...

Orion...

I turn my head enough to find him leaning against the wooden cot I'm on, his hands tugging his hair. Only his profile is lit by the glow from the cabin's potbelly stove. He stares into the flames, unseeing, deep bags under his eyes, sunken cheeks, and a five o'clock shadow that's at least a day long.

When was the last time he slept?

Actually, screw that. I do not care.

Determined to keep hating him, I shift to get up. The wood groans beneath me, and my muscles protest with it, dragging a whimper from my throat.

Orion lurches up, scrambling to face me.

"Luna?" His deep voice is a hoarse rasp. "You're... you're awake. Baby, you're *awake*. Thank *fuck*."

What looks like relief has him sinking back with a *thud*, raking both hands through his hair and pulling at the roots. If the spiky, haphazard mop is any indication, he's done it at least a million times.

Annnddd he's shirtless.

Jesus, like I need that.

I blink, forcing my eyes not to drag over the dark ink on his chest, the birthmark that matches the skull on my leg... and the trail of hair disappearing beneath the band of his boxer briefs.

"Where are your clothes?" I groan, slowly sitting up on my elbows, minding every throbbing bruise.

But the leather jacket slips down, wafting warm air over my chest. My *bare* chest.

I peek under the jacket, finding I'm only in panties.

"Where the hell are *my* clothes?" I gasp, snatching the jacket up to cover myself.

He doesn't seem to notice my crisis, his hand pressed over his chest and breath unsteady, like he's seen a ghost.

"Dadgum, woman. Don't do that to me again."

"Do what?" I quirk my brow. "Wake up?"

He huffs, holding up his heavy-duty watch. "You were out for twenty-one hours and forty-six minutes."

"A *day*?" I jolt up, and groan at the aches in my bones, catching the leather jacket before it falls again.

He nods, then winces. "The tranquilizer dart... it was meant for a man. I've never tranq'd a woman before."

"Gee," I grumble. "So happy to be your first."

His shoulders droop, features ragged. Is that worry and guilt I see? Good. He deserves it.

"I didn't think about how you'd already been drugged. Then you got a full tranq dose." His eyes drag over my body, and his voice cracks. "And you're so small."

I try to ignore the devastated remorse on his face and look away. "It's funny how you wanna marry me so bad that you're willing to kill me."

"Fuck, I'm so goddamn sorry," he rasps, bringing an unwelcome twinge in my chest.

"Apology not accepted." I cross my arms over the jacket and refuse to look at him, scanning my surroundings. Priority one? Clothes.

My outfit hangs from hooks in the rafters above the toasty cast-iron stove squatting at the back wall. Its rounded belly glows faint orange, filling the cabin with the comforting scent of wood smoke. My bodice and tutu look crisp and dry, but brown from the river. The ballet flats' satin is frayed and stained beside my garter.

"How do you feel?" Orion rumbles, and I relent, meeting his gaze again.

Those multicolored eyes shine in the light, and that voice— God, his voice. I try not to think about the way he taunted me when I ran away from him. The fact that I was turned on *and* scared will be all kinds of fucked-up fodder for my therapist. Maria's been through a lot with me, but she might cut me loose after that little confession.

Yeah right, she loves me.

"Let's see... how do I feel," I say sarcastically. Trying to focus. I shake my head, but pain screams back, making me grimace and press my fingers to my temples. "Oh, like someone who survived a maniac, falling off a cliff, and nearly drowning through two waterfalls. How do *you* feel, Orion?"

"Walked into that one." He sighs. "I feel like shit, Luna. None of this is going how I wanted."

"And how did you expect your kidnapping to go, exactly?" A whiff of stale dust hits my nostrils, distracting me from my rhetorical question, and my nose wrinkles. "Ew, is this mattress sanitary?"

"As sanitary as we could hope for at the moment. I found

fresh sheets in a tub that had layers of dust on the lid. Everything inside was fine. The mattress was covered with plastic too. You know, like the ones old grannies use to protect their couches in between Sunday suppers?"

"Um... not really?"

"Well," he mumbles, shrugging. "It was like that."

Then he stands, almost too tall for the low ceiling as he walks over to the stove. The fire flickers over the skeleton ballerina on his ribs, making her dance along his corded muscles. His boxers leave nothing to the imagination, so I snap my gaze away, pretending to study my nails. Unfortunately, there's not a speck of dirt in them to inspect—

Wait.

"How am I clean?" I muse. My eyes jerk up and I sing off key with a touch of anger in the tone, "O-*ri*-on? How the hell am I *cle-ean*?" I yank his black T-shirt up from my legs and put it on using the jacket as a makeshift curtain. "And I'd like to revisit the whole me-being-naked issue. You have some explaining to do, jerk."

Orion's reaches awkwardly for the stove like the grate might open up and eat him whole. I frown as he uses a cloth to deposit two long pieces of tin foil off the flat top to their respective plates.

"I found washcloths and a fresh bar of soap," he answers. "I didn't want you to have to sleep with that river dirt on you, and your tutu was practically freezing before I got the fire started." He scowls. "If you're worried about me doing anything shitty, I didn't. I'm a gentleman."

"A gentleman," I echo pointing at my sore butt cheek. "You. Shot. Me. In. The. *Ass*."

He sighs, like *I'm* the unreasonable one.

The nerve.

"Would a non-gentleman offer you dinner?"

As he peels back the tin foil, my nostrils flare at the scent of steamed fish stuffed with rosemary, thyme, and other herbs that he must've gathered from the bundles hanging in the rafters. I wince as I slide off the cot, drawn to the plate like a cartoon character to a pie steaming in a windowsill.

"Careful now," his low voice raises goosebumps on my skin. "Caught the trout this morning. Found a line and hook in another crate."

When I look up, heat reflects in his eyes as he watches me crawl toward him. I glance down to see the neckline hanging low. He can't see much, but I take delight that the bulge growing in his boxer briefs is thanks to me, and even *more* delight knowing he's not getting so much as a tug to relieve the pressure in that huge cock that I'm dying to have in my—

Jesus. Get it together, bitch.

I sit up, careful of my probably sprained ankle, and my eyes flick between him and the fish.

"What if there are spiderwebs in the herbs?"

He rolls his eyes. "There aren't. I checked first, then smoked them for good measure. Here. Eat. You're hungry."

My stomach growls, making any objection seem even pettier than I already have been. I take the plate and sit while he sets his near the cot, farther from the stove.

"Yeah, because *someone* kidnapped me two days ago and didn't even have the decency to give me so much as a protein bar."

"Come here." He ignores me, nodding to the space beside him. "Sit with me."

I pretend to think. "Hmm. No."

He doesn't even warn me before scooping me up in a flash. I yelp, but he just as quickly deposits me gently on the ground, well away from the stove.

"What the hell?"

"You were too close to the fire," he grumbles, setting my plate by his before plopping down across from me.

"Wow, dramatic? I wasn't even that close." My eyes narrow to slits at the over-the-top male until he circles back to my earlier argument.

"And I did have protein bars for you, actually." He peels back his fish's skin with his knife and pushes the herbs aside, then lifts a brow. "But if you'll recall, *someone* didn't even want the water I offered."

"Can you blame me?" I mutter, mentally taking notes as he separates the meat from the bones in one skilled move. The last thing I want is more "city girl" taunts after royally screwing up my escape.

But I'm brutalizing the already dead fish, and when Orion takes pity on me, taking my plate, I let him.

"No. I don't blame you. I expected it." He makes quick work of the bones. "And I wanted it. I want my wife to stand on her own at my side, and I knew I'd get that from you." He gathers a hefty bite of fish on his fork and raises it, eyes on my lips. "Open for me."

My mouth waters—for the fish, obviously. I really, *really* want that bite. If I take the fork from him, then the fish could fall off. And wouldn't that be a tragedy?

So that's why I don't knock his hand away.

Or maybe I like the way my belly flips and my nipples perk under his gaze as I lean forward, opening my mouth. His multi-color eyes dart up to mine as I close around the fork and take the bite before pulling away with a whimpering moan.

So. Damn. Good.

The rosemary and thyme coax the buttery, smoky smoothness from the trout, but it's Orion's smolder that warms me from the inside out.

Dammit, girl, stay strong.

As I sit back, shooting pain stabs up from my ankle and shin. My vision tunnels and I suck in a breath.

"Shit, Luna." He hurriedly places the plates aside to reach for me, but I stop him with a raised hand as I breathe through it.

"I'm fine," I lie, shifting to investigate the sprain.

My swollen ankle is as big as the massage balls we use after grueling rehearsals and bound in a makeshift wrap made of tulle, courtesy of Orion. Who would've guessed my kidnapper would use the same material he tied me up with to treat my sprain. How fucking thoughtful.

I grimace as I rotate one way then the other, the throb sharpening to knives between the joints. Yup. *Definitely* a sprain. Which blows, because even though I've danced on worse, any harebrained scheme to escape is shot.

"I did what I could to minimize the swelling." Worry carves Orion's brows, his jaw hard, and firelight sculpts his muscles into marble. "Of all the things I found here, a first aid kit wasn't one of them."

"Ain't that just the way it goes," I grumble, copying his speech pattern and looking around again. "Where is 'here' anyway?"

He twirls his fork, indicating the cabin. "A shine shack, if I had to guess."

"What the hell's a shine shack?" Parched, I grab the chipped mug of water beside him and sip.

"No, you don't want to—"

Fire explodes down my throat, and I cough, almost spitting it back out. He pats my back, chuckling as I catch my breath.

"A shine shack, aka a *moonshine* shack. Generations of bootleggers have run up and down these mountains since before Prohibition. You took the moonshine better than I thought you would."

"Moonshine, huh?" I rasp. "Benoit and I would've both lost our liquor poker faces. What do they make that stuff with? It's worse than the knockoff Hurricanes on Bourbon Street."

He nods to a green chalkboard that says *Po's Revenge???* in chicken-scratch chalk writing, a mix of crossed-out recipes and ingredients underneath, like that's supposed to mean something to me.

"I failed Chemistry 101," I deadpan.

He snorts. "No, you didn't."

"It's *so creepy* that you know that." I groan, then smack my tongue against the roof of my mouth. "It tastes like corn and copper pennies had a three way with"—I cough again—"rubbing alcohol."

"Yeahhh, I suspect there's no first aid kit because they were banking on this 'cure-all.' Drink at your own risk."

He sips the mug, sucking in a satisfied breath through his teeth as he places it beside him again.

Show-off.

Challenge makes my lips purse, and I snatch the mug. This time when I drink, I hold his smirking gaze through squinting eyes. The taste is awful, but the warmth filling my veins isn't unpleasant.

When I set the cup down again, my body shivers like a cold chill came over it, but my ankle doesn't hurt at the movement. I frown, twist it gingerly, and shrug.

"Huh, gotta hand it to them. It does feel better." I tilt my head, testing how far I can point my toes. "I barely feel anything at all, actually."

"Annnd *that's* when you stop." He snorts and slides the mug behind him. Then he hands me a blue glass bottle.

"Try this instead."

I sip warily, but it's pure, delicious water.

"Jesus, that's refreshing."

He laughs again, scooping more fish from the tin foil to set it on my plate.

"That's spring water for you. Water 'round here's 'bout as fresh as it gets, but I boiled it and strained it just in case." He places my plate in front of me. "Here you go. Got the fish out for you."

"Oh, um, thanks," I mumble, my cheeks heating at his kindness.

His grunt must be his version of "you're welcome," and we settle into a comfortable silence. Forks lightly scrape ceramic, the fire crackles, and the storm rumbles overhead. The ambience allows my mind to drift, and with Orion so intent on his meal, I inspect my kidnapper.

The last time I saw Orion Fury, I was sixteen. I'd walked into my parents' study to find Momma staring in horror at the TV with Dad beside her trying to comfort her in French. The documentary was titled *Wildes and Furys: The Appalachian Capulets and Montagues.* The headline was dramatic, but Momma's teary voice stopped any joke I might've made.

"The Wildes did this to them? How... oh my God, how awful. The oldest is hardly a year older than our babies."

The exposé on the Wilde-Fury feud focused on the "King" branch, complete with their crimes and mugshots, then scanned a graveyard burned to a crisp with blackened headstones. The program skipped to a blurry panning shot, taken by a nosy photographer, and paused on the three King Fury boys leaving a hospital.

Two looked like mirror images, flanking a younger one with black hair streaked white at the front. He walked stiffly, like he had steel for a spine, and the boys helped him, one with hands wrapped in bandages. Two wore sunglasses, but I could still see the rage and anguish filling their faces.

The tallest scowled at the camera, jaw clenched even in the blur, a threat in his eyes. If the photographer got any closer, the boy would've no doubt murdered him where he stood. The hate in his expression was way too much for someone his age and left me shuddering.

It was like he was glaring straight at me, and I'd stared back like I knew him. Because... I did.

The fever dream from the Troisgarde family meeting when I was twelve flitted through my brain. My parents never talked about it, I certainly couldn't admit I'd eavesdropped, and the Furys never returned to New Orleans. So I forgot, wiping it from memory like only children can.

But with the boy staring back at me through the screen, I remembered the curiosity and determination in those eyes as he flicked his knife open and closed, open and closed, before leading his mother out of the auditorium, protecting her.

"That's him, isn't it? Orion?" Momma whispered, pointing to the hate-filled boy. She shook her head. "It can't happen, Sol. They can't take her into that life. Use her as leverage. She can't be their hostage."

"They'll take her over my dead body, *ma muse*. You can count on that."

Finally understanding, I gasped. They turned, both their eyes wide, and Momma broke down.

They confirmed the pact was no fever dream, but Dad assured me it wasn't something to worry about. Even though the Wildes and Furys were dangers to themselves, no one could touch me in New Orleans. *He* was the most dangerous man in the South, the Phantom of the French Quarter, dead set on protecting his princess. I believed him. My father could do no wrong in my eyes.

And yet, here I am now. Alone in the stormy wilderness with the very man I was told wasn't a threat.

But as I eat the food Orion cooked for me, drink the water he gathered for me, and wear the shirt he used to cover me, I can't help but wonder if he's a threat at all.

Don't let him fool you. He kidnapped you, for God's sake.

I blink away from him, and a flash of silver under a net near the stove catches my gaze. My eyes flick to Orion, who's still focused on eating every last tender piece of fish. I slowly, *casually*, stretch my arms down my legs to hold my healthy ankle with one hand and sneak my other under the net, inching toward the knife handle—

It's snatched away from me, and my body snaps up like a rubber band. "Hey!"

He smirks, effortlessly rolling the knife between his fingers. "You thought I'd let you steal *my* knife right under my nose?" He tsks. "Come on, you're smarter than that."

I grumble, "A girl's gotta try. I'm Sol Bordeaux's daughter. If you think I'm gonna skip down the aisle over a little fish and some water, you've got another think coming."

"Good." His lips quirk. "I love your willful side."

Wings flutter in my belly, and I use that willfulness to squash them. "You won't love it when my dad finds me. He's going to kill you. If not him, then my brother will." I smile gleefully. "If not *him*, then my friends. Hell, my momma might even get in on the action. There's no way I'm marrying you, so whatever your plan is, call it off. Take me back to my dad now and *maybe* I can convince him to make it painless."

He nods thoughtfully, unfazed, as he points at me with the knife handle, the blade in his palm like it's no big deal.

"See, that right there? That's *exactly* why my father arranged this marriage. Our families need one another to defeat the Wildes and the fucked-up branches of the Fury family tree once and for all."

My breath stalls in my lungs. Why his family *needs* me.

I'm leverage, like Momma said. Everything he's doing is to force me to be their hostage so my father will fight by their side.

My chest aches at the thought, but I harness the reality. It's easier to remember he's the enemy and why I'm here in the first place.

I shake my head. "My mom told me the Wildes and Furys have feuded for generations. Why now? Why are the 'Troisgarde daughters' so special?" I ask, putting air quotes on the ridiculous name other families and societies call Brylie, Lucy, and me.

His lips thin as he sets the knife behind him and continues eating, answering between bites.

"Things have escalated again. It's been quiet for six years, but a Fury murdered a Wilde mother unprovoked. The victim's son killed her murderer, rightfully so. It should've ended there. The Wildes had exiled the boy's family years ago for other reasons, but we're all the same when it comes to grudges. The Fury he killed belonged to a northern branch that's got their hands in every government pot they can. The rest of us wouldn't take a dirty cop's hand if it was saving us, but they slip cash inside instead. Even though the Wildes didn't claim the boy, they still got all up in arms when he got sentenced to life. That's when the feud sparked up worse than ever."

"Jesus. No wonder they're after you."

"The King kin had nothing to do with it, and trust me, we have *every* right to call life for life," he scolds, then gentles while stabbing the trout mercilessly. "But no one cares about who deserves what anymore. No one even remembers how this war started."

"Yeah? Well, the Bordeauxs know exactly how we were dragged into it."

Orion doesn't take the bait, only eyeing me. "You know, I was gonna do this the right way. Win my bride over by dating the girl I couldn't stop wanting instead of"—he twirls his fork at the cabin again—"all of this."

I snort, trying to play off that those foolish butterflies are back. "So what changed?"

"You started dating a Wilde." His jaw tightens. "Not just any Wilde. Bossie Wilde's kin. You may hate me for how things went down, but if I hadn't stepped in, worse would've happened. Worse *did* happen when they drugged you."

I wince, and resolve fills his voice.

"They won't touch you again. King taught us to protect our wives to our deaths. That's what my brothers and I are gonna fucking do."

I swallow and hug my knee, tugging his long shirt over it. "This is too much. I just want to be free." Then I add the lie, "I don't even want to marry anyone."

He shakes his head, eyes softening at the edges.

"Yes, you do. I know what you want, and I've seen the way you look at your parents. You idolize them and the way they love each other. You can have what they have *and* freedom. *I* can give you both."

I bite my lip, then meet his determined gaze as I whisper, "You have no idea what I want."

Even as I say it, memories rush in. My favorite flowers, our dance, the way he touched me like he needed me...

Like he can read my mind, a knowing smile lifts his lips. "I know you better than you do, little bird. We established that the first time we met."

I shiver and glance around to think of *anything* else, taking in the little room. The shine shack, as Orion called it.

I frown. Sure, spider webs cling to the corners and the worn floorboards have seen better days. But the cot's comfy, the iron stove heats my skin, and moonshine and dinner warm me from the inside.

"Seems kinda rude to call it a shine *shack*," I murmur idly.

His head tilts before he looks around the room. "But... it is though?"

I shrug. "Seems more cabin-ish to me. A shack doesn't feel like a home, ya know? This room is small, but it's got 'home' potential."

Something flickers in his eyes, then he asks in a thick, velvet tone. "This feels like home to you?"

I don't know what that reaction's about, but I look around again before giving my verdict.

"If you spruced it up a bit, it'd be quite cozy." There's a pause between us, and I sigh. "Do we know where we are? You know, before we go all *Southern Living* magazine up in here?"

When I meet his gaze again, he clears his throat and quickly looks away. He takes one final bite and sets his plate on the wooden floor.

"Best I can figure is we're in a Lost Cove holler." He chuckles dryly. "Only you could accidentally find *the* lost cove."

"A '*holler*'?" I frown.

"A *hollow*, but we call it a holler. It's a small valley cut off from everything else." He dips a washcloth in a bucket, wipes his hands, then passes it to me. "I went as far as I'd let myself with you unconscious, but we're good and trapped, with rock walls all around. With your ankle and this weather," he huffs. "We're stuck. At least until the rain clears."

"Stuck." My eyes widen. "Wait, *stuck?*"

He sucks his teeth. "Yup. We're safe for now, but we're too close to Old Bridge, Wilde territory, for my liking. I reckon it's as impossible to get down in here as it is to get out, though. I set traps for good measure, but I want to get us to Dark Corner as soon as this 'Storm of the Century' passes."

"Are your brothers not hotshot trackers like you? Call them. Maybe they can come get us."

"Call them with what?" He points to a phone nearby, screen cracked to smithereens. "Turns out in a game of rock, water, SAT phones, SAT phones always lose. And even the best hunters can't win against washed-out tracks. I'll work on clearing a path while you heal, and as soon as you can walk, we're outta here."

"And then you'll take me back to New Orleans."

He sighs, scrubbing a hand down his face. "It's like you said. I've declared war between five families back there. The Troisgarde, the Furys, *and* the Wildes. We all want you for different reasons, and the only way you won't be trapped is with me. It's love or bondage at this point, little bird." He sips the water, then shrugs. "Better get used to it."

He hands the water to me.

"I don't have to—" at one sip, my bladder perks up after its long rest. "Oh my God, I have to pee."

He chuckles and grabs his jacket before holding out his hand. "I'll help you."

I swat him away. "The hell you will."

"I won't give you an inch so you can fly a mile again. Besides, you don't even know where to go."

"So! I'll figure it out." I wag my finger at him as I stand. "You may kidnap me, chase me, drug me, but I draw the line at watching—*ah!*"

Blinding pain shoots through me again at the slightest weight on my foot, and I land in his outstretched arms.

"Jesus, you reckless little bird. What am I going to do with you?"

I groan. "Take me to the bathroom, I guess. Oh God, this is going to be embarrassing."

He laughs again as he scoops me up in a bridal carry, making me squeal. I cling to him, and I have to admit, I hate him, but with his warmth and the muscles of his naked chest moving against the thin shirt I'm wearing, I don't mind this.

With my arms around him, he shifts so one arm is under my butt and he can grab a roll of toilet paper by the door. He hands it to me, then covers my head and body with his jacket.

"Don't worry. I'm not gonna watch. There's an outhouse with a door and everything out back."

My nose scrunches. "Like... a port-a-potty in the woods?"

"Trust me, an Appalachian outhouse is a million times better than a Mardi Gras port-a-potty." He snorts, already moving to leave. "And you better not do anything reckless."

"Like what?"

"Run away." He gives me a pointed look before grinning. "Well... limp away."

I scowl, an argument on my tongue, but he's opened the door, and a breathtaking mix of hot and cold gusts of rain-laced wind slams it against the wall with a bang.

"Shit." Orion rushes out, hurrying to latch it closed behind him as thunder cracks and lightning leaves the sting of ozone scent in the air.

"Okay, I see your point about running being reckless," I concede, yelling over the wind.

He hoists me up, pressing my head against his neck. "Gotta make it quick. Don't wanna be out here for long."

He holds me so tightly, I don't even bounce as he carries me down the porch steps, and I can't see where we're going with his jacket blocking my view. After several steps, he gently sets me down, keeping the jacket over my head as he opens another door.

My eyes widen at the pitch-black space inside. "*Here*?"

"It's either this or a hole in the ground!" He yells over the wind and uses his knee to keep the door open as he hands me the roll of toilet paper. "You gonna have a conniption, city girl, or suck it up?"

I can't even argue the "city girl" on this one.

"I'll be fine," I grumble and climb in.

He goes to close the door, but pauses. "I'll be right here, but if you hear somebody calling your name, don't come out."

I pause. "What if you're the one calling my name?"

He shakes his head. "I won't. Not your real name, anyway. First rule if you're in the deep woods: If you hear someone call your name and there ain't no one around, then no, you didn't. Don't answer."

I roll my eyes. "Sounds superstitious."

"It is," he says, shrugging. "Until it isn't."

He closes the door, leaving me bewildered in what's essentially a wooden closet. I wait for my eyes to adjust, and lightning flashes in the cracks to show a hole to hover over. He was right though. Any Mardi Gras or Saints' game port-a-potty is much worse.

I shrug, do my business, then open the door, hanging onto it so I don't fly away as I close it. Orion catches me as a strong gust makes me fall, wrapping his arms around my waist like we're in a pas de deux. He mutters a curse then pulls me against him, murmuring in my hair.

"Careful now."

Rain falls around us as I look up at him, clutching his neck. I swallow.

Butterflies, butterflies, so many butterflies, dammit.

Even in the dim light, I see his swallow trail down his throat, the water sluicing over his hard, bare chest. But he doesn't give me time to appreciate him as he picks me up again and carries me with the jacket over me.

Back inside, he sets me on the cot and fluffs the pillow. Just the thought of laying my head down has me exhausted. I haven't taken my medicine in four days, so normally I'd expect to be wired by now.

"I guess being drugged into sleep can really take it out of a girl," I mutter.

Orion winces, and I watch as he goes about tidying up our plates, washing them with water from outside.

"We'll leave as soon as the rain stops and you can put weight on your ankle," he sighs, hanging his jacket on a rafter hook like it's a million pounds. "Now we get some rest."

Damn, he looks worn out, even wavering on his feet.

I watch him in silence as I take one of the blankets from my footrest and spread it over me. It's nice, actually, soft and lightly smelling like firewood smoke.

Orion stokes the fire tentatively, jolting back when it pops, like he's afraid it'll reach out and grab him. Strange. This guy went toe-to-toe with my father—who's *much* scarier than fire—and didn't even flinch, yet something as harmless as embers makes him jump.

Before I can ask or tease him about it, he sets the poker aside and pulls down his crossbow from an exposed beam. Then he heads over, shoulders sagging as he pulls back the blanket, until I throw out my hand.

"What're you doing?"

His brow furrows. "Sleeping?"

"Not in this bed you're not. You'll take the floor."

He growls, "I'm not sleeping anywhere but beside my bride."

I cross my arms. "Then it won't be beside me. Because I—aka not your 'bride'—am sleeping in this bed, and you're sleeping on the floor."

"The fuck I am."

I shrug. "One of us is."

He groans but grabs a blanket from a storage container and plops onto the floor in front of the door. Then he levels me with a glare.

"If you think we're gonna be all *Pleasantville* with two twin beds back at the Fury compound, you're mistaken." I open my mouth to retort, but then he stops me. "And if you think you're gonna escape through the windows? That'll be a mistake too. If anyone tries to open them, they'll get rocked. Literally."

He points at the ceiling where a few huge stones hang by some invisible strings, presumably to barrel right into the windows and door.

"Fine," I spit. Laying my head on the pillow, I scowl at him. "I hate you, you know that?"

He closes his eyes, holding the blanket like a pillow in front of him. "You might. But you'll love me soon enough."

"How do you know that?" I yawn, wishing I could put some oomph into my anger, but I'm too tired to care.

My eyes, heavy from fatigue, narrow at him. His head tips back against the door, legs splayed, and brow relaxed.

Finally, when I've all but closed my eyes, he answers sleepily, "Because all you have to do is meet me halfway."

We're both asleep before I can ask what that means.

15
A STALKER'S NIGHTMARE

LUNA

"**M**omma!"

The ragged scream snaps me upright, my hand pressing against my racing heart. But other than the stove's crackle, silence greets me inside the cabin. Outside, the storm still rages, rumbling and slapping branches against the window.

Was that what I heard?

The twigs tap their fingers in an off-beat rhythm, scratching at the glass to be let in. I shudder, pulling the blanket tighter as I scan the room—stopping at Orion slumped against the door.

His legs are stretched out, head eerily tilted toward me, as if he can see me with his eyes closed. He clutches the blanket in his arms like a life raft, though if it were one, it would've popped by now from the force of his grip, his biceps bulging and tattoos rippling in the dim light. I don't think he's moved since we fell asleep.

Except his fingers twitch, and his body spasms in his sleep. His chest rises and falls too quickly. Is he hyperventilating?

His lips move in fits and starts, muttering words I can't catch. A jerk shudders through him, shoulders flexing, knees shifting like he's fighting off a monster.

Maybe it's Bigfoot.

I almost laugh, until a broken sound escapes him, tugging an ache from my chest.

"*Momma...*"

It was him. He's what woke me. Orion Fury is having a nightmare.

"*Please...*" he begs.

The pain in his voice is so raw, so anguished, there's no way his subconscious is dreaming up something from his imagination. I've heard the same torment the few times my dad has suffered night terrors. This isn't just a nightmare.

It's a memory.

The ragged whimper that slips out of Orion springs tears in my eyes. I wipe them angrily because I'm not supposed to feel anything for my kidnapper. I refuse to get Stockholm syndromed. And even though I'm always desperate for dark romance characters to just bang it out as soon as the villain shows an ounce of vulnerability, I'm not supposed to want that in real life.

Right?

I swallow, frozen. Do I let it pass or wake him? My dad only has them when he goes to sleep without my mom, usually on the couch after watching a game. As far as I know, she's never woken him, but as soon as she sits with him, he calms down. But I feel like that's way too intimate—

"*Help...*"

I whip the blanket off and ease down from the cot. Despite everything, including my own good sense, I can't watch him suffer like this.

My muscles groan, but I bite my lip to stay silent, crawling toward him on my knees. His every twitch nearly makes me turn right back around, but his eyes stay squeezed shut, his mouth muttering faster now, and I keep going.

He jerks again, twisting the fabric like he's pulling something. The movement dislodges the crossbow behind him, sending it skittering toward me.

I freeze. The dart is locked and ready. There are even extras laying around, having spilled from the quiver attached to the main frame. I could plunge them all into his chest, depress the triggers this time, and run.

"*No, please...*" he whimpers.

My breath catches. I quietly push the weapon aside and crawl the rest of the way to him.

"*No!*"

"Orion?" I whisper.

No response, but now I can see the sheen of sweat on his brow. Heat radiates off him, hotter than the stove's fire. Whatever's gripping him must be excruciating, twisting his body in painful contortions.

"*... fire. Get... out... save... Hatch... her... please!*"

The ache in my chest almost knocks the air from me. I sink beside him and do the only thing I can think of.

"Shh, shh, Orion, it's okay. You're okay..."

Leaning up against the door, I ease him down so I can hold him. Even in sleep, he tenses, then relaxes the instant his head rests in my lap.

I should be asleep myself. Not sleeping can be hell for me, but maybe it's okay since I've slept a total of a billion hours in the past forty-eight. And I don't know why, but... I can't leave him, not when some memory has him in its chokehold.

His face stays pinched, jaw clenched. My hands hover over his head, unsure what to do with them now that I'm here. He whimpers again. Moisture that had collected at the corner of his eye trails down his cheek, and I catch the tear with my fingertips.

I don't hesitate anymore, threading my hand through his hair and brushing it back from his forehead in soft strokes. Lightning flashes through the windows, flickering over the agony carved into his face.

"You're okay," I murmur again, barely audible over the thunder as I massage his head.

I saw Dad do this once for Momma when her illness ravaged her mind after a particularly bad depressive episode. I'm sure he did it other times, but I'd snuck into their room one night and found them this way.

The manic episode before that was a hesitant sort of fun. We exploded with laughs but still held our breath, all of us waiting for the shoe to drop. Momma had all the energy in the world to keep up with me and Nox—taking us for daily beignets, dancing with a brass band in Jackson Square, visiting the Audubon Zoo over and over again. It was great. Kind of. Because by then, Nox and I already knew it wouldn't last.

We were right.

One day she just... wouldn't get out of bed. The meds she hated taking for her mania, ones that seemed to torture her more than the mania ever did, had finally started working.

The tear stains on her pillow and the mascara streaks down her cheeks broke something in me, sparking dread and empathy I didn't understand yet. The highs lasted longer, but they felt brief when the lows went on for an eternity. She tried her damnedest not to let us see her like that, but my parents never hid her bipolar disorder, teaching us that it is a part of her. Still, it was hard at ten years old to see her go from on top of the world to the very depths of it. It still is. Especially now that I know what it's like.

That night I snuck in, Dad held her in their bed, whispering in French and singing lullabies Dad's mom, my grand-mère, used to sing. I never paid attention to the words. Now I wish I knew them.

I hum the tune instead, hoping it's enough.

The tightness in my chest releases the moment Orion's tension melts under my hand. He exhales a shaky breath against my thigh, then shifts. I still, but his eyes stay closed as one arm threads behind my back, circling my waist. His hand catches the wrist I've braced on the ground, and his other arm comes around my front to tug me impossibly closer, molding me against him like a pillow.

I frown at his hand wrapped around my wrist, finally close enough to analyze the rough, glossy webbing that spans both his palms. His grip is strong as I slightly turn my hand to better see the damage, knowing already that they're not callouses.

His skin is discolored in uneven patches, pale ridges and darker valleys melted together in a way that can only be from heat and flame. A pit forms in my stomach at the confirmation.

I've seen wounds like this my whole life. They're both gorgeous and terrifying to behold every time I look at my father's face and know what he had to endure. The pain he suffered.

Orion's palms are covered in burn scars.

A million questions flood my mind, but if he's anything like my dad, answers will come on his time.

Orion's head turns toward me, and my pulse races. Despite how wrong the reaction is, my inner muscles flutter at his closeness to the apex of my thighs. With my hurt leg stretched out and the other bent, his lips ghost dangerously over my covered sex. The thin T-shirt I borrowed and my panties do nothing to block his heavy, sleepy breaths coasting through the fabric.

I bite my lip, then after a few more of his deep breaths, I stroke his hair again, trying not to think about the desire tugging my core. I stay like that for a long time, long enough for the forbidden ache to settle and for my legs to go numb beneath him. But I can't bring myself to move.

"You're... here..." he mutters, words carrying nothing but relief.

I swallow, my gaze dragging from the fire and down to him.

"I'm here."

He squeezes me, tightening his hold on my wrist too. The FURY tattooed across his scarred knuckles shifts with the motion. Those marks should terrify me, the same way the skeleton ballerina inked on his ribs should. But they don't.

Instead, my gaze traces the letters like answers lie somewhere between the scars, as if they'll explain why I'm soothing the man intent on forcing me to marry him, all because I couldn't stand him suffering in his dreams.

"What am I going to do with you, Orion Fury," I whisper, echoing his own words.

I don't expect an answer, but after thunder rumbles and fire crackles, his deep voice pleads softly.

"Stay with me."

My pulse stutters. My hand stills in his hair. I swallow, not really sure what I'm doing until I've slipped my wrist from his grasp. His grip tenses before letting go, and I lace my fingers with his, holding his tortured palm. Leaning back against the door, I find way too much peace in the way the muscles relax in his jaw and around his eyes.

Then I tell the truth.

"I'm not going anywhere."

Maybe that's because he's trapped me, or maybe because he'll catch me if I run.

But then there's that other possibility. The one sneaking into every doubt cracking my resolve, growing bolder.

After everything my stalker in black has done to steal me, to keep me, the dumb jokes, the way he takes my insults with a grin, the adrenaline of all we've been through... how he saved me...

Maybe I *want* to stay.

Just yesterday, I was so sure I hated him.

But after tonight, I'm not sure what I feel.

ACT THREE

SWAN LAKE

16
LESSONS OF THE WOODS
ORION

She slept in my arms last night. Half-conscious, I thought her soft voice, her fingers combing through my hair, and her hand in mine had to be my imagination's escape from another night terror. There's no way a moment from my wildest dreams could be real.

But it was. Luna comforting me was as real as the stunning goddess in front of me now, bathing in a spring-fed pond. The waterfall feeding it tumbles down from a dizzying height. The fact that we endured that drop together makes me queasy, especially knowing we barreled over Cove Falls first, which is at least twice as high. Despite the odds, we survived, and this waterfall has delivered enough wayward trout for proper meals.

The rain's let up for now. Mist kisses my skin, leaving droplets in its wake. Far-off rumblings warn the storm isn't done, and the ground is still slick and unstable, a recipe for disaster with Luna's injury. We're stuck. Not that I'm complaining at this particular moment.

So I sit on the bank, switching between making sure the crossbow won't jam at the wrong moment and scanning the woods like a hawk. The forest's eyes watch back, encroaching on this moment between us. But all I can really focus on is the memory of her warmth around me.

Her Carolina jasmine and honey scent, heady at the apex of her thighs, the softness of her skin... Fuck. In my dream, I wanted to pull her panties aside and taste her again. My mouth still waters thinking about it. I'd have made sure she loved it, just like she did in the dressing room. Resting on her thigh, I felt the frantic pulse there against my ear. I have no doubt she wanted it too—or, at the very least, I had an effect on her being that close. She knows exactly what the man she hates can give her.

But now the lust is mixed with confusion, and I've racked my brain all morning with one question.

Why did she stay?

My crossbow was only a few feet away when I woke up, a mistake if I've ever made one. Had I trusted her that much to leave it lying out? Or was I so exhausted I forgot she's a threat? Hell, she could've emptied every dart left from my quiver into my heart and ended her captor once and for all. And yet, she didn't.

Was it the storm that kept her with me? Her ankle? The threat of my traps?

But no, none of that accounts for why she'd let me cuddle her waist, why our fingers were intertwined like we needed each other, or why her palm cradled my head like I was something fragile.

My heart was near full to bursting, but I got up before she could push me away. The rejection would've been a crack in my sternum I'm not sure I could've stitched back up. So instead, I carried her back to the cot, raised her sprained ankle on more blankets, and let her sleep while I went out to clear more trail.

I feel more refreshed after the best sleep of my life, let alone since my night terrors started at seventeen. But I'm sure I kept her up, considering whatever she heard was bad enough to convince her to soothe me.

And I can't muster an ounce of guilt over that. Not when I finally felt her arms around me. Not when I held her like I've wanted since I was too young to understand why.

But I do hold back a wince every time I glimpse the evidence of her poor sleep—sunken cheeks, dark bags against pale skin, reddened eyes. She keeps massaging her neck, where a knot seems to come back with a vengeance every ten minutes.

I want to rid her of the pain I caused, but I won't. The only kindness she's shown me so far was when I wasn't conscious to remember it, and I won't acknowledge it before she does.

When I returned to the cabin, Luna was up and demanded a bath in the small lake, seemingly desperate to get out of the cabin. I didn't blame her. I'm sure she was bored, and after our swim in the rapids from hell, I'd carried her into the shack to sleep off the tranq and scrubbed off the sediment that dusted every inch of me. With her passed out, though, all I could do was wipe her down with a washcloth, a poor substitute for the real thing.

I only took a dip in my boxer briefs, not wanting to freak her out, then set up shop on this water-slicked boulder, my clean jeans hanging from a branch for later. She splashes near the waterfall, probably passing time since she and her clothes are already scrubbed clean. Her bodice suns beside me, featherless in spots and stained from the muddy river. In the water, her tutu spreads around her like wings as she switches from lathering her skin to working the soap through the tulle.

With the storm-ravaged river beyond the waterfall, it's a miracle this pond is clean. And while it's chilly, the water still clings to the last heat of summer, and Luna doesn't seem to mind the cooler temperature. She's weightless, serene, her arms long and graceful as she rinses the bubbles trailing down her curves. When she rises to drape her tutu over a dry boulder, the sexy dimples above the swell of her ass flirt with the surface of the water. Each time she turns, I catch sight of the soft contour of her breast.

I shouldn't be looking, but a man only has so much willpower when it comes to his wife.

Her faint humming drifts like a memory, though I don't recognize the tune. She's talkative today, but these last few minutes have been her quietest all morning. Maybe it's nerves, or maybe she's trying to distract one or both of us. Either way, I like hearing her when I'm not looking.

I had to be on alert every moment I watched her from afar.

Finally having her nearby is a breath of fresh air. She's safe. She's *here*. And she's *mine*.

Almost.

I'll claim her soon enough, but not before the time is right.

"You don't scare me, you know."

I frown, blinking back into focus to see she's facing me now, dunked lower so the pond teases the tops of her breasts.

"Whatever you're doing with that thing." She nods at the crossbow in my lap. "All those broody, scowling, villainy looks. It's not working on me."

I look down, suddenly seeing it through the eyes of someone who has no idea how a crossbow works. I've been messing around with it, aiming it this way and that, testing the tension, checking for cracks along the frame, making sure the mechanism I designed for my hands still disengages properly.

No wonder she thinks I'm trying to intimidate her.

"I've figured you out," she continues. "I don't think you'd actually hurt me."

Rage surges through me at the mere thought. "Never."

I set the crossbow aside, keeping a blunt bolt from my quiver to twirl it between my fingers. The exercise is necessary to stretch the scarred skin and keep my palms from tightening up, but hopefully the movement is more playful than menacing.

She juts her chin. "So who taught you to use a crossbow?"

Pain slices through me, sharp enough that it takes me a second to realize the hit wasn't real. I clear my throat.

"I taught myself. My momma gave it to me for my seventeenth birthday."

Something furrows her brows before she spins away. Her voice is light when she replies over her shoulder.

"I'd ask what kind of parent gives a weapon for a birthday gift, but my Dad gave Nox a dagger when we turned sixteen."

I'm about to say I got one of those too, but she tosses her hair in a dramatic flip, smiling. "*I* asked Daddy for a sweet sixteen yacht party, naturally."

I chuckle. "Naturally."

She doesn't know I know the full story. As the NOLA grapevine tells it, Luna invited her whole class on that luxury yacht, something most of the kids probably wouldn't have even dreamed of experiencing. It was fairytale themed, and she gave crowns and costumes to anyone who wanted them, complete with professional styling and makeup. Not a soul was left out. The party was legendary for that alone.

People were still talking about it two years later at her eighteenth birthday. I'd been there less than a week when I heard the story, and I've been smitten ever since. My brothers and I grew up isolated in a county with a smaller population than the French Quarter, so it's entrancing to watch someone not only make so many people feel included, but actually include them. She's never met a stranger.

My father taught us every King kin carries a fight inside him that he'll never win until he finds the peace to his fury. Momma was that for him, his perfect opposite. When we find who's ours, Fate carves our mate's name into our souls. We feel that peace deep in our bones, but we won't be at rest until we claim it.

Luna is my perfect opposite. She's as reckless as I am vigilant, a city girl but freer than I'll ever be. Left to her own devices, she'll test her boundaries until she breaks, but as long as I'm there when she finds the sharp edges of this world, I'll make sure she doesn't get hurt. Once I claim her, I can give her the freedom she craves. With me, she'll finally be safe to stretch her wings. She'll fit right in as a Fury, as soon as I convince her to anyway.

"Why a crossbow, though?" she asks. "I'd think guns are a better gift for most hunters."

"Aimers," I correct, then shrug. "We have more guns than we'd ever need stocked in our armory, and every Fury gets a family dagger after completing Survival Week. I broke my 'baby's first crossbow' running from a momma black bear on day one—"

"Wait, wait, wait." She wags her finger. "None of those words should go together. Explain 'Survival Week' first."

"It's a Fury rite of passage. When we're sixteen, our parents blindfold us, drop us in the woods with a weapon and a prayer, and we have to last a week on our own before finding our way back."

"Oh, so casual child abuse," she snarls protectively, nearly making me preen.

I huff a laugh. "Not child abuse. Child abuse would be throwing a kid out here without teaching him how to survive first. By the time King was done drilling those skills into me, Survival Week was a cinch."

She harrumphs, unconvinced as she plays with the ends of her hair. "There's gotta be a better way."

"Probably, but it's the Fury way." I smirk, then toss back some of her sass. "We'll do it with our kids when they're sixteen."

She swings narrowed eyes on me. "The hell we will."

"Ah, so you *do* want kids with me."

"Ugh." She gives me a reprimanding look. "You tricked me."

She lets her hair plop to her shoulder and crosses her arms under the water. "Point being, I'm not sending my kids into the woods to die. I'd rather keep my little hellions around, thank you very much."

My chest thrums with the way this conversation is going, so I keep it rolling, wondering how far she'll let me go.

"Don't worry, I'll teach them everything they need to know before we kick our little cygnets out of the nest."

She frowns. "You'd have to teach the girls too, you know."

A flare of protectiveness sparks through me. No way am I letting any of my girls be put in danger. But... she's right.

"Deal," I relent gruffly. "The more my family knows, the better."

She seems to consider that as her gaze sweeps the woods before landing back on me.

"Would you teach me to live off the land?"

"You... want that?" Fuck, I love that question, but I can't help pointing out the obvious. "That implies you're sticking around."

She huffs. "*No*. It *implies* I'm bored as hell. All I did while you were gone today was twiddle my thumbs. If we're stuck here, I want to know everything I can."

"Hey, now, you did more than twiddle. It's squeaky clean in that there cabin."

She scowls. "Trust me, that was a one-time thing. I am *not* cut out to be a housewife homebody."

"Oh, I know." My smile is soft. "You were born to fly, little bird."

She hesitates, eyes dropping to my mouth for a split-second before she says nonchalantly, "Cool. It's settled. You'll teach me. We'll start with catching trout, following trails, shooting the crossbow, picking berries—"

I bark a laugh. "Don't speed past that crossbow part now." I waggle the bow in a "no" gesture. "You ain't touching this thing until I know good and well you won't shoot the messenger."

She sighs dramatically. "*Fine*, but I bet you'd feel pretttty guilty if I wound up dead, killed by whatever mysterious thing calls my name in the woods. A silly little city girl like me might head straight toward that danger."

I smirk. "You *are* pretty reckless."

That earns me another scowl, so I lift my hand in surrender.

"Alright, tell you what. I'll teach you a thing or two about a thing or two, how 'bout that?"

She whirls around, carelessly swishing water and revealing her dusky pink nipples. "Really?"

It takes every bit of my willpower to keep my eyes on hers.

I clear my throat. "Yeah, really." I point the bolt at her in warning. "But we start on beginner-level shit and work our way up."

She licks her lips, and I lift my knee up to block her view of the hard-on growing in my boxer briefs. I'm not embarrassed that my cock responds to her so easily—it knows who it belongs to— but I don't want to scare the girl away just when she's letting me in.

"So what's the first lesson?" she asks, then reconsiders. "Besides the whole 'if you hear your name in the woods, no, you didn't' thing. That still sounds like a superstition, by the way."

"Superstitions are, until they aren't. It's like getting a cold chill after stepping on a grave. Or when leaves turn over on a pretty, windless day, and then lo and behold, it rains." She looks at me like I have two heads. I wave my bolt dismissively. "Trust me. It's true. Dash can explain it way better than me."

"Sure he can," she mocks.

I snort, but think for a second, trying to figure out something she can see for herself that isn't just an old wives' tale.

Glancing around the trees, it hits me, and I almost kick myself for not explaining it sooner.

I sweep my bolt to point at the swaths of paint high up on some of the tree trunks.

"See those red markings?"

She nods quickly, so eager for information that droplets drip down her cheek with the movement.

"They mark territory. Black is for Dark Corner, Fury land. White's for Old Bridge, Wilde land. We're in Lost Cove, neutral ground, which is red. Because no blood should be spilt on neutral ground."

Her brow wrinkles. "Does that ever happen? We're safe here, right?"

"Of course we are." I scowl, offended she'd suggest otherwise. "The good thing about being unable to get out is that no Wilde can get in. No one knows we're here, and I've got traps set in every direction. I'll know if anyone gets within a quarter mile."

She skims her hands over the water, not looking at me. "Where are the other traps?"

I smirk. "*That* I'm not telling you."

She frowns like I've caught her.

"Don't pout. You're not going anywhere without me, so I'll make sure you don't trip any. But if I told you now, I bet dollars to donuts you'd try something reckless, thinking you could trick me. I'd somehow wind up knocked out and hogtied in tulle, butt-ass naked come morning so you could escape."

Her eyes roll, all but confirming my suspicion.

"I'd come back for you," she argues half-heartedly. "Eventually." Then she cuts me a sharp glance. "After you learned your lesson."

I chuckle, and she huffs, continuing. "But you know I wouldn't have to do any of that if we left right now. It stopped raining, so what's keeping us from getting outta here?"

As if the weather itself wants to defy her, she jolts and glares up at the sky, wrinkling her nose as she hastily wipes off what must've been a raindrop.

What's left of any path I could find is covered with collapsed trees, slick with mud that'd suck your boots clean off. Even I had trouble climbing through it to see the other side.

"Storm's still in the air. Not to mention you're still hurt, birdie." I shake my head, letting my concern show. "The only safe path out that I've found would kill that ankle."

She whines softly, "I said I have a high pain tolerance."

"Oh, believe me, I know," I tease lightly. "You haven't made so much as a peep about an injury half my high school football team would've cried like babies over."

"See? I'll be fine," she insists.

I force a playful smile, though it feels strained as my hand presses over the ache in my chest.

"Ready to get rid of me so soon, baby?"

She rolls her lips between her teeth, eyes seeing too much before finally murmuring, "Don't call me baby."

Then she slips beneath the water.

"The hell I won't," I mutter to the ripples she leaves behind.

I've seen the way she shivers at my nicknames for her, *that* one most of all. There's no way I'm stopping when it's the one button I know works every time I want her to feel *something* for me. At this point, with the slow, unenthusiastic jabs she's trying to throw my way, her rebellion and spite seem more like phantom limbs she thinks she's supposed to keep using against a man she's supposed to keep hating.

She surfaces with a breath, no longer facing me, and her voice is back to that devil-may-care tone.

"Well, if you're gonna hold me hostage in the wilderness, the least you can do is teach me which type of clay fits best into my seven-step skincare routine."

My jaw goes slack at that.

She's back to unserious Luna, but she didn't shut me down. Fuck, I'll take the win.

I stare as she slicks her wet hair back, strands now darkened to a deep plum. They tease her sexy skull tattoo on her upper back, spilling water over the ink and down her spine as she stands tall enough for me to see the beginning of her pert little ass.

The tempting nymph is daring me to look now.

But a flash of white at the edge of the lake catches my eye, and I straighten.

Before I can stop myself, I slip silently into the water, sinking deeper as I make my way to Luna. She tenses as I slowly cover her mouth with one hand while my other arm wraps around her slippery, naked waist. But she doesn't fight me as I pull her against my chest, trusting me.

Fuck. That feels good.

I lower my mouth to her ear and whisper, "Hold your breath, little bird."

She inhales through her nose as I dip us both farther into the water.

"And don't... make... a sound."

17
SWAN LAKE

LUNA

"...*D*on't... make... a sound."

My heart skips as we sink deeper, right up to my nose, then takes off into a sprint.

What are we hiding from? What's out there?

I'm terrified, but I listen, holding my breath and trying to ignore the spark of need unfurling low in my belly, heat drawn from Orion's warm chest against my back. It's the same confusing, intoxicating sensation I felt when he chased me through the woods.

His nearly naked body presses into mine, slippery against me, but every muscle is hard as stone, coiled to strike. Tension pulls taut between us, and I go languid in his strong, determined embrace, ready to move however he needs me to.

He turns us slowly. Confusion prickles my mind when his arm slips from my waist and breaks the water's surface, pointing toward something white at the edge of the lake.

My cheek brushes his massive bicep as I squint.

It's...

Oh my God. It's a *swan*.

His hand tightens over my mouth, anticipating my gasp, stifling it. Then his scruff-roughened cheek rounds in a smile against my temple as his grip softens and his arm returns around my waist.

The swan is big, much larger than I imagined the bird would

be. I slump against Orion's chest, watching in awe as the bird preens its pristine white feathers and glides along the water.

Orion raises us so my chin skims the water's surface. His lips brush my ear, and I will myself not to shiver.

"I've never seen them this close," he whispers warmly, his words light and gentle. "My cousins on the coast say they come around this time of year. Maybe they are stopping here to rest."

They?

On cue, another smaller swan drifts out from the shadowed trees hanging over the water. Excitement has me clutching Orion's forearm, my nails pricking his tattooed skin. I glance up to make sure he's watching, and his eyes crinkle at me as he nods in answer, mouthing, *his mate*.

I do a little happy shimmy in his arms. His chest rumbles with laughter against my back and he tightens his grip as he sits me on his bent knee. Entranced with the scene, I settle against him like he's a chair. His arm rests in my lap, thumb stroking circles on my hip, while his other hand still covers my mouth, like he knows I'm still on the verge of squealing.

The swans float farther away, rippling the surface back and forth like a silent conversation. One dips its neck, preening the other's feathers. I don't know why, but for some reason, my chest tightens.

"They mate for life." His words take root in my chest. "Once they're paired, they fiercely raise their young together. And when the time comes, they'll go back home. Together."

We stay like that, watching the pair meander through the mist like something out of a dream. Then the male flaps his wings, and his mate answers in kind before they vanish between mossy rocks.

Long after they're gone, we sit in the quiet. The rush of the waterfall, the buzz of cicadas, and the rustle of leaves filter back in before Orion murmurs.

"You okay?"

His hand drops from my mouth to rest at my collarbone, while his other arm tightens around me, like he's afraid I'll run.

I should run. My confusion over how I reacted last night combined with the charge of the moment we just shared is too much to handle. My mind races to find its footing but dusts up a jumble of random memories instead.

His mother's gentleness toward his father years ago. Orion's nightmare from last night. The reverence in his voice when he talks about his family. It feels wrong to ask about any of it, too personal for how I've insisted on pushing him away. So I stick to what's in front of us.

"What happens if a swan's mate dies?"

I'm unsure how it relates, but deep in my chest, I'm desperate to know. When he stiffens behind me, I wonder if he understands why I'm asking better than I do.

His voice catches before he clears his throat and speaks more firmly. "For many, that's it for them."

My sternum cracks under the weight of his answer. He swallows thickly before continuing.

"He waited for his soulmate. Without her, there's no one else."

His fingers squeeze my neck while his other hand slides lower, hesitant, like he's waiting for me to stop him. I'm achingly aware of the glossy ridges of his scars curving softly over my skin. The cool water flows around us, but his body flush against mine keeps me warm. *Inside* and out.

Earlier, I stripped down to tease and annoy him, to prove he didn't scare me and that big bad Orion was all talk. But I'd also wanted to lighten the mood after dealing with all the emotions brought on by soothing my stalker into a restful sleep I couldn't find for myself.

That lack of sleep is *not* good, and I could tell I was in trouble as soon as I woke up. I'm a live wire, energy vibrating under my skin, and I've had a hard time trying not to talk nonstop. He doesn't seem to mind, at least. I think he might even like it.

But he doesn't know the telltale signs. He doesn't know that when the high feels too good, I have a bad habit of chasing it until

I'm reined in, either by myself or by someone who loves me. Like now, I'm in control, and as long as we either get home soon or I get good sleep, I'll stay that way.

Even if I do slip, though, I'll still be *Luna*, just razor-sharp, braver, and quicker to act on impulses I normally wouldn't. The easiest way to explain it is that I know what I want, and I want it *right now*.

Up until this point—thanks to him, apparently—I've never acted on my urges outside my bedroom, and even then, only with my battery-operated boyfriend. But Orion is here. Ready, willing, and just as needy as I am.

With this buzz humming through me, encouraging me to move, I can't stop the inevitable even if I wanted to. And I do *not* want to stop.

Orion's hand ghosts down my torso while his other stays firm around my throat. My breaths grow heavy, and his heart races against my back, just as fast as mine. Instead of flying away like I should, I sink further onto him, feeling his cock hardening beneath me. Desire pools in my core, a want that's gone unsated for too long.

God, it feels good to finally do something about it.

He applies more pressure on my throat, making it hard for my nervous swallow to travel down my neck.

"Do you like me holding you like this?" His voice is hushed, despite the trees being our only audience. "My hand around your neck?"

His thick cock pushes against my ass, his boxer briefs creating friction between us. A whimper slips out of me. He curses into my nape, and my whole body trembles.

"Yeah, you love it." His words come out harsher through gritted teeth as he grips my hip and tugs down as he thrusts up, grinding against me. "You love knowing your life's in my hands. It turns you on, doesn't it, little bird?"

In answer, my hand boldly wraps around his on my neck, urging him to squeeze harder, restricting my breath.

"Fuck." He breathes the word like a prayer. "I bet running from me had you soaked too. You wanted to be claimed that day."

The truth taunts me, keeping me quiet so I don't admit he's right. As terrifying as it was to be hunted, more than anything, I wanted to be caught.

He takes my silence for the submission that it is, and his wicked chuckle rumbles down my back to my pulsing sex.

I need him. I need him. I need him.

He shifts, and his hand leaves my hip. Panicked at the loss of his warmth, I try to turn to beg him not to go. But his hand still around my throat clamps tighter, holding me in place as he continues to move behind me.

"Don't look at me," he orders, voice low, heavy, and... resigned? Then he murmurs, "Not yet."

The words sting, but I get the distinct feeling the command is for my benefit, and one he hates to give. But I understand.

Somehow, he knows that looking at him will make this too real for me. I already run from the mere threat of being vulnerable, something I *definitely* am in this moment, naked before him with his hand around my throat. If I meet my kidnapper's eyes, I'll remember I'm the captive. I'll drown in shame if I face the man keeping me hostage and I don't kick, scream, and fight like I know I *should*.

But like this, I'm only at the mercy of the man who makes me ache, the one who makes me feel safe in the wilderness. He feels... *right*. I don't want to screw that up by facing reality.

So I close my eyes, keeping up the ruse. I hear the slap of wet clothes against rock, then his hand returns to my hip while the other caresses my throat with his thumb. His lips brush mine, light as a feather, and I hold my breath.

"Be reckless with me, little bird."

I swallow hard beneath his grip. "Yes. *Please*."

His lips finally claim mine, and his body crushes into my back, sloshing cool water against my nipples. He's slick everywhere now, completely bare. I suck in a shocked breath that he greedily takes back, his hard, thick cock gliding along the curve of my ass. I moan, arching my back, and his hand at my hip slides to hover above my center, tantalizingly close to my clit.

He grinds into me, and I nearly sob for him to push between my thighs to ease the pressure building there.

"Do you remember what I promised before you flew away from me?" His hand loosens at my throat, giving me air.

"You said you'd show me how... how—" My cheeks burn at the phrasing teasing the tip of my tongue.

"Show you how...?" he prompts, voice like velvet.

"How I... I crave to be fucked," I whisper.

"Mmm," his feral growl of approval vibrates through me. "That's right, my good girl."

The praise racks through me at the same moment his fingers ghost over my clit, and I jolt.

"Open for me, Luna."

He doesn't wait, his knee spreading mine apart, tipping me off balance. My eyes snap open and I hold onto the rock wall in front of me. He's snuck us past the waterfall into a small alcove where the water is shallow enough for me to stand on the slick stones. I rely on his hand at my throat to keep me upright, my fingers digging into the boulder's crevices as his impossibly thick cock glides along my sex between my thighs.

"Fuck." His mouth grazes my collarbone, raising goosebumps. "I can already feel how ready you are for me. You want to be fucked so bad by your husband, you'd let me take you right now."

Not a question, just the desperate truth.

My teeth carve into my lip, and his grip tightens on my throat as his other hand finally, *finally* circles my clit, making me whine.

"All this fighting, rebelling. It's an act," he murmurs. "You're glad I saved you from your white knight, aren't you, little bird? One day you'll admit you're mine."

His cock stills along the crease of my ass, and he sinks a finger into me, stretching me. My muscles clench around him, making me suck in a sharp breath.

"So needy. You wanna feel how drenched you are?"

He lets go of my neck to wrap his arm tightly around my waist, lifting my hips out of the water. I stretch on my tiptoes, enough for his finger inside my channel to slip free above the surface. Then I feel him stroke his cock, hear him grunting his pleasure, before reaching around me and tracing his slickened fingers on my lips.

"Feel that? That's us. I'm about to come just from fucking your thighs, and you're already slick enough to take my cock and all I've had to do is barely touch your clit."

He grabs my hip with his other hand and sinks us back beneath the surface.

"That's how this could be between us. So fucking easy. All you have to do is let me treat you right. Can you imagine how good we'll feel when I'm actually inside you?" he rasps as he smears the proof of how much we need each other across my mouth.

My tongue sneaks out to lick his fingertip.

"Jesus, yes. Taste us, Luna."

He curves his finger into my open mouth, and I obey instantly, wrapping my lips around him, tasting water laced with our arousal.

"Taste the difference between spring water and us. There's *nothing* pure about us. We're sinful perfection."

I don't know which flavor is him or me, but my eyes close again on a moan. His finger moves in and out of my mouth in sync with the way his cock has begun to move between my thighs again, taunting my opening.

"One day, I'm gonna fuck 'I love you' out of these pretty lips, little wife."

My heart stutters.

I should argue with him, push back.

But I can't seem to care. Not when he's bending me forward

for a better angle on my clit. Not when he whispers things that make me want to beg for him to make good on his promises.

"Every time I thrust, I'm *so close* to sinking inside you, and I'm *aching* to fill you up. You know how hard it is to hold back right now? Once I'm inside my wife, I don't know if I'll be able to restrain myself, and I don't think you'd want me to. You'd want everything from me. You'd beg for me to come inside you, wouldn't you, baby?"

His cock pulses between my thighs, sliding along my core. Each thrust leaves me breathless for more, the shock of cold water rushing in to replace the heat he leaves behind.

"Don't you want that, Luna?" he asks again, popping his finger from my mouth to join his other hand to grab my hips. His grip bites into my skin possessively, like he'll never let me go no matter how I answer.

"Yes," I gasp, not sure of the question, just wanting him to keep ending each thrust with that little pulse against my clit.

"Mmm," he growls, kissing my jaw before dragging his teeth down my throat. His canines lightly bear into the flesh at the crook of my neck, and one hand glides up to pinch my nipple, drawing a gasp from me.

"You've been teasing me all morning. Don't think I didn't notice," he accuses, but there's not a hint of disapproval in his dark tone. "You didn't have to strip down, but you did. And you sat naked in the cold water, right in front of me and ripe for the taking during the longest bath in history. I had to keep myself from diving in after you to latch onto these perfect tits."

He squeezes my breast roughly, making me cry out. Then his hand glides down my side, every inch of his touch slow and deliberate before resting over my clit.

"I wasn't trying to tease you," I pant, lying through my teeth. "I just... wanted a bath."

And now I just want is release.

He bites my neck, and my yelp ends in a moan when the gentle caress of his lips soothes the wound.

"Liar." He chuckles darkly. "Someone needs to put you in your place."

Rebellious heat flares in my chest.

"And that's gonna be you?"

But his fingers circle my clit again, harder and faster this time, and I moan, putty in his arms.

"It'll only ever be me. You want to be tamed, and I'm the one who'll do it."

He thrusts hard between my thighs, clapping our skin in the water, and I whimper. "Take what I give you for now. Neither of us is lasting long."

My nerves are on fire. "Are you... are we gonna...?"

"Are we gonna... what, baby?" he taunts, his low laugh bouncing against the rocks.

Anticipation and embarrassment lodges the words in my throat. I'm *never* like this. I'll say whatever I want to say, whenever I want to say it. But right now? I can't form the words, and my cheeks heat.

"Can't finish that sentence for me? Is my reckless little bird finally shy?" His voice lowers, rich as honey as his warm whisper caresses my cheek. "Good. You never have to put on a show with me."

Something unravels in my chest, releasing a tightness I hadn't realized was holding me back. My vision blurs before I slam my eyes shut. The waterfall's mist will hide any tears that fall, thankfully. He's already seen too much of me. I already *feel* too much with him. And he's not even inside me yet.

Orion Fury will ruin me if I'm not careful.

I brace myself for him to do it. My muscles tense, ready for him to pull back and slam into me in one brutal thrust.

But his fingers on my clit keep their steady circular rhythm that's driving me mad. His thrusts slow, though, and he croons over the waterfall's roar.

"Relax, I'm not gonna claim you. Not yet." He kisses my tattoo on my upper back, making me quiver. "When I finally take you, there won't be a single doubt about me in your mind. Now stay still and let your husband do the work."

He shifts us over, catching me as my feet slip on the stones. I wonder why he's moved us until my hands find a better grip on the new boulder in front of me, and my feet find purchase on a flat rock. The waterfall breaks on his back, splashing over mine as he bends over me.

One hand returns to cup my breast firmly, while his other hand zeroes in on my clit faster and with merciless precision. His cock pumps between my thighs again, slick with our arousal, and I whine at the sensations pulsing through me.

He works me brutally, tweaking my nipples, teasing my clit. But his tantalizing thrusts never give me the one swift plunge inside that I'm craving to ease the ache that I instinctively *know* only he can.

Every circle of his fingers over my clit builds tension in my muscles, tightening them as I clutch the boulder and become one throbbing heartbeat begging for release.

"Orion, *please.*"

He curses against my nape, but I can barely hear him, his name now a needy chant on my lips. My muscles coil tightly, straining to climb the peak, and I chase the high like I never have, rising with it, pleading for it, begging to reach it, until I finally... finally...

... break.

My climax slams into me, forcing a breathless cry from my chest. Waves of pleasure rack through me, and I collapse forward. Orion catches me, his arm banding over my chest before I hit the slick stone as all tension leaves my body.

"I got you." He holds me to him, keeping me upright, cradling my throat with his palm again and steadying me.

His thrusts between my thighs grow frantic, his grip on my throat gentler now, while the one back on my hip is punishing, so desperate to claim me I know I'll wear his marks. I swallow against his palm, and glance down at the hand on my hip. The FURY tattooed across his knuckles strains white as he clings to me through his frenzy.

He told me not to look at him, but I *need* to see the way he needs me, even if it's only a peek.

When the hand at my throat leaves to grip my collarbone for a stronger hold, I glance over my shoulder and—God, am I glad I do.

Orion Fury is falling apart over me, face creased with focus, jaw locked, a vein bulging at his temple. His eyes fix on his cock sliding between my thighs, and he sucks in ragged breaths every time he thrusts.

Then he looks up.

His dark green and brown mismatched gaze captures mine. His lips part as his hips stutter almost to a stop. One heady breath passes between us, then he picks up speed again, eyes on me, letting me see the ecstasy my body gives him. His chest heaves, abs contracting over his inked stomach, and his cock thickens, teasing my entrance more and more with every stroke.

I brace my hands on the stone and bend lower, changing the angle to offer more of myself as I squeeze my thighs around him.

"Fuck, Luna. Fuck, fuck, *fuck,* baby," he groans, one final thrust surging through him as he comes.

But his cock slides too high, the very tip slipping inside my channel before he lurches to a stop, hands digging into my collarbone and hip. His thick head lodged just past my entrance, his cum pulses into me, heat flooding my channel.

"Oh my God, Orion!"

"*Shit*," he hisses low, looking almost as shocked as I feel, even as his hips keep pumping shallowly, spilling his seed into me.

"Orion, are you—are we..."

I drift off, panic, pleasure, confusing exhilaration—everything colliding in my chest at the sight of Orion's awestruck face as he comes inside me.

A voice deep in the back of my mind tries to fight for reason, but something primal takes over instead. I suddenly want things I shouldn't. *Need* things I shouldn't. The adrenaline brought on by this risk draws me to him like a drug.

My virginity teeters on a knife's edge. He's coming inside me, and worst of all, I *want* it.

God, what's wrong with me?

"Orion?" My voice trembles, heart racing, torn between fear and need. Rebellion and surrender. The urge to flee, or to fly straight into the forbidden.

More, please. Break me only for you. Make me yours.

I try again, fighting for better judgment. "We shouldn't, Orion. I... I'm not on birth control—"

"Shhh, baby." His thumb starts slow, comforting circles on my hip. "It's okay. I already know. Trust me."

His reassurance quiets the storm in my mind even though my pulse still thunders. My body bends easily for him as his hand on my neck arches me back, bringing me flush to his chest.

He whispers against my neck. "We want this, don't we?"

I swallow, unable to argue.

His teeth scrape lightly over my skin, the promise of a bite.

God, am I crazy? This is careless, impulsive... everything I shouldn't be. And yet the feral part of me craves for him to mark me, to claim me fully.

"*Please*," I whimper, not sure if I'm begging him to trap me or free me. Or both all at once.

"Soon," he murmurs. "Soon I'll give you everything, Luna. Every goddamn thing."

He lifts my hips, angling to allow his cock to nudge deeper. I gasp as he taunts my body's resistance.

"Fuck, I can feel where you kept yourself for me," he whispers reverently.

"What... what are we doing?" My voice wavers, but his gaze steadies me, sure serenity wrapped in raw hunger.

"Every part of me belongs to my wife, Luna," he growls, unrelenting. "Everything I am belongs to *you*."

My heart skips painfully. I bite my lip, tilting my hips to let him rock into me, stretching my opening. Not enough to break me, but enough to destroy me all the same.

I could move. I *should*. But I don't. And we both know I don't want to.

Because this part of him, the instinctual way his body dances with mine, the bites that almost pierce my flesh, the way he's claimed me in almost every way... Orion has unveiled something deep within me, something I didn't know I needed, but now I'll crave forever. From *him*.

His thumbs press into the dimples above my ass as he flexes forward again, halting right at the barrier he refuses to cross. Then his hand circles my waist, and his other lifts my damp hair to drape it over my shoulder, revealing my tattoo.

He kisses it with possessive heat in his gaze, evaporating the splash of fear trying to trickle in. With one look and a touch so tender it feels as intimate as being inside me, he stokes a terrifying wildfire of emotions inside me.

"One day I'll break you, my reckless little bird. I'll wear your blood like a vow, making you mine forever." His gaze sears into me, dark with promise as his palm settles over my belly. "If I haven't already."

18
THIRTY-THREE *Fouettés*
ORION

As much as I hate to admit it, I think I fucked up today.

The second I slipped out of her, I saw it happen, watched her shut me out in real time. Weird thing was, she kept talking. But it wasn't *to* me. It was *at* me.

Rapid-fire sentences came at breakneck speed, as if her orgasm high set her on fast forward. She had to expend the energy somehow, and her mouth was her best bet—saying nothing and everything all at once, piling on words like she was trying to bury what we did beneath the noise.

And yet in all her breathless conversation, she hasn't breathed a word that we might've made a little Fury together.

Goddammit, what the hell did I do?

And is it fucked up that I'd do it again?

I'd feel less fucked up if we could just *talk* about it.

But I gave her space instead, letting her avoid what needs to be said a little longer. The timing worked out, because I had to clear more trail before either nightfall or the storm swallowed my daylight. I didn't make it, though, and worked well into the night. The machete I found in the cabin is duller than a butter knife now, and rain drenched me clean of the mud and grime I earned.

Luna hadn't wanted me to leave without her, sassing me that I was overprotective about her sprain. But there was nothing for it. No matter how many times she insists, her ankle is *not* fine.

So when I return around one A.M., I don't expect to see my little bird fluttering around, twirling in the firelight.

She's shoved all the furniture aside, and the cast-iron stove radiates a halo around her as she spins, arms above her head. Her tattered tutu lifts, revealing the sexy tattoo I designed for her, and her satin slippers are frayed to mere threads while her bodice slips low on her perky, round tits.

I stop in the doorway, awestruck. She's hypnotic as she dances, though a little off-kilter, like the broken ballerina in my mom's old music box. But unlike the little figurine, Luna's legs are cut up and bruised, her tangled curls bounce down her back, and she clutches a jug of moonshine in one hand. She whips out fouetté after fouetté, just like her *Black Swan* solo. Each one is perfect, controlled, and I count out of habit.

... Twenty-nine.

Thirty.

Maybe her ankle's better than I thought.

Thirty-one.

Thirty-two...

Wait, she's still going.

Thirty-three—

She sways on the extra turn, laughing, and I drop the machete and crossbow to lunge just in time, catching her before she cracks her head on the mantel behind the stove.

Her giggles are infectious but seem pressured, her smile is too bright, and the firelight flickers in her pupils, so wide I can barely make out their clear blue rings.

Something's off with my girl.

"Luna," I say gently. "Doesn't your ankle hurt?"

"Nuh uh," she chirps, leaping out of my hold before I can set her upright. She points her toes, showing off the tight bow at the top of the tulle-wrapped limb. "See? I even made it cute."

"So you did," I chuckle, peeling off my sopping wet shirt and hanging it on a rafter. "I was worried—"

"Well, don't be," she snaps.

My brows shoot up.

"Okay…" I scratch the back of my head. Cold droplets roll down my nape, making me shiver. "Uh, it's kinda late to be up, isn't it? I'm assuming you ate dinner?"

I don't actually assume that, since I cooked her trout before leaving earlier and the ceramic plate still sits on the stove with tin foil over it.

"Nope." The word pops on her lips. "Couldn't sleep. Wasn't hungry."

I force a smile. "Aw, even though I picked the bones out for you and everything?"

But she's already humming to herself, off somewhere else in her head as she sways again. That's when I see the mason jars by the hearth, the jug that rolled out of her hand when I caught her.

I run my tongue over my teeth. The jug's corked, but I can't tell if it or the jars have been cracked open. Honestly, given what I've put her through, I wouldn't blame her for taking the edge off. I've never seen her quite like this, though, the franticness in her eyes much different than her normal party buzz.

"You been drinking, Luna?"

She grins. "Nope."

I hesitate. "You sure?"

Her jaw clenches before she grits out, "I'm sure." Her smile is brilliant except for those eyes, accusing and sharp. "Your *baby* is fine."

"Jesus." My chest cracks. "It's not about that."

"Then what is it about? Wait. You know what?" She waves me off. "I don't care. Come dance."

She reaches for my hand, but I pull back. "What the hell, Luna? *I* care. What's going on right now? This isn't like you."

"Nothing's going on. This is just the *real* me."

I shake my head. "No. It's not. You don't talk like this."

"Like what?" She picks up the jug, letting it dangle at her side.

"Like you don't give a shit about anything." I swallow. "Like you don't give a shit about what happened between us."

She hesitates, then shrugs and points the jug at me.

"Maybe I do, maybe I don't. But you wouldn't know. There's a *lot* you don't know about me. Like how I'm not drunk. My ankle's just being dumb, and the jug helps me balance." She makes her point with a pirouette and a wicked smile. "Or that I wish you'd just finish what you started earlier."

Her free hand slides down my damp chest before her plush lips suddenly crash to mine in a hungry, messy kiss. Sure enough, no hint of moonshine, though.

What the hell?

Her nails rake down my abs with feral abandon and sink past the waistband of my jeans, already slung low from water weight.

"Whoa, no... stop," I mutter in a half-assed order. If my jeans come off, it's game over. I'll take her eager ass right now.

But she's fumbling with my belt, trembling and frenzied like a woman possessed. Like she *has* to do this.

I growl, clawing up willpower from the depths of my black heart. "I said *no*, Luna."

She freezes. I exhale and place firm hands on her shoulders to guide her away from me.

"Let's take a beat, okay?"

She doesn't make a move for me, but her tongue darts over her lips as her gaze trails down my heaving chest.

I groan. "Don't look at me like that." My cock throbs in my jeans, but I force myself to focus. "We need to talk about today before we do anything like it again."

She blinks, then tilts her head and smiles thinly.

"I don't want to."

Worry needles the back of my skull.

Okay, pivot.

"Fine. We won't yet." I let go of her and back up, giving her space. "So, what'd you do today?"

"Oh, you know. Literally *nothing*." She huffs. "Oh, wait, I danced in the rain. That was fun."

"The rain? It didn't start raining until nightfall, and it's been thundering and lightning ever since. Luna, that's dangerous."

"Jee-zus, you're a buzzkill. I stopped before it got really bad." Then she grins impishly. "Or *did* I? Maybe lightning was my spotlight. Maybe the thunder was my applause. Maybe I was *reckless*. You know, my M.O.? Doing all the wrong things. Giving in to all my impulses. Or maybe I got it all *that* out of my system by almost fucking my *kidnapper*."

"Back to that, huh?" I tongue my cheek, then nod once. "Alright, baby. You said you don't want to talk, but obviously you do. So let's talk about it."

"No," she flings back. Using the jug and the mantel behind the iron stove for balance, she turns her feet out and bends at her knees. "I don't want to."

I blow out a frustrated breath. "So you're choosing to be passive-aggressive instead?"

She flinches to a stop, and I wince.

"Fuck, I'm sorry. That was harsh—"

"It was fine! I'm fine. You know why? Because I. Don't. Care." Her voice flutters like silk but cuts like steel. "I said I don't want to talk, and I don't."

"Well, *I* do."

She pushes off the mantel to spin, faster this time. "Too bad. There's nothing to talk about."

"Yes, there is." I catch her hand. She scowls at our touch like the connection personally offends her. "We need to talk about earlier. It seems like it's bothering you. The lake. How it ended..."

Her eyes widen, then her lips press into a thin line. "I *definitely* don't want to talk about that."

I search her face for anything that could tell me what's going on. After watching her for years, I *know* this girl. But it feels like she's trapped somewhere behind this wall, a defense I can't sneak past this time.

"Why don't you wanna talk about it?"

"Pick a reason!" she explodes, dropping the jug. "You

stalked me. Murdered someone. Kidnapped me?! And earlier? God, you might as well have fucked me. Get a girl pregnant without so much as taking her virginity? I might've been a tarot hack, but I can assure you dying a virgin wasn't in my cards. Why didn't you just finish the job? It's not like any of it matters."

I stumble back, letting her hand go. Stabbing me with my own knife would've hurt less. Somehow, she's found my softest spot and pressed the bruise mercilessly.

I swallow hard. "You might not think it matters, Luna... but it matters to me. I've done so much wrong when it comes to you. Us. Making you mine, doing it the right way, that matters to me."

For a second, vulnerability softens her eyes, but it's gone in a blink as she props her hands on her hips.

"So you think getting me pregnant *before* taking my virginity is 'doing it the right way'? Spoiler alert. You're wrong, because it sure felt like the right time to me!"

I pause. The way she phrased that... she's not upset over the possibility of carrying my child. She's furious I didn't claim her.

Hope puffs in my chest, where a literal growl builds as I step forward.

"I'm going to take you, wife. In every way I can." My voice deepens, gravelly and possessive. "Having a baby with you is just one of the ways, so I'm not sorry for coming inside you today. Not when I'd do it again in a heartbeat. And I won't apologize for wanting to savor the moment I make you mine. When I do, there won't be an ounce of doubt that it matters to you too."

She shivers, the fight slipping from her shoulders. Then she shakes her head. Her voice is pained when she finally speaks.

"No. No, this feels too much. I was right. I can't do this."

Dread gnaws at me, and I approach her as gingerly as I would an injured bird, further closing the gap between us with another cautious step.

"Look, I don't think any of this is what you're upset about. Not the lake. Not me coming inside you." I watch her carefully.

"Something happened while I was gone. But if I had to guess, something started happening before that."

Fear reflects back at me in her silver-blue eyes like a mirror. "What do you mean?"

"You've been talking nonstop. You didn't eat. Your pain tolerance is unreal. You're not tired, meanwhile I'm exhausted. And your moods—"

"What about my moods?" she challenges.

I grimace. "I hate to sound like a dick, but they feel all over the place. You're happy one second, pissed the next. Sad after that."

She turns away from me, fists clenching and opening, over and over again. As if she's trying to burn off energy any way she can. Her legs vibrate with it, and I have no doubt if her ankle was healed, she'd fly away from me before I could catch her.

My brow furrows. Try as she might to keep herself under control, it's like she can't help unveiling a part of herself she's not ready for me to see. I don't know if she needs me to stop it or help her through it. Or if there's anything I can do at all.

Fuck, if I feel this helpless, I can't imagine how she feels.

My voice cracks. "What's going on, Luna? Are you okay?"

She snorts, still facing the wall. "Naturally, he wouldn't think about the hypersexual component—"

My pulse spikes. "The what?"

"Nothing. Forget it. I don't want to talk about it."

"Luna—"

She wheels around, shouting, "I'm *fine*!"

The venom she spits would knock anyone else back, but I've already braced myself for everything she's got in this hidden arsenal of hers. I might not know what's going on, but I'm a quick learner when it comes to my girl.

"Baby," I exhale. "I don't think you are."

"You don't know a goddamn thing about me, alright? You think following me around gives you all the answers? You don't *know*. You haven't been... *here*." She stabs a finger into her chest.

"You haven't seen what I've fought like hell to keep out, and within one week, it's all up *here*."

Her finger jabs her temple so hard that I curse and lunge to grab her hands. A desperate cry rips from her, and she clings to me even as she tries to push me away. Emotions drown her, and her eyes plead for relief, still untamed but *hers*.

"It's too much, Orion. I *feel everything*. I'm not *me*—"

She cuts off the last with a sob that absolutely *guts* me as she shatters against my chest.

"It's okay. I'm here. You can talk to me. Just slow down."

I try to wrap my arms around her, but she pushes me away.

"No, no, no, *no*." Her tears spill freely now as she grabs the jug again and holds it to herself like it'll protect her. From me, what's inside, or both, I don't know. I physically ache to comfort her, at a loss for what to do as she rocks back and forth on her feet.

"Don't make me, please. If I talk, I feel. I can't feel any more. I've felt too much. It's too much, Orion, *please*—"

"Okay, okay," I say softly, stepping back and trying to ignore the guilt hollowing me out. My heartbeat and thoughts race for ways to help her, when instinct answers loud and clear.

"Then we'll dance instead."

She starts at that. My heart pounds as I hold out my hand.

"May I have this dance?" I ask for the second time, more nervous than I ever was the first.

Her teary eyes turn skeptical, flicking down to my palm and back up again.

"You... you want to dance with me?" Her voice is so, so small, the uncertainty and hope in it splitting my chest open like a bloom through pavement.

My vow is strong, more sure than I've ever been. "I'll always want to dance with you, little bird."

Her glossy gaze sparkles as she shyly bites her lip. Then a slow smile tugs it free, and Luna Bordeaux takes my hand to dance.

19

BLACK SWAN PAS DE DEUX

ORION

Luna's trust nearly makes me crumple with relief. I exhale slowly through my nose, calming myself so I don't spook her. I'm so afraid she'll fly away from me again that it takes all my restraint not to yank her into my arms. I gingerly pull her to my bare chest, while my other hand rests at the small of her back.

Her brows are still drawn together, wary. But she lets me lead her into a slow, modified waltz with steps small enough to fit the one-room cabin. I hum a folk tune, one that reminds me of a winding river, and turn her gently. She lifts the jug and spins once on her good foot, proving the moonshine does help counterbalance her body weight so she can avoid her bad ankle.

But when I draw her close again, I slide the jug from her hand and set it on the mantel.

"You don't need that anymore. Use me instead."

Her eyes flash right before I guide her into a turn, my hand steadying her waist. She spins so fast her tutu flares, light as air, like she's flying. When she returns to my arms, her face has softened, the tension in her body nearly gone.

"Dancing helps," she whispers, resting her head on my chest.

Pride fills my lungs, loosening the vise around them, and I press my lips to the crown of her head.

"Then we'll dance as long as you need, baby."

In all the time I've watched her, I've seen Luna carefree,

happy, angry, mischievous, sassy... just about every which way I can.

But this is new. This soft, fragile side. If what I just saw is another facet of her, one I have a feeling few people have had the privilege to see, then I want to know that side just as much, maybe more. I want to be the peace to Luna's fury, and the fact that she curls into me now, seeking me for comfort, is all the confirmation I need to know Fate has named her mine.

I can practically feel the energy buzzing through her, and I wince every time she shudders like she's trying to visibly rein it in. I let instinct tell me how to ground her—humming, singing, talking about nonsense—filling the silence like I can tell she's fighting not to do.

"Let's see," I say. "Another rule of the Fury hollers..."

Her eyes flick to mine, and I bite back my smile. She'd gone somewhere deep in the recesses of her mind, but I knew that'd return her to me.

"We already went over the leaves, name in the woods, paint marks," I continue. "Oh, here's one. If it's silent, you're not the only predator."

She repeats it softly. "Silent... not the only predator..."

"That's right," I nod. "So if I ever tell you to run, you run, alright? No matter what. I'll find you."

She frowns. "Promise? I'm not very good at the woods yet."

I can't hide my grin this time. "Yeah, I promise."

"Okay. Then I promise too."

If I have anything to say about it, she'll never have to run from danger again. But nothing out here is ever guaranteed. Her trusting me is half the battle. The other half is arming her.

She's retreated back into her mind, staring unseeing at the embers in the cast-iron stove, so I clear my throat.

"By the way," I start. "I don't think you'll kill me anymore."

"What?" She blinks, dragging her eyes away from the fire.

"I don't think you'll kill me anymore. Which *means*, I think you've earned crossbow privileges tomorrow."

"Oh."

Damn, I was hoping that'd work. But she doesn't play back, and she searches my face for so long I nearly miss our next step. Finally, she breaks her silence.

"I'm sorry I've been off."

"It's okay," I say quickly. "No one can be *on* all the time. You've been through enough the past week alone."

She winces. "Yeah. Well, this happens sometimes. It's just never been this bad. Today was too much." Her voice wavers, then drops to a whisper. "It was terrifying."

"Fuck, if all this is because of what happened at the lake—"

She shakes her head, wincing. "I'm not talking about that. I don't *want* to talk about it yet. It's too much right now. I need to feel everything quietly before I feel it aloud."

I nod, chest tight. "I can't say I totally understand. But we'll need to talk about it eventually." Guilt carves deeper in my chest, and the words tumble out before I can stop them. "I got carried away. I haven't been able to stop thinking about you since I woke up beside you this morning—"

Her eyes widen, and I stutter to a stop as she stills.

"I know what to do." Her gaze snaps to mine. "I need to go to sleep."

I frown. Something in the way she said *need* doesn't sit right with me, but I let it go.

"Okay, we'll go to sleep."

I walk her to the outhouse and back, never letting her out of my sight. She's calmer now, but she still fidgets like her skin doesn't fit. I can't help being on high alert, analyzing her every move.

I've *never* seen her like this. On edge. Euphoric one second, vicious the next, breakable last. Like she could implode or explode at any moment, the slightest wrong touch enough to set her off.

When we're back inside, I pull my dry shirt from its rafter and hold it up.

"Put my shirt on, baby."

She doesn't argue, just strips down to her panties and walks into the opening I've stretched for her, letting me help without a word. Not that she needs me to help her get dressed, obviously. But for me, doing *something* eases the tension in my muscles a fraction.

The hem flutters to just above her knees. There's no flirting. No sly jokes.

Just... silence.

Jesus, I hate this.

When she sits on the cot, I undress to my boxer briefs with just as little fanfare. My pulse is a heavy lump of concern in my throat as I lean against the door and slowly slump down to my "bed."

"Orion?"

"Yeah?" I freeze mid-sit.

She scooches back on the cot, making herself smaller, and fidgets with the edge of the blanket. She looks so innocent when her shy question whispers out.

"Sleep with me?"

My heart stops painfully.

I swallow, but my voice is still rough. "You sure?"

She nods without hesitation, but I'm already moving, sliding in under the blanket beside her.

The second I'm close, something primal takes over, but not lust. Need. The need to touch her, hold her, save her from whatever monster claws her up inside.

As I lie down, I loop one arm around her waist and roll her into me. Wanting to be pressed along every part of her that I can reach, I hook my hand behind her knee and pull her leg over mine, brushing my hand over her tattoo and keeping it there. She instantly rests her cheek on my chest, like it's the most natural thing in the world for her to find comfort a breath away from my Fury birthmark. As it should be.

Her soft hand drifts over my pec. "What happened here?"

I don't have to look to know she's tracing the jagged scar that I had inked into her thigh tattoo.

Where to begin? Where to end? That's the thing about this feud. There's neither.

I don't want to burden her with anything else tonight, but it *is* a part of my past—a part of me— she'll find out soon enough. She's given me so much already tonight, she deserves whatever I can give her back.

"It happened when I was seventeen," I murmur. "I was stabbed."

Her fingers still, but I go on. "It was the worst night of my life. I got these then too." I raise one hand, turning it in the firelight.

My fingers and the tops of my hands were left relatively unscathed, but my palms? With the fire flickering out of focus behind them, the ridges and glossy divots look alive with movement over the dead nerves. Ironic, really.

"The burns were bad. I'm lucky I have feeling in my hands at all."

My eyes drift to the fire, my mind to the memories that always flicker behind the flames. Luna traces a horizontal ridge, bringing me back to her and saving me from descending into hell for the millionth time. Then she laces her fingers in mine and holds them to my chest.

"Is he dead?"

She doesn't pity me. She doesn't whisper "I'm sorry" or cry for me. And I don't want her to.

Luna was born into this life and understands its brutality without needing an explanation. She intuitively knows those exchanges feel more like peeling off a scab than the half-assed balm they're meant to be. As much as I want to protect her from this world, she belongs in it too. She belongs to *me*, and one day I'll convince her of that.

"He's dead," I answer simply, even though there's way more to that story. Like the fact that two got away.

"Good."

She settles against me, and her next question comes out with weighted tenderness.

"Orion?" I feel her cheek shift as she worries her lip, thinking. "Do your scars have anything to do with your nightmares?"

My breath stills.

"My nightmares?"

She nods. "Like the one last night."

The nightmare that changed everything between us. I made more progress with her while unconscious than I ever had awake. Something about it cracked open the door to her soul just enough to let me in.

And tonight did the same for me.

I knew I cared about her, but now that I've seen an unveiled glimpse of Luna when she's afraid someone's watching, I want *all* of her. I want to seep into her lungs, become every breath, learn every thought, and understand her down to her marrow. I want to know her better than the backwoods I grew up in. By feel, by instinct, in daylight, but especially in her storms.

I kiss her forehead, grateful she let me this close. Terrified it won't last. I've begged her for honesty. I owe her mine.

"Yeah, baby," I swallow, but my throat is still raw as I whisper into her hair. "My scars have everything to do with my nightmares."

20

DON'T STEP ON THE GRAVE

ORION

I don't leave her alone this time. After last night? Not a chance.

The storm's let up some, but the path's still wrecked, slick with mud, scattered branches, and loose rocks. It's hell on her ankle, but leaving her behind felt like the more terrifying option.

I hack through the brush with the machete, booting stones off the path so she doesn't trip. I still can't tell if this was once a man-made trail or one worn down by animals. Either way, I hope it leads us outta here so I can get Luna home.

Behind me, she holds my crossbow like she was born with it. One hand grips the modified handle I designed, the other aims the bolt down and away from us like I taught her. She's vigilant, head on a swivel, even as her mouth never quite stops.

Her stream-of-conscious narration rolls on like eerie background music. Pressured to the point of discomfort for both of us, rambling, chaotic. But she's in good spirits, excited that I've gone over more "rules of the holler" with her.

I've taught her a lot already, the first being how to walk out here. Her dainty feet clomped like a Clydesdale when we first set off, crunching anything and everything we encountered. So I showed her how to read the ground, roll heel-to-toe, and find stable footing so she wouldn't tumble down the drop-offs inches from us—an ever-present danger in these mountains that I never truly feared until I had precious cargo limping behind me.

She listened, thank Christ. Having to focus seems to help whatever storm is spinning inside her. She's still vibrating with energy, but no longer on the verge of combusting. As far as I can tell, she might even be tiring out, steadily relieving some of the tension in my chest too.

I think the forest calms her, like it does me. People weren't meant to be so accessible all the time. Out here, it's easy to escape from the world's gray chaos and get lost in nature's rich hues and the grounding feel of rough bark and crumbling dirt under your fingers. For me, the scent of earth and flowers brings thousands of happy memories. My future wife being settled the same way is like a balm on the nerves she fired up last night.

She tossed and turned in my arms until instinct told me to thread my fingers through her hair. As soon as I started massaging her head, her breathing slowed and she finally drifted into a deep sleep. I followed soon after, waking up refreshed.

No night terrors. No flashbacks. No burning screams that left my throat raw. Just peace in Luna's arms. That's two nights now that I've held her, and two nights the nightmares were kept at bay. Luna can call me superstitious, but I know better. That shit ain't coincidence.

I don't bring up how fucking *right* sleeping in her arms felt, and of all the things she's chattered on about, she hasn't brought up any part of last night either. I sense she's more embarrassed than anything, so I leave her be, pretending I'm not hanging on every word for signs she's slipping again.

Another thing I don't mention... the fact that she shouldn't be able to keep up with me. Not with frayed slippers, a shredded tutu, and a bodice that must be stabbing her ribs by now, and certainly not on that ankle. But she tightened her makeshift tulle wrap and she's managing the trek remarkably well. I don't think she's even cold in the morning mist. She wears my jacket only at my insistence, but it slides off her shoulder as if she doesn't notice its warmth.

Every sign that she is *not* okay wears on me, but I try to take the good, not focusing on the bad omen it feels like. Her energy is too electric, her pain tolerance alarmingly high. The kind of tolerance you only see in fighters who don't know they're bleeding out until it's over. I'm worried, but if she insists she's fine... I have to trust her. So for now, we walk comfortably in tandem.

Until I realize she's suddenly quiet, unnerving after hours of her reassuring voice. Then there's a thump.

"Son of a..." Luna grumbles.

"You good?" I halt and ask over my shoulder, scanning for danger. We've come up on a verdant meadow, its colors muted in the hazy fog. Something about it feels... familiar.

"Yeah, sorry," she answers. "I thought I saw something and bumped into—I think it's a little fence?"

"A fence?"

"Yeah, an iron one. Got my shin a little. No big deal. But... whoa, cool."

The coast clear, I lower the machete and turn to find her shifting the crossbow to her back, inspecting a mossy stone. It's half-sunken in leaves and tall grass, surrounded by bent thigh-high, rusted iron fencing. She brushes dirt away with careful fingers.

"I think this is a gravestone," she murmurs.

My heartbeat stutters.

"What?" I ask, breathless, looking around with new eyes.

Fog crawls heavily through the meadow, and dark stones reach from the ground like skeletal fingers. My pulse slows, my machete going slack at my side, suddenly too heavy to hold.

"Shame it's all overgrown," she continues, not realizing my vision is tunneling and I've gone still. "I hate seeing them go without care. It's sad, you know?"

"I... I know where we are," I whisper.

"Oh really? Where? That means we're close to some kind of

civilization, right?" she asks lightly in that stream-of-conscious-ness way again, brushing off more moss that's collected for six years. "Wow, the stone is even blackened. Like there was a—"

"Fire," I finish softly, staring blankly at the charred tree trunk, crumbled to ash and no longer blocking the fence's only outlet. "It burned... everything."

Her hand freezes over the headstone, where she was tracing the last name I already know is there. The energy that's ridden her all morning goes calm. Her gaze rises, cautious now.

"Orion," she whispers. "How did you know there was a fire here?"

I stare at the stone my family has avoided for six years.

"Because this is where my momma died."

21
CAGED BIRD OR BURIED BODY
LUNA

I didn't realize how loud the wilderness was until it went completely silent.

Late-season cicadas buzzed in waves, the wind rustled dying green and gold leaves, and rain was still pitter-pattering onto rocks and pine needles.

But that all stops at the edge of this graveyard, nature itself going quiet, paying its respects to death, the ultimate predator.

The surname FURY is etched into the gravestone as clear as day, but moss is embedded in the first name, and I can't bring myself to peel it back. I'm afraid to after what he just said.

"It's not her," Orion answers my unspoken question. "My aunt is buried there. Flora Fury. My dad's sister. We were visiting her grave that day." Grief grates his voice like gravel, so raw it hurts my throat.

"Flora Fury," he repeats, his voice unwavering. "Names are important around here. Say them aloud and they live on forever."

"Flora Fury," I echo softly.

Deep pain slashes across his face, replaced by rage and sorrow that carve his features and etch into his bones, dragging his shoulders down.

"The graveyard at Whitby Rose Chapel is neutral ground. Always has been. Wildes and Furys buried our dead here for generations, even before the feud began. The only place kept sacred." His jaw tightens before he spits, "But it became her pyre."

He shudders, then steadies, chin raised and machete fisted at his side. "We scattered most of Momma's ashes on Fury land, so she could be close to King. The rest," he gestures to his aunt's grave, "we left here beside her best friend."

He scans the abandoned graveyard, shaking his head. "I guess no one's come back since."

I bite my tongue to keep my racing thoughts from flying free, waiting, listening.

"It was supposed to be a normal visit. Like always. Just in case..." He chokes like he's drowning in a memory. "I was supposed to be the lookout."

My breath hitches.

Orion, no...

"At seventeen, I was old enough to protect us. But Dash was hanging with me while I learned the new crossbow she'd given me for my birthday. I was distracted."

His scarred hands curl tighter at his sides. In his next ragged breath, I can almost feel the moment everything went wrong.

"We heard glass shatter. Then a scream." His voice breaks. "She and Hatch were attacked."

"A mom and her child?" My chest strangles the words out. "*Why?*"

"Why do Wildes do anything? And Bossie Wilde's kin is some of the worst," he snaps bitterly. "I don't know how it started, Hatch won't talk about it, but the next thing I saw was the dry brush going up in a flash."

My heart climbs into my throat.

"Flames were everywhere. A tree fell across the fence in front of the exit, trapping Momma and Hatch against the gravestone. And Bossie Wilde's boys... fuck, they just *stood* there. Watching." His eyes flick to mine. "Rufus's and Bart's father, along with two other bastards I never knew."

Rage boils hot behind my sternum. Orion's gaze returns to the gravestone, like he sees it all again in his mind's eye.

"Dash went straight to Momma and Hatch, but I... I saw red.

Two fled. I didn't give the third coward the chance. I stabbed him, but he cut me back before he went down." He presses his fingers over his heart, his birthmark. "I didn't even feel the pain. Not then anyway."

He swallows, and his voice gets even quieter, reverent.

"Momma protected Hatch, shielding him against the gravestone with her body. When the tree cracked"—he points to a broken section big enough for someone to fit in—"she pushed him out before it fell on her. I went in, not thinking. I got her out."

His hands flex in the air like a tactile memory, and my heart hurts at the sight of the roughened palms that have only ever been soft with me. The burn scars. I never asked the specifics. My dad hates when people ask about his, so I learned early to let people tell their own stories.

But I don't think I would've ever been ready for Orion's nightmare.

His voice trembles. "I was too late. Dash did everything he could, but the trunk crushed her thigh. She never stood a chance." He nods to the gravestone. "This is where Momma bled out in our arms."

I trace the FURY on the headstone, a new reverence in the touch as another Fury name I didn't realize I remembered comes to mind.

"Ruth 'Queenie' Fury," I say, the words choking my throat.

He waits a beat, then takes my hand, lifting me up.

"I've protected you ever since. One way or another. At first from here, making sure no Wilde crossed the Louisiana line. Then when you turned eighteen, I went to New Orleans. *I* was your shadow. I honored the pact by staying away as much as I could, but I still protected my wife. Always."

My heart pounds as he steps closer, and with the dark promise clouding his eyes, for the first time, it fully resonates how far he'd go for that vow.

"But when I saw Bart and Rufus, the sons of one of the

monsters who killed my mom... I couldn't risk it. I couldn't prevent my mom's death. But I'll be damned if a Wilde, if *anyone*, takes you too."

The graveyard seems to hold its breath with me.

"This," he gestures broadly, "is why our families need the Troisgarde-Fury pact." His scarred palms close over mine, as he says gently, "This is why I need you. You may think this pact is a curse. But *you're* my salvation."

Those words weigh heavy between us, pressing against my chest.

He scans the stones again, then exhales. "And Sol is one of the most dangerous men in the country. The King kin want to bring him back into play."

I'm shaking my head before he finishes. "And I'm supposed to accept that? That I'm some... bargaining chip in a blood war I have nothing to do with?"

His jaw hardens. "The Wildes won't stop with us. Your father's denial doesn't change the reality that your family's already in this war. The Bordeauxs are the closest to our feud. If the Wildes wipe us out, y'all are next. The Troisgarde fathers pledged themselves into this alliance. If they're honorable men, their word is their bond, and so is mine. I'll do whatever it takes to protect the people I love from getting hurt again."

Love?

Thick, humid mountain air catches in my lungs.

Does he mean me? His family? Both?

"What if I'm the one you hurt in the process?" I ask, almost too softly to hear. "Would you still do 'whatever it takes'?"

"If it saves you from *this* fate?" His eyes flick to the burned gravestone. "I would, Luna. And I wouldn't lose a wink of goddamn sleep over it."

I cringe, the words cutting deep. "But... couldn't my family just agree to protect you? That's how it is with the Troisgarde."

He shakes his head. "They've had decades to strengthen their power. We need you now, and there's nothing to ensure the

Troisgarde will make good on their promise. Not without marriage."

My stomach drops. "So that's why marriage is so important to the Furys?"

He studies me for a moment before answering. "Marriage is the only thing that guarantees nearly unbreakable alliances. The only sacred bond anyone respects anymore. The Troisgarde daughters are the key to ensure every family is pledged to side with the King Fury kin."

My blood runs cold, and an icy laugh stabs through my sternum. "The daughters are the key, huh? So none of you care which daughter you claim, so long as she can be trussed up and used as a weapon or shield at your convenience?"

Orion's hands tighten on mine in a possessive grip as he tries to draw me to him. His voice drops into a growl.

"After everything, you *know* it's not like that, Luna. *You* are mine."

God, I love the sound of that. But I shouldn't, and my feet stay firmly put. My eyes fall to the grave, away from him, before I lose the fight against the whirlwind of emotions already trying to consume me.

"I'm sorry about your mom, Orion. About everything you and your family have gone through. It's tragic in an unimaginable way, and my heart breaks for you. But..." I draw in a shaky breath. "She was a martyr in this feud." I exhale and finally meet his eyes. "It's cruel to ask me to be the same."

He jolts back, dropping my hands like they burned him. His lips curl, and his words struggle to escape through clenched teeth.

"Are you comparing my mother's sacrifice to you being asked to honor your marriage vow?"

"Of course not. It's a far from perfect comparison. But you have to see this is wrong. It wasn't *my* vow."

"Jesus." He scrubs a hand down his face, then lets out a low, bitter chuckle. "Do you really think marrying me is the worst thing that could happen to you? Have you not been fucking listening?"

I blink at him, stunned as he backs up with heavy steps, the gravestone becoming a wall between us.

"My family is dying, Luna. Like it or not, you became my family the moment your father bet your life and put a target on your back. Which means, I don't care if you don't want to marry me, not when this union is the only thing that can keep you safe."

I force myself to focus, my emotions spiking to new heights, hatred over this situation and his words burning in my veins. Yet the determination and dedication in his voice makes me melt for him. The confusing mix destroys me like acid.

"There's no 'if' I do or don't want to get married, Orion. I think I've made it pretty clear that the Troisgarde daughters don't want to be forced to marry Furys. I'll run again if you try."

His caustic laugh singes me, making me wince. "And *I* think it's pretty clear the Furys do not give a fuck. You're acting like you have a choice. Sorry, birdie. You're stuck with your black knight. Try flying away from me again, and I'll clip your wings to keep you."

The words hang like a noose between us.

"Doesn't that make you just as bad as the Wildes?" I ask sharply.

His nostrils flare. "I am *nothing* like them. Wildes take what they want and don't give a fuck about anyone else."

"Unlike you?"

He falters, then doubles down, his voice so calm and resolute I want to scream. "Yeah, birdie. Unlike me. This is different. There are casualties in every war."

"My freedom is just a *casualty* to you?" My voice raises despite myself. "You want me to be—what? A bird in a cage?"

He doesn't answer right away, just sweeping his gaze across the graveyard.

"Look around you. Be glad you're not a body in a grave. Without me, that's what you'll be."

I huff like the wind's been knocked from me. "You're a monster."

His voice deepens. "If I'm a monster, it's because they made me one. Tell me you understand the difference."

"I didn't promise myself to anyone. Your family is black-mailing mine. *See the difference*?" My voice breaks and tears burn my eyes at how trapped and invisible I feel. "I could've been anyone."

His growl is quick, erupting goosebumps over my skin. "You weren't *anyone*. You're my Luna. You might not have promised yourself to anyone, but I promised myself to you. It was always and will only ever be *you*."

I freeze.

"What do you mean?"

He closes his eyes, his chest rising and falling with a deep breath, before they open again, softer now. "I waited for my soul-mate. Without you, there was no one else. I saved myself for you."

I stare at him, unable to process what he's saying.

"You've never had... you've never been with anyone?"

He shakes his head. "The only woman I'll ever be with is my wife. *You*. That's why I wanted to do this right between us, the best I knew how with the little control I had." His lips twitch into a small, helpless smile. "With you, all my discipline cracks. I become as reckless as you are."

I shake my head. "But why? You didn't even know me."

"Didn't matter. If you tell me something's mine, I guard it with my life. That happened the moment King told me I was marrying you. But since then, watching you—getting to know *you*, Luna Bordeaux—has only proven you're worth the wait."

His gaze pins me in place, but a floating sensation still flows in my limbs. "You're my fiancée. My future wife. And if something belongs to *you*, I'll guard that just as fiercely." He leans closer, his voice a caress on my cheek. "I am yours to claim, just as you are mine."

I shiver, caught between the dwindling anger I'm clinging to and the primal possessiveness flooding through my veins and rushing to my core.

"Which means you're stuck with me," he adds in a lethal tone. "For life. I've tried waiting for you to understand the danger you're in, the danger our families are in, but we're running out of time. I won't let you run from me again, and I'll let you hate me if it saves you, so get fucking used to it, bride."

My thoughts splinter. He watches dispassionately, face blank, as he breaks my heart, clipping my wings. Hurt and anger heat my skin, and I hold onto the latter like a lifeline.

"Fine then. Have it your way, and hear me loud and clear." I swallow before putting all the venom I can into how I wish I felt. "I *hate* you, Orion Fury."

Only the slight jump of a muscle in his jaw tells me the words affected him at all.

"Good," he finally says, barely a trace of sadness in the word. "I see I've finally hit my mark."

And then he moves on, pointing at the trees.

"There," he says, less harshly this time. "That white steeple is Whitby Rose. There's a dirt road nearby. Now that I know where we are, I can get us out."

Even though the next-to-last place I want to be is at his side, the very last place I want to be is alone with my thoughts. I scare myself more than Orion, or the truth, does.

"I'll come with you," I mutter.

"No. I'm taking you back first."

The finality in his tone makes me flinch. "What?"

He shakes his head. "I can't have you be a liability."

"I'm not a liability. I've kept up with you just fine, and it's only misting now. The storm's gone."

"This time of year, storms come and go on a whim," he replies. "And the drenched ground will be one hundred times worse in the dark. The dirt road from the church to the main road is at least seven miles, and I don't even know how far my car is past that."

Then he steps closer, his voice softening back to the Orion I know. The deceptive kindness almost coaxes my shredded emotions into thinking we're safe again, but he's already battered my heart bloody.

"You need to sleep. Something's up. I haven't pushed, and I've tried to respect your space. But last night?" He rakes his hand through his hair. "Fuck, it scared me, baby. You seem less keyed up today, so best I can figure is that sleep must've helped. But you're still nowhere near as exhausted as you should be. As *I* am, if I'm honest. I need to take you back and do what's best for you. I can find you when I get the car."

Tears prick at my eyes, and humiliation crawls hotly up my neck. What's worse is he's right. I do need sleep. If I don't get it, I won't be able to hide what's going on anymore, and I'm not ready for that conversation. Not yet. Not until I get a handle on it. Not until I know he'll still see me as *me* when it's over. If he finds out, I want it to be when my head's on straight, not when I'm losing it.

I tip my chin to the sky, blinking fast to keep the tears from falling so this jerk can't see me cry. A flicker of movement in the trees pulls my gaze to the swath of paint slashed across the bark. The hair on the back of my neck rises.

"Orion... what does pink paint mean?"

He stills. "Pink?"

I nod, pointing at a trunk across the graveyard. "Red is neutral, black is Fury..." The red mark ahead has been sloppily painted over with white.

Pink.

"Those motherfuckers." Orion's jaw clenches as he takes my hand, fisting his machete with the other. "They're trying to claim what isn't theirs."

"I thought Whitby Rose graveyard was neutral ground."

"It was," he growls. "Both Wildes and Furys buried kin here. We *used* to respect the dead."

"Until six years ago," I whisper.

"Until six years ago," he echoes.

His hand tightens around mine. Thunder rolls in the distance, and a chilly breeze strokes up my spine like a ghostly finger. The touch felt so tangible, my gaze darts around the graveyard, trying to make sure I only imagined it. But my search doesn't help. The woods have eyes in the dark.

"Come on," he murmurs. "The cove is a few miles into neutral territory still, and I've got traps there. The plan doesn't change. We're getting the fuck out of this place, come hell or high water."

22

THE *Forest* IS SILENT

Orion still hasn't come back.

I went to bed without him, curling up in a cot that felt strangely empty, and made myself sleep as long as I could. But when I woke up to find him still gone, my nerves went haywire. Hours later, and I've taken up pacing, staring out the warped windows to watch the tree line, listening after every branch snap, and praying the renewed storm hasn't swallowed him whole.

I'm still furious with him, half-tempted to kick his ass when he shows up. One good knee to the balls is all I'll need to remind him I'm not some delicate bird to cage and guard.

But every minute he's gone, worry evaporates more of my anger. And as much as I wish those words I slung at him in the graveyard were true... I don't hate him.

I didn't realize, though, just *how much* I don't hate him.

He's fought for me, saved me, treated me with care and respect when I was fraying at the edges. Not only that, but now that I've witnessed graves blackened from burning hate between the Wildes and Furys, I finally understand the stakes in this feud. Which means I finally understand Orion better too.

Not the way he talked to me, obviously, because fuck him for that. But I get his instinctual need to protect everyone he loves, the urgency running like a current under his skin. We're alike in that way. Bordeauxs would set the world aflame for our family. Unlike me, though, Orion's already had everything burn to ash once, right in front of him. From the scars on his hands to the scorched gravestone that failed to shield his mother, I believe him when he says he'll do anything to keep his loved ones safe.

And... I think that includes me.

What do I do with that?

Right now? Nothing. No, I'm taking the coward's way out, falling back on my usual M.O., aka distracting myself with literally anything to avoid emotions that are too deep to wade in.

At the moment, I'm stationed right in the trajectory of one of Orion's traps, watching the fishing line glint like spider silk in the stove grate's firelight. One wrong twitch and a boulder the size of my head could swing down and crush my noggin. The adrenaline of "will it-won't it come crashing down" is enough to keep my mind from drifting where I'm afraid to go.

Is it messed up that I'd choose potential death over figuring out how I feel about Orion? Yes. Have I still dragged my finger over the wire like it's Nox's cello, wondering how much pressure it'd take to keep me from ever having to confront my feelings again? Also yes, and I do realize that my therapy appointment truly cannot come soon enough.

Like always, though, distraction only lasts so long before anxiety pushes in. Scattered rain dances across the tin roof, a kind of white noise that usually lulls me to sleep like a baby. But nothing feels soothing without knowing Orion is safe, and the longer I stare into the stormy wilderness, the less safe I feel too. Will he return before whatever *thing* I *swear* stares back finally emerges from the shadows and devours me?

Luna...

I freeze at my name on a hushed whisper, so faint I almost think I imagined it. My heart instantly hammers so loudly that I'm afraid I can't hear if it happens again. Orion's superstitions echo in my head, but a reality check reverberates back.

Momma has auditory hallucinations. We thought her illness

was different from mine, though, and I've never gotten to the point of psychosis before. This can't be psychosis. It just can't be.

Right?

I swallow.

"Luna?"

"No," I whisper, pressing my palms over my ears. "No, no—"

"Lu, you in there? It's Benoit."

My hands peel away. I hold my breath to listen.

"Come on, Luna. It's cold out here," my friend grumbles.

Relief and excitement shock through me, urging me to the door to fling it open.

Benoit's hand is frozen mid-knock. He's soaked to the bone in a jacket, green tee, and black cargo pants, his black hair plastered to his forehead. But that lopsided smile I've known all my life is still there.

"Hiya, Lu."

"Benny!" I half-whisper, half-squeal, leaping at him and knocking the wind out of him.

"Oof," he laughs, catching me like always. Then he squeezes tight, saying into my hair, "Been worried about you, *cher*."

Tears of relief spring to my eyes at the warm familiarity of his hug. His embrace feels like home in a way nothing else has since this nightmare began. He's family and safety. If he's here, my father and rescue can't be too far behind. A few tears slip out as he lets me go and gasps.

"Holy shit, what happened to you?" He holds my hands as he steps back to look at me, brows furrowed. "You're covered in scratches and more bruises than that time you and Lucy tried pole dancing. And your *Swan Lake* costume is holding on by a feather and a thread. Literally."

I glance down at the ripped tutu and nearly-featherless bodice, then try a smirk to downplay his concern. Benoit would have a heart attack if he knew all the details.

"I'm okay. That pole hurt worse, I promise. Orion and I... took a tumble down a waterfall or two."

"You..." His eyes bug out. "You *what*?"

I wave him off. "I'll tell you everything on the ride home. How long have you been following us? Since before the graveyard? I *knew* I saw something. I figured it was an animal or one of the superstitions in the woods he talks about—"

"Wait, wait, what graveyard?"

"Whitby Rose, obviously. That's where you found me right? You tracked us there? How did you find us? Were we loud? I tried walking quietly like Orion said, but it's hard and—"

"Luna, slow down, will ya? It's been a while since you've talked this fast. I've forgotten how to keep up." He massages his temple and jerks his thumb over his shoulder.

"When a few of us shadows found the tracker from Orion's car way down the riverbank, we spread out, with me sticking to the river. This cabin was the first sign of humanity, and there weren't any *Deliverance* banjos playing in the trees, so..." He gives himself a flourish ending in a slight bow. "Here I am!"

"*Deliverance*? Really?" I cross my arms. "That was offensive, Benoit."

His shoulders lift in an innocent shrug, smile mocking. "How about I stop being offensive as soon as these assholes quit fighting over you, yeah? Anyway, enough chitchat. We need to get this show on the road."

He takes my hand, pulls his phone out with the other, and swipes until my dad's caller ID pops up. Then he hands it to me.

"Here, call him and tell him we're on the way. He was on the other side of the mountain when we split up, so it'll take him a while to come grab us. I slid down this ravine during the storm, but if we move now, with the weather letting up again, we can maybe make it out the same way I came. Hopefully he'll be there by the time we get to the main road."

My brain takes a second to catch up. "Wait..."

"It's not exactly a smooth trip back along the river." He grimaces at the stormy sky. "Does it always rain this much up here?"

He tugs me forward, but I tug back. "Wait. What about Orion?"

His expression darkens. "You mean Fury? Don't worry. He's a dead man. Sol will start hunting him the second you call to tell him you're safe."

He gestures to the phone like he'll make the call for me, but I snatch it out of his reach.

"No!"

"What the—"

"You can't hurt him. And we have to wait for him to come back. I don't want to leave without him."

The words slip out before I can stop them, and Benoit's bewilderment and hurt register too late.

"You don't... want to leave him? Luna, we're here to save you," he says slowly, the same tone he used the time I confessed to lifting a gun off a cop. "You okay, *cher*? If this is one of those I-fell-in-love-with-my-stalker Stockholm-y things, let me help you out. He *kidnapped* you. Killed a guy behind Masque—"

"No, he—"

He did that for me, hovers on my tongue, but I swallow my words this time. If anything would make Benoit think I've fallen for my captor, it'd be that.

Then again... *did* I fall for him?

Orion Fury is possessive and ruthless. But he's also protective, thoughtful. The only times he's ever been harsh with me is when it came to my safety.

Damn. Maybe I have been Stockholmed. Wouldn't that be just my luck? I mean, *why not* add one more cherry-on-top diagnosis to my fucked-up sundae?

Except... just thinking that way makes guilt pang through my chest. Orion's been transparent about how much he cares for me, and my own feelings are becoming just as clear.

"I wouldn't be alive if it weren't for him," I say instead, sticking with the safest truth I've got.

Benoit studies me, then explains firmly. "He can survive out here on his own, Lu. Furys are practically born feral."

"I..." My chest twists. "I'm sorry. I just can't leave yet."

"Luna," he groans, half-exasperation, half-plea.

"Stay," I beg. "Please, Benny? He'll be back any second. After you talk, you'll see what I mean. There's a lot you don't know."

I step aside, inviting him in. He hesitates at the threshold, drumming his fingers on the doorframe, lips pressed together as he thinks. After a few beats, he nods to himself and steps back to slip an orange pill bottle from his jacket.

"Your dad made sure we all carried some," he begins carefully, but irritation stains my vision red. "This way, whoever found you would be able to help you. Maybe... maybe you could take one now before Fury gets back?"

It's all I can do not to knock the pills out of his hand. But that sure as hell won't help my case, so I cross my arms tight against my chest.

"I'm not out of my mind, Benoit. I know what I'm doing. Just because you don't agree with me doesn't mean I'm '*crazy*.'"

"Sorry, sorry. Reading you loud and clear." He winces, hands lifted in surrender. "Jesus, you know I'd never call it that. Hear me out, though. Maybe not now, but at least on the way back? It's been days without them. That's bad enough on its own, but then pile on what you've gone through?" His voice gentles. "Your parents are worried about you, *cher*. We all are."

I shift on my feet, staring at the bottle in his hand, unable to confront the concern I know is written all over his face. He's right, but there's something he doesn't know.

My cheeks heat, and I worry my lip.

It's only been a day, and I don't know if anything I can do will affect it, or if there's even an "anything" *to* affect, but I won't take the risk.

"Do you think they're safe for pregnancy?" I ask quietly.

Benoit freezes. Every muscle in his face hardens as my meaning slams into him.

"Luna... did that motherfucker ra—"

"No." I cut him off fast. "I... I wanted it."

The words come out easier than I would've expected, and once that truth is out in the world, peace settles over me. I wanted everything that happened yesterday in the waterfall. I want Orion.

Benoit's posture sags, and pity creeps into the rest of his features. But not judgment. He nods his acceptance, and my breath releases from my chest.

I don't know why I was worried. He's never judged me before, and, even now, when he believes I've done the unthinkable by sleeping with the enemy, my friend still loves me the same.

"We'll look it up together, okay?" He slides the medicine back into his jacket pocket. "But we don't know when Fury will be back, and we *need* to go."

"What's the rush?" My eyes narrow. "It's been days. Why do we need to go *now*?"

His hard swallow bobs down his neck. "I... can't tell you."

"Can't?" My brow raises. "Or won't?"

"Can't. Orders." He winces. "Your dad didn't want to worry you."

"Benoit," I warn. "You know I hate when you shadows get all secretive."

"All I can say is"—his hands go up, palms out like he's trying to calm a spooked animal—"since that Wilde got killed outside Masque, things are getting heated. People are getting... jumpy."

"Okay, what's 'heated' mean? Like arguing in the streets? Tourists getting rowdy? Bar fights..." I run through more scenarios, letting my stream of consciousness flow with questions, until his tight-lipped silence makes a brittle, frustrated laugh huff out. "Come on, Benny, tell me already. You're scaring me. Are my parents okay? Nox, Uncle Jaime? Oh God, it was the car chase. Did Jaime get hurt——"

"Okay, chill, Lu. Your parents, Nox, Jaime, they're all fine," he rushes to say. "The car chase was child's play. We've done worse on the track. But the sooner we get home—"

"Benoit." I step up to him. "Tell. Me."

He closes his eyes, bracing himself for me to blow up on him. He's quiet for so long, I have to physically bite my tongue to keep my racing thoughts in check.

His eyes open on a sigh. "It's about the other daughters. Us shadows are watching them like hawks, closing ranks to make sure they're protected. Brylie's pissed as per usual, but Lucy..."

"What about her?" Dread pools in my stomach as he grimaces.

"She's scared. To *death*. You being kidnapped majorly triggered her. Panic attacks, breakdowns, the whole nine. I'm sure she'll be okay once you're safe and sound, but we're worried she'll go rabbit on us again. Like she used to after she was... you know."

Cold sweat prickles the back of my neck. He doesn't need to elaborate. When we were kids, we were told to never, ever, *ever* bring up Lucy's kidnapping. Just mentioning it would send her spiraling.

"But she hasn't run away in years," I say, guilt building in my chest. "Benny, that'd be literally the worst thing she could do in this situation."

Her parents were always able to find her before, but she got better and better at hiding from her anxiety, not to mention the rest of us. Trauma taught her it was the only way to save herself.

Sure, Lucy and I would fantasize about leaving to find our own paths, out from under our parents' and the public's watchful eyes. But the only reason I even entertained those thoughts is because she'd grown out of the habit and hadn't run away in years.

"Panic isn't always logical." He sighs, the sound jarring in the quiet forest.

Wait.

"And she was good at hiding as a kid," he continues while my ears perk up. "Imagine what she can do now that she knows what she's doing—"

"Shh," I cut him off, straining to hear.

He jolts. "What?"

I tap my ear, mouthing, *Listen.*

He stills. The world stills. I hold my breath for the cawing of birds, the rustle of scurrying animals, or even a trumpet from one of the lake swans calling to their mate. Anything.

But there's just... silence.

"I don't hear anything," Benoit murmurs.

"Exactly." My eyes sweep the dark woods beyond the porch. "Something's out there—"

"Luna, look out!"

The shove knocks me back just as two deafening bangs rip through the air.

Benoit jerks twice, twisting under the impacts. Blood blossoms across his green shirt, each bloom with a gaping cavity in his chest.

"Benoit!"

He stares down at the wounds in disbelief, then at me, eyes wide, unfocused.

Nonononononono—

"Benny?" The world slows into a warped, muffled blur as if I'm underwater. My chest is tight as I sink.

I can't breathe. This isn't real. It can't be.

He staggers toward me. My breath hitches with every step, each one smaller and slower than the last, until his legs buckle. I lunge in time to catch him, the role reversal a sickeningly familiar dance that sends my stomach lurching up my throat.

"No! Come on, Benny, don't fall. Stand up with me—"

But his weight, *so* heavy, folds into me. We collapse to the ground together, slamming my knees hard onto the wood floor.

"Okay, it's okay, we'll try again later." I fight for the words he's said to me a million times. "You... you just need to rest for a minute, that's all. Then we'll get back up. J-just hold on until then, okay? Someone will come. I-I-I'll call for help. Your phone —" I look around frantically for where I dropped it. "Your phone is somewhere. I'll call my dad. He's close, right? He can get help. And when Orion gets here, he'll know what to do—"

"Luna?" His plea stops me cold. I watch in horror as his hand comes away slick with blood. His lips tremble. "I think... I think I'm dying."

"*No.*" Pain like I've never known punches into my chest. I shake my head frantically, muttering the word over and over again.

He can't die. Not him. Not my Benny who's danced me through thousands of rehearsals since we were four. Who started as much trouble with me as we escaped. Who swore to protect me with his life since that fateful day in the auditorium ten years ago.

"Don't worry, cher. *Nox and I will protect you with our lives, I promise."*

It'd seemed so ridiculous then.

Benny's been my shadow for years. My friend my whole life. Family. He took a vow right beside Nox to protect me, to be my shield against the worst of the world. But he wasn't supposed to make good on it.

He was almost out.

Being one of my father's men isn't a life sentence anymore. Shadows protect. They don't bleed. They don't fall. They don't...

They don't die.

Tears glaze his eyes, and he gasps softly. His signature lopsided smile breaks through as he sees something beyond me. Something I can't see.

"They're here, Luna... my parents. I finally... I finally found them."

Peace softens his brow, and he's just my Benny again, more carefree and hopeful than I've ever seen him.

A heartbroken wail strangles my throat, and hot tears streak down, landing in a fresh puddle of blood. He blinks and looks at me again. One hand still pressed to his heart, he seems to use all his strength as he lifts the other to cradle my jaw. I capture his wrist to keep him there, and his thumb brushes gently over my cheek, but I can't tell which he's wiping away. My tears or his blood.

"Don't cry for me, *cher*. I... I died protecting my family. I did what I never could," he murmurs softly, voice fading with every word. "And now... I'm going home."

"Benny, wait!" Pressure builds in my chest, cracking open my sternum and freeing a panicked shout. "Please, stay with me. Don't—"

His hand goes limp in mine and I tighten my grip. Life leaves his eyes in a blink, and his final breath slips out on a sigh.

"*No!*" The scream rips my throat raw, ending in a sob that racks through me. "*Please*, no."

The words echo uselessly, choking out of my lungs only to get lost in the woods—

Wild blond hair flashes between the trees. A man steps out, gun raised, stalking toward me with a cruel, triumphant grin slashed across his lips. Like he's already won the battle my friend never got to fight in.

Instant, white-hot fury sears through my grief. My shadow, my *friend*, died to keep me alive. I won't let his death go in vain.

I close Benoit's eyes with shaking fingers, then lift my chin at the man who took my friend from me, every muscle coiled tight as the coward points the barrel at my head.

23

NOT THE ONLY PREDATOR
ORION

Two things survived my car being scorched. Crossbow bolts I'd stuck underneath the driver's seat, and the blush rose, wildflower, and feather bouquet I gave Luna. The rest? Melted tires, frame twisted like ribs of an animal picked clean, and windshield a spiderweb of fractures.

I should've known what I'd find as soon as I saw smoke mixing with clouds over the treetops. The acrid stench of burning rubber was my second clue. And yet, here I am, a pathetic fool standing by a metal husk, like if I stare long enough, I'll figure out how to bend everything back into the shape it once was.

I keep fucking things up. Reaching the car too late, being unable to find a way out for days, the way I spoke to Luna... The way I *threatened* my future wife into submission. My momma would be ashamed. I know I am. I have half a mind to bring this bouquet back to Luna as the start of my apology tour, not that I deserve forgiveness.

The flowers do remind me of her, though. When I found them half-buried under one of my old, burnt-to-a-crisp leather jackets, I was entranced by its singed petals, ash-dusted feathers, and brittle stems held together by a black-streaked white ribbon.

How could something so delicate survive such chaos?

My Luna could. She'd stand toe-to-toe with me and we'd both come out stronger, so long as I don't break her wings. Helping her soar has always been the goal.

So why am I failing her every chance I—

Wait.

My car is torched. Someone knows we're here.

And I left Luna alone.

Fuck!

Everything comes back into focus, and for the first time, I see what might be the most chilling sign of all, high up on the closest tree by the smoldering skeleton of my car.

One swipe of fresh, dripping white paint streaks over the red underneath.

The Wildes.

I snatch my bolts, slotting one and filling my quiver with the rest, then take the most direct route I found while canvassing the area. It's a straight shot descending the steepest slope, and I half-tumble, half-skate down the rain-slicked ridge, the grade so sheer I might as well be falling. My boots skid through wet dirt and moss, and my scarred hands tear as I catch myself on bark and branches to stay upright. Rain peppers my eyes, weighs down my jacket, and slips cold fingers down my spine, but I ignore it all because I'm this close to making sure Luna is—

Bang—I snag a heavy branch, wrenching myself to a stop.

Another shot cracks the air.

My lungs seize before my adrenaline kicks into overdrive. I take deep breaths while molding the fear and terror into something useful, focusing on what I need to do to make sure Luna is safe, and leashing the predator within me so I don't lose myself to wrath.

A desperate, heartbroken scream shatters me from the inside out. I've heard one like it a thousand times in my nightmares.

No!

It takes everything in me not to call out for her. The "name in the woods" lore is partly bullshit, but regardless, it's dangerous to reveal yourself without knowing who's around. A mistake like that could get me killed before I can save her.

I move silently, clinging to the forest's shadows until the cabin peeks through the leaves. Then I drop into a crouch, crossbow at the ready. I only have so many bolts, so as much as I want to run in, crossbow blazing, I have to be smart about this and make every bolt count.

My breaths push against my sternum, wanting to escape, but I control them as best I can with my crazed heartbeat. When I finally manage to get feet from the mist-coated, warped window, my soul aches at the visual inside.

Blood smears Luna's cheek and stains her feather bodice and tutu, nearly driving me feral over the thought that it's hers.

But she cradles someone in her arms, rocking them.

Shit.

It's Benoit.

He's still as a corpse, sprawled over her and across the floorboards. Luna's shoulders curl protectively over him, and tears trail in cleansing streaks down crimson-splattered cheeks.

This will *ruin* her, and there won't be a damn thing I can do to help her.

Don't think about that. Help her now.

Luna's head lifts, and her eyes narrow as she drags them toward a man I didn't see at first. His blond hair is a mess on his head, and he's got a beard as thick as my father's. His camo is a durable brand, but worn from obvious use. Like mine is back home. He's not just from the land like I am. He's a Wilde.

And he's pointing his goddamn gun at my girl.

"Did I hear you right?" the Wilde chuckles. "Did that Fury scum fuck a baby into you? Maybe I should end it before it begins." He drops the gun down to her belly. "Sure would hate for you to be pregnant with another man's baby at your wedding."

Luna scowls. "I don't know what the fuck you're talking about."

Pride and terror consume me as she boldly takes her eyes off the man threatening to kill her, shocking electric fear down my spine.

But she's turned my way now, and her eyes flash as they meet mine, barely noticeable even if you're looking straight on. Unless you stalked her for years and can read every twitch of muscle in her facial expressions.

She sneers at the Wilde. "You know what? I don't know, and I don't *care*. Fuck the Wildes!"

What is she doing?

The Wilde barrels toward her. "You little—"

Crack.

It happens so fast, the sound of her whimper registers before the slap against skin. Her head jerks to the side under his palm, and red-hot *fury* filters over my vision as he lords over her.

But she's given me the opening I need.

I grab a rock and hurl it at the window, breaking the glass and tripping the wire attached to the frame. And because Luna lured the fool into coming farther into the cabin to strike her, the rock trap I positioned on a ceiling rafter slams into the side of his skull.

His curse is a garbled moan as he stumbles, clutching his bloody temple, and Luna takes advantage of his moment of weakness.

She lunges with the fluid grace of a dancer, grabbing two loose tranquilizer darts I stowed beside the door and driving them both into the bastard—one in the quad, the other near his groin— depressing the plungers.

That's my girl.

The Wilde howls and tries to raise his gun, but it clatters to the floor from paralyzed hands. His knees buckle, body slumping forward as his limbs seize. I rise fully and send a bolt through the open window and into his chest. He drops in a heap.

Righteous anger vibrates through Luna as she slams her foot into his neck, and I hear his spine crack from here. My lips twitch between a smirk and a frown, torn between pride and guilt for her being in this position at all.

I'll analyze that later. After I make sure she's safe.

"You Fury *bitch*!"

Anddd that's my cue.

I slip out of the trees on silent feet, loading my crossbow with another bolt in one fluid motion. Another figure rushes from the shadows, knife raised high. I don't think. I don't even aim, and my crossbow fires like the extension of me it is.

Thunk.

The bolt sinks into his throat with a wet, choking sound. His body folds, twitching as he reaches for the arrow's shaft. Ain't no way that thing's coming out, though, especially with the blood slicking his fingers. He hits the sopping wet ground on his knees, sinking partway in before collapsing face-first, driving the broadhead deeper.

The cabin door flings wide to reveal my pretty white swan painted in blood that isn't hers, holding my knife and poised to strike. Pure rage and agony flash in her eyes, warring over which one will win out. My little warrior, ready for battle.

The rain dampens her tresses, but she stays focused as another Wilde surges from the woods.

His eyes lock on the blade she wields like it was made for her, and he falters, no doubt eyeing the *F* initial on the handle. Recognition flares.

"The Fury gave you his knife?"

She doesn't know what that means, not yet. But every Wilde does. They're after her because they don't want her to become mine. But we're past that. She's already becoming one of *us*.

He doesn't wait for her answer, charging at her. He's fast, but she swivels out of his reach in a move I've seen her perform a thousand times on stage, and I bulldoze into him before his blade can graze her shoulder.

We slam into the ground shoulders first. My knuckles crack against his jaw. His elbow hammers my ribs, but I punch his throat. He lands one to my face, flooding blood into my mouth, iron tainting my tongue, but I don't stop. I can't. Not until I've taken out every last one of these bastards.

We roll through mud and stones, fists flying, grunts muffled by thunder. His knee aims for my stomach, but I twist, driving an elbow into his sternum and slamming him down on a gnarled root.

He wheezes and writhes in pain.

"Luna." I whistle, holding out my hand, and in the next second she's tossed me the knife. It arcs through the air, and I catch it by the hilt, fingers closing over the *F* at the top. I plunge the blade into his chest, relishing in the sound of his last breath rasping from his body.

A crow shrieks overhead, circling once before vanishing into the branches. I blink up after it but quickly snap my eyes back to Luna.

She shakes as she comes to me, chest heaving, blood and dirt streaking her skin. Her eyes are locked on mine, their glint as dark and twisted as the sensations thrumming in my veins and down to my cock.

I step toward her.

"Orion," she whispers, swallowing, her voice carrying the same desperation flooding through me.

She's alive. She's mine.

I'm alive. I'm hers.

And it's time to make that true.

I can *feel* that she's about to ask me for what we need, the adrenaline riding us both.

She steps closer, trembling. "*Please...*"

"Fuck, baby." I barely recognize my own voice. "Come here—"

A guttural scream pushes us apart as another Wilde bursts from the tree line, followed by a second.

Shit.

I intercept the one going for her first, just as steel flashes in the other's hand, and shove Luna behind me, roaring.

"*Run!*"

She hesitates for one brief second, until one of their daggers nicks me and I can't afford to look at her anymore. Out of the corner of my vision, cherry cola curls vanish into the underbrush.

Good girl.

I turn back in time to see two blades mid-flight. There's no time to think or dodge. There's only a gleam of silver—then the sound of my own breath choking out of me.

24

FLY AWAY LITTLE BIRD

LUNA

I flee like I'm being hunted, like something's breathing down my neck, chasing me through the storm-ravaged forest. But the reality that I'm leaving Orion behind is so much worse. And then what happened with Benoit—

Guilt squeezes my chest to the point I can barely breathe.

That's why I'm doing this. *That's* why I'm running. I refuse to die when Benoit gave his life for me, making his sacrifice go in vain.

I hope Orion didn't sacrifice himself for me too.

I can't die. I can't die. I can't die.

Runrunrunrun.

Blood pounds in my ears louder than the thunder cracking overhead. Rain lashes my face, mixing with tears. One cheek still stings from that Wilde bastard's slap, the other burns with shame for running instead of fighting. But I made a promise, so I grit my teeth and harness my frustration and turn it into determination.

No matter how hard I try to navigate the forest like Orion taught me, fear and hate make me reckless. I slip and stumble through mud and underbrush, one satin ballet flat clinging to my foot by sheer force of will, the other frayed to shreds, held together only by my ankle wrap of tulle. Adrenaline dulls the achy sprain enough to keep me moving.

At first, my own terror is all I hear—my pounding heartbeat, ragged breaths, and the chaotic slap of mud under my feet. But then the telltale pounding of boots joins in behind me. Steady. Determined. They slide with the grade instead of fighting it like my city feet do. I don't know who it is. All I know is I have to *fly*. If it's a Wilde, I can't be caught.

If it's Orion, he'll catch me.

Please God, let him catch me.

Branches whip at my arms like they're punishing me for leaving him behind. I welcome the sting, letting it scratch and tear into my flesh like a physical manifestation of my guilt.

Is he okay?

He was fighting off two Wildes when I left. I was dying to help, but they only got the jump on him because I distracted him. My aching need for him to touch me and prove we're still alive and breathing was too much. He wouldn't be fighting for his life right now if we'd stayed vigilant. So I did what I promised I'd do two nights ago.

"...if I ever tell you to run, you run, alright? No matter what. I'll find you."

Please, Orion. Find me.

I keep going, even as every step away from him drives the knife deeper into my traitorous, cowardly heart.

Vines and roots claw my ankles, threatening to twist them to their breaking point. Fog thickens, blurring my vision, but I search the trees anyway for some sign I'm heading toward safety. Red paint mars the tree trunks—but red isn't safe anymore, so I keep sprinting through every wheezing breath.

Red.

My head swims as the naked branches and dead vines all begin to look the same in the mist.

Red.

Spots darken my vision, as if the trees themselves are marked...

Black.

Relief surges through me, and my knees nearly buckle.

Fury land. Orion said I'm safe here.

Then again, we were supposed to be safe in Lost Cove too.

But no Wilde should follow me here.

And yet... someone is.

Footsteps I've been trying to block out continue to crash through the undergrowth, louder and closer than before. Prey-like panic takes over, propelling me faster. A scream claws up my throat, but I swallow it down. Orion said help wouldn't be able to hear me past a quarter mile, and as far as I know, the only ones nearby are my enemies.

Lightning scars the sky, blinding me. The hollow opens beneath my feet without warning.

I tumble.

Down, down, down.

My limbs flail like a rag doll, slapping against clay that snatches and rips my costume as I fall. The decline spits me into a shallow bog, and I splash onto all fours into cold water as dark as spilled ink. Mud curls like icy hands around my knees and wrists, trying to tug me deeper while my tutu clings heavy to my legs. My hair coils into dripping, snakelike tendrils around my face.

Head spinning, I silently sip measured breaths through my nose, forcing them past the pain to focus on the slowing footsteps still dislodging pebbles up the hill. Nearly bare trees stand watch in the swamp, their gnarled, exposed roots rising from the ground and cradling mounds of soft moss. I grip a root that's thick as an arm to help me stand as quietly as I can, pulse jackhammering while the footsteps get louder. Too loud.

Wildes and Furys know how to sneak through these woods. Whoever's after me is being this noisy on purpose.

Who's hunting me? Is it an enemy? Or Orion?

Is there a difference?

He doesn't know I've forgiven him for the way he talked to me, or that I desperately needed him to show me how *alive* we are after witnessing my friend get mur—

My hands fly up to silence my sob as Benoit's death flashes in my mind. My eyes slam shut against the memory I'm still coated in—the blood still streaking my forearms, soaking feathers and staining tulle with desperate handprints. The end of my friend's life clings to me thicker than the mud threatening to drag me under.

Tears pour hotly down my cheeks, a contrast to the chilly rain, and my heart aches. My soul begs for relief it knows only Orion can give. He's the one person who's seen me teeter on the edge as bad as I did the other night, yet he held me anyway.

And I might have just left him to die.

Orion's a danger to everyone else, but he's a safe space for me. Right now, I crave both. My emotions may drown me if he doesn't lead me to the other side. I need the man who chased me. The man who saved me. The man who asked me to dance, even when I was terrified he'd run away.

Please catch me.

Beyond the fog and out of my vision, boots splash as someone heavy jumps into the bog. His loud, steady huffs are more animalistic than man. Until they go silent.

Mist stalks lowly through the trees, and I can't see more than a few feet in front of me. Sound, though, comes from all directions, disorienting as it permeates the fog.

And yet, I can't hear *him* anymore.

I go still as water ripples in a gentle current toward me and around my calves. My body shakes from fear and anticipation. The predator in the dark tugs at something deep in my core.

A man's low growl rumbles through me, all the warning I get.

An adrenaline-fueled scream tears from my burning throat, and I turn to sprint through the watery sludge, but I'm scooped up from behind, strong arms like iron caging me in before we collapse into shallower water. A large hand cradles my head in the fall, but cold water seeps over my shoulders. sending my body into full panic.

I'm going to drown. I'm going to die here. I can't die here. I can't. I can't. Ican'tIcan'tIcan't.

I slam my fists against a steel chest, blindly kicking and thrashing, until a scarred hand pins my wrists above my head and easily stretches me the few inches necessary to get up and over a soft bed of moss. Another hand clamps around my throat, squeezing and cutting off my scream. Warmth presses over me as he lays on top of me, keeping me from hurting us both.

"Shh," he murmurs low, letting go of my neck to wrap tightly around my waist and hold me to him. "Shh, little bird, I've got you."

"Orion," I whimper, and he squeezes tighter.

"You ran." His teeth graze the sensitive skin under my ear, making me shiver and curl into him. "Good girl."

He buries his nose into the crook between my neck and collarbone, breathing me in like my scent is all the oxygen he needs. Relief and terror still hammer against my sternum, and I writhe, unable to stop struggling underneath him.

"*Fuck...* don't fight me, baby," he groans through ragged breaths. "Not right now, or I swear to God I'm gonna fucking lose it."

His feral rasp coils tightly in my belly. As soon as I melt in his arms, his mouth crushes mine, teeth scraping in a brutal kiss that makes me cry out. He lifts me into his chest, and I kiss him just as needily until tangy blood stains my tongue.

Lightning flashes, outlining his massive form above me, his chest rising and falling in heaving breaths that heat the air between us. But my relief curdles in my stomach at the seeping, bloody hole in his shirt right over his heart.

"You're... you're hurt," I whisper, fresh tears burning my eyes and fear splitting my chest wide open. My head shakes, first slowly, then violently. "No, no, *no*. Not you too, *please*."

Not again. Not someone else I love dying for me.

He follows my gaze, then fixes his back on me as he moves to cup my cheek.

"Luna," his voice gentles. "Baby, I'm okay. Don't go there."

But I've already slipped out from underneath him, scrambling up on trembling limbs to escape the truth.

"Not you too," I repeat over and over, focused solely on his wound as I stagger backward until a tree stops me. Benoit's last breath floods my mind and my vision swims. Sobs tear through me. "*Please*. Not you, Orion, not *you*. I *can't*. I can't lose *you*."

He cages me in against the bark, shielding me from the terrifyingly cruel world with one arm around my waist and the other braced by my head on the tree trunk like a wall, keeping me from running.

"Luna, stop. I'm right here."

"You're hurt, you're hurt, you're hurt." I choke, doubling over and clutching his shirt like I can tether him to this world, my body racked with soul-deep agony. "What if you die too? I can't lose you. I can't, Orion, I just can't. *Please*. Don't l-leave me."

He curses low and grips me harder, forcing me upright.

"Hey, Luna? Hey, hey, hey. Listen." He moves to cradle my head, tilting my gaze upward as he towers over me, becoming all I see.

"*Listen* to me, baby," he commands, giving me a little shake that makes me hiccup. His grip on my waist and the back of my head tighten, his voice fierce. "I will *never* leave you. *Never*. I promise. See?"

He shrugs out of his jacket, tossing it to the side, and yanks his shirt over his head with one hand to join it. My cries deepen at the sight of the bloody gash.

"*No!*" I try to wrench away, but he snatches my hand and slams it against the cut cleaving his skull birthmark in two.

Blood warms my palm, and his grip on my waist turns punishing to keep me still.

"Feel me, Luna. I'm *alive*. *We* are *alive*."

My eyes lock on our hands, his heartbeat fast but strong underneath my fingertips. Blood doesn't pour around my fingers like it should from a stab wound to the chest. Has it already stopped bleeding?

I stop, my gaze flicking up to his in question. He pulls my hand away, revealing the slice through the thickest ridge of scar tissue at the top of the skull.

"Bad aim," he answers. "And good luck. The strike was shallow enough that my scar saved me."

His sad smile gives way to determination that darkens his eyes and sets his jaw.

"I'm here, and I'm not going anywhere."

"You're here." My voice breaks, and my eyes trace the thin, crimson rivulets dipping in and out of muscular valleys and hills as they contract with each breath. It's not a life-threatening amount. If anything, it proves he's still alive.

Hope accompanied with something needy and feral settles deep in my core before I meet his gaze again.

"You're *here*."

He nods, then repeats, voice steady, "And I'm not going anywhere."

Rain sluices mud from our bodies, dripping heavy onto my lashes as I finally, *really* see him. The truth in his vow, the adrenaline still riding us both.

His desperation.

His hunger.

His need.

I shiver. I'm so in tune with him, and him with me, that I can see, *feel*, the moment everything changes.

His grip tightens, bruising my waist and hand as he holds me like we're in a dance. I embrace the pain because it means two things.

He's alive.

And so am I.

"Show me." I bite my lip, letting my own desire bleed through my expression before I beg, "Please. Show me we're alive."

His jaw ticks. Then, with a curse under his breath, he lets me go, backing up to the edge of the small, mossy bank. His hands flex open and closed before they slice through his hair and grip the back of his head. Every muscle in his body seems to fight against his restraint, hardening as his heated stare strips me bare, unveiling everything I've hidden all my life... and wanting me anyway.

My pulse flies when he exhales through his nose, drops his hands into clenched fists at his sides, and finally speaks.

"I can't be gentle. Not right now," he growls. "Not when I've waited for you for so fucking long just to almost lose you."

He's nearly vibrating with something darker than rage, deeper than lust. Something I recognize, because it thrums in me too.

"I don't want your gentle," I vow. "I want your fury."

"Fuck." His jaw clenches. Then he shakes his head once. "You asked for this, little bird."

He prowls forward, gaze dropping to my chest. His fingers trace my soaked neckline before gripping it with both hands. With one brutal tug, my bodice rips in two, and I gasp as my breasts spill into the cold rain.

"Orion!"

"Quiet." His eyes flick from me to the mossy ground and back again. "Turn around."

I swallow, my pulse thundering like the storm. Slowly, I turn, anticipation making me lightheaded.

"Good girl. Now get on your knees."

"Wh-what?" My heart stutters. I start to twist around, but his hand captures the nape of my neck.

"I *said*..." his voice is a warm, commanding rumble in my ear. "Get on your knees, *wife*."

My breath catches. Fear swirls with adrenaline, tangling with reckless need. Before I can move, he guides me until I'm kneeling on the pillowy moss.

He lets go, and in the next breath, his belt jingles behind me and wet leather slips free with a hiss. When I risk glancing back, his eyes devour me as he unzips with trembling fingers. His shaking hands shove his soaked jeans and briefs down, freeing his already long, hard cock. He fists his length, giving himself one deliberate stroke, ending with a hard squeeze at the leaking tip.

Then he kneels close, his body heat burning the few inches between us, raising goosebumps along my skin. He grips my nape again to slowly push me lower until my palms sink into the damp earth. I breathe in the earthy scent as he brushes aside my wet tendrils, revealing my tattoo on my upper back and making me shiver.

He turns my chin slightly, just enough for me to see him.

"I caught you, my reckless little bird." Wicked hunger blackens his eyes. "There's no escaping me now."

25
I CRAVE THE HUNT
ORION

My fingers tremble as they caress the gift kneeling before me, Luna submitting on all fours, fair skin wet and gleaming in the fading light. I stroke my hands down her spine and rest them on her lower back right above her Venus dimples.

"This isn't the way I intended to claim you... but it's the way it's supposed to be, isn't it?"

She nods, shifting her legs wider for me.

"Please," she whispers, vibrating under my touch and hardening my cock to steel.

Jesus.

I shouldn't take her like this. She's covered in blood, dirt, and it's cold even in the humid, foggy rain. Feathers scatter around her from the bodice I ripped off. Her tutu clings to her thighs, more tatters than tulle after running for her life.

But that's why she begged me for this. She's wrecked from watching her friend die, and after staring death in the face, she needs me to show her we're alive.

And fuck, I need it too.

I drag the remains of her layered skirt up and over her hips, then easily tear her panties in two with both hands. The sight of her glistening, bare cunt makes me groan.

"Orion," she whimpers, shivering from the chill over her sensitive, exposed flesh.

I grab the globes of her ass, spreading them to serve her up for me. She yelps as I bend low, then moans when my tongue swipes through her dripping arousal. Her heady Carolina jasmine and honey scent is as addictive as sin.

"You liked running from me, didn't you?" I rasp, barely able to contain the urge to bury myself inside her. "You liked being scared."

I slip a finger in and flutter it over the bundle of nerves that make her writhe. Her breath catches, and I murmur.

"Don't be shy. Your body tells me all I need to know. You loved it." I withdraw my finger and suck, relishing her delicious flavor. "I can fucking taste it."

She wiggles against me as I slide my finger back in and add another. Curving my body around hers, my fingers play with shallow strokes, and my mouth brushes the shell of her ear.

"One thing I can promise? I'll always catch you, birdie, and you'll always want to be caught. You wanted to be caught that first night too, didn't you?"

"Yes, I wanted it tonight too. So badly. I..." She swallows. "I-I'm sorry for what I said at the graveyard." She hiccups, and my heart stutters, waiting as she continues softly, "I don't hate you. I never did."

After everything, she was worried about this? Hurting me with words I knew were never true?

I'm trying to wrap my mind around the fact that she cared so much about my pain when she begins to shake again, like she's trying to hold it together for what she says next.

"I don't know... I don't know what I would've done if you died thinking that."

The sob finally bursts out, bowing her body. I catch her before she falls, kissing her temple.

"Shh, I know. I know. My sweet, sweet girl. I'm gonna take good care of you, alright? For the rest of our lives."

A breathy cry of relief shudders from her, and the same tension releases from my chest.

I want to love her so hard I break her, then put her back together again with splintered pieces that only fit when seared with mine.

Teeth clenched, my willpower is in tatters, as shredded as the bodice lying like fractured wings by her side. It's time my broken angel and I make the devil blush.

When I tease her opening, she whines and pushes back against me.

"Not yet. I'm too big, and I don't want to break you before you're ready."

She bends lower, curving her spine and presenting herself to me with a whine.

"I don't care, Orion. Please, make me yours."

"Goddamn, little bird."

I suck in a breath as pressure builds at the base of my shaft, my cock hardening to a painful degree. I don't know how much longer *we* can take it, but I withdraw my fingers and resist.

Going back in, I revel in one more taste, lapping up her arousal from her clit to that tight little pucker I plan to claim one day, and she moans. I thumb her clit in slow circles while I straighten on my knees and stroke myself with my other hand, spreading the precum from my tip along the rest of my length.

Blood from my wound drips onto my shaft, slickening me more with every glide. The sight alone nearly makes me come undone, and without thinking, I press my palm to my cut, holding back a curse.

I played it off earlier, but this hurts like hell. There was no way I was going to let her see my pain, though. Not after what she's been through. Not after Benoit, and not with how crushed she looked, terrified she was going to lose me too.

But now I use the pain, sliding the warm liquid up and down, coating my cock with it. My breaths quicken knowing my lifeblood is about to be inside her. When the ache to claim her is finally too much, I drag my tip through her sex. Rain falls between us, but I curl over her body, shielding her from the cold drops, and to make sure the blood I spilt for her doesn't wash away before I can fill her cunt.

"I bled for you, and I'd do it again. It's only right I mark you with it from the inside out."

"Do it. Mark me. Make me yours."

"I'd do anything for you, you know that?"

"Yes," she breathes instantly. "I-I know."

I notch myself at her entrance and settle both hands at her hips, steadying her. Then I slowly, *painfully* slowly, push forward, feeling her stretch around my head. Still, she flinches, making me wince. It's both our first times, and I'm dying to be inside her, but hurting her in any way will devastate me.

"Relax for me." I knead her upper thighs, trying to encourage her.

"O-okay."

I grit my teeth as I pull out, never leaving her warmth before sliding back in, inch by inch. Every shallow thrust works her open, but when I meet that tender resistance, her muscles turn to stone. She whimpers when I try to push.

"Luna?" I say low, watching her. Her back rises with an inhale... but doesn't fall. My chest aches, and I bend over her, careful not to force myself farther than she can take.

I kiss her neck, ghosting my lips up to her ear. "Don't hold your breath, baby."

She nods and lets out a shaky exhale. I wait until she inhales... exhales... but then she stops again.

"I don't want this to hurt you. You have to let me in."

"I... I want to. I..." She swallows, shaking her head, fingers clawing the moss. "I'm afraid. I'm trying, but I can't..."

"It's okay," I murmur and sit up, racking my brain for what to do as my bloody palms easily glide down her rain-slicked spine, so wet at this point there's zero resistance...

That realization hits me.

"Shit," I mutter under my breath.

My jaw clenches, knowing, and hating, what I have to do to

claim her. I press my wound again, pouring blood into my palm before slicking the rest of my cock until I'm not just using it to mark her, I'm dripping with it this time. Then my hands rest at her hips, my fingers dipping into the waistband of her tutu to get the perfect hold. My cock never left her, still lodged right up against her resistance.

"After this, you're mine, and I'm yours, okay? Remember that."

She nods and bites her lip, but I don't wait for her to answer out loud. Accepting the guilt that will come, my fingers tighten into a bruising grip, the shock of it forcing her to suck in a breath before I slam forward past her barrier, seating my length fully inside her.

I'm already bent over her, arms wrapped around her torso to gather her up in an embrace when her cry of pain rips through me, murmuring into her nape.

"Good girl. Such a good fucking girl. You did so good for me. I'm sorry. I know it hurt. Dragging it out would've been worse and warning you would've made you tense up more. But I've got you. You're mine. And now, with my blood, my body, all of me... I'm yours."

I don't move until her trembling subsides and her tight walls begin to soften around me. Only then do I finally let myself bask in the moment. Bask in *her*. My wife.

I waited for Luna Bordeaux my whole life, never touched another, and goddamn, was it worth it. I'd wait forever all over again to feel this claiming one more time.

After breathing through all the sensations bulldozing through me, making me lightheaded, I ease her back down onto all fours, and sit up. Holding onto her hips, I withdraw and watch where we're connected. The blood I used to make it easier on her is gone, replaced by her glistening arousal and a faint swirl of pink around my shaft. Possessiveness and something stronger, something that's only grown the more I've been around her, claw through me.

"You're only ever going to be mine, Luna Bordeaux," I vow. My grip tightens on her hips again as I slide back in. "Say it, baby. Say what I want to hear and mean it."

"I'm only yours, Orion," she moans, no hesitation.

I watch myself disappear inside her again, and fuck, her walls contract every time she sucks in a sharp breath to take my invasion. She's supple in my hands, and I massage down her spine over the delicate muscles she's honed for years. My tanned, scarred hands paint her fair, soft skin with crimson until they rest in the dimples above her curved ass, my fingers delving into the waistband of her skirt.

Thrusting one more time, slow but deep, I rest my forehead to her tattooed shoulder blade and groan.

"God*damn*, Luna."

I force steady breaths, determined not to ruin her first time by coming too soon. So I force myself to relax, wait, taking this in so I can do things right by her for once.

Her pulse pounds around my cock, and my smile brushes her skin as I speak, "Want to know a secret?"

"Hm?"

"I like you scared. I like the way your moonlight skin flushes bright red under my hands, the way your breasts heave toward me, begging to be sucked." I release her hips to cup them, tweaking her nipples with my thumbs.

"Orion!" she cries, writhing in a way that is absolutely *counter*productive to my aim of slowing this down.

But I can't be bothered to care as she rocks back and forth against me, not realizing how naturally we've melded together, or that she's not in pain anymore in the slightest, chasing her own high. Her breaths come in pants, and I tease her more with my words alone as she tries to take what she needs.

"I love you breathless and trembling like prey. Know that every time you run from me, you're begging me to claim you." I sit up, holding her hips again and pumping in agonizingly slow thrusts as I deliver each word. "Just. Like. This."

"Yes, *please*," she moans, glancing back at me through wet lashes. "Please fuck me just like this."

That one desperate look, her voice quiet but loud amidst the rolling thunder...

Her pussy clenching me *hard*.

I fucking lose it.

Snatching her hips, I snap mine forward, impaling her on a brutal thrust. Her shriek of half-pain, half-need calls to the deepest, darkest, most feral parts of me, and I answer with my own roar. My thumbs dig into the dimples on her back as I thrust with ruthless abandon. A true fucking.

Claiming my wife.

Her body trembles in my hands, and instinct tells me she's close as her cunt tightens like a vise around my cock the higher she climbs.

But then I see it. Blood trickles down her arm. Fresh blood. It takes me a second to realize it's not mine.

It's hers.

I fist her hair, wrapping my arm around her front as I pull her back to better see the slash on her shoulder I didn't notice before.

"When did this happen?" I snarl. "Who did this to you?"

Her eyes narrow with rage back at me as she spits the answer, "A *Wilde*."

The fight plays in a flash in my mind, stopping on the moment I thought I'd saved her from the knife grazing her shoulder. I'd failed her.

My fury explodes in my chest. I lick the cut, making her hiss, then glare into her eyes as I cleanse the metallic stain. Her pain tastes sharp, like steel and hate, and once I've lapped up every trace of what they did to her, I crash my mouth to hers. She moans, lips parting to take the bloody offering, our kiss a frenzy of hunger and vengeance until I can't tell where her anger ends and mine begins.

I finally wrench myself away, leaving her breathless as I confess how the fight ended.

"They're dead," I promise. "All of them are dead by the same knife they cut you with."

Gorgeous brutality flashes in her eyes. "Good."

Pride fills my chest, but my voice hardens. "That goes for anyone who touches you. If anyone hurts you, a shallow grave is all they'll get."

She cups my cheek. "*Good.*"

I growl at her ruthlessness that rivals my own, and pull her in for another kiss, teasing her clit with my fingers while I thrust into her again. She braces against the tree trunk, completely at my mercy, until her thighs tremble and her muscles lock around me.

"Come for me, wife." She tries to close her eyes, but I shake her. "No. Eyes on me. Let me see you come undone."

Her eyes flutter closed, but I tap her clit as punishment, and she *shatters*, sobbing as her body bows over. My grip in her hair keeps her upright so I can witness her break for me. Gorgeous tears spill down her cheeks, but her clear blue gaze stays on mine. My name falls from her lips on a long, low moan of surrender. Her pussy strangles my cock with rhythmic clenches, so tight I nearly tip over the edge with her, but I maintain my speed and thrusts as her hips push back against me, meeting me stroke for stroke.

"There it is," I encourage her, my voice deep. "Ride my cock. Fuck, you're so beautiful falling for me like this. You were made for me to catch you."

I do just that as she goes limp in my arms, totally sated. My thrusts slow but never stop as I ease her forward onto the soft bed of moss, then prop her hips high, opening her wide so I can take her the way I need. I pull out only to slam back in again, over and over, until I lose all sense of time watching my wife's face twist in ecstasy.

Blood seeps from my wound, running down my chest and abdomen until it slicks my shaft again. Her virgin blood mingles with the blood I sacrificed in her name, blending together as I claim her, and I'm suddenly overcome with the aching need to fill her with everything I can give.

I hook one hand over her clavicle, my palm resting over the skull tattooed on her shoulder blade. The Fury mark. My other grips her hip, fingers digging into the cracked skull I designed. *My* mark.

My thrusts quicken, an unforgiving pace as my fingerprints stamp into her flesh. She arches and rocks back against me, on the verge of another round of pleasure, strangling my cock with her tight little cunt. I drag my tongue up her spine and nip her neck beneath her ear.

"Again, Luna. Come for your husband."

She shrieks, convulsing around me. My hand clamps her throat as I snarl.

"I'm going to come inside my wife. Always your cunt, do you understand? I'll fuck my seed into you for the rest of our lives, until you're good and fucking bred by your Fury."

"*Yes*," she begs. "Please. Come inside me, Orion. Give me everything."

She's mindless right now, and will probably hate me later, but I can't care, too primal to think of anything other than claiming her from the inside out. I've made my stance on possessing her in every way possible pretty damn clear, so I take the invitation for what it is.

White-hot sensation explodes through me, and I go blind with pleasure as my balls draw up. My cock surges, and I press my hand to her lower belly to drive deeper against her sensitive channel.

"*Orion!*"

Fisting her hair, I twist the tendrils aside to sink my teeth into the crook of her neck. She screams as I bite to bruise, to mark, to scar, all so she can never forget me. Copper teases my tongue, and I come harder than I ever have, buried to the hilt inside her.

I release her on a roar, and she jerks in my arms, another orgasm racking her body until she comes undone again like a woman possessed. Because she is. She's mine, and what we just did sealed it, binding us in mind, body, and soul.

We're riddled with aftershocks, and it takes a while for my racing heartbeat to finally slow as adrenaline bleeds out of me. I gather Luna before she can collapse, pulling out with a hiss at the loss of her heat. She clings to me, sobbing into my neck.

"Fuck, baby, come here," I murmur, even though she's already as close as she can get.

Holding her tight, I sit on my shirt and lean against the trunk, then guide her to straddle me. Raising her hips enough to slip my cock back inside her, I bite down a groan as residual spurts of cum leave me, coating her channel. Once I've got a handle on my shit, I cradle her against my chest and wrap my jacket around her trembling form. The sight of blood welling where my canines pierced her, bruises already darkening to a rich purple around them, makes my cock stir again, but I tamp it down and lave the marks gently, making her shudder.

I hold her to me, keeping us joined, the connection necessary not only for her, but for me too. I could've lost her today, and it's a miracle she survived.

No. Not a miracle. It was a sacrifice. The loss of one of her best friends.

I feel the exact breath when her cries shift to something that's no longer from ecstasy. A pained wail escapes her chest, and she sags into me, depending on me to hold her together as the weight of everything she's gone through tears her apart. Unfortunately, I know some of the emotions too well.

Pain. Grief.

Guilt.

No matter how Benoit died, even with the Wildes the clear enemy, Luna will wear the blame like an anvil on her back. I'll hold her through it until she forgives herself. Maybe one day, she'll help me do the same.

Rocking her slowly, I massage her scalp and whisper fiercely against her temple, saying all the things I wish had been said to me.

"It's okay."

"I've got you."

"You're safe now."

"It's not your fault."

I repeat them, wondering if the words even register, hoping she internalizes them somehow if they don't.

Eventually, her sorrow releases its chokehold, letting her breaths even, and she goes fully limp in my arms. When sleep finally claims her, I hold her impossibly tighter and make the same vow I have every night so far.

"I love you, wife." I kiss her forehead, pouring everything I am into her. "I love you, and I'm never letting you go."

26
GUARDING HER CYGNET
ORION

Luna is killing me.

Those watery, clear blue eyes have been fixed in a hollow stare since we got back to the cabin, the sight of Benoit's body no doubt bringing back fresh hurt and guilt. I know that feeling. Seeing the burnt graveyard was a sucker punch to the chest, and it's been six years since I confronted my mom's death, not little more than six hours.

Luna collapsed at her friend's side as soon as we walked up, her tutu fanning around her like broken wings as she tucked her legs beneath her and pulled him into her lap. She's still wearing my jacket and the crudely fixed bodice laced together with ripped tulle. The blood from Benoit's gunshot wounds has dried, rust-colored flakes crusting the holes in his shirt and speckling her fair skin. But she wouldn't have cared if she'd been soaked through.

Benoit looks worse now, despite the rosy glow of early morning creeping in through the cabin slats. His skin is pale and waxy, slick with October dew, lips an unnatural bluish-gray. The only saving grace is that his eyes are closed. You don't come back the same after looking into dead eyes. That image never stops haunting you. Luna's silent, catatonic, and cradling him like they might open at any moment.

I'd do anything to take away her pain, but all I can give her is a few minutes to mourn in peace. So I check the traps that ended up being useless, confirm we're alone, then hide bodies in the brush so Luna doesn't have to see them. When I return to the cabin, she's in the same position, a portrait of grief frozen in time.

I crouch beside her and rub small circles on her back. She leans into me enough that I feel the quake of her sobs as she lets them free. I press a kiss to her crown, reveling in the trust she has in me, trust I don't deserve, and hating myself for ruining it with what I have to say next.

"I need to check him, little bird."

She recoils, hissing and wrapping around him like a swan guarding her cygnets. "No."

Exactly the reaction I predicted. My girl's fiercely protective over the people she loves, one of the many reasons I fell for her. But that devotion is also how I know she can't handle watching me search her dead friend's pockets for anything useful.

Out here, we can't count on anything but surprises. Everything is used and nothing is wasted. A practical, sometimes harsh rule of the woods I would've hoped to teach her in much better circumstances. But it's a lesson that might keep us alive, especially with Luna still hurt and the possibility of the Wildes hiding anywhere in the Lost Cove trees.

I don't say that, though. Her emotions are an exposed nerve right now, and I'm afraid one wrong word will set her off into a devastated spiral. So I rub my thumb at the nape of her neck and offer a truth she can digest.

"I have to make sure there's nothing on him that can hurt you."

Her eyes narrow. "Like what?"

"I don't know. But I won't take chances with you." I tip my chin toward the door. "Go, please. I promise I'll be quick, but you won't want to see this."

Her eyes well up as she holds him tighter. "You won't hurt him."

Way to break my damn heart.

I shake my head. "I promise. I'll treat him like my own."

She waits a beat, then nods slowly and passes him to me,

holding his head like a baby's. I take him just as gently and watch as she limps to the porch with barely a grunt of pain. She doesn't go far, stopping at the railing. Her fingers dig into the wood as she stares out across the lake where the mist lifts in the sun's meager rays. Her back is straight, jaw clenched. The soft wind wafts through her hair and ripples her skirt like water, and she visibly shudders, as if from a cold chill like a ghost passing by.

The guilt weighing on my chest makes it hard to breathe.

My strong little bird is wrecked. Black, blue, and purple marks paint her fair skin, some I'm proud of, like my claiming bite and the fingerprints mapping my touch. Others make me murderous.

The welt on her cheek from that Wilde's backhand is the worst of them, the cut on her shoulder a close second. I wish I could drag him and his knife-wielding friend back from the grave to fuck them up again, toy with them like a cat with its prey. At least Luna helped take out the first one, cracking his neck under her foot.

But it's not just her wounds that'll worry me until I get her safe in Dark Corner. It's been almost a week, but she's already losing weight she couldn't afford to. Her spine is more pronounced, cheekbones sharper. The bodice I ripped still fits, but only because of my hack job stitch-up, threading tulle like a corset through slits I cut. It hugs her lean frame and pushes her breasts up so high it's a wonder she can breathe. I want the thing off her as soon as we're safe. The once-white fabric and remaining feathers are nearly black now, stained by bog mud and dark crimson blood.

Forcing my gaze away from my girl, I focus on Benoit, laying him on the floorboards to work swiftly. I don't touch the gun he never had a chance to fire. No matter how helpful it could be, the bad luck that comes with a dead man's weapon ain't worth the risk. But I pocket his cracked phone, keys, and an unlabeled pill bottle. Then I zip up his jacket, covering the bloodstains so she won't have to see them again.

"I'm finished," I murmur.

She appears before the last word's out, dropping beside him and gathering his body into her lap again to rock him. Her face returns to that blank expression I *hate*, churning my stomach.

I slowly rise and step outside, giving her space she probably won't even notice. Glancing back at her, I pull Benoit's phone out and swipe through it, then bring it to my ear to make the call I've been dreading.

It's answered on the first ring.

"Benny? You okay, kid? You missed your check-in."

Fuck. Me.

The casual tone slices through my resolve deeper than I'd expect. I suck my teeth, rub at the pang in my chest, then let out a hard sigh.

"Bordeaux."

There's silence before Luna's father answers gruffly.

"Explain."

27

FOREVERMORE

ORION

I move farther down the muddy path toward the lake, as far as I'll allow myself away from Luna, keeping her within my line of sight but out of earshot. Still, I lower my voice.

"Benoit is dead."

"You mother—"

"I didn't kill him." My eyes flick back to my distraught girl, still exactly as I left her, then sweep the woods again. "But I'll give you one guess who did."

A pause, then Sol grits out. "The Wildes." Rage roughens his voice. "None of this would've happened if you'd never stolen my daughter."

My grip tightens around the phone.

"Let's get one thing *crystal* fucking clear. *You* made a vow. King Fury's kin kept our end, and we didn't tell a soul. But *somehow* the Wildes found out. The only reason I had to 'steal' her in the first place is because you've got snakes in your own garden."

I give him a second to choke on that before twisting the knife.

"You didn't even know that Ozias was a Wilde, did you?"

"The hell he is. What did you do with him? He's been missing since that night."

Missing? He was supposed to be at the hospital...

I blink, pushing past that question to answer him, my voice firm. "I handled Ozias because *you* didn't. And his cousins? Bart and Rufus? They slipped right past your precious shadows too. They drugged her, Sol."

He sucks in a sharp breath. "No way that happened in my city."

"I'm telling you... It. Did. If you don't believe me, ask my brothers for the photo of the Pining blister pack we found on Rufus. There was some plan between him and Bart to take Luna. Maybe Ozias was even in on it too."

Silence stretches between us, but I can practically hear him connect it all.

"We found Rufus dead," he finally admits, less hostility in his tone. The enemy of my enemy is my friend and all that, I guess. "What of Bartholomew and Ozias?"

"This is the first time I've had signal in nearly a week, but last I heard from my brothers, Bart's in the wind."

Luna's dad grunts his disapproval. "And Ozias?"

"My brothers were supposed to drop him off at the hospital, but if you haven't seen him..." I let the words drift before continuing. "I'm not sure how much he had to do with it, honestly, if at all. Hurting women's usually off-limits with Zy. But just in case, I gave him an invitation to fuck right off." My lips quirk wryly. "He won't be smiling about much from now on."

"Good." Then Sol mutters, almost to himself. "I still can't believe this."

"Believe it. This is like King predicted. You've underestimated the Wilde-Fury feud. I was under your nose for years protecting Luna. You really think someone just as determined to do the opposite couldn't pull off a long con too? I didn't take her to fuck with you, Bordeaux. I took her because she's mine, *and* she was in danger. If I hadn't, who knows how far they would've gone. Benoit's death proves the lengths they'll go to."

"I'll shore up my defenses, then. We've never needed Furys before, and we won't now."

I seethe. "We're in a war, don't you get that? Luna's not just your daughter anymore. She's *my wife*. The Wildes will do whatever it takes to stop the pact between our families. Without me, she's a sitting duck."

"She's not your wife unless she chooses it," he snaps. "You're forcing her into something she doesn't want."

I shake my head, eyes returning to the cabin. Luna finally looks at me, and as soon as our eyes meet, her expression softens.

"I don't think that's true anymore, Solomon."

"We'll see about that," he grits. "Turn on video and give Luna the phone. I need to speak with my daughter."

"Only if she wants to," I shoot back, needling him even as I'm on my way back to her.

"You little..." He rattles off what I'm sure is a string of New Orleans-style French curses.

I mute him as I take the porch steps in two strides. When I'm beside Luna, I squeeze her shoulder and crouch to meet her gaze, phone extended.

"You wanna talk to your dad?"

She releases a ragged exhale, then nods, taking the phone and switching to video. My jacket's fallen off her shoulder, so I tighten it around her. One because even though she says she doesn't feel the cold, she's trembling now, and to hell with my wife being cold. And two... Solomon Bordeaux will kill me if he sees the bite mark I left on his daughter. I'm not afraid of the guy, but there's nothing wrong with having a healthy respect for your father-in-law, especially when he's the most dangerous man in New Orleans.

I pull Luna's head in to kiss her temple as the phone's signal stabilizes. Sol's scarred face appears on the grainy screen as I release her.

"Luna?"

She breaks.

"Daddy?" she sobs, voice fracturing into jagged pieces that tear my heart in two.

"Oh, *ma luné*," he croons gently. *My moon*. "Are you okay? Are you—wait. What the *fuck* happened to your cheek?"

She gasps, covering the welt, and I pull her into my chest.

"Watch it," I snarl, my rage yanking at its leash. "Don't talk to my wife that way."

He ignores me. "Did that Fury boy do that to you?"

"The fuck I did."

Luna shakes her head quickly. "No, Dad. I promise."

I glare at him but force myself to back off, brushing her hair aside so I can meet her eyes.

"I'll be right over here," I murmur, pointing outside with my thumb.

She nods, and I step off the porch, giving her the illusion of privacy while keeping watch for her safety. No way I'm going far when Wildes know where we are. We already stayed too long, and it cost us too much, a mistake I'll hate myself over for the rest of my life. But now Luna needs to say goodbye, so I'll hold our enemies at bay while she gets what she needs.

I doubt they'll attack again. We've all got wounds to lick, and with the Wilde-Fury feud, there's honor among thieves. Or there's supposed to be. If we can't take care of our loved ones even in death, then what the hell are we fighting over in the first place?

"I'm okay." Her whispered voice is raw from crying. "Just a little banged up."

She pauses. I peer back to make sure she's okay, and her eyes lock on mine with an emotion that makes my pulse skip.

"Orion saved me."

The words tug my heart toward hers, right until her father snaps.

"*Saved* you? Luna, he kidnapped—"

"I know," she cuts in, looking back at the phone. I face the lake again, arms crossed. "Trust me, I'm *still* pissed about that. But it's complicated now." Her voice softens, and I feel her gaze warm my back. "He's kind, Dad. Thoughtful. He's saved my life more than once."

"Are you serious?"

"Like *you* have room to talk," a soft voice interrupts.

"Momma?" Luna's pitch rises to a childlike hopefulness. "You're there?"

"I'm here. Your dad put me up in a hotel while he was looking for you. He's been out all night but came back to check on me." Luna's mom huffs, then orders firmly, "Come on, Sol, give me the phone already."

My brows shoot up, and my grin widens. I've never heard the Phantom of the French Quarter get ordered around before, but it makes sense that Luna wouldn't get all that sass just from her father.

Sol grumbles, and something rustles on the other end before Luna and her mom exchange teary hellos and updates between sniffles. Luna's voice lightens as she recounts what's happened, thankfully leaving out some crucial, *damning* details. By the time she's done, my feisty girl even lets out a wry laugh.

"So, um, yeah. That's all."

"Oh, Lu, you've been through so much." Her mom sighs, not letting Luna downplay it. "Tell me, really. You've seen your dad and me. You know what good looks like. Is he... is he good to you?"

"Yeah," I hear Luna's shy smile as she answers. "I know that's strange."

"No, honey... I've felt the way you do." Her voice lowers to that hush only a momma has, the softness hardening a lump in my throat. "Those feelings are confusing. Terrifying even. Don't get me wrong, I don't like this, not one bit. This life isn't what I wanted for you."

"That's an understatement," Sol scoffs.

"But don't feel ashamed for caring for him," Scarlett insists. "Bordeaux women have a knack for falling for the black knight."

I pretend to scrub my chin, hiding my smile behind the ruse. Fury wives tend to do the same thing.

Luna chuckles. "Yeah. That's another understatement."

Wait. Falling for the black knight is an understatement?
Does that mean...?

My heart soars.

They talk a while longer with snippets about her friends making their way back to me on the light breeze.

Brylie's pissed, apparently, insisting she should join the search even with her parents telling her to stay put and stay safe. None of that's a surprise from what Dash has shared about her. Lucy's anxiety is through the roof. Hopefully Hatch is in the know about that one. Nox is murderous and protective over all the Troisgarde daughters now, something I can respect. And everyone's worried for Luna, desperate for her to come home.

Not gonna happen.

Eventually, Luna says her goodbyes, but then she calls my name, lifting the phone.

I'm already on the porch steps, stretching up to take it. The second it's in my hand, I switch off video.

"Yeah?" I ask, walking back to the lake.

"Take care of her. I'm... I'm trusting you with one of the three people I'd burn the world over. If you hurt her—"

"It's not even a question."

He exhales a grudging sigh. "After talking to her, I think I know that now."

Pride swells in my chest, until he adds, "Which is why you need to do something for me."

"Okayyy," I hedge. "Only if it helps Luna."

"It will," he rushes out and continues reluctantly. "But she might not like it. Not if it's too late."

My jaw clenches. I glance toward the cabin, where she's still curled over Benoit, and take another casual step farther down the path.

"*I* already don't like this. What do you mean?"

The phone exchanges hands with a shuffle before Scarlett takes over.

"She needs her medicine. Especially after everything."

Something in her voice makes my mouth dry.

"What medicine?" I rasp.

"Benoit should have it. All the shadows Sol sent out carried some. We wanted to get them to her as soon as possible. According to her pill organizer, she already missed two days even before Bon Temps Night."

"What are they for?" I rake a hand through my hair, pacing, the slim pill bottle burning in my jeans pocket. "Is she okay?"

"I hope so. She needs them soon, though. Abrupt withdrawal can trigger symptoms. But how or to what degree isn't predictable. It's a tricky diagnosis."

My pulse quickens. "Mrs. Bordeaux—"

"Scarlett's fine."

"Scarlett, I'm trying not to freak out here."

She swallows audibly. "My daughter... She has what I have. Bipolar disorder. Type two. It's a little different than mine but can still be just as difficult."

My breath catches. The Bordeauxs keep certain things tightly under wraps, with their medical privacy at the top of the list. As fucked up as it was to stalk Luna for so long, I didn't feel right asking Dash to hack into those systems. I figured out Mrs. Bordeaux's bipolar disorder type one diagnosis from word of mouth and rumors about episodes a long time ago. But nothing, *nothing* even hinted that Luna has it.

Or did I miss it?

Emotion is thick in my throat. "Okay. How can I help her?"

She exhales what I'm pretty sure is relief, like I passed a test.

"It's really encouraging that's your first question."

I frown. "What other question is there?"

She huffs dryly. "You'd be surprised what people say."

My brows raise, but she continues, "Let me give you a quick rundown. First thing you need to know is stress and poor sleep are major triggers for our Luna. Emotional overload's one too. What would make someone else crack might shatter her. Any combination of those could trigger a depressive or hypomanic episode, and the other will almost always follow. Or, like I said, she could be completely fine."

My gaze drags back to Luna, still mourning her dead friend... in an abandoned shack... one I've basically held her hostage in... and kept her up with my nightmares... after kidnapping her.

Well shit.

"Alright." I shut my eyes, grimacing. "Hit me with it."

She walks me through the symptoms Luna experiences during episodes, starting with depression, none of which I've clocked.

But when Scarlett moves on to hypomania, certain hallmark signs have my chest tightening to the point of pain. I have to fight the sensation that I'm drowning, trapped deep underwater.

Pressured speech. Check.

No sleep but tons of energy. Check. Check.

Impulsivity. Triple check for my reckless girl.

Irritability, frustration, mental acuity, and even pain or temperature toleration that can all either be blunted or heightened. Quadruple fucking check.

"And then," Scarlett hesitates. "Sol, do you mind?"

"Scarlett... no. You can't think they'd—"

"Just go, Sol, please?"

"I'll kill him," he grumbles, ending the rest of the threat in French.

But a door slams and Scarlett sighs.

"Orion?"

"I'm here," I answer, my pulse racing as I hold my breath.

Her gentle voice drops low. "Another symptom is sexual impulsivity. She may be more... *forward* than usual. Or act on feelings that—to be clear—are still *her* feelings, but whether she would've acted on them otherwise is a different question."

My heart stutters to a stop, aching. I stumble backward, landing against a tree.

Fuck.

Fuck. Fuck. Fuck.

I don't want to go there, slapping my hand over my eyes and desperately trying to push the image away, but my mind pictures Luna open and begging, *needing* me to claim her.

My dick shrivels, my heart along with it. What if I twisted a moment meant to be sacred? What if I took something she didn't really want to give?

I'm lightheaded, so I try to breathe past the agonizing guilt ripping through my chest, but there's no use. And honestly, I don't deserve the relief. All I want to do is rush back to the cabin and beg Luna to tell me that the best moment of my life wasn't the worst thing I've ever done.

But I can't even look at her.

Scarlett blows out a harsh exhale. "I sense you and my daughter need to talk."

I slide down the tree, landing in a crouch, my shame so heavy I can't hold myself up under the weight.

"We do."

She sighs. "Since we were prepared because of my own condition, Luna's managed hers quite well from the beginning. She takes her medicine, practices good sleep hygiene, and the girl couldn't be serious or stressed if she tried." She chuckles lightly. "Luna's a free spirit in every sense. Some of that comes naturally. But some of it's on purpose."

All the pieces I've missed snap together into the gorgeous, intricate puzzle that is my Luna. The way she's the life of the party and carefree, even when she doesn't want to be. She's always included others, no doubt because she knows what it's like to be different. How she tried so hard to avoid talking about her emotions with me the other night...

"Sometimes hypomanic episodes can be exhilarating, and Luna's been known to 'ride the high,' as she calls it. But that rollercoaster is *not* safe. Her decisions could accidentally hurt her or other people, and long-lasting hypomania is bad for our brains."

"What do I need to do?" I ask quickly.

"Episodes are different for everyone, but for Luna, she comes out of them fastest with the help of sleep, mood stabilizers, and exercise. Interestingly enough, though, nature grounds her more than anything. Running the Garden District has helped, but I always wished we could take her hiking again. She loved it. We used to go up to the mountains all the time, until…"

"Until the Furys called on the pact," I finish, another awful pang of guilt splitting me in two.

She doesn't answer. She doesn't have to. We both know the second King called Sol on his debt, Luna's life changed forever.

"You got anything else for me, ma'am?"

"No. That's the quick and dirty of it," she says, then her voice softens. "Take care of our girl, Orion. I think you just might be the one to do it."

My chest warms, that one piece of encouragement making it hope that we didn't fuck everything up beyond repair.

"Thank you, Mrs. Bordeaux. Can you put Sol back on?"

In an instant, Sol's gruff voice returns.

"What?"

"I'm guessing y'all hooked up a GPS tracker on Benoit's car? I can find it through his phone?"

"Yes? Why?"

"Good. I've got his keys, and I need a car since the Wildes torched mine."

He curses.

"I'm sure you have our location by now thanks to our call." I soften my tone. "Come get your man for a proper burial, Bordeaux. I'd do it, but I have to get Luna home." He starts to argue, so I clarify, "*Our* home. In Dark Corner. Don't come after us without a treaty."

"Always about the Troisgarde, I see," he snaps.

"The fuck it is, Bordeaux." My grip tightens on the phone as I stand. "It's always been about *Luna*."

"And you think I don't know what's best for her?" Sol grinds out. "You're talking about my daughter, Fury. *My daughter*."

"No. My *wife*."

My thumb smashes the screen, ending the call.

I lean back against the tree again, blowing out a breath, letting my head hang. I tap the phone against my forehead, trying to figure out what the hell to do next. Then I pocket it and walk back to Luna, still where I left her, cradling what's left of her past.

Foregoing the meds talk for now, I settle on a slightly less shitty conversation instead.

"We can't stay here."

A beat of silence passes us before she murmurs, "I know."

Her eyes lift, clearer now, but sorrow still carves into every exhausted feature. She slept in my arms last night, but it can't have been enough. I'll have to make sure she gets as much as possible when we're home.

"We'll get Benoit's car," I say. "His phone's GPS will lead us there."

Her nose wrinkles. "What happened to your car?"

I suck my teeth. "Let's just say it's beyond repair."

She winces. "The Wildes?"

I nod. "The Wildes."

"They're really the gift that keeps on giving," she mutters, then sighs and shakes her head. "I don't want to leave him."

"I know." My hand squeezes her shoulder. "I know."

Her voice turns watery, emotion pressing hard against the floodgates. "What am I going to do when I get back? Everything's changed."

I don't tell her she's never going back, at least not without her husband as her personal shadow. Or that death like this is one of those things that changes you at a cellular level.

Before, she'd built a life as pure and bright as the white swan costume she ran from me in. Now the darkness of our worlds has stained every inch of her, inside and out. I would've saved her from the wreckage if I could've. But now that the veil's lifted from her eyes, there's only one way forward.

So I try to give her the comfort I can. With the only truths I know.

"You take it day by day. Give all the love you've got to the ones who are still here."

"And the ones who aren't? How do we go on without them?"

The rest of the platitudes burn to ash on my tongue. I shake my head, my throat dry, the words thick.

"We try our best."

A tear slips down her cheek. I brush it away with my knuckles, catching it on the letters tattooed there. Her arms tighten around her friend, like she can will him back to life just by holding on harder.

Moisture stings my own eyes at the sight of her pain, its familiarity buried deep in my marrow. I wouldn't wish it on my worst enemy, let alone my wife. It's an ache that nothing but time will dull but never erase. Sometimes, not even that works.

Still, urgency claws at my sternum. I hate to tear her away before she's ready, but we have to get out of here. I have to keep her safe.

She leans against me, another tear streaking through the dirt lightly dusting her cheek.

Fuck, I have to give her *something*. We can't even put her friend to rest yet, and she won't feel any kind of relief until she's had some way to say goodbye.

An idea sparks. It won't repair her heartache, nothing can, but it's a comfort that's generations old for a reason. Maybe the Appalachia in her soul will connect with it, giving her at least a thread of peace.

"I have something that may help." I grab a moonshine jug from the corner marked "P.R." in black sharpie.

Her brow lifts in question, and I raise my hand. "Hear me out. We've got a ritual around here. A goodbye toast."

"A toast," she asks skeptically, eyeing the jug.

I nod. "I can't explain why, but saying goodbye like this helps. It still hurts like hell, but paying respects in our way heals something, I think."

I offer my hand, like I have every time we've danced together, hoping she'll trust me enough to take it.

She gazes down at Benoit for a long, painful heartbeat. Then her voice is barely above a whisper as she answers.

"Okay."

She lays him gently, reverently back on the floor. Then she slips her hand into mine, my pulse thrumming from her touch outward. I help her to her feet, guiding her to the stove, the untended embers inside having all but gone out.

Curiosity flickers in her eyes as I raise the moonshine toward the mountain in the north.

"For the dead who've gone before," I say solemnly, tapping the bottom of the jug on the mantel. Then I lift it again, this time to Benoit, and pour a careful ounce onto the hearth before the stove. "Rest, dear spirit, forevermore."

Her eyes shine as I pass the jug to her trembling hands. Her voice cracks as she repeats the tribute.

"For the dead who've gone before..." She turns to Benoit. "Rest, my friend... forevermore."

ACT FOUR

FLIGHT OF THE WILDES

28
A CONFESSION
LUNA

Orion has been quiet. Not "me talking his ear off" quiet like a couple days ago, and not because I've also been quiet. No, his silence is as heavy and loaded as the world after a gun's gone off.

Meanwhile the cicadas are having entire conversations of their own, their constant buzz filling the night with white noise as I try to figure out what's going on. There's an undercurrent of emotion that thickens the air between us, the kind I'd have sprinted away from in the past.

But my friend just died. In my arms. Any emotion after that is child's play. I couldn't avoid them right now if I tried anyway. And I don't want to. Not anymore.

The toast soothed some of those raw nerves, and like Orion said, I can't explain why. Just that it felt like the kind of finality Benoit would've wanted and a much-needed stopgap before the funeral.

The only way to fully mourn him is to get back home. Which means climbing this mountain to his car in a threadbare *Swan Lake* outfit, an oversized leather jacket, frayed satin ballet flats, and an ankle swollen to the size of a baseball, wrapped in tulle that hangs on by a thread.

So yeah, Orion's silence wears on me, if at least because I need something to take my mind off the fact I'm turning into one giant blister. Sitting in front of the fire he built, safe in Fury land, I'm still racking my brain for what changed between us.

First I blamed the fact he hasn't been able to get in touch with his brothers, every call going to voicemail. But he seemed to chalk that up to "single-minded Fury men when it comes to protecting their wives," which is kind of hilarious when I think about it. The way Brylie would absolutely fuck Dash up if he ever called her that. Lucy's scaredy-cat behind would flee if Hatch ever looked at her the way Orion looks at me.

Once I knocked that off my list, I went to the Wildes. Orion's worried about them, certainly. That's why we're going at a speed that's as breakneck as my body will allow.

My pain tolerance is dwindling back to normal, sheer exhaustion burning off my hypomania like the sun to the mist this afternoon. Hypomanic episodes aren't ideal, *obviously*, but the reality of this disorder is there are some perks to riding the high... until there really aren't.

That last part is something my mom has drilled into me, and I've seen it firsthand. In the middle of the wilderness, an extended episode could've been disastrous, so I'm glad I'm coming down. I just hope we can get to safety before my mood does what it always does. Plummets.

I guess there's plenty on my mind too. If I can't figure out why he's being so quiet, maybe I can at least find out answers to my own questions.

"One of the Wildes seemed shocked that I had a knife," I begin. Orion's gaze drags from the fire to mine. "Why is that? It's just a knife. Women can have knives too. Do Wilde girls use spoons for everything?"

He snorts, but there's little humor in it. "It's not 'just a knife.' It's a Fury knife. There's rules about weapons out here too. The first is don't touch a dead man's weapon. The second is that family knives are sacred. The Furys get ours after coming home from Survival Week. From that moment on, we never, ever give them up. Not unless it's to someone we trust and care about."

My knee stops bouncing as that sinks in. "And you gave yours to me."

"Yeah, little bird. I gave mine to you." He tilts his head sadly. "I hope by now, you realize that I'd give you anything. That you can *trust* me with anything too. You know that, right?"

I nod slowly, unsure why that sounded like a vow and a plea all at once.

After a moment, he sighs like he's disappointed. His gaze returns to the fire, and we fall back into a wordless discomfort. I'd hoped to distract him with the question, get him out of his own head like he did with me the other night, but I'm afraid I only made it worse.

The bags underneath his eyes are deeper in the flickering dark. His beard looks soft to the touch but hollows his cheeks. He sits across from me on the stump he dragged to our camp, elbows propped on his knees, hands hanging between his legs.

There's something that's eating him up from the inside, and the catalyst I've tried to avoid confronting comes to a head.

"What did my dad say to you?" I ask a little sharper than I intended.

Something like guilt flickers with the firelight in his eyes.

"Shit." He swallows, then swipes a hand down his face. "It wasn't so much your dad." My nose wrinkles in confusion as he continues, "It was your mom."

"My *mom*?" I chuckle. "What on earth could she have—"

The words lodge in my throat as he slips a pill bottle from his jeans pocket. The one Benoit carried.

Dammit.

Orion turns it over in his hands, idly studying it, then holds it up between his index finger and thumb.

His voice is rough when he finally speaks. "Why didn't you tell me you have bipolar disorder?"

For the first time in days, I'm speechless. My tongue literally won't move, my lips glued together, teeth clenched. My burning cheeks have nothing to do with the fire.

But he doesn't relent, waiting patiently as ever.

I swallow. "She told you?"

He nods, then lightly tosses the pill bottle from one hand to the other.

"That wasn't her story to tell," I snap, grasping for anger, indignation, anything other than humiliation I *know* I shouldn't feel.

"Nah, don't give me that," he chides. "She's a momma worried about her daughter. And she wouldn't have had to tell me"—he points with the pill bottle, voice firm—"if *you* had. So..." His voice gentles. "Why didn't you?"

My tongue stays stuck to the roof of my mouth.

He rolls his lips between his teeth, gears clearly turning as he tries to figure me out.

"You know you don't have to be... embarrassed, right? I care about you. In my family, marriage means what's mine is yours and what's yours is mine. Good. Bad. Sick. Healthy. I'm there for it all."

My heart takes flight, words that are way too freaking soon to say bounce around my mind, and not an ounce of pushback is left in me.

He takes my silence as encouragement, continuing, "And if anyone ever does make you feel embarrassed, I'll fuck them up. Having a disorder ain't nothing to be ashamed of."

"I'm not embarrassed about having bipolar disorder," I insist, but my eyes drop to the fire. "That's not it."

"Then what is it? Come on, baby, talk to me."

I bite my lip, then release it slowly.

"I was embarrassed because... I've never *had* to tell anyone about my bipolar disorder."

My eyes flick to his furrowed brow and pursed lips. The back of my neck burns as I force the truth out, starting from the beginning so hopefully he'll understand.

"My family and friends know. It's no big deal with them. Genetics sometimes play a part, so my parents were on notice that either Nox or I—or both of us—could have it. Nox hasn't shown symptoms, but we figured out mine pretty early after a rough go of it at eighteen."

I idly brush away a crunchy brown leaf caught in the tulle of my tutu as my knee bounces at a frenzied tempo.

"We figured out meds, gathered a good medical team. Dance helps channel my energy and gives me a routine. My symptoms have been mild, all things considered. I'm lucky too. I have support that a lot of people don't have. I couldn't do it without my family, my friends... not to mention my psych is also a therapist, and I trust that saint with *all* my secrets. Which, I mean, aren't that many. I'm kind of an open book. Lies are just another thing to stress over."

Shame itches under my skin about what I have to say next.

"So when I felt the hypomania coming on this week, I sort of freaked out. I thought I could white-knuckle through it. Ride it out until we got back to civilization and skip the whole 'woe is me, I have a mental health condition' convo. I've never *had* to have the conversation. It's the first time I've failed at taking care of myself."

"Luna, you didn't fail."

My head shakes. "Logically, I *know* that. It's just that, I've seen people find out my mom was bipolar because she was mid-episode." Tracing the dirt, I admit my worst fear. "People look at you differently when you tell them while you're sick versus when you tell them while you're well."

"What do you mean?" he asks.

"Well, they look at me like..." I lift my gaze to find Orion's brow furrowed and his wary eyes waiting for my answer. "Kind of the way you are right now, if I'm honest."

His jaw goes slack, then he shakes his head hard.

"I don't see you differently because of this. I mean, sure, it fits together a few puzzle pieces I hadn't realized were missing. But I love finding those."

"Then why are you looking at me like you don't know whether I'm going to pop off or break down?" I counter.

He winces. "If anything, what you're seeing is me pissed at myself. You felt that you couldn't trust me with this—why would you after what I've put you through? And besides that, you shouldn't have *had* to tell me. I should've put the pieces together."

I frown as he rakes a hand through his hair, gripping his nape before gesturing toward me with a defeated exhale.

"I know everything about you, birdie. Literally everything." His voice softens. "At least, I'm supposed to."

His lips quirk up at my scowl. "Go on and be irritated if you want, but don't act like you don't love it."

I roll my eyes, and he chuckles, though it fades fast. He glares at the fire like it'll tell him what to say next. The flames pop twice, making him flinch before he finally speaks.

"This week, I knew something was off. But I chalked it up to stress. Or me being an asshole that deserved a good ass-kicking."

I snort. "You're not *wrong*."

His fleeting grin makes my heart skip, then vanishes. "Point being, I missed this, and I shouldn't have."

"It's not your fault. My family and I kept it under wraps pretty good," I say with a shrug. "Like I said, I've managed it well."

"Well, for the record, I'll probably feel shitty about the way everything's gone down for the rest of our lives."

Before I can joke, agree, or even argue, he blows out a breath. "Alright. You managed it well before I came along. Let's keep the streak alive, yeah? I already fucked up enough with you this week."

I wrinkle my nose at that, but he keeps going, tapping the bottle lightly. "What's the dosage on these? Can you take one now?"

I hesitate. I *just* told him I was okay. Will I sound like I'm lying if I say no?

Trust him. Go with the truth.

"I..." God, I hope he believes me. "I can't take them."

He eyes me. Concern and ember shadows carve deep lines across his brow before he pleads. "Come on, baby..."

"I'm not on birth control."

His head jerks. "What does that have to do with anything?"

"What if..." I worry my lip. "What if we've made a baby? You never know."

"I hope we did." A smile tugs at his mouth, and my stomach flutters with need. Then that smile turns wicked. "You'll be a lot less of a pain in the ass to catch if you're waddling away from me down the aisle with a beach ball under your gown."

I don't laugh, though, and he sobers fast, clearing his throat before asking the right question. "But what does being pregnant have to do with your medicine..."

Understanding softens his face. He shakes his head. "Baby, it's so early, that's not even on my radar. I don't think we need to worry about that."

"How could you know?"

"I *don't* know, but I do know that you're what matters most to me. Don't get me wrong, anything we create between us matters to me too. But you're the most important person in my life. Whatever you need to do for your health, I want—no, I *need* you to do it. So please. Take the medicine."

My skin tingles at everything he's saying, all the right words. It's not enough, though.

"I'm already coming down. I can feel it. And we'll make it to Benoit's car by tomorrow afternoon, right? Where we'll probably have good cell service again?"

He keeps studying me as he slides my friend's phone out, then thumbs through the screen. "We should."

"Then I'll be fine. You may not be worried, but *I* need to know. I can wait another day to call my psych." His lips thin, and my voice gentles. "Respect this. Please. I already have to fight for that sometimes with this disorder, even against people with the best intentions. I don't want to have to fight for it with you too."

His shoulders slump as my plea seems to break through to him.

"Okay, baby. I trust you. But if I feel like it's something you're not catching yourself, will you trust *me*?"

I give him an earnest nod that ends in a laugh. "No problem. I already have that setup with everyone else. I suppose for the man that knows 'everything' about me, I should give *some* thought to your opinion."

"Yeah, yeah." He pockets the pill bottle, rolling his eyes.

I give him a cheeky grin. "What? Don't blame me. *You're* the creep."

It's a joke, but I swear, even in the firelight, Orion's tan face pales. His eyes drop but not before I catch some awful, horrible emotion crumpling his face.

I freeze. "What is it?"

He refuses to look at me, studying the ground and curling in on himself as he nervously pops each lettered knuckle.

"Orion?"

When he finally looks up, his eyes are glassy with tears, and my heart drops to my stomach.

"Luna, did I..." he clears his throat, but his voice is still ragged. "Did I take advantage of you?"

"*What?*" I blurt, nearly laughing, but I keep my reaction sort of in check. "Where the hell did you get that idea?"

Okay, not in check at all, but *seriously?*

He swallows, his eyes dropping again. "Something your mom said."

"Oh my *God*," I growl my frustration, leaping up and off my seat with all the angry energy thrumming in my veins. "I'm gonna shoot that messenger right in her dainty little damn foot." I'm pacing the fire's edge when I turn on him. "What could she have possibly said that would make you think you—"

I stop, my blood running cold. All the fight leaves my posture, and my voice softens. "She told you about the lowered sexual inhibitions part."

He nods once, eyes still on the ground.

I round the fire slowly and kneel in front of him, taking his hands. They tighten around mine like his been desperate to hold me, and he finally meets my gaze.

"Orion," I murmur, keeping my tone careful but firm. "Listen to me loud and clear. And if there's ever something you need to trust me on, it's this, alright?"

His multicolored eyes blaze in the light like a forest fire, begging me to tell him he's wrong. I lick my lips nervously, hoping what I say next resonates so he never, ever has that question again.

"Everything... *everything* we did, I wanted. Do you understand?"

Hope glimmers across his destroyed expression as the tightness around his eyes and jaw eases.

"My inhibitions might be lowered, but they're still *my* feelings. *My* desires. I've tracked my disorder like my life depends on it. I know the difference between being impulsive and unsafe and being run-of-the-mill reckless Luna," I joke, but it lands flat, so I squeeze his large hands, brushing my thumbs along the glossy scars. "What we did together was none of those. I haven't regretted a single thing with you. Ever."

A hard swallow trails down his throat as he leans forward, silently hanging on every word.

"I wanted you last year when you gave me my first kiss on my birthday and I was totally healthy."

His eyes glint with memory, and I smile.

"I wanted you the night you asked me to dance, before any symptoms even showed."

His face darkens now with the same hesitant hunger burning in my lower belly. My heart pounds as I release his hands to place mine on his hard thighs, sliding closer to the heat radiating from him.

"I wanted you when you came inside me under the waterfall..."

"*Fuck*, Luna," he mutters through clenched teeth. His hands fist on his knees, but he lets me keep exploring.

I breathe deeply, getting my nerves under control. His gaze flicks to my breasts nearly spilling out of my bodice, then back to my lips, landing on my eyes with reverent softness.

"And I wanted you when I *begged* you to claim me in the forest."

He growls low, and his hands slip beneath the jacket, finding the curve of my waist.

"And I want you right now."

Closing the gap between us, I kiss him without hesitation. My nails dig into his jeans as I bite his lip then soften the nip with my tongue. A curse rumbles from his chest, vibrating the air between us as he pulls me into his heat, flush against his hardening cock. He lifts my face to deepen the kiss, curving around me for a better angle, his tongue dancing with mine in a pas de deux of sexual tension and need.

I sneak my fingers under his shirt, willing them not to tremble despite my excitement and anticipation. My nails scratch his abs, and he groans as I follow down the light trail of hair leading to his waistband.

He kisses me like my truth healed his soul, and maybe it did. His singular obsession with consuming me means he doesn't even register when I unbuckle him. Not until I drag my lips from his. He tries to move with me, but he seems to finally realize I've already unbuttoned his jeans, and he starts as I slowly draw his zipper down.

I whisper against his lips, and he shudders when I repeat a version of what he said a lifetime ago in the dressing room.

"Let me show you. Just. How. *Fucking*. Badly. I want *every-thing* with you, Orion Fury."

29
BEGGING FOR HIM
ORION

This is a bad idea. Right?

But with Luna looking up at me like this? For the life of me, I can't remember why.

My wife kneels before me in the firelight, every bit a sinful angel worshiping her devil. Embers cast her silhouette in gold and smoke. Her full pout glistens, tongue peeking out to lick her lips, and her cherry cola hair burns in a hellfire halo around her flushed face. My leather jacket drapes over her shoulders, its shadows darkening her stained, feathered bodice, while her dirty tulle skirt spreads around her. She's my black swan on her knees for her black-hearted Fury. I don't deserve it, I don't deserve her, but somehow she sees me for the villain I am and still finds me worthy.

Fuck, I'm about to lose every ounce of good, goddamn, gentlemanly sense I've ever had.

She told me to trust her, and she does seem better, the symptoms having eased before my eyes since the graveyard.

So if my wife says sucking my cock is what she wants, then my cock is gonna be what my wife fucking gets.

She finishes unzipping my jeans but doesn't free me yet. Instead, her nails drag up my abs, scratching over my ribs, pecs, and teasing me until I rip my shirt off over my head. The night air prickles goosebumps across my skin before her warm palms smooth them down.

Her hands pause on the tattoo at my side, nails tracing the dancing skeleton ballerina.

"This one's for me, isn't it?"

The quiet question comes out unsure even though she has to know the truth by now. She's always been mine. Her eyes are wide with awe, softening in a way that cracks me open.

My voice comes out deeper than I've ever heard it. "Everything's for you."

She bites her lip, and the sight makes me throb at the base of my cock. Emboldened, she digs her nails into my skin harder, dragging them lower, somehow already knowing I like the pain. The fact that she's learning me, reading my body like a dance she's rehearsed in secret, damn near undoes me.

Her touch trails the lines of my Adonis belt to the edge of my boxer briefs. Delicate fingers tremble over my hard bulge as she curves them around the elastic. The tremor is slight, but it reverberates in my veins and ricochets doubt in my mind. What does hesitance mean? Anticipation? Fear?

I catch her hands. "You don't have to do this."

"Are you *kidding*?" She huffs a laugh that releases the tension in my chest. "I need your cock in my mouth, or I'll perish this very instant."

But then she adds sheepishly, "I've... never done this before."

Relief washes through me, with overwhelming desire flooding in right on its heels.

Of course I knew that, but god*damn* does it still sound good. I've already claimed her, but something about this being entirely her decision? It hits differently. It's trust and vulnerability all wrapped up in one gorgeous, stunning, breakable piece she's never given anyone else. Another gift, and I'm going to treat it with the reverence it deserves.

My heart pounds so hard I swear it echoes through the forest as I take her hands, steadying us both.

"Remember, neither have I, birdie. Anything you do will blow my mind, trust me on that."

She licks her lips, and my cock jolts behind my briefs.

"Can you... show me what you might like then?"

Christ. If I could lay her down and devour every inch of her, I would, right fucking now.

But that's not what she wants, and with her hands in mine, familiarity teases my mind. I've held them like this before. Once when I led her across a shimmering lake dance floor at Masque, and again on the worn, firelit floorboards at the cabin. I've always led her in our dance. It makes every sense to lead her in this too.

So I nod.

"I'll show you everything."

My fingers guide hers, tugging my boxer briefs down over my painfully hard length. Her eyes widen when I spring free, glistening at the tip. Firelight licks every vein and ridge that wrecked her yesterday, making her come over and over again during my claiming.

It takes me a minute to remember she's never seen me this close, never even held me. The way she takes me in right now is a heady sensation, making me feel like I'm actually worth a damn. Maybe with her, I can be.

Her tongue slips out to wet her lips again, and she lets me circle her careful fingers around my hot length, one hand stacked over the other. Her fingertips don't quite meet as I stroke them up and down my cock. I hiss when I round her palm over my crown, sparks ripping through me already. Her eyes flick up to mine, watching me, no doubt mentally noting every muscle twitch of pleasure, just like I do with her. I don't look away as I show her exactly how to give me what I want.

"Stroke me like this. Don't be gentle," I murmur, tightening her grip. "Fuck, that's it. Almost as tight as your pretty cunt was for me yesterday."

"Only for you," she breathes.

My pulse stutters, and I grit out. "You've got that right."

She takes over, and I gather her curls in one hand. They

slide like silk over my knuckles as I twist the mass of them around my fist at the base of her head. My other hand cups her jaw.

"You ready to take me, sweet wife?"

She shivers, then nods.

"Good girl. Hold me at the base… open for me."

My thumb presses her chin down and she obeys, lips parting as her hands shift lower on my shaft, waiting for my lead. Her trust in me builds heat in my chest, pulsing through every vein, already full to the brim with need for her.

"Tell me again you want me, Luna," I beg.

"I want you, Orion."

No hesitation, just like when I claimed her. But the eagerness in her eyes is also like the time I came inside her under the waterfall, when I feasted on her in the dressing room, and when I kissed her on her birthday. She was telling the truth. She's wanted me in every single moment we've been together.

And now? I've dreamt about those words for so long, and she's finally brought them to life. Making me believe that maybe, *maybe* I didn't fuck this up beyond repair. Maybe she can love me too.

The last bit of concern leaves my body on an exhale.

"Thank fuck," I mutter.

I cover her hands, angling myself into her mouth. Her lips close around the head, and the first wet heat of her tongue—

"Shit. Wait—" I choke out, pulling her off too abruptly, but I was about to lose it.

She sucks in a breath, uncertainty tightening her features. "Did I do it wrong already?"

"No," I groan. "Hell, no. It's just that, last night? It was all I could do not to blow the second I slid into your perfect cunt. The only reason I lasted more than two pumps was because I needed to make it good for you." I shake my head. "I won't make it tonight unless you go easy on me."

She blinks in confusion. Then challenge sparks in her eyes,

and her smile slowly shifts into something absolutely, positively wicked.

Oh, fuck.

"Luna," I growl in warning.

Her lips latch around the head of my cock, and I fucking *whimper*, my whole body jolting like she's a live wire. I hiss through my teeth as she sinks down, stopping where her fingers cover the base of my shaft. My head tips back with a moan I don't bother holding back.

"Shit, shit, shit, *Luna*."

My fist tightens in her hair, my other hand flying to the back of her head as I surge forward, unthinking and overwhelmed. But my girl takes me, her mouth made for my cock. She breathes steady, tongue twirling over my crown, and my thighs lock beneath her.

I try to pull away, I *need* to pull away or this will be over before it's started, but she's not done. She cups my balls, massaging them with tenderness I didn't know I needed, while her other hand claws into my upper thigh. The sting is electric, shocking every nerve, pulsing in sync.

She teases this sweet spot I didn't even know I fucking had, and I nearly black out.

"Jesus Christ, little bird," I groan. "Where did you learn to do that?"

She only shrugs, like she doesn't realize she's making me come undone just by instinct. That thought alone almost does me in.

I force myself to slow her, gently pulling her off. Her lips slide wetly along my length, tongue teasing the underside all the way up until she comes away with a *pop*. I'm shaking as I keep her in place, my fingers firm on her chin.

"Okay, baby. You gotta slow down. You're making it too good, too quick. I don't want to spill down your throat. My cum only goes in your pussy, got it?"

Her eyes flare, but ultimately she nods.

"Got it," she agrees hoarsely.

I swallow then guide her back down. She goes eagerly, eyes locked on mine, her hand back to gripping my base while the other continues teasing everywhere else.

We find our deliberate, tight, mind-blowing rhythm, and I massage her scalp as I set the pace.

"There you go, that's my good fucking girl," I murmur, almost mindless, the praise coming so easily. "Nice and slow, just like that. You're so good at sucking your husband's cock, aren't you?"

She gazes up through long lashes, lust-filled pupils swallowing the irises surrounding them. Instead of pushing back, my sassy vixen stays submissive, finally letting me worship my wife while she worships me. The sight steals my strength, my legs trembling and my breaths quickening. If she wasn't before me right now, I'd be in her place, kneeling at her altar in one stuttering heartbeat.

In the eyes of everything that truly matters to me, this forest, these mountains, the Fury legacy, she's not just finally home with me, she *is* my home.

Anyone from here feels the roots deep in our bones, no matter how far we wander. The blue mountains are a tether, pulling us back with the same certainty as the river running through these hills. The fact *my home* is where her instincts led her to safety yesterday told me all I needed.

"You ran to me yesterday, to my land," I whisper, brushing her curls back from her temple. "All on your own, you found Dark Corner like it calls to you the way it calls to me. Fury territory was your safe space. And when I found you here, goddamn, I was proud. Your soul knows where it belongs. With *me*."

Her eyes soften, and she hums her agreement around me, her throat opening as my cock nudges the back. She tries to slide down further, but gags, and I still her movements with a light tap to her jaw.

"Easy. You don't have to take all of me. Even this is already about as much as I can handle."

I know fuck all about directing this show, but like everything else between us, we're acting on instinct and raw, desperate need.

Which is exactly what ignites when her whole body relaxes, even her throat, and she sucks. Me. *Down*. All the way to the base.

Both my fists now grip her hair as I barely hold still. My girl somehow knows how to deepthroat, and I'm out of my damn mind.

"The way you worship your husband's cock is sinful, wife."

Her moan vibrates around me as I lose it, panting, trembling, teetering on the edge. My hips jerk forward, thrusting into her as she works me faster, every tight muscle in her throat squeezing the life out of every inch of me. My body begs to finish in her mouth. But I can't. I refuse.

"*Fuckkkkk*. Okay, that's enough. I need your pussy."

I try to pull her off, but her lips tighten around my base, and she swallows against my head.

"*Luna*," I choke, every muscle locking against the pleasure as she bobs her head faster and faster, my abs seizing until I'm left with no choice but to give in.

I drive deeper, mouthfucking my wife like she was made for it. She's my first, I'm hers, in *everything*, and primal possession pumps in my veins, desperate to mark every inch of her inside and out.

Tears well at the corners of her eyes, dripping down, and I love the sight of her crying for my ecstasy. But when she fights me mid-thrust, I stop instantly... only for her to swallow against my tip one... last... time.

"*Luna!*" I roar, plunging into her, filling her throat with my length.

She can't breathe. Somewhere in the back of my mind I know that. But neither can I.

Hot jets of cum pulse through me, and I feel each drop as it spills down her throat. My hips stutter every time she swallows, my vision fading at the edges, my muscles losing all strength as I become helpless under my wife's power over me.

When my locked muscles finally release, I zero back on Luna and find her face darkened in the firelight, her features strained from lack of oxygen.

"Jesus."

I tug her off me, and she gasps, my slick cock popping free from her swollen lips. The chilly air envelops my hot length, making me shudder, but I'm already lifting Luna and straddling her over my lap, savoring her warmth. Spent or not, my cock twitches against her heat, bare for me since her panties became nothing but a memory after I tore them off in the bog.

"You broke the rules," I tsk, only half-pissed. "I said my cum goes in my wife's cunt."

"Better punish me then." Her voice is roughened from taking me so deep, and her giggle vibrates against my chest as I pull her flush to me. "I couldn't resist drinking you down. Guess all those shots taught me something."

I chuckle, sliding my hands up her thighs and past the garter that's somehow held on through everything.

"My reckless, *bratty* little bird, what am I gonna do with you, huh?"

She licks her swollen lips, eyelids heavy as she meets my gaze. "Fuck me... *husband*."

"Anything for you, wife," I vow and stroke her clit with my cock, her words alone hardening me for another round. Her breath hitches as the head circles that sensitive bundle of nerves, then I position myself at her entrance, teasing her. "You feel me? You feel how fucking hard I get for you? This is what happens when your husband waits for you. I already need you again. Hell, I'll *never* get enough of you. But let me make sure you're ready for me, hm?"

I plunge two fingers into her soaked cunt, making her moan. My mouth closes over my deep purple and blue claiming mark at her collarbone, sucking hard. She grinds against my palm at her clit, and I murmur against her skin.

"Patience. I'll take care of you."

I drag my fingers from her channel, line my cock at her core, then grip her hip to guide her—

I freeze.

The hairs on the back of my neck stand straight.

I don't know how I know, but something's not right.

No... it's not just that.

Something's out there. Something that doesn't belong.

Something *watching*.

30

THE WOODS HAVE EYES

ORION

L una stills, lips on my jaw, breath caught.

"Ori—"

"Shh, baby," I breathe, voice low in her ear. "Don't stop."

Her body trembles as she forces it to relax, molding tighter to mine, arms slipping between us but keeping my hands free. She peppers quiet kisses down my throat like nothing's wrong, tucking my now deflating cock back into my boxers with shaky breaths but steady fingers.

She buttons, buckles, zips, all with slow, *silent* care. Her hips roll over me like we're fucking, while I palm the garter around her thigh, reminding her what I gave her. My other hand slips into the inside pocket of my jacket.

I pull back, cup her nape, and kiss her hard enough to pull a real moan from her—

My gun's drawn before leaves rustle behind her.

"This is a courtesy," I growl into the dark, my other hand cradling the back of Luna's head and holding her to my chest. "Come on out, or you're dead."

I scan the trees, keeping Luna close, my aim steady.

Chick-chick.

A shotgun.

Behind me.

Luna sucks in a breath and goes rigid with fear.

I hold her tighter, curving over her body, shielding her as best I can with my gun still aimed forward.

Out of the corner of my eye, a bearded man with brown hair and a shit-eating grin steps into view, a sawed-off shotgun level with Luna's face.

"Oh, don't stop on our account," he drawls with an accent like mine. "But how 'bout you go on and drop that gun before getting to the good part, yeah? I'd hate to see Bordeaux's pride and joy bleed out all over Fury scum. Killing a pretty thing like that would be a waste of a good cunt if you ask me. Don't you agree, cousin?"

Rage boils under my skin, but fear for Luna's life douses it as good as ice water. I ease my finger off the trigger, lifting the pistol skyward, my jaw still clenched tightly. My other hand releases Luna, dragging away from her to slowly rise in surrender.

Leaves whisper in the darkness I aimed at, and a tall, broad shadow in blacked-out camo finally emerges.

Bart. Fucking. Wilde.

He locks his pistol on me and whistles. "Y'all were putting on *quite* the show."

Luna shudders. She's still straddling me, covered by my jacket draped over her shoulders but still terrifyingly vulnerable before these monsters. Her thighs tighten around my hips, doing anything to shield her exposed flesh. The fact that *I* turned her into prey by not paying attention, by destroying the only scrap of fabric that could've concealed her, all because I couldn't control myself... It hollows my chest out worse than the shotgun next to me ever could.

"Too bad we can't finish the porno," the other Wilde sneers. "Go on, girl. Put his shirt on. We don't wanna be seeing all that."

Luna's fingers tremble as she gathers my shirt and yanks it over my head, so fast my glare only breaks for a blink. She tugs the sleeves down my arms and torso, movements efficient despite her shaking hands. I ache to ease her fear, to end these two bastards for putting that terror in her eyes, but I have to keep my head on straight and focus on our captors.

"Hurry up," the Wilde barks. "We've got places to be."

Bart gives us a wolfish grin. "And a wedding to attend. *Mine.*"

My stomach lurches. "The fuck are y'all talking ab—"

The butt of the shotgun cracks against my skull. White-hot pain explodes behind my eyes, shattering my vision, and Luna's scream pierces through the ringing in my ears.

Then everything goes dark as rough black fabric scratches down my face.

"Stop! Get off him—*Ah!*"

She's torn from my lap, and I roar, lunging for her blindly, but something pierces my left shoulder. I stagger at the impact, landing hard on my knees, head reeling.

Luna shrieks a curse, igniting new hatred in me, and I claw the sack off my head. I don't know where my gun went, so I reach for my crossbow instead, but...

...my left arm...

It won't. Fucking. Move.

I grit my teeth, trying again, but it hangs uselessly at my side.

Not even a twitch.

Luna struggles across the fire against both Wildes, my jacket ripped away as she fights tooth and claw. She's *right there* and I can do nothing to help her. And her screams... they're so far away.

What the hell is happening?

My heartbeat thunders in my ears. I reach behind me with my other arm, fighting the numbness. My fingers brush the hilt of something foreign lodged in my deltoid. A dart. A *tranquilizer* dart.

Fuck.

My mind shouts against the darkness pressing in, nerves sparking and misfiring as my body turns traitor. I twist to wrench the dart free, but I can't control my grip. Luna shrieks again, followed by a grunt that isn't hers.

She's fighting back.

Equal parts relief and terror flood through me.

"*Orion!*"

"Luna..." I inch forward, searing my palm on hot coals, but I keep moving. "I'm—"

A boot slams into my ribs, and a sharp *crack* drives me into the mud, gasping through the pain. I draw a ragged breath and reach for her, only to close around something soft, a point at the end.

A feather. It's one of hers, stained black, bent, and ripped from her bodice.

Protect her. Protect her. Protect her.

It's the mantra I swore to years ago. It's all I've ever done, all I know. And it's always worked.

Until now.

"Stop! You're hurting him! Orion, please get up. You have to—"

Her voice cuts off on a scream.

"Leave her alone! Take me!" I roar into the night, but my plea is swallowed by the woods and the sudden flapping of wings.

"I'm okay," she gasps, suddenly at my side. "It's okay. Stay with me. No—don't! Please don't—"

A final kick slams into my skull.

"*Orion!*"

The last thing I hear is the woman I love begging for my life.

31
THE QUEEN

LUNA

The black bag comes off with a harsh *whoosh*, yanking on strands of my tangled hair. Half-blind, I kick the bastard in front of me, slamming my foot right in his dick.

He jolts, clutching himself as he crumples to his knees on a pathetic, high-pitched keen. I rear back to strike again, but an iron grip jerks me backward against a broad chest that reeks of sweat and cigarette smoke.

Bart.

"Where the *hell* is Orion?" I scream at him over my shoulder, swinging my legs anyway, not caring that pain shoots up my ankle like I'm learning pointe all over again.

My victim, the other bearded brute that helped kidnap me, wheezes. "You. *Bitch—*"

"*Travis*, you best stop right there."

A woman's voice cracks like a whip, freezing me in place. "You ain't above a whupping, even at your age."

I blink several times until my eyes adjust to the dim lantern glow, revealing the white painted wooden walls of a chapel. My gaze lands on a single pew with armrests. It's more throne than church seat, made all the more surreal by the regal woman holding court from it.

She's perched like a wise, elderly queen, so ancient I'd believe it if she'd been here longer than the Appalachian Mountains themselves. Her pale, gnarled hands rest on a hooked cane, and she wears a prim, black dress buttoned to her chin, faded blonde hair wound tightly into a bun at her collar.

"Excuse him, baby," she drawls, her cadence and accent eerily like Orion's. "My boys know better than to speak ill of women and the dead. But even though he's one of my grandbabies, his momma ain't raised him right. Just look at that unkempt beard. Hairier than Bigfoot." She ends with a disapproving click of her tongue.

Beside her, an older, barrel-chested, clean-shaven guard grumbles. "Now that ain't nice neither, Mama."

She glares up at the man nearly twice her height. "Ain't my fault, son. You married her even after I told you she weren't right for the Wildes."

Her rheumy blue eyes narrow at the drama king still rolling on the floor. "Apologize, Travvie-boy."

He groans. "Sorry... Mama Bossie."

Oh. My brows shoot up, eyes darting from him to her. So *this* is Bossie Wilde.

The frail woman stretches slowly—her frame all skin and bone—then whacks her cane across Travis's back with enough force that he cries out and I flinch. Maybe Orion's "bit of a ruthless bitch" description was an understatement. Gotta admit, I'd be impressed if I wasn't a little terrified.

"Don't apologize to me, fool." She points her cane at me. "To our guest."

"Ugh... sorry, Luna," he rasps.

Bossie's eyes land on me again, full of wry amusement as she sits back again.

"Men never do learn, do they? That's why us womenfolk gotta stick together." She juts her chin at Bart. "Let her go, Barty. She ain't gonna cause no trouble now. Are you, child?"

My heart pounds like I've taken another high dive off a short cliff. There's more than a hint of warning in her question, and my eyes flick to her bone-white knuckles tightening around her cane.

I shake my head.

Bart releases me roughly from his meaty grip, and I stumble toward her.

"Careful! Goodness gracious, Barty, you're gonna break the poor girl. She a little bitty ol' thing already…"

I stay silent as she berates him for manhandling me, taking in my surroundings and trying to figure out my best play.

We're on a church stage with dingy red carpet and warped wood that creaks beneath our feet. Wind rattles through the slatted walls like the chapel itself is breathing through cracked ribs. Smoke stains climb toward the rafters from flickering lantern sconces, their light casting shadows in the corners like restless spirits. Behind Bossie, the faded imprint of a cross is flanked by arched stained glass windows, their biblical tableaus fractured to hell. A small plaque near the lectern catches my eye.

Whitby Rose Chapel

My stomach drops.

The church by the graveyard where Orion's family is buried… The shadows I saw in the forest that day weren't ghosts. They were Wildes, and they followed us from here back to the cabin.

Where they killed Benny.

Anger blasts through me, incinerating any semblance of my self-control over "my best play."

Concern deepens Bossie's sun-weathered wrinkles, her grandmotherly smile returning. "How you doin', baby? They treat you nice on the way here?"

I square my shoulders, lifting my chin.

"Oh, they treated me fine for being *kidnapped*." My voice cracks with rage. "Where. Is. Orion?"

Bossie eyes me for a beat before a raspy chuckle huffs out of her, churning my stomach. "Shoo-wee, Barty. You gon' have a *time* with this one."

"It'll be my pleasure to break her, ma'am." He snickers behind my back, his tone mocking. "Although judging by that bite mark, looks like she's already been rode hard and put up wet. It might take a while to get the Fury stench out."

My blood runs cold, but I refuse to let them see me shudder, so I seethe. "Fuck you, Bart—"

"Nah-ah-ah, I won't allow that language from you neither, missy." Bossie tsks, lifting her cane, silencing me. "And no whining now. You could've had the nice one. Ozias would've been good to you. But he ain't here, and I wouldn't ask him to be." She glares daggers over my shoulder. "Not after the Furys stole his smile."

I follow her gaze—

My world shatters like the stained glass around us.

"*Orion?*" I whimper.

He's slumped in a chair, his ankles roped to the legs and wrists bound together in front of him.

My feet move on their own, heart pounding painfully behind my sternum.

He's not moving. He's not moving. He's not—

"Orion?"

Tears blur my vision.

Is he...

"No!" I scream, lunging for him, but I'm yanked back. "Let me go! Let me—"

He stirs, and my shouts die on my lips.

"Orion?"

His head lifts slowly like it's too heavy to hold up. He blinks, eyes glassy and lost as he searches the room.

"You're... *alive*," I cry, my knees buckling with relief. "You're alive. Thank God."

But he's barely able to sit up straight, breaths shallow, blood glistening a sickeningly pretty crimson on his black shirt. A man stands on either side of him, one aiming Orion's crossbow at his back, the other scowling with his arms crossed, pistol loose in his grip like he knows Orion is in no shape to fight back.

Not yet, you bastard.

I saw Travis Wilde shove the loose dart into his shoulder, and I also saw it jam before Travis could fully depress the plunger. *If I can just stall...*

Orion's gaze locks on me, and he exhales. "Luna?"

My heart strains to go to him, but I force myself to stand still so Bart's grip doesn't tighten further.

"I'm here. It's okay. You're alive. We both are."

"Alive," Bossie spits, unleashing her anger. "Unlike my grand-baby, Rufus."

Orion zeroes his focus on Bossie as he growls, "You mean the 'grandbaby' that drugged Luna?"

Bossie waves him off. "He did what had to be done. Ozias had his plan to win her over." She rolls her eyes. "That boy never had it in him, though. The fool fancies himself *in love* with someone else already."

My breath catches at the confirmation, but before I can fully register that information, Bart sneers bitterly.

"If he'd just taken her from the start, my brother would still be alive. The Bordeaux branch of the Troisgarde would've been secured ages ago. Instead, Rufus and I had to step in and grease the wheels, so to speak."

"Wait," I blurt, putting things together. "Did Ozias have anything to do with drugging me?"

"Nope. That was all me and Rufus," Bart answers so casually, I want to stab him. "Goody Two-shoes should've at least done what the Fury did."

He jerks his chin at Orion, speaking to him, "You're more a Wilde than he is, far as I'm concerned."

Bossie slams the bottom of her cane on the floor, splintering the rotten wood through a shredded hole in the carpet.

"I'll have none of that talk now. Kin is kin. You know that."

"But see? All that means Ozias wouldn't have wanted this," I try, grasping for her humanity. "He's nice and kind and—"

"Weak," Bossie finishes flatly. "And this feud ain't for the weak. He knew what had to be done to make up for his branch's sins, and he failed. He'll live with that. He also understands life for life. Blood for blood. And after all the bodies that boy—" she jabs her cane toward Orion "—left behind in Lost Cove, if Ozias doesn't see our side by now, he never will. And we ain't got no use for him."

There it is. The wolf beneath the grandmotherly skin. The matriarch even the Furys fear.

This time, I can't hold back my shiver at the coldness in her eyes.

"It's within our rights to call on the lives of both of you," she hisses at me, the venom in her voice turns my blood to sludge. "And we will."

"No!" Orion strains forward against the ropes. "You won't touch her!"

The guy with the gun smashes his fist into Orion's jaw, snapping his head sideways.

"Orion!"

"I'm okay, birdie," he huffs, forcing himself upright. He works his mouth, then spits blood at the man who hit him.

"You motherfu—" The man cocks his arm back again, but a high-pitched whistle through Bossie's teeth halts him mid-swing.

"Cut that out, you two," she says in a tired, even tone. Then she pins Orion with a look like she's scolding him for acting out during Sunday service. "Don't worry. Our proposition is more than fair. She's not the one we want dead."

She fixes her eyes on me, spiking my pulse. "We've decided to go a more... creative route."

"What are you going on about, Bossie?" Orion snaps.

Bossie's lips curve. "We want her to pledge her life to the Wildes."

Orion scoffs, "That's fucking worse."

Bossie sighs, a barely-there wheeze in her lungs. "Looks like you got as much sense as your daddy, boy." She nods toward the other guard behind him. "Go ahead, Vaughn."

He cracks the butt of the crossbow into the back of Orion's skull. I smother my shriek as he slumps forward, only breathing again when he hisses and lifts his eyes to mine.

Bossie drums her fingers on the hook of her cane. "Now, is everyone gonna behave? Fury, you're alive for one reason, and I won't have you acting out in front of our other guests."

My skin prickles. "Other guests?"

"Haven't you figured it out, child? There's gonna be a wedding." She leans toward me like she's letting me in on a secret. "And *you* are the lucky bride."

My jaw falls slack.

She chuckles. "Your little outfit's already white and everything."

Her eyes scan my black and crimson stained swan costume. "Almost anyway."

Anger and fear vibrate through me, but before I can scream, run, fight, do *anything* at all, the chapel doors slam open, banging against the walls.

Every weapon shifts toward the two men barreling in like they're ready to set the world aflame. One's the dangerous King of New Orleans, the Phantom of the French Quarter himself, rage carved into his scarred face. The other, NOLA's prince, his father's furious, lethal spitting image.

Despite the knives raised, the guns cocked, and the crossbow aimed, Solomon Bordeaux strides in, staring them all down without flinching. Thunder rumbles, vibrating the walls as he stops in the center and growls.

"What the *fuck* is going on?"

32

A STORM AT WHITBY ROSE

LUNA

"Daddy? Nox?" I breathe.

Nox looks murderous, and my dad's chest heaves like he's run through fire just to burn everything down behind him. Which, considering his history, wouldn't be that off-brand.

"Ah, Mr. Bordeaux." Bossie claps once, her time-worn voice syrupy sweet like a Southern belle at brunch. "Everyone simmer down now."

All weapons lower a fraction, but the air stays charged, like the chapel holds its breath right along with me.

"So glad you got my invitation, Solomon."

"You mean this?" Dad lifts bloody stationary between two fingers, his hand slightly trembling. Not from cold or fear. From *rage*.

A pit forms in my stomach as he snarls, "You've got a lot of nerve, Ruth."

"Call me Bossie, hon. Everyone does," she chuckles, but he ignores her.

"You left this on one of my men's bodies. A man *you* killed." His hard voice falters. "A *boy*. Benoit was like a son to me. And you—"

He chokes like he's drowning, and his sorrow drags me under with him. My chest swells, my eyes burn, and I ache to reach for him, Nox, and Orion, to hold on for all of us. But relief and adrenaline have drained me, leaving my body weak. It's all I can do to keep standing. Collapsing now would break their concentration when it seems they're already hanging on by a thread.

Because I see it now. I see everything Dad and Nox are trying to bury beneath rage. Red rims their eyes, their jaws twitch from being clenched too long, fists curled around their guns, knuckles blanched. And underneath all of it lies raw, bone-weary grief.

Dad hadn't reacted much when Orion told him about Benoit, but I think I know why. With my arms literally holding my grief at the time, he must have forced a brave face for me.

And then he had the impossible task of breaking the news to my twin that his best friend is dead. Murdered. I have no doubt Nox has been changed fundamentally, irrevocably, in ways I'll only understand on the surface.

Now Dad holds the evidence of our heartbreak in his hand, drenched in Benoit's blood, all because this woman ordered it.

"I am sorry about that," Bossie says like she's commenting on the storm that's opening up outside to drown us all. I want to fling her tiny body out the window and let the elements finish her. "But he stood in the way of my family's business. And nothing gets in the way of family business. Surely you understand."

"Family *business*?" I hiss, my skin hot. "Benoit *was* family. *Our* family."

Dad snarls with me. "And what the hell do the Bordeauxs have to do with Wilde 'family business'?"

Bossie tuts. "You've cursed in my presence for the last time, Mr. Bordeaux. I won't have that language in a house of God."

Dad's nostrils flare, and for a second I swear I see smoke curl out of them. My own breathing sounds loud in my ears as I wait for him to combust.

But then his gaze finds me, dismissing her. He softens and beckons me with one hand.

"Come on, *ma luné*. We're getting the fuck—"

Click.

Every weapon in the room snaps toward him and Nox.

"Stop! Please!" I scream, lunging for Bart's gun. I'm easily shoved aside like I'm nothing, and pain shoots up my ankle as I hit the ground with a cry.

"Luna!" Orion shouts along with my dad and Nox.

"Quiet." Bossie lifts her hand.

A heavy, weighted silence follows for a full breath. Then she shrugs, a genteel smile cresting her lips like she's helpless to stop the violence *she* set in motion.

"Until your daddy speaks with respect, I can't help my boys defending me. They're only doin' what they've been taught." Her narrowed eyes slide between me and my dad. "Miss Luna, I don't think he quite understands the gravity of our little situation here."

His eyes slam shut, a vein throbbing in his forehead as the rest of him vibrates with rage. My tongue turns to ash, on the verge of begging him not to push further. It takes him several long, controlled breaths before he lifts his gaze again. His real eye is as flat and cold as the prosthetic beside it.

"You're right, Bossie. Please. Enlighten me."

Her tone gentles like my grand-meré's when she chided me about pralines before dinner.

"We're here to make a truce, dear."

"A truce?" Orion scoffs hoarsely from across the room. "After *this*?"

"I have to second that," Dad growls, thunder punctuating the rumble. "This is a joke, right?"

"I don't joke over truces, Solomon." She gestures toward me, and the hair on the back of my neck rises. "From what I hear, your daughter's a mighty important piece in this here feud. We couldn't pass up the opportunity to finally beat the King Furys once and for all. We've been playing children's games thus far."

Her eyes glitter as she leans forward. "But allies like the Trois-garde would *destroy* the Furys' power once and for all." She chuckles, leaning back. "And to think, we considered attacking you. Almost threw the baby out with the bathwater. Good thing rumors fly like crows around here. We wouldn't have known about the Troisgarde daughters pact at all if one hadn't squawked."

My lip curls at the thought of a Troisgarde snitch. The flare in Dad's eyes is the only sign that he's shocked she's confirming everything Orion warned him about. No one wants to believe they have a traitor in their midst.

The flicker is gone in a blink before he seethes. "I've already told King, but I'll tell you too. A drunken bet does not make a pact. The Troisgarde wants no part in your feud. We've fought long and hard in our own territories, but after two decades, we've finally achieved peace—"

"*And we have never known peace!*" Bossie explodes from her seat in a fit of speed that makes me scramble back.

"You speak of decades, Bordeaux?" Spit flies from her lips, a sliver of hair escapes from her bun. "Try *centuries.*"

She stands regally now, posture straight, her cane forgotten against the throne. Her wrinkles vanish in flickering firelight and shadows, like her hate has forged her into something immortal.

"You have felt pain. You wear it clear on your face, and I commend you for that." She nods toward the side of my father that will forever remain burn-scarred. "But until *you've* felt the spirit leave your *child's* brutalized body on one last breath..."

She shakes her head. My hands clench tighter at the memory of Benoit's weight, suddenly too heavy in my arms.

"Until you've felt *that*," she whispers. "Do not speak to me of decades. Do not speak to me of fighting. Do not speak to me of *peace*. I have lost more than you could ever imagine and clawed my way out of hell more times than I can count, all before you were even born. You know *nothing* of war."

She returns to her throne, the tremble of her fingers the only thing betraying her age. The clean-shaven guard slips the cane back into her hand, and she lowers herself onto the white pew with a long, breathy sigh. Her chin lifts as if a crown were placed atop her head, a queen presiding over judgment.

"So now... we're doing it your way. You promised to hand

over your firstborn daughter in a dadgum drunken card game. That might not count as a pact in the Troisgarde's eyes, but 'round here, we've been enforcing moonshine vows for generations." She flicks her hand like that point doesn't matter. "Even so, your daughter was in her right mind when she agreed to marry a Wilde."

Her words rattle the rafters and settle in my bones, and Orion's growl rips through the thick air.

"No! She didn't know. She never would've been with him if she'd known the truth."

I would've been with you, I want to say. Regret surges through my veins, so quickly it makes me lightheaded. If I weren't already on my knees, I'd crumple to the ground.

Bossie doesn't acknowledge him, her focus staying on my dad.

"Those are the terms of my truce. You'd be wise to agree to them. Life for life is meant to be much, much worse for her."

"Luna is innocent," Orion insists, his raw voice scraping me from the inside out. "If life for life is what you want, then take me instead."

"Orion, no," I whisper, my heart twisting.

"I got you into this feud, Luna." His eyes find mine. "I never wanted the pact to be your curse, but that's all it's been for you. That's all *I've* been for you. Let me break it." He swallows hard, and my hand presses to my throat in sympathy. "Let me set you free."

"*No.*" A painful shudder racks through me as I shake my head.

Bossie huffs. "Believe me, young Fury, we're gonna get to you."

Dad's measured gaze drags from Orion to glare at Bossie. "My daughter's not marrying anyone she doesn't want to. And I have a feeling that boy—" His jaw clenches as he points to Orion who's straining against his ropes. "—and I will both burn this church to the ground with all of you Wildes in it before letting that happen. Your truce would go up in smoke, and I'd use every resource at my disposal to annihilate the rest of the 'Bossie Wilde kin.'"

A shiver runs through me at the cold venom in his voice, but his defiance and the agreement in Orion's eyes steadies me. I believe every word, but Bossie just chuckles.

"You highfalutin folks always think you've got the upper hand. But look around you, Mr. Bordeaux."

She sweeps her arms over the chapel, and my eyes track them automatically. My stomach knots as I finally register how dire our situation actually is. It's my father, Nox, Orion, and me... against twelve armed men. Bart towers over me, two guard Bossie, and there are two more behind Orion. Seven others stand watch near Dad and Nox, looming from the shadows among the pushed-aside pews.

The back of my neck burns like a spotlight's fixed on me alone. It might as well be, since the death of my freedom is the star of this shitshow.

"Your money don't do you no good when you're outnumbered," Bossie says. "And after the Lost Cove massacre, your daughter and Orion owe debts money can't repay."

Dad's eyes narrow before he finally grits out. "Then we'll side with you."

My jaw drops so fast it clicks. "*What*?"

"I pledge our loyalty. My family walks out of here unharmed, 'debt' paid. Do what you want with the Fury—"

"No!" The word tears from my chest, and I surge to my feet, not caring about my ankle. "Dad, what're you *doing*?"

He doesn't look at me, gaze hard as steel on Bossie as he drives a knife into my back.

"The Furys have only brought my family grief. You don't need my daughter. Go back to your feud. You've got your life for life and the truce you wanted."

"She's playing you, Bordeaux," Orion says evenly. "Luna won't be safe. She'll always be a bargaining chip to them."

"Just like she is to you," he lashes out.

My chest caves in.

"It's not like that, Dad, and you know it." My voice cracks as he blurs in my burning vision. "You can't throw Orion to the wolves. I'll never forgive you."

He shakes his head, finally looking at me, but I see no cracks or weakness in his hard gaze. "You'll get over it, Luna. You hardly know him."

"*What*? Who even are you right now? You always talk about Fate." My voice shakes, but I refuse to yield. "What I feel is Fate."

Bossie cuts in, smug. "What you feel isn't *Fate*. It's the Furys. They can con even the smartest of women, slick as the snake in Eden. I hate to say it, child, but you fell for their wicked ways. Sure as Eve to the Devil."

"*You* are the Devil," I spit—

Crack.

My head whips sideways before the pain even lands, the force making me collapse. I gasp, ears ringing, heat trickling down my cheek. I press the tender flesh lightly, grimacing at the sting. My fingers come away crimson, my mind zeroing in on the sight while everything else around it becomes a hazy nightmare.

When my vision finally realigns, Bossie's watching me impassively. Her face is calm while her knuckles and gold ring glisten red. A drop of blood plops onto the warped wood, a sound I think I imagine in my muffled head, but it snaps the world back into focus.

Voices clash like swords as the men in my life roar their threats. Their rage is deafening, yet all I hear is Bossie.

"Let that be a learnin' to you, child. That mouth a' yours is gonna get you in trouble. That ain't no way to talk to your elders, least of all your future kin."

My hand trembles as I wipe my cheek, but I force my shoulders straight, meeting her eyes.

She nods toward Dad and Nox, both restrained by three men each. Their faces flush red as they strain uselessly against the grip.

Orion's not much different, except for the new slash across his brow.

"I trust your 'loyalty' about as far as I can throw you, Bordeaux," Bossie replies like the church isn't on the verge of imploding. "Marriage is the only way to ensure alliances. Luna will marry my grandson. That's final."

I hate the trembling waver as I plea. "But Ozias doesn't want this either, Bossie."

"You're right." Her bony hand waves toward Bart. "Another grandbaby of mine will do just fine."

My stomach lurches.

Dad snaps. "You can't do this."

"Actually, I can. I'm ordained and everythin'." She levels him with a glare. "If you want peace, Bordeaux, then you'll bear witness while your daughter wins it for you. You should be grateful I invited you here at all. I didn't get the same courtesy for my daughter's wedding thanks to the Furys. And you." She points at me, her long nail gleaming like a talon. "*You* will do as you're told, girl."

My cheek burns, blood already going tacky on my skin, but I slowly stand and square my shoulders, raising my chin. "And why on earth would I do that?"

Lightning flashes through the stained glass, splashing muted colors over Bossie's toothy, malicious smile.

"Because I reckon you like your little Fury boy alive, don't you? That ain't gonna last long unless you say 'I do.' Right here. Right now."

Thunder growls, the storm a feral beast rattling the chapel to the studs. It takes me a second to realize the sound is Orion's bark of bitter laughter.

"There's no fucking way she'll do that. Not over my dead—"

"Boys?"

I scream as every gun whips toward him, one pressing against his temple.

"Stop! Please!"

Bart jerks me backward, stopping me before I can run to Orion, and shoves me to my knees. The splintered wood bites my skin and his grip grinds into my shoulder, but I twist anyway, meeting Bossie's placid expression with watery eyes.

"Please, Bossie. *Please* let him go."

But she doesn't flinch, eyes cool and lips pressed flat. My lungs catch on jagged sobs as I turn to Orion, my heart physically breaking at the sight of him, one twitch of a finger away from death.

He was seething a moment ago, eyes feral. But when he sees the desperation crumpling my face, his jaw locks and he visibly gulps.

"Luna..." he warns, shaking his head.

"You know what to do, child," Bossie murmurs.

Blinking back tears, my gaze never leaves his as I force the question through my tight throat.

"If I do this, he'll go free?"

"Don't." The word cracks with Orion's panic.

"It's a life for life in our world," Bossie answers. "Pledge yours to the Wildes, and my boys will release him. You have Bossie Wilde's word."

"*No*," Orion's rough plea makes me flinch. "It's a trick, baby. Don't listen to her."

"You have my word," she repeats.

Hot tears fall down my cheeks.

"I'm sorry."

"*Please*, little bird. Don't." He battles the ropes, chair rocking violently until one of the men wrenches his shoulder back. "*Luna!*"

Every muscle in him strains, but all the fight leaves my bones.

"*No!*" he roars as I turn my back on him to face the matriarch. My voice is steady as my heart breaks.

"I'll do it."

33
THE CHOICE

ORION

My voice is hoarse from screaming. My head's on fire from every blow these bastards behind me landed. My ribs grind like broken glass every time I breathe.

But nothing compares to the agony of watching the woman I love say vows that were meant for me. She's marrying my enemy, holding his hands when he'll use them to hurt her the first chance he gets... and it's all to save *me*.

I'm not worth it.

Bossie had it all planned out too. She brought vows, the guests, hell, even a white veil. Somehow she knew she'd get us here one way or another, and now Luna trembles beside Bart on a dais that feels as high as a mountain from where I'm bound.

He's clutching her hands tightly enough to bruise, and the veil mocks me, hiding tears I know she's trying to hold back for my sake. I see them anyway, shimmering at its gauzy edge, firelight mirrored on the drops as they trail down her chest with every silent, hitched breath. She's trying to be strong, trying not to let me see her heart break, trying to keep me from drowning in guilt over ruining her life. It isn't working.

"Please, baby," I rasp for the millionth time. "You don't have to do this. Please, Luna, I'd rather die."

And goddamn, do I mean that.

I twist my glare on Bossie, rage tightening my jaw. "You better think real hard about letting me go. The second I'm out of these restraints, I'm coming for every single fu—"

"Too little. Too late, don't you think?" Sol sneers nearby, his voice slicing through me as sure as any blade. "You were supposed to protect her, Fury. Short of a miracle bursting in and saving the day, we have to sit here and watch my daughter sacrifice herself. For *you.*"

His scowl sears my skin, his unscarred side giving me a pointed look. If he didn't hate me so much, I'd think there might be a message beneath his words. But even if there was, my mind is too fucked up to figure it out.

All I can think is... he's right.

I failed to stop a woman I love from falling to the Wildes.

Again.

Don't give up.

Protect her. Protect her. Protect her.

I blink hard and summon all the will I have left to focus and search for any way to get her out of this.

A Wilde digs my own crossbow bolt into my shoulder, mocking me, and Sol and Nox are disarmed now too. Nox paces like a caged animal inside a ring of five guards, and Sol stands stock-still with fists at his side, the only tell he has that he's on the verge of exploding.

Two more guard the chapel entrance, while the ones on me might as well be posted up on a pissed-off rock for all the damage I can do trussed up like this. Another pair stand by Bossie, who's back to her bullshit Sunday school teacher act as she prattles off the vows.

My throat seizes when she reaches the final question.

"And do you, Bartholomew Wilde, take Luna Bordeaux, to have and to hold, from this day forward, till death do you part?"

His grin stretches wide. My stomach churns at his lecherous gaze sliding up and down my girl like she's a slab of meat.

"I do."

Lightning cracks. Thunder booms immediately after, shaking the chapel's ancient bones.

Bossie turns to Luna, her expression suddenly unforgiving. "And do you, Luna Bordeaux, take Bartholomew Wilde, to have and to hold, from this day forward, till death do you part?"

"No!" The word tears my throat raw, bursting a metallic tang on my tongue. Another punch slams into my skull, lurching my jaw to the side.

"You promised you wouldn't hurt him!" Luna's voice clears the fog threatening to take me under. I fight to focus on her, to hold on. She's lifted the veil to see me, and I suck in a breath.

Even now, eyes glittering with fear and pain, face crumpled with defeat, she's breathtaking on a stage. My chest aches to kiss her tears dry.

"Don't pay him no mind, boys. I already skipped the 'who objects' line," Bossie laughs dryly, all mirth gone as her eyes cut to me. "I didn't gag you because we've got some things to discuss. Don't make me change my mind." Then she clasps her hands over the crook of her cane and fixes that glare on Luna. "Now. I believe I asked you a question, honey."

Luna inhales, opens her mouth—

"You know what? That's enough. If you think taking my daughter hostage will unite our families, you're delusional," Sol snaps. "You think we'll be allies? I'm warning you, if you force my daughter into this farce, I'll rain hell on every last one of you."

Bossie's smile twitches. "Threatening to hurt people is some blasphemous talk in a house of God. It's a mighty fine threat, though, I'll give you that. But it ain't got no teeth. Once your daughter's in Old Bridge, we'll take care of her well enough. So long as you play nice when we call on you to stand against the Furys. The rest of the Troisgarde will follow suit once we have their daughters too."

Fuck.

Dread hangs my head. I was afraid of this. My brothers are gonna go ballistic.

Luna's breath hitches. "Wh-What do you mean?"

I swallow past my dry throat. "It means your sacrifice is just the beginning, baby."

Luna's eyes meet mine, worry creasing her brow, but Bossie's chuckle snaps her attention back.

"He's right. We ain't stopping at the Bordeauxs. It's the Trois-garde *daughters*. The three of you are part of this, and if we don't finish the job," Bossie says, narrowing her eyes at me, "the King Furys will."

"No," Luna chokes. "You can't cage Brylie like this. And Lucy... Lucy's not strong enough for this life, Bossie. Let's end it here. None of this has anything to do with them."

Bossie leans forward, a copperhead ready to strike. But her position is all the more chilling as she replies calmly.

"It has *everything* to do with them. The King Fury branch attacked my kin. Murdered us. It's *them* who tried to destroy us from the roots up."

"Really?" Rage hurls out my accusation. "Tell her what y'all did. Tell her how my mom was murdered by *your* sons."

"You mean... *her* brothers."

I open my mouth to shout back, but the words hit their target.

"What?" I breathe.

Bossies sighs and shakes her head. "Figures no one ever told you about your momma's side of the family tree. Can't say I blame them. Before she was your 'Queenie,' she was my princess. My namesake... my Ruthie."

"Wait." I can barely form my mouth around the words. "My momma... she was a Wilde?"

As far as my brothers and I knew, she had no living family. Never talked about it. We didn't think much of it, since my dad had family to spare. But to hide something like *this*?

Bossie nods. "Wilde through and through. Until she was bewitched under your King's spell. The moment she set foot in Dark Corner, she was no kin of mine."

"You exiled her?" I spit.

It's the Wilde way, to cut off your family like that. But how could anyone be so cruel to someone as good as my mom?

"Your *momma* cut *us* off. She knew the consequences of running off with your daddy and she still spit in our eye, choosing Fury."

Jesus, no wonder her branch of the tree in our books starts with her and ends with...

Us.

My eyes widen at Bossie as she slowly nods.

"Which makes you and your brothers my grandsons."

She says it with zero warmth, and I feel the same. But I can't help throwing her own words back at her and raising my bound wrists.

"Then what's this, huh? What happened to 'kin is kin'?"

"It's the reason you ain't already buried out back and the last courtesy I'll give my late daughter," she counters, hands tightening on her cane. "I have no love for you, boy, and I'll do what I have to for this family. Her line is rotten to the core, and rot's gotta be cut off or the whole tree falls down. I won't have y'all's traitorous blood continuing your line and infecting mine. The Furys *will* be defeated, and King Fury's direct line *will* end with you, Dashiel, and Hatton. We're stealing your precious Troisgarde daughters for our own, like King did with mine. *He* started this. *I'm* finishing it."

"He knew what was coming," Sol muses low, then raises his voice. "*You're* the reason he made this pact in the first place. To ensure his line was protected by us, and that his legacy would live on."

I wince. He makes it sound so... *calculated*. And maybe it is on paper, but it certainly doesn't feel that way at the heart of it. Not to my brothers, and certainly not to me.

It feels like Fate. Destiny. The Fury call we get when we meet the ones who give us peace, the call I *know* my father felt for my mom. But whatever the motive behind King's plan was, our wives are *ours*, and no Wilde can stand in the way of that.

Bossie nods then levels me with a hard stare. "King tried to ward us off, but he gave us an opening instead. It's life for life, young Fury. Your father will rue the day he crossed Bossie Wilde."

I'm stunned, slack-jawed and vision tunneling, but even as I face off with Bossie, my senses quiet, trying to register everything in my periphery.

The guards surrounding Nox and Sol are dialed in, listening to the argument and not giving the Bordeauxs nearly as much attention as the deadly men deserve. Sol studies me and Bossie like he's tracking the storm raging inside the church, while Nox has stopped pacing, bracing to weather it.

Even Luna's posture has straightened, her expression carefully blank aside from narrowed eyes she's pretending aren't solely focused on her brother and father. The Bordeaux family vigilance thickens the air. Does Bossie feel it too? Or is it because I've watched them for so long that I can tell something's up?

"Now then, that's quite enough family story time, isn't it? Luna!" Bossie snaps her fingers, redirecting everyone's focus back to the sham of a wedding. "I asked you a question. Do. You... take my grandson as your husband?"

"I..." Luna closes her eyes, gathering courage, and breathing hard through her nose.

Bossie's eyes flick beyond Luna, and she nods to her kin.

Then it happens exactly how I knew it would.

Like wolves rising at their alpha's command, every barrel slowly, *silently* lifts to aim at me. Even my own crossbow digs harder into my shoulder.

My eyes close. I lift my chin, ready for my judgment. As soon as Luna says yes, it's over. I just hope some trigger-happy bastard puts me down before then. I can't watch the woman I love sell herself for me in vain.

"Answer the question!" Bossie's shrill voice cuts through the chapel, no doubt to mask the sound of guns cocking...

"I—"

...but someone's too slow.

Luna gasps at the *click*, then screams.

"*Don't!*"

She's airborne before anyone can react, leaping from the dais like it's a cliff. Bart grabs for her, but only catches her veil, tearing it free. With just a few strides, Luna crashes into me, her skirt fanning out like wings as she wraps her body around mine.

The woman I love is shielding me.

Saving *me*.

And now every fucking weapon in the room is pointed at her.

34
RECKLESS LITTLE BIRD

ORION

"Stop!" Sol roars. "Hold your *goddamn* fire!"

"What the fuck are you doing?" I rasp, panicked. My chest caves in underneath her small, trembling, defiant body.

She whispers strongly against my neck, "Protecting my husband."

"No," I beg, voice breaking as my arms strain against the rope, desperate to shield her. "Get off me, Luna. *Please*, baby. *Please*."

She only squeezes tighter, curling around my neck like armor.

"Fuck, *fuck*. My reckless, *brave* little bird..." I couldn't give a shit about me, but Luna? I'm terrified, and my question comes out as a harsh plea against her soft neck. "What am I gonna do with you?"

"Let me save you."

Those words knife through me, and my eyes burn.

"No. Not me." I shake my head. "Don't do this for me. I won't let you die for me. I'm not worth it."

Her hand cradles the back of my head, and her lips graze my ear. "You're worth everything, Orion Fury."

"Hold your fire," Bossie finally orders, irritated now. The weapons ease up, including the crossbow and gun lifting off my back. A fraction of adrenaline leaves me on a shaky breath.

Luna presses harder against me, tulle pooling over my lap and tied hands. I grip the bottom of her bodice where the tutu's waistband overlaps it, pulling her closer even though every other fiber of my being wants to push her away. My wrists graze her garter as she breathes in my ear so softly only I can hear.

"Don't forget how much you trust me, Fury."

Of course I trust you, almost rolls off the tip of my tongue, but I bite it back.

I keep my expression the same, hoping the swelling and bruises hide my confusion as I try to piece together what she means. When she shifts her weight, tightening her thighs around me, her meaning becomes clear-cut.

Literally.

My brave girl isn't just shielding me.

She's arming me.

Wasting no time, my bound hands work nimbly over the garter strapped to her thigh to free the Fury knife from the makeshift lace and tulle holster. The Wildes made a mistake not frisking my reckless little wife.

Her real tears mix with big ol' crocodile ones, spilling down her face and onto my shoulder as she plays the biggest role of her life. She exaggerates loud, racking sobs to camouflage my awkward movements underneath her tutu while I saw at the rope around my wrists.

"Lawd have mercy, child. Pull yourself together." Bossie snaps her fingers. "Go on and go get her, Bart—"

Click.

Sol's gun cocks with a deadly finality as he aims it at the throne.

"If anyone lays a finger on my daughter, son, or Orion, I'll paint this white church red."

How he got another gun I have no idea, but the room falls silent. The men holding Nox back let the younger Bordeaux go.

Luna twists to look at her dad, but the sudden movement slips the knife from the rope, nicking her thigh. Her eyes flick to mine, and my heart stalls out at the pain I caused there. My girl's quick, though, and disguises the whimper into another sob as she squeezes me tighter.

"Sorry, baby," I murmur, aching with guilt, but I get back to cutting. I won't let her sacrifice be for nothing.

Sol and Bossie keep up their verbal sparring, with Sol's voice rising over the thunder, echoing through the small chapel. I can't focus on them, though. Luna's cut slicks my wrists, helping them slide free from my restraints. I love and hate that it's always Luna's blood that saves me.

Please let her be okay.

I keep moving, pooling the rope in my lap. Then slowly, so fucking slowly, I lift my hands out from under her tutu to move onto the restraints at my chest.

"Closer," I breathe under her ear. "Almost done."

With the tulle no longer providing cover, Luna cries louder and grips my shoulders, her arms now concealing what I'm doing.

"Mr. Bordeaux," Bossie sighs. "It's hardly necessary to make threats in the Lord's house."

"Isn't that what this stunt is?" he seethes. "You're threatening my family, the Troisgarde. Hell, I don't even like you intimidating the Furys at this point. Not when my daughter's involved…"

He rages on, spitting French curses and lighting into the stoic matriarch like a preacher in a fire-and-brimstone sermon. The words blur together, and all I hear is Luna crying. All I feel is her warmth against me. All I can focus on is *my wife* and the knife between us.

Sol's tirade distracts every eye in the room, buying me time. I sever, twist, and pull until one of the ropes is frayed enough that it'll give when the time is right to escape. Luna shudders against me, relief racking her body, but she doesn't let go, keeping alive the illusion that I'm still bound. My heartbeat races against her chest as I grip the knife tightly.

"You know what, Bossie?" Sol snaps. "Before all this"—he gestures toward everything but me and Luna, ending at the pulpit

Bossie reigns from—"I'd hoped you were the reasonable one in this feud. But I don't think you and I are the type to see eye to eye with one another."

Bossie settles back in her throne, smug. "Sure seems that way, don't it?"

Sol sucks his teeth, and Nox shifts on his feet behind him, getting closer.

Using his father as cover.

No one else seems to notice, so I shift my gaze away from him. But from the corner of my eye, I catch the flash of Nox's phone screen as he checks, then pockets it again.

What are you up to, Bordeaux?

"That's what I was afraid of, Bossie. But now that you're not only the enemy of my enemy, you've become mine as well. So when my getaway driver insisted he come in with me..." Sol juts his chin toward Nox, before smirking at Bossie. "I took the liberty of calling in a new one. Turns out, there's a couple of brothers who were champing at the bit to help out. You know, your *other* grandsons?"

My eyes bug out along with Bossie's, and Sol laughs at her shock. "Figured they'd want to be in on this, wouldn't you say, Orion?"

I take that as my cue and stab the pistol-wielding guard to my right in the thigh as Luna, still sitting in my lap, yanks the rest of the ropes off my chest. The guard's shriek drowns out Bossie's orders, and chaos breaks loose as the double doors explode inward, Hatch barreling through, snapfiring into the two men flanking them.

The wind howls behind him, slapping the doors against the walls and whipping rain at his back. Outside, a blacked-out SUV revs in the raging storm, nearly invisible but for Dash aiming his gun through the half-cracked window.

Until Bossie's voice tears through the chapel.

"Kill them! Kill every one of 'em!"

My stomach drops at her unhinged hatred, and the room

erupts in gunfire as Sol, Nox, and Hatch let bullets fly. The man behind me drops, still reeling from the stab wound in his thigh. I pivot around Luna to give his friend the same treatment, only to find myself staring down my own crossbow.

The guard jerks the trigger back... but my custom rig jams it, and he looks down, dumbfounded. I grin right before driving my blade into his gut.

He howls, doubling over. Luna snatches the crossbow from him, flips the mechanism like I showed her, then swivels on my lap to fire with all the aim that I had time to teach her.

Which was, unfortunately, absolutely none.

The bolt flies wide, missing both Bossie and Bart by a mile, snagging a lantern above the altar and sending it crashing down. Oil and fire splash on the carpet, lighting up the dry wood like a Christmas tree in March.

Oh shit.

"Time to go, baby." I grab Luna's waist to steady her, keeping my reckless bird from flying straight into danger, and cut the ankle ropes, not caring that the blade slices into my skin.

Then I grab her and *run*.

It's hellish mayhem in all directions, every man locked in a fight, while two Wildes drag a spitting mad Bossie from the chapel like she's the Holy Grail. Retreating cowards or not, they're right to guard their matriarch.

And I need to protect my wife. *Now.*

"We gotta get outta here."

"Yup, yup, yup. Totally agree."

We trade weapons, right as the guy we took the crossbow from stretches his bloody hand toward her, now with a pistol in his slippery grip. Luna screams, but I wrench it from his hand and shoot him point-blank in the head. He plops like a sack of meat, and I drop the gun onto his back.

With my fractured ribs, split cheek, and swollen eye, I should be knocked out from pain. But my mantra thunders in my skull, drowning out everything else.

Protect her. Protect her. Protect her.

It jolts through me, and I clamp my bloody grip on Luna's hand, hauling her toward the doors—

She's ripped away from me, screaming.

"Orion!"

Bart drags her kicking and screaming up to the dais, trying to steal my wife and carry her through the same doors they took Bossie through. The last feather, black and bloody, drifts from her bodice like an omen, and all I see is red.

I yank back the steel cable on my crossbow in one brutal pull, the string biting into my scars as I force it to cock faster than it's meant to, and slot another bolt. I ignore the pain and lock my sights on him.

"Luna! Duck!"

She instantly goes limp, becoming dead weight in his arms and exposing him as she drops. I let the bolt fly. In the next blink, the bolt's buried in his throat. He chokes and claws at it, trying to get a grip on the white feathers. But my little bird takes flight, spinning up on her good ankle to plunge the Fury knife into his chest with a dancer's grace.

"I'm not *yours*." She rips the knife free before he falls to his knees.

I hop up onto the dais and smirk. "She's *mine*."

His shocked eyes beg for mercy, but I kick the stab wound in his chest, sending him flying off the dais and into the fire on the other side.

I hold out my hand.

"Come with me, wife."

She grins brilliantly and reaches for me. If I were an optimistic man, I'd say the smile she returns might even mean she loves—

A groan cracks from the ceiling. Luna's eyes widen in terror as a beam teeters over her head... and falls.

35

WHITE SWAN PAS DE DEUX

ORION

I scoop Luna up, one arm around her waist, the other hand shielding her head, and sprint just as a tree-sized rafter crashes down behind us. Fire, ash, cinders, and smoke explode in a cloud, singeing the air while more wood splinters and groans, the chapel collapsing piece by piece.

"Oh my God, we're trapped!"

I curse.

She's right.

Two beams pen us in on the stage. We could maybe climb between them, but the larger beam wobbles, on fire and still suspended from the ceiling, ready to fall with the next gust of wind. One of us may be able to slip through in time. But not both of us.

I search the gaps beyond the burning beams, but there's no help in sight. Only fire.

Nightmares rush in with the heat, choking me worse than the smoke and making my hands ache. Blinding orange and red, the cloying stench of charred flesh... screaming flames.

"What do we do?" Luna cries, snapping me out of it.

Fuck. *Luna.*

I couldn't hold back the fire then, but I have to get her out now.

"Orion?"

"Shh, it's okay," I murmur into her hair, rounding over her, protecting her from the heat already whipping my back as I analyze the best way through.

"Luna! Orion!" Nox's voice breaks through the wood's crackling groans.

Relief floods in my veins. I peer through the small opening between the flames from him to her, then lie through my teeth.

"We can make it. I'm going to lift the beam, you're going to jump through, and I'll be right behind you."

She searches my face warily, eyes rimmed red from smoke and weeping. I wanted to wake up to that clearwater blue every day for the rest of my life.

I guess I did.

Something slams across the church, making Luna yelp. We're running out of time.

My heart pounds as I look at my promised—but never to be—bride.

"You have to go first."

She shakes her head, panic swimming in her glassy eyes. Tears wash streaks through the ash on her cheeks, drying as fast as they fall to the ground.

"No, we go at the same time. I'm not leaving you."

"Please, baby..."

"You said you'd never leave me. *You promised*," she begs, lips trembling before she crashes into me in an unbreakable embrace.

Almost unbreakable.

"You promised. You promised. You promised."

Her tears cool my neck as she repeats it through coughs, her voice so shredded by smoke that every plea only hardens my resolve.

The fire dances around us, closing in. I'm trying to shield her, wrapping my body around hers, but do the flames bite her skin too? Is she already burning?

Is this how Hatch felt when our momma sacrificed herself for him?

I can't let it happen again. I won't.

I tighten my grip around Luna and find Nox through the inferno. His eyes are wide with the kind of terror that sparks rage instead. It's an emotion I can clock from a mile away, especially now with it coursing through me too.

He finally catches my stare, his gaze locking with mine. A moment spanning an eternity passes between us. It ends with a silent promise, and I nod.

Take care of her.

His hard expression softens with understanding, knowing what I have to do. What I'm about to give up. He exhales with the weight of it, then shakes out his limbs, preparing for the most important catch of his life. When he raises his arms, they're loose, ready.

I gather Luna closer to me, covering her nose with my shirt, and inhale her sweet jasmine and honey scent one last time.

"Hold your breath, baby."

She sucks a breath in through my tee, obeying me on instinct. My hands drop to her waist, and I steal one hard, selfish kiss, savoring a final taste of the woman I'd burn for, then whisper against her lips.

"I love you, Luna Bordeaux. But I'm sorry. I can't keep my promise."

Shock makes her go limp, and I move too swiftly for her to get her bearings, scooping her into my arm. I wedge my shoulder under an unburned section of the beam, muscles screaming from the weight, and spin her in one last dance.

Only this time, I let go.

My heart drops with her as she falls through the crevice. Her eyes widen with betrayal and terror, and the image overlays the horrible memory of her plummeting from the cliff.

For a split second, my legs twitch to dive after her again. Maybe I could make it.

But Whitby Rose gives up another of its bones as a rafter cracks and thunders to the floor, exploding pews before crashing onto the far end of the beam I'm holding, crushing my shoulder. I grunt, muscles tearing as I fight to keep it from toppling onto Luna.

She screams as she flies, her skirt flaring out like wings before she lands safely in her brother's arms. I roar, rolling the beam off me, raining embers down my back. It crashes below, a wall of cinder and flame between me and them. Between death and life.

I stumble back, catching heaving breaths that burn from the inside out, and watch her through the fire.

She fights like I knew she would, writhing like a feral, furious little thing, clawing her brother to get back to me. But he cages her in his arms, then lifts her like she weighs nothing and sprints through the sanctuary. I blink, and they're gone. Out of the church, out of danger, and into the darkness on the other side.

Relief makes me lightheaded, or maybe it's the smoke. Either way, hazy images of Luna come easily. I picture her safe in the car with my family and hers, Dash flying down mountain roads like a bat out of hell, taking her back home. Back to New Orleans.

My thoughts cut to her being there, surrounded by everything and everyone she knows and loves. The terror squeezing my heart eases at that, because if I'm not with her, with her family is the safest place she could be. Sol and Nox will make sure of that.

Which means Luna is truly safe. And I... I'm gonna die.

And that's okay. Maybe this, saving the woman I love, is what I was meant to do all along.

Smoke thickens around me, and I collapse under its weight. My skin begs for a balm as my nightmares burn into me like a fresh brand, the kind of pain that drags time to a halt.

Until a shadowy hand stretches through the flames.

I know that hand.

I blink. But it doesn't go away. I smile up knowing who I'll see, and I breathe past the smoke scorching my lungs.

"Momma."

Her soft, blonde hair wafts in a phantom breeze. She brushes it back, giving me the sweet smile I've never forgotten.

This isn't real. It can't be. Lack of oxygen has gotten to my brain...

"Come with me, Orion." Her voice is a whisper through Dark Corner pines and a gust in a wildfire all at once.

But even as she reaches for me, even as I'm desperate to follow, I hesitate. If I go, Fate will have decided, and Luna will be gone for good.

Momma smiles. "Trust me."

She offers her hand through the flames. I exhale.

I loved you fiercely, Luna Bordeaux.

I push the emotion out with one final breath, hoping Luna can feel it. Gathering my courage and every ounce of my strength, I surrender, reaching for her to accept my bittersweet end—

Momma's hand is too rough, callused, and strong for such a small woman as it snatches mine in a painful grip. Her sweet face morphs, unveiling a furious demon in her place. His scars are both armor and a weapon, his smile twisted into something vicious, and his eyes fathomless midnight pits.

The demon roars, heaving aside the fallen beam. Ravenous flames devour everything but his void as he yanks my arm... and drags me with him to hell.

36
I SAVED YOU

"I thought you were a demon, you know," I grit out, my voice rough from smoke.

Sol snorts. "You're not that far off. My wife calls me her *démon de la musique*, after all."

"Fitting," I cough.

I don't mention how hallucinating my mom ushering me into the afterlife then transforming into the man I thought hated me might be one of the top five most traumatic things that's ever happened to me. The fact that he carried me out of the fire, got me to the getaway car, *saving* me, and now I'm in my own bed with Luna sound asleep in my arms? Nothing short of a miracle from the devil himself, and I ain't about to look that gift horse in the mouth. Especially if he's more apocalypse than pony.

"You were stalling too, weren't you? When you argued with Bossie before my brothers showed up?" I clear my throat and take a swig from the water bottle on my bedside table, trying to wash the metallic taste of blood off my tongue. "All of it was a tactic. You and Nox were waiting until they could get there."

Sol nods. "About five minutes in, I realized playing Bossie's game would be the only way to keep everyone breathing." He sighs. "Luna's probably going to hate me for the things I said, at least for a little while. She'll understand, though. She knows I'd sooner cut my own arm off than be strong-armed into a truce. Of course, all that was *before* Luna tried to sacrifice herself."

He grumbles the last with a mix of anger and disappointment that only a father can master. A combination my brothers and I know all too well.

Then Sol has the audacity to cut me a glare, as if the whole thing was my fault.

I lift my hand. "Hey, don't look at me like I'm not also mad as hell at your reckless daughter. She and I are having words." I look down at the little hellion resting in my arms, and my voice softens as I stroke her back. "Later, obviously."

Luna's long lashes fan across her pale cheeks, bags under her eyes and remnants of soot I couldn't scrub clean before she drifted off on my chest. Her even breaths flutter over my bare skin, and I cherish each one.

She's alive. With me. Right where she's supposed to be.

Her father gazes at her, leaning forward in his wooden chair, elbows on his knees and hands steepled between them.

"I wouldn't have expected anything less. She's a Bordeaux through and through, but her ability to think on her feet is unmatched. I trusted she'd come up with a plan or figure out mine and Nox's. Either way, stalling seemed like the best stopgap."

"Nice." I smile weakly.

He grunts his agreement and reaches for her like he might brush her hair back, but I shift her away, hooking my hand behind her knee and pulling her closer, ricocheting pain through my bones.

Our local vet provided a makeshift boot cast for Luna until she can go to a real doctor. It's meant for a calf but heavier than it looks, doing a number on my bruised shin fractures.

"She's *sleeping*," I hiss. As soon as her meds kicked in, she passed out from a bone-weary exhaustion that's all my fault. I'll be damned if anyone wakes her after the week she's had.

"Jesus Christ, you're almost as bad as I am," Sol mutters. I barely register his griping as I focus on breathing out the agony pulsing in my veins.

King Fury kin don't use heavy pain pills if we can help it. Addiction runs in our bloodline, and those types of drugs are already pushed too hard around these parts, leaving more devastation than healing. We stick to over-the-counter as long as we can, although at the moment they're just not quite cutting it.

But I don't care. I'll endure this pain every day if it means Luna's safe.

"You're alive," King's voice arrives before he does. "That's good."

My father's deep rumble fits him perfectly, unlike his larger-than-life presence in this cozy room, which now feels suddenly cramped as Dash and Hatch file in behind him. Other than our father's thick beard and thirty years, we all look nearly identical, our Fury genes strong. With their massive frames combined with mine and Sol's, my room has all the makings of a clown car inside a fun house.

My brothers have already checked on me, but this is the first appearance from dear ol' dad. Even Grandma Fancy called this morning, taking time out from visiting our family on the coast to see how I was doing. She's eager to meet Luna when she comes back next week, and I can't wait either. They'll be two peas in a pod, both spitfires who take no shit.

Hatch plops into a corner chair, black hair, scars, and his rose tattoo shielded by his backward ball cap, and sprawls out like he doesn't have a care in the world. But his usual feral grin has flattened into the tight-lipped smirk that always signals he's stressed, and his eyes keep flicking to his phone, jaw tightening each time it apparently disappoints him.

I've only seen him like this a few times, the first after Momma died. Now, if I had to guess, he's worried about two things. His future wife. And Dash.

Over the years, Hatch and I have been the ruthless ones, happily doing the dirty work so Dash could have a shot at something better. I think we wanted med school for him—hell, any future beyond this feud—more than he did.

But everything he's done since New Orleans has given him a taste of the brutality Hatch and I have lived for years. I can see it in his hollowed cheeks and the darkness around his eyes that it's haunting him like it did us, before we got numb to it. He stares off, unseeing. Probably plotting. Knowing Dash, Brylie's presence in New Orleans won't last long before he pulls the same shit I did.

Father's as stoic as ever. His salt-and-pepper hair and beard add to his wise, regal air. Those shrewd eyes appraise me, no doubt finding me lacking. All the kindness Momma ever brought out of him died with her. He'd never say it, but he's always blamed me for my mom's death. That guilt is one of the many reasons I've been hell-bent on being the first to make good on this pact, protecting all our families. Every other reason is Luna.

"How are you feeling, son?"

I swallow past the dryness in my throat. "Just peachy."

He nods, then turns on Sol, all business.

"Clearly, you see the importance of joining our side."

"No. We're not doing this now," I hiss, my eyes darting to the only innocent one in all this.

Sol's tone gentles. "Don't worry, she won't wake up. When she's *asleep*"—he emphasizes the word, honoring Luna's privacy—"she stays that way for hours. We'll fill her in after she's rested."

Luna texted her psychiatrist on the way home to check if it was safe to take her medicine. When the doc gave the go-ahead, Luna took it right there in the car. Poor thing's been basically out like a light ever since.

I nod to Sol, then settle in and resume my light finger strokes down her back. I still glare daggers at my father for not having the decency to wait, but I don't interrupt.

"You should've called me," King narrows his eyes at Sol, serious expression so like Dash—with a beard—I almost double take.

Sol scoffs. "I trust you even less than your boys, King. Why the fuck would I call you?"

My father scowls but straightens. "In any case, the Wildes

have gone after Luna as I suspected they would. We need to discuss next steps for the Troisgarde daughters."

"You mean *ex*-pected," Sol sneers. "You set my daughter up for the slaughter by insisting your legacy live on through strong alliances."

"It's not about legacy," King counters harshly. "You may question my motives, but never question my wife's. We wanted our children to have a chance at what we had, something a Wilde target on their back would never allow without the blood of three and power of many behind them." His chin raises proudly, meeting Sol's height. "You don't know my sons, but I do. This isn't about legacy for them either. Their Fury blood has already chosen who they belong to."

The words rest in the air. Dash stands taller where he leans by the door, Hatch sits straighter, and my hands flex over Luna, closing over her shoulder, all of us in silent agreement. The explanation apparently resonates with Sol too, his gaze darting over us with curious interest.

King clears his throat, a glimpse of the man he used to be gone in the matter of a heartbeat.

"Without the threat of the Troisgarde backing us, Bossie and other Wilde kin will try the same stunt again, or worse. It's only logical to seal the Bordeaux part of the truce now. Luna must marry Orion—"

"I'm not making her marry me."

"Oh?" my father's brow lifts at me, his expression hard.

Sol's jaw drops, "Are you kidding me? After everything you've put my daughter through—"

"Shh," I cut them off as she stirs, then lower my voice. "Look, I get it. But it took me making all the wrong decisions to realize they should've been hers to make all along."

Sol grumbles, "And if she makes the 'wrong decision'? At least, according to you?"

"I'll wait for her." I shrug. "You heard King. She's it for me. I know how she feels too. But no matter what she decides, I'll still protect her."

"That's sweet," King says dryly, the man who would've preached that same sentiment six years ago nowhere in sight. "But feelings are irrelevant now. Solomon, you've seen what my boys can do. They came in to save you—"

"From a mess *your* family created," Sol says. "This is your war."

King wags his finger. "Except the Wildes know she's killed one of theirs. According to you both, she helped dispatch more than one at the church, not to mention her role in what they're now calling the Lost Cove massacre. You and your son are now targets as well. The Matriarch let Luna off easy with a marriage proposal. Next time, she'll want revenge, and so will her boys."

The unscarred part of Sol's face tightens. "It was a mutual fight. They took their lumps and ran scared. It's over. That's how it works."

We all shake our heads slightly as King answers. "That's not how it works here. With a feud that started centuries ago, life for life and blood for blood are the only ways we keep score anymore. You're all on the board now, like it or not, and they *will* collect. Unless we push back. Without your help, you and your loved ones are more in danger than ever."

Sol growls low, "But they're the ones that started this."

"Technically... I started this round. With my wife." King's posture, usually so strong, suddenly sags with defeat. Dash and Hatch's ears perk up as he continues, "She was a Wilde, and I took her."

"*What?*" Dash and Hatch whisper-shout, somehow remembering not to wake Luna.

"I'll explain more later," King mutters.

But Sol and I don't react. A reaction in itself.

"Ah." King's lips purse. "So Bossie told you." He hesitates. "Did she say anything else?

My eyes narrow. "Like...?"

He watches me for a second, then shifts on his feet, face reset-ting to neutral.

"Bossie has a tendency to tell Jack Tales," he says, referring to our tall tales and fables. "Best to take anything she says with a grain of salt."

"But the part about you stealing her daughter away? That was true?" Sol crosses his arms. "Seems to be business as usual back-stage for the Furys, all things considered."

"I didn't *steal* her. I fell in love," King narrows his eyes. "I acknowledge my part in this feud, but I won't apologize for it." His gaze slides from me to the woman sleeping in my arms. "Surely by now you understand the lengths men will go to for love."

"Even start a war," I whisper.

He's right. I can't fault him. Not only did I love my mother, the woman he risked everything for, I started a war for Luna too. And as far as I've heard, that's Sol's story as well, first with his wife, then again when he refused to follow the pact, and lastly by protecting Luna from the Wildes.

Which is probably why Bordeaux doesn't argue, only moving on with a gruff voice. "So what now, then?"

"A truce," King answers. "Between the Furys and the Troisgarde."

My brothers freeze, other than Hatch's knee, bouncing quicker than a cottontail on the wood floor, like all his anxiety is ready to run off without him.

Sol shakes his head. "I cannot and will not speak for the McKennons and Lucianos. Lucy's barely holding it together. She told her parents she refuses to leave her house until Luna is safe. With her history..." He winces. "This brought up a lot of... emotions for her."

"What do you mean?" Hatch asks, an urgency in the ques-tion. I know that feeling too. It drove me crazy realizing there was something about Luna I didn't know.

"It's not my story to tell. But all I can say is while my family is getting dragged onto the board, the McKennons and Lucianos may hold out. I don't blame them for wanting to keep their daughters as far away from this as they can get. They already disagree with me for even considering an alliance with you after everything you've put me through." He sighs. "Ultimately, what you're asking for will threaten the Troisgarde, not strengthen it."

"But it's not a choice anymore, we have to work together." Hatch hunches forward, resting his elbows on his knees, hands clenched around his phone as he locks eyes with Sol. "You saw how they treated Luna. And her friend?"

"Don't bring Benoit into this," Sol snaps. "He gave his life for my daughter. I won't have him be used as a manipulation tactic."

But Hatch only leans in further. "It's not manipulation, Bordeaux. It's facts."

Sol scowls. "The Troisgarde is learning from its mistakes. Now that Luna is safe, Brylie has agreed to return to Italy with her parents—"

"She's what?" Dash breathes, pushing off the wall. "But her twenty-second birthday's only a couple of months away."

Sol's left brow raises. "Which, as you Furys seem to continuously forget, doesn't. Fucking. Matter. She'll be safe there. The Lucianos have even deeper ties in Italy than here. Good riddance to any Wilde who tries to fuck with the mafia. That goes for Furys too," he adds with a wry smirk.

Dash's jaw flexes, but he leans against the wall again, shoulders slouching like something in him has loosened its grip. Maybe fear and relief all in one. Or maybe the calculating motherfucker is biding his time.

No matter how he plays what happens next, I get it. That instinct a Fury has to claim his woman is in constant battle with the even more desperate need to protect her, whether that's gluing her by our side, like I did, or letting her go. Like I'm willing to do now.

That inner fight, though... It's why Dash is hyperfocused on med school, why Hatch pretends not to give a shit, and why I left my home to stalk and kidnap a woman I then had to convince wasn't my enemy. We've all had to protect our girls from afar, which means we've had to figure out how to survive the gnawing pit that distance creates without letting it eat us alive. Avoidance, dissociation, confrontation. We've tried everything, but the ache still thrums through us like a second pulse under the skin.

None of us know how to explain the phenomenon, but among the King kin, the certainty that our women are *ours*, sometimes at first sight, comes as surely as the skull birthmark we're born with. As isolated as life gets in these mountains, you're born believing in things bigger than yourself, and devotion to our future wives becomes gospel. Maybe that mark of Fury DNA carries some primal gene, because the second King told us the Troisgarde daughters were ours, something in us shifted.

Back then we were too young to know what to do with those instincts. But when Momma died, that drive to protect turned feral, like keeping our girls safe could be our second chance. After last night, I don't think we were wrong.

"Wait a second, Brylie's leaving?" Hatch asks. "So Lucy's gonna be all by herself? For how long?"

"Not that it concerns you, but Brylie left for Boston less than an hour ago to join her parents." Sol's irritation hums throughout the room.

"But what does that mean for Lucy?" Hatch's tone is more venomous than I've ever heard it. "Are Lucy's parents going to take her back to Vegas? She shouldn't be alone."

Sol's left eye narrows, tugging at his scars. "Like I said, it's none of your concern what their plan is, and the last person they'll tell is *you*."

Anger reddens the small scars peppering Hatch's own face. "So she's still in danger. You said yourself that she was freaked out about Luna. She's scared out of her mind and all alone. She needs someone with her—"

"Let me get this straight," Sol laughs coldly. "Lucy asked her *own parents* to give her space because her anxiety was so bad, but you—what? Somehow know her better than they do?"

Hatch stills. "Are you saying Lucy hasn't talked to her parents?"

Sol scoffs like he's disgusted. "Let me give you some advice, kid. Whatever you're doing, Hatton—watching her, stalking her, tapping her phone—stop it. Kian will have your head. The *McKennons* know their daughter. *You* know nothing. If the Wildes come, Kian and Lacey will handle it."

"Oh yeah?" Hatch rises to his full height, nearly an inch taller than Sol, but Bordeaux doesn't flinch. "Like you did?"

"What did you just say to me?"

Hatch doesn't back down, stepping up to him. "When—not if, *when*—the Wildes come for Lucy, it won't be the *McKennons* who figure out how to save *my wife*."

I blink.

Well, shit.

I've never heard him call her that out loud before.

Hatch can get intense, but in a chaotic, unhinged way. I've never seen him this deadly serious.

"The McKennons don't know the Wildes. None of you do. You haven't fought them like we have. Orion's the muscle, Dash the mind. *I* run the underground, so I know how far and wide their network goes, and it's filled with people who'd die before they ever gave their family up. From what I've heard, that's not the case with you."

He lets that sit, and Sol's face twists with rage the longer the breath goes on, until Hatch huffs.

"Nah, don't look at me like that. It's not the Furys who fucked up. The Troisgarde already failed one daughter, even after we warned you, and still you won't accept our help. You *will* fail again, because despite what your arrogance tells you, the Wildes. Won't. Stop." Hatch seethes, shaking his head. "Not until everything we love burns to ash."

Those words sear a hole in my chest, but Hatch is gone in the next breath, shoulder-checking Sol on his way out. Dash follows after him, his face a dark cloud of rage too. Whether that's at Sol's arrogant naïveté, or Hatch's storm of emotion, I don't know. If I didn't have Luna cradled against me, I'd be going after them too, or lighting into him myself.

Guilt has made Dash overprotective of Hatch since that day in the woods. He still thinks our scars are his fault, but we both failed Hatch, almost just as much as we failed our mom.

He just managed to live.

King shrugs like his son didn't mouth off to a third of the most powerful crime dynasty in the country. Maybe the fucking world.

"As you can see, growing pains are expected with any shift in power. But Hatton is right. The Wildes will target the others next. My boys will do what they can to protect the remaining daughters, but the Wildes are dogs with bones."

Sol's nostrils flare, his chest rising and falling in quick succession. But he gives King one stiff nod.

"The Bordeauxs are on your side. For *Luna's* safety. But know this. I don't trust you. If I knew my family would be safe tomorrow in a world without you or your boys in it, I'd finish you off like"—he snaps his fingers—"that."

"But you won't," King says, gaze drifting to Luna. "Because now she'd never forgive you. And you know it."

Sol's jaw ticks as he glances between the three of us, finally landing on Luna, sleeping safe and sound now that we're home.

"I love her, Sol. I'll let her make her decisions, but whether I get to love her by her side or from a distance, I won't give her up without a fight. No matter what, though, she'll be safe."

I pause, letting that truth settle, then deliver the rest. "But she's *your* daughter. Which means I can't make her do anything she doesn't want to do. If she chooses me, it's because she *wants* to, and you'll have to respect that."

I'm pretty sure his molars crack, but before he can bite back, King speaks with finality.

"Work this out with the other families. They need to accept our resources and knowledge. Until they do, their daughters are in danger." Genuine concern furrows his brow. "Don't take too long to make the right decision."

King leaves on that note. Sol glares daggers at his back, his expression so deadly I have no doubt he's already mapping out which grave to bury him in at Lafayette Cemetery #2. Meanwhile, my thoughts couldn't be more different.

My eyes narrow at the scars rising out of the collar of the black Henley he borrowed, then slide to the fresh burns peeking from the cuff. Burns I don't have, all because he came back for me.

I clear my throat. "How were you able to pull me from the fire?"

He frowns, eyeing me like he's weighing how to answer. But then he slowly rolls up the sleeve. Every inch reveals old glossy scars, now marred by new raw, puckered burns.

I'm careful to school my expression. I hate the looks I get when people see my hands. His wounds are like mine. I hadn't realized they covered so much of him. Like Hatch's do. We're each so different, but in our wounds, this fucked-up life made us the same.

He holds his arm to the light, twisting it, rolling his hand into a fist like he's studying it all for the first time.

"I mastered the fire a long time ago, young Fury. Its pain, its scars, the fear of it." His low voice is steady like a teacher's. "Once you do that, you can do anything."

He rolls the other up to join the first, that side untouched, roughly yanking the last inch of sleeve to fold it over.

"*Except* keep his daughter from a man just like him, apparently," he mutters dryly, shaking his head. Then he sags into his chair and sighs. "I never wanted you for her."

I swallow past the strange lump in my throat. "So why'd you do it, then? You hate me, so why save me?"

He watches me carefully for a minute, then juts his chin toward his daughter.

"Because of her. *Ma petite luné.*"

"Ah... makes sense. I've saved her, you saved me." I nod. "Life for a life."

"No," he says firmly. "I took your name off my hit list because you saved her."

His face softens as he looks at his daughter. Then he meets my eyes.

"I saved you because she loves you."

My heart nearly stutters to a stop. I already suspected how she felt, but hearing her own father confirm it makes everything I've hoped for—*wished* for—all the more real.

The emotions suddenly clogging my throat are too much, and not for him to witness. I clear them away and play everything off with a smile.

"Aw, gee, you think she loves me?"

Sol looks irritated all over again, crossing his arms.

"Much to my immense dismay." His gaze flicks away from me and back to her. Then his voice lowers. "I'm afraid she'll choose you."

My jaw works, as all the times I fucked up flash like a heat storm in my mind.

"I'm not so sure about that," I whisper.

Almost like she's arguing with me even in her sleep, a faint furrow creases her brow, and her bottom lip juts out in an adorable pout. So rebellious, and yet still so, so soft.

"I am."

My gaze snaps up to Sol's. "How do you know?"

He huffs wryly. "Call it father's intuition. She's a lot like her mother, but more... spirited, as you know. We've been white-knuckling Luna's love life since she turned eighteen, terrified she'd pick a masked, stalking asshole."

He gestures to me. "And lo and behold."

I almost snort, but hold it back in time as his face stays serious.

"So, when she chooses you—if not now, then later—take care of our daughter. And better than you did this last time," he growls.

"I will. I promise."

"I'm serious, Fury. If you hurt her—"

"I won't."

"But if you do…"

"I'll give you the gun myself, Bordeaux," I finish evenly. "Locked and loaded."

He holds my stare for a beat longer, then rises to stand. "Her mother's on the way. In the meantime, I'll be downstairs. Send my daughter to me as soon as she wakes."

I will *not* be doing that, but I agree with a grunt anyway as he leaves. He doesn't need to know I plan to soak up every second I have left with Luna, just the two of us, until the world and everyone else in it crowds back in.

Right before he's gone, Sol pauses at the doorway, hand on the doorjamb. He taps it like he's thinking, then speaks over his shoulder without looking at me.

"And Fury? If I see another bite mark on my daughter, I will rip your fucking head off with my bare hands."

Then he's gone.

It takes a second before I finally snap my slack jaw shut. Not gonna lie, the murder in his voice was alarming. There's no way on God's green earth I'll stop marking my wife, but I might ask Luna to carry a scarf whenever we're back in New Orleans.

I give a two-finger mock salute to the empty doorway and smirk as I whisper to the ghost of him, "Yes, sir, Phantom, sir."

My smile softens as I brush Luna's hair back, caressing the mark beneath the neckline of the shirt she borrowed from me. The mark that, one day, might very well get me killed.

But the proof of my claiming settles something in me that's been on edge for a long fucking time.

I breathe her in and, ignoring the pain radiating through me, snuggle her closer. My heart thumps under her cheek with desperate hope. Hope that, when I give her the choice, she chooses to claim me too.

37
MEET ME HALFWAY
LUNA

"Ugh. Where am I *now*?" I rub my eyes, grumbling. "I keep waking up in new places..."

A delicious scent wafts in my nose as I shift. Maple, bourbon, and pine settle me.

Orion.

"You're in our bed, baby." He laughs hoarsely against my hair, and memories rush back in a sleepy haze.

Fleeing Whitby Rose. Going to Orion's home on Fury land. I was a total zombie when we got to the gorgeous cabin by a lake, and this must be where I wound up after Orion led me inside. His bedroom. And not a cot. *His. Bed.*

Wait, no. He said *our* bed...

Butterflies take flight in my stomach only for it to instantly seize, writhing with cramps. I wince.

Ugh.

My psych gave me the okay to take my medicine, but I figured out pretty quick that I hadn't needed to worry. Because after being drugged twice, getting kidnapped twice, losing my virginity one-point-five times, and nearly dying thrice over, of course I would get my period.

Pity party aside, I took my medicine and half-sleepwalked my way onto Orion's chest. Somehow, I'm moderately clean and finally out of my *Swan Lake* outfit, wearing Orion's comfy shirt instead. RIP the boxers he let me borrow, though, because Aunt Flo takes no prisoners.

"Mmm, an honest-to-God mattress," I murmur lazily, one eye squinting open and landing on something I never thought I'd see again.

"Is that my bouquet?"

He shifts under me and nods. "We passed the car on the way back. Everything in it was burned up except them. I couldn't resist stopping to grab it."

The wildflowers and blush roses are dry, but no less gorgeous.

"Thank you," I whisper, choking on all the emotion clogging my throat. I squeeze the rest of my gratitude into him. Until he groans.

My eyes snap open, and one look at him makes *me* groan.

"Oh my God, are you okay? Your bruises. They're even worse!"

Everywhere he's not tattooed, I see more bruised skin than healthy. I'm queasy thinking about the injuries hidden underneath his ink. He got these wounds fighting for his life. Fighting for me.

Fighting for *us*.

"I'm okay." He grins, waving me off. "I bruise easier than a peach. I'll heal by tomorrow."

I roll my eyes and resist the urge to poke one, the thick bandage protecting his ribs making me feel guilty for even thinking it.

"How are *you* feeling?" he asks, sliding his hand into mine.

Jesus. Where to begin? It's been one hell of a week. I'm banged up, in an ankle boot, and my head is killing me after taking my medicine for the first time in days. Orion nearly died saving me. We... killed people—something I'll for sure have to unpack later.

And then there's the worst part of all.

One of my friends died.

"Luna?" Orion prompts, tone laced with worry.

"Sorry, I'm trying to figure out how to answer that. My next therapy appointment is going to be one kick-ass soap opera season."

"Just one season?" He snorts, then sobers. "Alright, fair. How do you feel after taking your medicine, though?"

"Pretty good. Not too groggy other than the usual headache after missing a couple of days. My mind seems... normal. Whatever that means." I giggle. "How long did I sleep?"

"Fourteen hours, maybe?" He yawns. "It was still night when I carried you inside."

My jaw drops. "Did I lay on you that entire time?"

His brows pull together in confusion. "Well, after you freshened up in the bathroom and got the ankle boot on... pretty much, yeah. Why?"

I scan his battered frame. "And you just laid like a mummy for fourteen hours straight while I slept?"

"Well, you did sleepwalk to the bathroom one more time. I had to help you there." He winks.

"Ugh, embarrassing," I grumble. "At least it wasn't an outhouse this time."

"Hey, just you wait. After squatting over a hole on a camping trip with me, that outhouse will look like something outta *Southern Living*."

I sigh. "You're right, you're right... It wasn't all bad."

My fingers drift over his bare chest, trailing lazy patterns. "I think I already kinda miss it."

His bent arm rests behind his head, getting more comfortable. "Yeah? Was it the outhouse or the moonshine that struck your fancy?"

I snort, dropping my gaze and focusing really hard on tracing his birthmark, avoiding the new cut while even more studiously avoiding mismatched eyes that see everything.

"I think it was you."

The words leave me before I can second-guess them, and for a breath I want to snatch them back.

But they're true.

It wasn't the quaint cabin, the quiet peace, or even the adventure. It was Orion that made me feel more at home than I ever have. His soft gaze in the firelight, his gentle patience, our banter and steamy moments that'll forever live rent-free in my head. Even my fear felt different with him, charged and eager when I was at his mercy. I've never felt more alive than after facing death with Orion.

So yeah, I already miss the good we had before everything went to hell. And maybe I'm scared that we may never get that back.

"The cove..." I continue, trying to explain in his silence. "It was scary, and strange, and every moment was a scene from an Appalachian horror romance. But it was quiet. And peaceful. And just... us. Ya know?"

I bite my lip as a couple of calm, weighted breaths go by before he squeezes gently, minding my scrapes and bruises. Then he presses a kiss to the crown of my head.

"Yeah, little bird. I know exactly what you're talking about."

I can't see his face, but I swear I can taste those three big-little words he confessed before sacrificing himself for me at the chapel.

I should rip him a new one for that. He'd be burnt to a crisp if my dad hadn't pulled him out. But I'll let it slide for now. Besides, I technically did the same thing when I hurled myself off that pulpit and leapt onto him like a spider monkey. I'm sure he'll have some choice words for me too.

So yeah, I'll bask in the afterglow of Orion's "I love you" instead.

"Your mom is on her way to Dark Corner," he murmurs. "Nox went to go pick her up from the city."

My heart twists twice. Once for Nox, for losing his best friend, killing to free me, and dragging me out of that chapel to save me. And then it aches again, because, after everything, there's still something about a momma who can kiss any kind of hurt and make it better.

I almost share all that out loud, but I stop short, glad Orion can't see my face. Not only can he not share that same joy with me, he also had a bomb dropped on him about his mom and his dad last night. I'm sure his brothers know by now. How are they dealing with it?

Jesus, what a mess. I need to ask my therapist if she does group specials.

"Good," I answer simply. "It'll be nice to see her." Then, searching for anything else, I take in the room for the first time fully awake.

"So, we're in your room," I muse.

Smooth.

"Yup. And back on Fury land," he says proudly. "Home."

It's comfy in the most heartwarming, cozy way. The bed is huge, with a light blanket over us, a thick quilt folded at the bottom for cold nights. Everything's apple red, pine green, and rich woodsy brown, and it all *smells* deliciously like him.

"You built it, didn't you?" I ask, knowing instinctively. This entire house screams Orion, especially this room.

His slow smile is all the answer I need, but he continues, "Our land's been with us for generations. The government or big business is always trying to 'take it off our hands.' Some beyond the mountain have had to sell off pieces to make ends meet, but we've been lucky enough for all of us to stay. Our dairy farm does well, but our Fury... side jobs have done us good over the years too."

"Let me guess. You made your money in moonshine."

He snorts. "Among other things. We've perfected our smuggling techniques. That and protection are my job. King's the head of the family and our business dealings. Dash is focused on school. And Hatch... Hatch does a little bit of everything."

Huh. Wonder what *that* entails. Not that my father's much different.

"So if it's King Fury land, where do they all live?"

"King lives at the top of the hill. My Grandma Fancy's in a little mother-in-law suite off the back of that. You can't see it from here, but out on the land, you can't miss it. It's Southern gothic meets European castle. Dash's is almost its spitting image, with a tower and everything."

"Dash has a house here too?"

He nods. "We each built our own. I built mine the summer before your eighteenth birthday. It's more like a mountain cabin, as you can see. I... had a feeling that my future wife would like it." I bite my lip as he juts his chin toward the picture window. "Especially with the view."

I sit up on my elbow, and my jaw drops. We're at least on a second story, so I can see far and wide. Cows graze a green slope down to a shimmering lake that's nestled between two "hills," really mountains compared to flat New Orleans. The water mirrors the yellow, red, and green autumn trees hugging the edge.

"It's like the cabin," I whisper, then wince at the last memory I have of it. "The best parts anyway."

Earlier when I talked about our time together, I only had Orion in mind. Now with the view in front of me, more images come unbidden. I swallow and focus on the present.

"It's gorgeous. You should be proud."

"You should be too. It's yours," he says softly, raw vulnerability shining in the myriad of colors in his eyes. "If you want it."

"If I want it?"

He holds his breath, then exhales. "You can leave. I won't keep you here. But fuck, do I want you to stay."

I gasp. "You'd let me leave?"

He nods. "Under the caveat that I'm still protecting you until my dying breath. But if I'm not the one you want at your side, I'll do it from the shadows again. If you want to finally get your way..." He smiles ruefully. "Then I'll grant you what you wished for in that tunnel. I'll let you fly away."

"I thought you said my wish would never come true?" My chest pounds. "You know, because I told you what it was?"

Wow. Smooth again, Luna.
Why the hell did I say that?

But he's right. That's all I wanted going through that tunnel. Freedom.

I gnaw at my lip, gaze drifting from the mountains protecting the glittering lake to the man who's waited years to do the same with me.

He's carried me, sheltered me, nearly died for me too many times. He's made me laugh when I wanted to stab him with a tranq, shown me beauty in the quiet when my mind was too busy, and dove off cliffs and into fire for me.

And I'd do the same for him.

I'm his reckless little bird, after all.

My heart teeters over the edge, ready to take the leap.

"What if I don't want that?" His face starts to fall, so I rush on. "What if I don't want you in the shadows anymore. What if... what if I love you?"

His lips part, sucking in a breath. Then a soft smile brightens his face.

"You're finally meeting me halfway, huh?"

It's suddenly that first night in the cabin again.

"I hate you, you know that?"

"You might. But you'll love me soon enough."

"How do you know that?"

"Because all you have to do is meet me halfway."

More certain than anything I've ever been, I cup his face and whisper against his bruised lips, careful not to hurt him.

"I love you, Orion."

He swallows, then smiles slowly. "*That.*"

My eyes dart between his. "That what?"

"*That's* what I wished for."

"You wished way back then that I'd fall in love with you?"

His lips tick up. "I wished that'd you love me back."

My eyes water, and his smile widens.

"But, you know, now that I'm thinking it over, it seems awful reckless of you to fall in love with your stalker, little bird."

I huff an overwhelmed laugh and echo what he said beneath the waterfall.

"Then be reckless with me, Orion Fury."

"Have you already forgotten? I'd fucking jump off a cliff for you."

He crushes his mouth to my grin, wrapping his arms around me. I'm careful of his injuries, but he's doesn't care, gripping my nape while his other hand hooks around the back of my knee, lifting me higher onto his body to kiss me deeper.

I follow his lead, toying with the waistband of his gym shorts. My nails graze his abs and his Adonis belt, wandering to where the soft trail of hair disappears. His breath catches as I follow it down.

"You're too hurt to have sex," I murmur, "but there's something else I could do that's my second favorite new thing."

His growl vibrates my chest. "I could be in a coma and still want to fuck you. I swear to God, if you don't come here and get on top of me right—"

The door flings open.

"Have you talked to her?"

We jolt apart like two teenagers caught red-handed. Orion groans at the jolt, but Hatch doesn't seem to notice. He fills the doorway, chest heaving, hands braced on either side like the frame's the edge of a hole and the hallway behind him might suck him down if he lets go.

"Have you, Luna?" His frantic begging clogs a lump in my throat. "If she doesn't want me to know, fine, but just tell me something."

"Hatch, slow down. What's wrong?" Orion asks, sitting up with a grunt.

Hatch breathes deeply through his nose, then pushes it out in a woosh. His wild, black hair, a shock of white in the front, stands on end, pushing up his snapback. Sweat shines underneath the bill, glistening along the rose tattoo framing half his brow. The ink is gorgeous, tucking underneath his shirt and winding down his arms, and I can't take my eyes off it as I try to make out the intricate lines. The odd pattern looks like the roses are formed into the shape of a—

"Luna!" he cuts in, voice urgent. "Have you heard from her?"

I blink. "Heard from who?"

"Lucy," he growls. "Who the hell else?"

"Watch it, Hatton," Orion snaps, but Hatch doesn't even spare him a glance, intense stare locked on me.

"When was the last time you spoke to her?" he presses again. "Her parents haven't heard from her in hours—and she talks to her mom all the time."

My cheeks flush as I scramble to think. She's one of my best friends. I should know this, but I wince.

"Honestly, after everything I've been kind of distract—"

"How. Long."

I almost mouth off, but there's something in him, on edge, *desperate*, and it makes me answer him seriously.

"My birthday," I admit.

"*Fuck*." One hand yanks off his worn cap, crumpling it while the other drags through his two-toned hair, and he paces, muttering to himself, "She would've called you once you got back. Sol told her, so she would've found out, unless she heard about what went down at Whitby Rose first... and then there's her cat..."

His voice trails off, talking about cat food, how long since she's been home, how his cameras aren't—

He slams his fist against the doorframe, and the cap he'd been abusing slips from his hand and falls to the ground.

"Fuck, fuck, *fuck*."

"What?" I breathe. "What is it?"

His face crumples. He stumbles back, hitting the frame hard, then slides down in defeat.

"Hatton, man, what's going on?" Orion demands.

"She's gone," he says flatly, voice raw. He swallows like it physically hurts before his eyes meet mine. "Lucy's missing."

FINALE

LUNA

We gave Benoit a Second Line that rivaled Mardi Gras on Bourbon Street. Then we buried him between Madam G and the memorial to his parents in St. Louis Cemetery No. 2. Exactly where he'd want to be.

"I'm going home."

Even now, six months later, the memory of his peaceful smile before he took his last breath comes too fast. But here, standing inside the cabin again, I don't feel the guilt, rage, or shame like a hot poker in my chest. It's still an ember. It probably always will be.

But time has healed me enough to let something soothing settle in too.

I'm proud I knew him. Thankful I was there for his final breaths. And grateful that Orion brought me back here one last time to truly say goodbye.

The pool of blood that soaked into the floor is gone. Each board has been sanded so smooth you can't tell where Benoit bled out in my arms.

I have no doubt Orion did that in anticipation of bringing me back here. He knows no amount of healing could ever make me brave enough to see the shape of my friend's death stained in the wood.

I lightly kiss my fingers then place them on the spot where I laid his head.

"Rest, dear friend, forevermore."

I sit back on my heels and sigh, letting go of as much grief as I can after everything that's happened since.

The Troisgarde doesn't sleep, investigating who betrayed them while fending off attacks from Wildes and rogue Furys that get more dangerous by the day.

And Lucy? We still haven't found her. Six months have passed, and still, nothing. All we know is she withdrew a large amount of cash from her account, hasn't used her cards since, and she left her cat enough food to survive for a week—as if it'd take us that long to realize she was gone. It didn't even take Hatch an hour.

We're operating under the hope that my kidnapping was so triggering, she had no choice but to run. She's so good at hiding, I doubt we'll ever find her, not unless she wants to be found. She's probably safer that way. The war is worse than ever, and Brylie suffered the most.

Does Lucy know?

If she did, nothing would've kept her from coming back. I have to believe she has no idea, because the alternative, that she knew and *couldn't* come back, is too much to bear.

I haven't gone home since Benoit's funeral. Dad doesn't want me to take so much as a single step off Fury land. Not without Orion.

If only they'd made that rule before Brylie.

My eyes slam closed. I can't think about her. Not here. Not when our friend's finally at rest.

I quickly swipe my eyes and blow out a harsh breath.

Orion crouches beside me, then bumps my shoulder and nods farther into the cabin.

"You remember how you took down that one Wilde? The darts to the leg?" He whistles. "Served him up on a platter for me to come in with the assist."

"Yeah." My laugh is watery, but it comes easy, like it always does with him. "We're a good team."

"That one was all you, reckless girl. You were quick on the draw with those darts. Almost like you already had it planned." His eyes narrow. "I've wondered how many times you'd thought about doing that to me."

I snort. "Too many. You really should've paid more attention around the girl who hated you."

"Nah, you never hated me." His lips twitch playfully. "You wanted to, sure. But you didn't, did you?"

My mouth tugs up. "Well... I *tried*."

"Thought so." His grin makes butterflies flutter in my chest.

That's the thing about Orion. That grin? It's rare for everyone but me. I'm the carefree party girl, the free bird, the one everyone counts on for a good time. But I get to be quiet with him. He's serious with everyone else, *so* freaking serious. But with me, he laughs. He keeps me down-to-earth. I help him soar. We're the perfect balance.

Benoit would've loved him for me.

My eyes drift back to the floor, and I exhale.

"You ready?" Orion rises slowly, still reverent for my fallen friend, and holds out his hand.

I take it without thought. My gaze lifts, pausing where we connect, then travels up to the gentle concern furrowing his brow.

I clear my dry throat. "I'm ready."

He helps me stand and hooks an arm around my shoulders, leading me toward the lake.

As much as I don't want to move on, we've done everything we can do by this point. I hate this holding pattern—God, I hate it—but I have to live. I would want that for them if they were in my shoes, so I know they'd want the same for me.

So I am ready. Ready to find happiness where and when I can, and that's always been in the man who looks at me like I'm his whole world.

The one who's now grinning like a fool, leaning up against a tree by the lake with the waterfall behind him.

"You said before we got here that you had something you wanted to tell me?" I frown, looking around to see if I can figure out his plan.

His lips purse before he looks from me to the tree and back again.

"Don't you see... ah." He snorts. Then he picks me up and twirls me, making me squeal and my dirt-speckled tennis skirt whirl around like a tutu. But at this height, I finally see it.

Black paint is slathered over the tree trunk, hiding the red that was underneath.

By the time he's put me down, confusion creases my brow deep enough for my future Botox injector to have a conniption. Meanwhile, Orion looks pleased as hell.

"This is Fury land now?" I ask, pointing up.

"Not just that." His lips quirk up. "It's our land. Once my family claimed it, I bought it."

My jaw drops. "Just like"—I snap my fingers—"that, huh?"

His smile turns predatory, and he stalks toward me in that way that makes me feel deliciously like prey.

"Just. Like. That." His eyes darken. "I hope you realize by now, I'd do anything for you. Walk through fire. Jump off cliffs... give you back the place we fell in love. I couldn't stop the bad that happened here, but I want us to relive the good, make new memories too. We haven't had that feeling of 'just us' since we left. I wanted to give that back to you again."

His intensity makes my heart swell and my lower belly throb with a tantalizing swirl of feeling cherished and desired all at once. I open my mouth to thank him, but a tree is suddenly at my back, and Orion's hands brace on both sides of my head. His slow, deliberate steps had backed me into his trap without realizing.

I bite my lip because he looks positively feral—jaw tight, eyes dark, tanned biceps straining his T-shirt and inches from my face as he cages me in. Like giving me this gift has turned him on.

That, combined with his hungry gaze, and I'm ready to climb him as if he's the tree behind me.

"What happened to Lost Cove being neutral?" I murmur, hot and bothered, but also needing reassurance we're safe. I trust him, but with the reality of this war, I need to hear it.

His expression clouds. "Bossie Wilde happened. They desecrated generations of family graves—on both sides, took over Whitby Rose, *and* went after you." He shakes his head. "We finally pushed back. The 'cove' in Lost Cove wasn't near lost enough for my liking. So every inch of this place is secure—physically and digitally—with Dash's state-of-the-art camera systems."

"So..." My eyes scan the treetops. "They're watching?"

"The fuck they are." He scowls. "And wipe that excited grin off your face, because, baby? That ain't happening. Your orgasms are mine to give, taste, hear—all the damn senses. Exhibition's off the table, got it?"

I giggle, and he keeps his disappointed warning glare as he slides out his phone from his pocket, checks it, then returns it. "The system updates me every time someone crosses into a new section of Fury territory. If we don't confirm it, the alert pings to Hatch and Dash too. While we're here, it'll notify me if anyone's coming. I installed the app on your phone too."

His face grows serious, the way it always does when he talks about the enemy. "Bossie's Wilde boys have been pushed back. As far as we can tell, they're not even in Old Bridge anymore."

I don't tell him that doesn't make me feel better. If they're not in Old Bridge or Lost Cove... then where are they? Are my friends and family in danger?

Pushing the worry that's constantly in the back of my mind aside, I nod. There's not much else I can do but trust him.

Trying to bring back the sensual playfulness we always have, I give him a cheeky grin.

"Is the waterfall 'ours' too?"

He jumps on the mood, smile crawling across his face again as he leans in. "Hell yeah, that's ours. And this time, I won't stop from coming inside you."

His nose trails along my jaw, making me shiver. I tug him closer by his cutoff tee while he nips down my collarbone to my breast through my racerback tee and sports bra.

"It's all ours, Luna."

Ours.

It feels so good to pretend that it really is *ours* and not just his, especially when his voice drops to that deep, primal, territorial rumble.

"Just like every inch of you is mine," he continues. "Every inch of this place is yours. Fury land, all the way to the bog, along our new border—"

"New... border?" My eyes fly open, and I grab his collar and tug him up. He blinks at me, eyes hazy with lust and confusion, but I'm seriously pissed.

"Orion Fury, you mean to tell me that during my 'Survival Week,' I wasn't just walking Fury land, I was covering Lost Cove too? The only ground *you* had to cover was Fury land! No wonder it took me so long."

He holds back a laugh. "Well, not *all* of Lost Cove. But around here, yeah. Don't forget, I had to do it all on my own. And I was just—"

"Sixteen, yeah, yeah." I wave him off. "You're the big, bad Fury. I'm the feisty, little Bordeaux. We get it."

I roll my eyes but when they get back to him, his face has gone serious again.

"You don't have to be, you know."

I frown. "Don't have to be what? Because let me tell ya, I've tried not being little *and* feisty. One's out of my control. The other I've got plenty of ballet tutors who'd say other—"

Orion drops to one knee and fishes something out of his back pocket.

My eyes go wide, my heart beating a mile a minute. "Orion... what are you doing?"

"Doing it the way I should've a long time ago."

Oh my God, is he...

Anticipation rockets through me—

He holds out a small sheath wrapped in brown paper and holds it out to me with both hands.

My racing pulse stutters to a slow waltz of confusion, but I'm still here for whatever he's got in store. His broad smile is infectious as he juts his chin toward his offering.

"Open it."

My grin grows again as I tentatively take the sheath like it could bite me. The weight is solid but balanced, easy in my grip. Like it was made for me.

I unwrap the paper, my eyes flicking from him to the gift, my palms embarrassingly sweaty. His gaze never leaves my expression, and as I unveil what's underneath, I gasp.

"It's..."

"A Fury knife." He finishes for me with all the gusto of a man who's hopeless at gifts but has finally found the perfect one. Not that I'll ever mention Christmas *out loud* or anything.

I slide it partway out. Black lace wraps the hilt, with rubber grips for my fingers so they won't slip. Other than the lace, it's almost a replica of his... down to the engraved "F" on the hilt, "FURY" etched into the blade.

His last name.

I try so hard not to look disappointed, but my smile wavers, and my voice is hoarse when I respond.

"This is amazing. Thank you. I've been dying for mine since Survival Week, but..." I swallow, hating that I have to say it out loud. "I'm not a Fury."

I love being a Bordeaux. It's literally in my veins. I'm a near carbon copy of my momma with my dad's sass. But I want more. I want *Orion*.

We haven't discussed the arranged marriage or how he's not enforcing it anymore. But he still calls me "wife," when I'm not even technically his fiancée anymore. The word—as much as I wish it to be true—is starting to feel less like an endearment and more like a wound Orion keeps prodding, reminding me that's not what I am at all.

Orion's voice drops lower, and his fingers stroke my hand over the knife sheath. "Open for me, Luna."

God.

That one phrase? In that *tone*? Jesus, it goes straight to the center of my core every time.

Arousal pools between my thighs, and I resist crossing my legs. It's like he's got his own "turn Luna on" button at this point.

With the sudden pulse between my legs, I hold his gaze with a sly smile as I do what he says. So I'm too busy eye-fucking him to notice when something falls out of the sheath, and I'm not prepared to catch it.

But Orion is.

He snatches it mid-air.

Before I can see it, I laugh. "Presents in the knife sheath? That's a new one. Most people just use wrapping paper, you know." I chuckle, shaking my head. "What am I gonna do with you, Orion Fury?"

He holds up a diamond ring.

"Marry me, little bird."

My jaw drops. At first, I can't take my eyes off of the lips that just asked what I've been desperate to hear for months.

Well, I guess, he didn't *ask*. But I wouldn't expect him to.

When those same lips curve into a smile, mine follow as I hold out my hand. But I still joke.

"Not gonna give me a choice?"

"Nope. Not when I know what's best for you." He slides the ring over my ring finger easily, but it's snug enough that I don't think it'll ever come off. Just the way I like it. "This is a done deal. It has been all our lives. This—" He nods to the ring, a cushion-cut stone set in a silver band with gorgeous leaf embellishments. "—is just a formality."

Then he takes my hands. "You are mine, Luna Bordeaux. You always have been, and you always will be. Forever."

I wrap my arms around his shoulders and lift myself up. Before I can even cling to him properly, his hands are under my ass and he's carrying me to the cabin.

My heart pounds the second we cross the threshold. I was too single-minded about Benoit earlier to even look at the rest of it. The memory of what happened, who we were, what we lost, it all rushes to the surface again.

But then Orion lays me down on the softest, most comfortable—

I gasp. "You changed the cot!"

Looking around, I finally see everything Orion's done for us —for *me*. The mattress, linens, the freshly lacquered walls, the cleaned hearth. And everything is decorated in the same rich, deep reds and greens I love in his home. *Our* home.

"Gave everything a little upgrade," he says proudly.

I eye him. "The outhouse?"

"You'll have to wait and see," he jokes, taking off my shoes and socks then toeing off his own. He growls, every word punctuated by removing a new piece of clothing. "Right now... I just wanna fuck my wife. *Good and slow*. I'm gonna savor every inch of your warm, soft pussy."

"I'm your fiancée now, you know," I whisper, licking my lips.

He shakes his head. "You've always been my world."

On the last, he frees his rock-hard cock from his boxer briefs, and my mouth waters to taste the bead of precum gleaming at the tip. His eyes darken as he takes himself in hand. I lick my lips and flick my eyes up to his.

"Please, Orion?"

He groans and threads his other hand through my hair to cradle the back of my head. "Only a taste."

I nod eagerly as he brings me closer, my mouth open and tongue waiting. The way he looks at me when the smooth, velvet head glides past my lips—eager, focused attention on my mouth, jaw clenching with restraint—makes me moan. The slightly salty flavor hits my tongue, and I wrap my mouth around him tight.

He hisses and pulls me slowly down his cock. I hollow my cheeks, opening my throat to take him deeper, and he tilts his head back.

"Goddamn, Luna," the curse comes out low and rough, making my nipples perk.

I swirl my tongue around the underside, but then he's suddenly tugging me off by my hair. I suck as hard as I can as he withdraws, popping out of my mouth.

"I said a taste, don't make me fuck your mouth so hard I choke you again."

My lips curl. "But I liked it."

"No." His voice brooks no argument, but his other hand caresses my cheek as he leans down. "Right now, I want my cock where it's supposed to be. Inside my wife's perfect cunt."

He crawls over me on the bed, then peels off my tank and sports bra with one motion. Curling his fingers around the waistband of my tennis skirt, he pulls it down, and I lift my hips to help him slide off both it and my panties.

Then he's on me, one hand around his cock as he notches himself at my entrance, the other gentle on the back of my neck as he whispers against my lips.

"Okay. What I said earlier, that question that wasn't a question? You can answer it now."

I smile. "*Yes.*"

He pushes into me slowly, making us both groan. Just when I'm ready for him to plunge inside, he pauses halfway. I push up my hips, but he nips my bottom lip.

"Nah, ah, ah. Say the rest."

"Yes," I answer instantly and he pushes in a few more inches as I breathe. "Yes, Orion Fury, I'll marry you. I want to be reckless with you too."

"That's a good *fucking* girl," he groans as he seats himself fully inside me.

I hum my appreciation and wrap my arms around his shoulders, eager to feel him move. When he does, he's slow, deep, intentional, and possessive in every stroke. They end with a curve of his hips, hitting that spot inside me, and even though he's easing in and out of me more deliberately than ever, it's no less primal.

His gaze, green and brown, brown and green, the perfect depiction of duality, takes me in like I'm precious, and the words I've grown to feel more of each and every day roll off my tongue.

"I love you, Orion Fury."

Those words are his own button, so to speak. His eyes flash, like he's still surprised I'm head over heels for him. Then he grabs my ass hard, and his wicked grin goes straight to my pulsing clit, followed by a possessive growl that envelops me in a full-body shiver.

"I love you too, Luna Fury."

My heart stutters, and he must take pleasure in my expression because he thrusts faster. His hips move with mine, his cock stroking the bundles of nerves inside me, while his pelvis grinds against my clit. My nails dig into his upper back, and I bite my lip to keep from crying out.

"Don't be shy, little bird," he rasps. "Let the forest hear my wife come on my cock."

His permission frees my moan as heat coils in my belly. My muscles tighten, my legs lock around his waist, ankles hooking behind him.

"Fuck, Luna, fuck. I love when you hold me like this. Your cunt's so tight and needy at this angle. Practically sucks me in."

I can't answer, my body giving into the throes of one of the most intense orgasms he's ever given me. My breaths come fast as I squeeze and climb the high.

"That's it, baby," he growls. "Chase it. Run to it. Fly to it, little bird. Come on your husband's cock."

Husband.

That's what does it.

My whole body convulses, clenching around him so hard it's

painful. His grip on me is agonizingly delicious, and I drift with pleasure before soaring down, down, down. My breaths come out ragged as I try to catch them in my ecstasy and I'm a puddle in his arms.

He picks my languid body up and seats me in his lap, moving me like I weigh nothing while he finds the perfect angle and rhythm—

Oh God.

"I'm com—"

My second orgasm rips through me, shattering me even more than the first. I scream as lightning explodes behind my eyes, thunder in my bones, and he's still pounding into me, deeper, faster, frantic now.

"Chase it, husband," I murmur.

"Luna!" He roars my name and yanks me down, somehow pushing even more of himself into me. My legs tighten around his hips as he holds me still, spilling inside me. His hand cups the back of my head while his hips roll, slow and deep, making sure every last drop stays in me.

"Fuck, fuck, *fuck*."

He bites into my neck where my bruise never really heals, making me cry out in agonizing pleasure-pain. I moan until he releases, then hum against his neck and kiss him over and over until he pulls my head back and dives his tongue inside my eager mouth. He doesn't let go, doesn't even let us move, only devours my mouth with the same fervor and intensity he does everything between us. Finally he rests on his calves, keeping me flush to him as he stays inside me and presses our foreheads together.

"Think we made a little Fury that time?"

A tired, sated chuckle falls from my lips.

"Not unless your cum can swim past an IUD."

He snorts. "I've defied worse odds."

I laugh, my breaths rising and falling against his chest.

"I love you, wife. My reckless little bird."

"I love you," I whisper. "Thank you for being reckless with me."

He smiles against my lips.

"Over a goddamn cliff, baby."

~ The End ~

<u>Read the Bonus Epilogue here</u>

https://bit.ly/UnveilBonusEpilogue

Can't wait to continue the Tatterverse?
Start from the beginning: *Phantom*, Scarlett and Sol's story.
Next: *Dishearten,* Lucy and Hatch's story!

ALSO BY GREER

WELCOME TO THE *TATTERVERSE*

<u>**Tattered Curtain Series**</u>

Phantom

A *Phantom of the Opera* Retelling where the villain gets the girl

Rouge

A Dark, Billionaire Moulin Rouge x Romeo & Juliet Reimagining

Dreadful

A Dark, Revenge Sweeney Todd x Medusa Reimagining

<u>**Frayed Satin Series**</u>

A *Tattered Curtain* Second Generation Legacy Series

Unveil: A Dark Swan Lake Reimagining

A *Phantom* legacy story where the villain steals the girl

Dishearten: A Dark Alice in Wonderland Reimagining

A *Rouge* legacy story where the villain steals the girl

Faded Ink: Coming Soon

Follow Greer on Amazon for updates on new releases!

FROM THE VAULT

<u>**Conviction Series**</u>

Escaping Conviction

Fighting Conviction

Breaking Conviction

Healing Conviction

Atoning Conviction

Leading Conviction

<u>**Standalone**</u>

Catching Lightning

An Enemies-To-Lovers College Sports Romance

Acknowledgments

Hi hi hi! I can ramble for ages about all the people who have made this book possible, but the list is literally longer than my TBR. SO in honor of Luna and Orion, here's the quick and dirty of it!

To whom my many undying thanks goes to includes, but is in no way limited to:

The hubs, my MAD TATTERS!, Jay from Simply Defined Art, Christine George, Kayleigh King, Lynda Hambright, the Dinner Divas, my wonderful & supportive family, Maria the Therapist, Athena the side character who thankfully has continued to stay silent as the backseat driver, Beck Literary Agency, Vajona, Lyric Audio, Valentine PR, The Inkfluence Agency, my wonderful artists: sovana.art, s.seidel.art, snowarox, ajn_art, niass_art, The GRiv Team (Erin, Carlie, Bre), Hambright PR, Bookish Girl Services, Bound to Love, Ever Amazing Betas (Erin, Carlie, A.V., Carrie, Kristen, Rosa, Whitney, Zainab, Isabella, Aimee, Bre), the Library Team...

I'm sure I'm missing approximately a billion people, but that's definitely a good start. I am immensely appreciative of every single person on this list and in my life, and it's safe to say that if you know me, you're on my list of awesomeness and I luff you.

Last, but not least, the Hubs again, because golly this book could not have been possible without you holding down the fort.

Love,
The Mad Queen G

$\mathcal{A}$LL ABOUT $\mathcal{G}$REER

Greer Rivers, The Mad Queen, lives by the mountains with her real-life book husband and their three furbabies. Obsessed with history and folklore, she's also a sucker for reality TV and proudly owns her titles as a messy eater, shirt ruiner, and steadfast non-sharer of food and wine. She adores romance, especially the dark and twisty kind, and her main goal as an author is to create a safe place for readers to feel too much.

Stalk Greer like you mean it...

Become a Mad Tatter and join her Facebook group,
The Mad Tatters' Tea Room.

www.ingramcontent.com/pod-product-compliance
Lightning Source LLC
Chambersburg PA
CBHW030341120726
47901CB00007B/1865